SILENT DAWN

Second Half

The Beyond Chronicles

I0562282

PONO FREEDOM

For my friends—those who witness my every high and low, yet choose to remain.
Without them, this story would never be told.
You have them to thank for this book.
I owe you my gratitude, weirdos.

Teddy Baker, my nephew.
I wonder when you'll be old enough to read this.

GOTNOECH

UNBEQUITH

HARLDÍOF

RANITORL

Map of the world, Beyond: by Maile A. Baker

OH, YOU'RE BACK.

I F YOU CAN RECALL, this is no ordinary story, nor frivolous tale of fantasy. This is real, and my foe has captured the pieces. Paun is... trapped, encased in an icy pocket dimension. Adela is being held as a prisoner, forced to confront a darkness she was never meant to face.

Nevertheless, I intend to save them.

Confused? Get in line. We're all learning here. Even I, the Oather, am struggling with the identity of my role in this world and its purpose. Deep down, I wonder if I'm as in control and influential as I think I am... or if I'm merely another puppeted character.

What of you, O'Reader? Surely, you have a role to play in this story, but... who are you in your story? What sort of character are *you*? Don't look at me—I haven't a clue.

Either way, I suppose we'll find out together.

Won't we?

CONTENTS

CHAPTER ONE

ZWISCHENZUG

ADELA STARTLED TO THE sudden commotion sounding outside her confine. Crawling to the wall in spasmodic trembles, she pressed her ear against the stone and strained to listen. Yes... those were voices. She may not have been able to discern its muffled words, but she could very well hear the responding reply.

"Is that a *threat*, soldier?" asked the gruff voice of a man. "And to whom would you report? I'd very much like to know!" Adela couldn't quite hear the response, but if she listened real hard, she might— "Alright," interrupted the gruff voice, "who are you and what the *blazes* are you doing here? You've picked the wrong disguise for this job, what with *that* rank of armour. However, if you follow Jon here, we'll be sure to sort out this—"

A clamorous racket of shouts, groans, and clanging metal followed suit, reaching an abrupt silence in mere moments. Adela sat still, waiting for more sounds, but to her disappointment, nothing occurred.

Biting her bottom lip, she leaned closer to the door; a different sort of quiet had settled in. Not the disparaging variety which had so haunted her these past weeks, but... an *anticipating* silence—as though the sound's voice wasn't quite through yet and still lingered in the air. Adela shivered against the cold stone. Had she *really* been here so long, she could tell the difference between the pitches of silence? Truly, it was both as depressing as it was—

Adela fell forward, the wall swinging outwards. Before she could pick herself up, armoured hands swooped beneath her armpits and did it for her. Her legs shook as she was set upon them, aching from the small quarters of her containment. Staring down at her quivering limbs, she noticed various guards sprawled out across the floor, unconscious. Her eyes widened and her skin paled upon hearing a voice.

"Adela..." it whispered.

She caught her breath as his armoured hand fell across her shoulder. Catching it by the wrist, she twisted it and forced the guard to his knees. A sprinkle of symbols sparked across her right shoulder in raging intensity. Before the soldier could process her actions, she whirled about, planting a spinning kick to his helm and knocking him to the ground. The soldier quickly raised his hands, crying: "*Wait*, wait—*wait*, Adela! It's me, it's—" He tore off his helmet to reveal his concerned features. "It's I—it's Resil! It—it's me!"

Adela sniffed, her eyes hazing over.

"I know." Falling to the floor, she covered her eyes. "No, I didn't, I..." Her trembling voice broke away. "I'm sorry..."

"Adela no, *please*, no..." Resil groaned as he picked himself up. Placing a gentle hand on her shoulder, he said: "I'm fine—you didn't—are you alright?"

Adela shook her head, smirking at the question.

"No, not really." She sniffed. "No, I've been..."

"Oy, it's alright, you needn't—Adela, did I upset you?"

"No, it's just, no..." Adela sniffed again, smiling. "For some reason, people are certain the sky weeps when it rains, without considering whether it merely sheds tears of joy."

Resil mirrored her pained smile.

"I know that quote from somewhere... Quinten, was it?"[1]

"I'm pretty sure... pretty sure I just made..."

"Here, never mind that." He ducked under Adela's left arm, raising her to her feet and leading her out from the dark passage. "Come now. We've a more suitable setting for discourse."

Adela's head whirled about as she studied her passing surroundings. It looked like anywhere else in the vault, what with the elegant, yet warlike, designs of the halls and various displays at patterned intervals. From the multiple levels of stairs they encountered, Adela guessed them to be coming up from the vault's lower halls and, for whatever reason, there were no windows to be found. The only light source was the eerie blue flames of lanterns lining the halls.

"Resil..." whispered Adela. "How—" She cut herself off as two soldiers strode in their direction from across the hall. Resil casually nodded at them as they approached. Passing by, they acknowledged his presence with friendly smiles and not a single word of Adela.

1.

"Fret not," said Resil. "They don't answer to the same allegiance. Most are loyal to Lord Monbel, but others... Well, you'll find out soon enough." Emerging from a spiralling staircase, they entered a hall hosting windows to their right. Resil slowed their stride to carefully study each door and corridor on their left, talking as he did so: "Sorry, Adela, but... what were you saying again?"

"How... how'd you find me?" She faltered, somewhat distracted by the windows' light and warmth. "And what of the Guild? If you're here with me now, does that mean you settled the pledge of your oaths?"

"In truth," began Resil, "I initially ventured to this cursed dungeon in hopes of settling said oaths and qualms—as commanded by the higher brethren. In settling the qualm, I learned from the Swindler that *you* were here as well. It ails me so to consider what you must've been through, *but* I'm still somewhat relieved to find all three aspects of my mistake here and ready for resolution."

"And what of the higher brethren, were they not... upset?"

"Oh they *were*, initially. It wasn't until I explained the motivation of my disloyalty that they began to understand... *somewhat*. They're still quite upset over what my actions could imply for the Guild's impeccable renown... *ness*. Reputation and all that. Nonetheless, they understood my logic and dispatched me accordingly."

Adela shivered as Resil veered left: down a dark passage and away from the windows' light.

"And..." She sighed, her gaze now resting on Resil. "And what logic was that?"

"I broke honour to my enlisted pack for the greater honour I have already long held to you. Therefore, if I repair the severed wound of my old pack, then I shall remain in the Guild's ranks, holding honour to her whomst'd honour overrides all."

"That's... quite a lot of honour," she said and chuckled.

"Yes, I'm afraid so. *But*, in the end, I never lost said honour—*conceptually*—and continue to remain unbranded by shame."

"That's jus' bonnie, luv..." Adela nodded, her eyelids blinking leisurely. She hadn't understood a single word. "So... what now? Are they gonna reinstate you elsewhere or are you... y'know..."

"Prohibited from the Guild's services? Oh *no*, hardly. After—or *if*—I settle my mistakes here, they predict a bright future of prospects awaiting me. They'll try to use this... eh, *incident* to promote me as... virtuous—or some madness of the like. If so, I should have multiple packs bidding for my service as their patron."

"Truly? Well, I'm happy... happy for you then." She forced a grin, asking a question she knew the answer to: "So where does your honour lie now, I wonder?"

"I must pursue the new allegiance, for it was to this allegiance that I forsook the other. In this logic, I may remain unscathed without staining the Guild's stature." He paused before a wooden door. "This is it." Turning about to face her, Resil set both hands on her shoulders. "Adela Windcatcher, you are my pack master to whom I pledge."

"What?" Adela's chuckle was chopped and raspy. "And what if I don't *elect* to have you as my patron?"

"Then... I suppose you'd have no choice but to banish me from your pack and shame me and my long line of beautiful heirs to come." He smiled. "I know you're a monster and that you'd only want the worst for me, so I—"

"Oh, you mustn't tease so." She slapped his hands, grinning mischievously. "For all you know, I *am* a monster."

"Well then, blast it all if I have a bleeding *monster* for a pack master."

"Yeh, I'm a terrible beasty." She coughed, old tears falling from her eyes as she shut them. "Yeh." She wiped her eyes, forcing another smile. "Lil' Monster. That's me."

"Very good, Ms. Windcatcher." Resil spun about to face the door, but... his hand hesitated mid-air before knocking. "Adela... I... might I inquire of your health?"

"If you will," she answered, eyebrow poised in an arch. "From what I can tell, I've certainly been better—mentally *and* physically. Though... though it's nothing to trouble about, not *really*."

"And your strength?" he persisted. "What of that?"

"I..." She shook her head, grinning through her perplexity. "I think I can walk on muh own now... though if you'd ask me to sprint, I'd simply collapse at the request."

"Mm... under normal circumstances, I'd be enraged at the condition so harshly brought upon you. However, in this instance, I am somewhat grateful for your weakness."

"And... might I ask... why that is?"

Resil paused, his mouth frozen halfway open before it clamped shut.

"I'll open the door now."

"Resil, what—" Adela was cut off by the swinging groans of the door's hinges. Shuffling to Resil, she peered over his shoulder and into the room. "Ooh! Is this one of those waiting rooms I've heard about? Why, it truly does have a bed and—" She gasped in delight. "Oy, and *you're* here too!" Adela darted forward and fastened her arms about a rather surprised Swindler. He refused to embrace her back, but it mattered not; by then, any familiar face might as well have been family. "I'll be," said Adela, finally releasing her hold. "So *you're* the one Resil came to settle his score with, eh?"

The Swindler's eye twitched, his head nodding from side to side.

"I... in part I suppose, but not nearly the central core to his motives, no."

"Then... then who—"

A voice spoke up from the shadows behind, deep, dark, and deliberate.

"*That...* that would be *me...* miss... Windcatcher."

All emotion seeped from Adela's features as she turned to behold the first of men she had truly come to hate; he sat reclined in an ebony chair, his posture, comfortable, cool and collected. His venomous-green eyes shone through the shadows falling across his features. "And... I *dare* say," he continued, "it is truly a... *delight* to so... *remake* an acquaintance such as yours. Mm... why... you are so... *extraordinarily* different from our first... *encounter*." Cormurants sniffed, scratching the underside of his bearded jaw.[2] "Yes, indeed... it truly does *feel...* as though I'm... remaking the acquaintance of a new... *person*." He smirked from beneath the shadows. "For I do not believe you were so ready to kill me then... as you are *now*."

Adela shook her head, eyes shut tight.

"Resil," she whispered, barely able to push the words though her pursed lips. "Resil... *please...* he can't be here."

"I know, Adela, but he—"

"But... I *am* here," interjected Cormurants, rising heavily from his chair as though it were some kind of throne. "And the living reason why *you* are here... for I do not believe

---

2. **Cormurants**: Former pack master of the Tree Crowned and member of the Grey-Circle. He's a sorcerer pirate from the same world as Aresmas and travelled to Beyond by accident. After discreetly roaming about Beyond, he discovered he was in another world. He used this knowledge to his own ends, stealing items from the Grey Marsh to grow in power. His actions aroused the attention of the Silent Legion, who contacted him and aided in his endeavors. Since then, he wore a dark mask, concealing his glowing eyes, so that no one could gain knowledge of the Grey-Circle or the existence of other worlds. The only power he's able to keep from his old world is his discernment. Cormurants can read the surface of one's mind—the reactive part, the part which holds the next words one intends to say, and the surface emotions. If he focuses on someone within his presence long enough, he can catch glimpses of memories, feelings, or intentions. He can apply this skill in combat, considering how every attack or defence is thought of in the moment and therefore reactive.

Resil would have paid dear Vault Tahagorah a visit if I had not been... so *swiftly* betrayed to *this*... place. Mine own pack... if you believe it."

"Mm, sounds rightfully so," began Adela, her features steadily developing into a frown. "No sane person in their right *mind* would ever serve the likes of you for long—not 'fore realisin' the *wicked* person you truly are."

"Or... how terribly wealthy *other* wicked persons are, but... *tsk*. We need not trouble over needless details or passive exchanges. Soon... Resil shall repay his honour owed to me and *we*... we shall never cross paths again." Cormurants smiled down at her. "Does that... *somewhat... ease* your mind, Ms. Windcatcher?"

"No, it doesn't, I—" Adela spun around, facing Resil. "And how *are* you going to repay your *honour* to him—hm, Mr. Saberheart?"

"I intend to free him from this wretched mountain. Him, *you* and Lesander."

"But you *can't*," she hissed, seizing the gorget of his armour. "Men like him are the very *reason* this place was constructed. Please, I beg you, you can't just... *abscond* the man from his natural habitat!"

"Oh... but you really *don't* have a choice," said Cormurants, circling about her to stand beside Resil. "If you're ever to... *escape* this vault... *unscathed*, you'll be in dire need of my... range of... *talents*... aye?"

"Aye," echoed Resil, shuffling away from Cormurants, "we'll need his abilities to—"

"*No*," interrupted Adela, "we won't, yeh? See, we'll—I know a man, a *good* man—high-ranking—one who long promised my release and cares *deeply* for m'safety. Yeh, he'll pardon Lesander as well—I *know* it." Her pleading gaze fell on Resil. "Find Aivon Seeker, *please*. He's a warlord—of Giltpool! If you find him, tell him of me, I'm certain he'll find—"

"And this... Aivon... Seeker." Cormurants cocked his head to the side. "If he is so... *concerned*... for your wellbeing, then why did... why did *Saberheart* here... find you alone... *rotting* in the *dark*."

"Well..." Adela said, her expression scrunched up, "Aivon couldn't... I don't think he could have—"

"Oh, but you *do* think... At the very *mention* of his name, my question rose to the surface of your... muddled thoughts. Truly, how could... *any* of us ever expect... aid from... such a man?"

Adela frowned.

"If you only peered further into my mind," she said, "you would have seen the doubt I held against such questions, for a man of his quality would never be so quick to forgo his word... unlike you, Master Cormurants."

"Ms. Windcatcher," said Lesander, speaking up from behind, "Ms. Windcatcher, your confidence in others is truly admirable and—in of itself—convincing enough. However, there are many Redfolk who are not what they seem, their loyalty devoted to a cause beyond us."

"I... what do you mean by that? Are you implying—"

"That this man may not be who you think he is?" Lesander nodded. "Aye, many in Unbequith and even other *regions* are... of another... allegiance."

"Another world..." whispered Cormurants. "They know not the morality of your time."

"Nor the conviction of honour," continued Resil, eyeing the bracers of his armour. "From what Cormurants has gathered, their true loyalty is bound to the Hand of Unbequith. I... *we* are not yet learned enough to know who this may pertain to."

"So..." Adela paused, taking the time to process their words. "I do believe I know what you mean. And... and I also believe I can tell the difference between them. Pen Wishton for example, he—"

"He's the hand... of a hand," stated Cormurants. "The primary overseer of the Redfolk's underground plot against the throne. Charming insurrectionist to be sure. However... it is not our place to... *interfere* with said conflicts, but to... *utilise* such secrets to our immediate... *advantage*."

"He speaks the truth," said Resil, calmly setting his hand on her shoulder. "Our objective is to *escape* Unbequith. To speak with any official is to become *wound up* in a web of political plots *not* of our immediate concern. In the least—for *now*—we must utilize what knowledge we've scrounged to aid *ourselves*. Every region is not without their own individual struggle, we can't—"

"I understand, I *gettit*," huffed Adela, shrugging off Resil. She was somewhat irritated by how he spoke to her, as though she wasn't bright enough to understand why they were sharing such information with her to *begin* with. *Honestly, just plain condescending.* "I jus' think... *that*... there has to be another way, one that doesn't involve... *that*... swindling fellow."

Lesander flinched ever so slightly, as though struck in the gut by her words.

"I hold a favourable position with the guards, and you'll need me if we're to—"

"Not *you*," she growled, "I wasn't referring to *you*."

Cormurants sniffed, amused by the harsh tone directed at his person.

"Well..." he began, turning his back to them and striding about the room. "Well... I *know* you'll need me if you're to escape. My... perception and... *persuasion* of tongue is reason enough... I should very well think. In any case... it's an infeasible fantasy, for we have long discussed our escape. The next phase was merely a matter of... *your* sway."

"Oh, I'm convinced enough," said Adela, crossing her arms. "And I still think we should tell Aivon."

Lesander shook his head.

"Tell Aivon *what*, pray tell?"

"Why... *everything!* He'll set us free the instant we ask for his name! Why, it'll be set in *stone* if we tell him of Pen and the plot against Unbequith or—"

"I'm sure he already knows," muttered Cormurants, casually reclining in a chair.

Before Adela could retort, Resil spoke up.

"Despite whatever you may believe of him, he can never know of our plight. By the dispatch of the higher brethren, I am still bound to the duty of mine honour. I *must* see to it that the old allegiance is settled. And Aivon—if he truly *could* be trusted—would never release Cormurants, for anyone whom you trust would surely possess a keen discernment of character."

Adela sighed, glancing at the smug villain in the shadows.

Cormurants.

The trouble and pain he had caused her... Adela still had nightmares from it: waking up in a cold sweat, struck in the middle of the night with the crushing horror that she had just killed her friends. Who was to blame for their deaths? Who was the man holding her hand as she drove her blade into their hearts?

Cormurants. Cormurants was *always* to blame.

She scowled at him now, too engulfed in her own furious thoughts to hear what anyone else had said. But no... he shan't get the best of her. He didn't deserve her attention, nor her anger. Such was the low esteem she held for one of—

"Adela."

She detached herself from her thoughts with a swift shake of her head.

"Yeh, Resil?" She reddened upon realising everyone looked to her now for some sort of answer. "I'm... terribly sorry, luv', but could you repeat that for me again?"

"Oh, well, I was only stating how we should wait for you to recover somewhat before proceeding in any way. I don't... I don't think you possess enough vigour for what we expect of you."

"That... depends," she said, trying to control her shaking limbs. "Do you... need me to subdue a legion of troops or... swipe a key?"

Resil shook his head.

"Before you can advance any further in the vault, you'll require a disguise of some variety. Cormurants here has already nabbed one from his bloody lurkings, so you and Lesander will have to acquire your own set." Resil shrugged. "I'd nab it for you myself, but this armour is rather... rather specific to one's, ehm... personal physique."

Adela dismissed his awkward look with a wave.

"Oh, that's fine, I—oh..." It finally dawned on her what he was referring to. "Well... *right*, well I'm sure Lesander knows where the armoury is, 'cause I haven't the foggiest o'notions."

A piece of rolled up parchment flew over the table, striking Resil's face.

"That's a layout of the vault," said Cormurants. "I... *acquired* it from the captain's office. He owns... quite the little library..."

Adela frowned at him over her shoulder.

"If yeh can wander about so freely, I'm left to wonder why you don't merely slip away from this place without our assistance."

Cormurants sighed.

"I lack the force and... *number* to execute my vision."

Adela glared, unconvinced by his ambiguous answer.

Cormurants shrugged in response to her glowering disposition. "I can't be everywhere at once mind you. If I could... *well...*" Cormurants chuckled darkly to himself. "Well, that's a fond story from another time."[3]

Adela sealed her lips, turning back to unroll the parchment across the table.

"*Moving on,* what are me and Lesander supposed to *do* once we've acquired said disguises?"

---

3. I haven't the slightest clue what the old knave could be referring to. No doubt it's some dark tale from his old world. Perhaps in the future, I shall visit his birthplace. Mm, another book, another time.

"Don't talk to *anyone*," said Resil. "There's far too much procedural jargon for you or any of us to memorise. That's Cormurants' job. Simply keep your traps shut and we'll rendezvous with you *here*. This bridge'll take us straight to the stabledocks where we'll use the feyldor tokens Cormurants snatched to flee on the iron dragons and escape."

"And this armoury..." Adela squinted at the map's meticulous illustration. "I don't think I'm, eh, *sneaky* like Cormurants, nor as... *efficient* as you. Besides, won't they suspect a girl like me in a place like... like that?"

"No..." murmured Cormurants, "not if Resil and I... *alert* the sentinels of a rather... *violent* breach in the western wall. In the least, they'll assume it's some *drill* or whatever nonsense of the like. And others... others will be all too... *delighted* for any form of... *excitement*."[4]

"Even so," continued Resil, "it won't be all of them. Some may very well stay behind, lingering at various primary stations, so mind yourself."

"Alright..." Biting her bottom lip, Adela studied the map. "And... and I don't suppose there's a place where they'd stow my effects, is there? I... they took something from me that I'd like to have back if it's all the same with you two."

Cormurants scoffed quietly to himself.

"What, a mask? Oh... but, no... this one is... *personal*. Why... did it belong to dear ol' Aresmas? Oh, *heavens*... in that case... of *course* you *have* to retrieve it!" He dusted his dark moustache with a thumb and sniffed. "You'll find it in the second holding room with some... *accoutrements* of the other prisoners." Cormurants rose from his seat and jutted a finger at the map. "I've been there myself." He fell back into his chair. "Nifty place."

Adela refused to return his stare; by now, to acknowledge his very existence was well more than he deserved. Even so, Adela could still feel his delight in the hatred she held against him. Releasing her breath in a careful sigh, Adela returned her focus to Resil and the finer details of his stratagem.

Took a while, but she's back on track. It's only a matter of time before I save Paun as well.

---

4. Considering this world is still in the early stages of developing its society's morality and general principles, it's safe to assume there's little to do for those guarding a near-empty prison. I believe the vault itself was constructed long before the four lords were elected, in a time when a certain king had many enemies and few friends.

What? Nothing to say?

CHAPTER TWO

WINTER GAOL

T HE COLD NUMBED HIS mind's perception, forcing him to behold the impossible and strange. Initially, it began as nothing more than a shimmering outline—a vague mirage of his own delusions no doubt. But... *presently*... at present it was a whole *creature*.

Well... that's it for me then.

Paun's mind belonged to the whims of madness.

The cold had all but *delightfully* served its cruel purpose. He couldn't react if he wanted to as the giant lizard nuzzled his head.

Paun... The word echoed across his mind like a deep bellow of thunder. *Paun Truvalson...*

A shiver ran up Paun's spine as a wisp of hot air ruffled his hair. There was something almost electric about it, buzzing and crackling through his entire being. The very sensation launched him to his feet with a bouncing jolt. Shaking the snow from his hair, Paun found himself in direct eye contact with the abnormally large lizard—although... no, it looked more like a dragon now, though not nearly as colossal. If anything, its height was similar to that of a wyvern. *You are warm now. There is no need to hoard the shards.* The dragon's shimmering form reminded Paun *somewhat* of the spinners' haunting appearances... just not quite as ghostly. In truth, there was something almost physical to its snowy-white scales and deep fiery-blue eyes. *Paun... you wish for freedom. Grant me but one shard and I shall free you from this casket.*

"I don't even know who—*what* you are," said Paun, warily backing away from the creature. "However, if you truly desired these shards, I'm pretty certain you could've bitten my head well off and simply claimed them."

Or rend thine flesh with breath alone.

"What do you—" Paun fell back against the ice as the dragon shrieked in his face. Arching its head downwards, it pummelled the ice before his feet with a torrent of pure heat. Its white flames were laced with cackling bolts of black lightning. After a few seconds, the creature snapped its mouth shut, a sizzling wisp squeezing from the corners of its jaws. Paun raised an eyebrow, leaning forward in faint recognition. "Is... is that you Vincent?"

The dragon snorted.

I am my own.

"Oh... that, sorry. Just seems like something Vincent would do if he were a... ehm, small dragon, at least, small in regards to how large the usual saurians are... yeh." Paun released a pent up sigh. "I'm sorry..."

The one you address as Vincent is outside this casket, waiting for us. Waiting for me to return to mine sword.

Paun nodded.

"By all means."

A shard then.

Paun's hand hesitated as it reached into his shirt.

"Still, I don't think—"

Very well. Before he could react, the dragon's form dissolved into a shimmering radiance of blue which poured into Paun's chest. Clutching his heart, he looked down to see a single shard illuminating beneath his shirt's lining. As its crimson light grew, Paun felt his essence expanding and the world about him shrinking till nothing remained but darkness.

And then he blinked.

Sharply inhaling, Paun felt the ground thud beneath his feet as it came into lurching contact. His breathing doubled over and the pressing weight of reality swelled over him. Falling to his knees, he felt a secure grip seize his shoulders.

"Ay now... slow and sure does it. There we are..." Vincent tried to hoist Paun back to his feet, but he remained rooted to the floor, his fingers feathering a small object of stone and wood. Raising it from the floor, Paun beheld a palm-sized box. He couldn't tell whether it was crafted from rotten wood or dirty, grey ice.[1]

A shimmering blue radiance wafted from the box and engulfed Vincent's drawn sword. "Ah, much thanks, Chulian." Vincent lowered his blade to study Paun. "And how about our lil' buddy here, huh? How might you be faring?"

"What... what do you mean by that?"

"*You*, are *you* alright?"

Clearing his muddled thoughts with a shake of his head, Paun gradually rose to a trembling stance.

"I'm... *fine* now. But what... *what*—" He fell back to the stone as Vincent struck his cheek with a well-placed slap. Paun's limbs were currently too weak for a swift retaliation. Rubbing the sharp pain in his cheek, Paun scowled. "The *blazes* was that for?!"

Vincent held a finger against his lips before jabbing it accusingly at Paun.

"You *dare* ask me what that was for? I might first like to know what killing *Oleander* was *for*. That was *her* bloody brother you know." Vincent jutted a thumb over his shoulder to a stern, yet blushing, Malvolia. "I know very well he may have been a rascally devil, but one of your skill could have *easily* subdued him—and don't you *tell* me it was a bloody accident."

Rubbing his eyes, Paun pressed a hand against his temple; a rather severe headache was developing. Not only that, but his throat felt raw... it hurt to swallow.

"It wasn't, I—do you have any water?" Upon receiving no answer, Paun tucked the grey casket into his coat. "Listen. We need to prioritise escaping this pit-of-a-temple."

"*No*, Oleander was her brother and you *killed* him!" Vincent flinched at the reverberating volume of his own voice. "You *do* realise he was the *only* person who ever beheld her true self? Why, deep down under all that monotonous visage is a decent being who happens to be *quite* affable and *bloody* loyal."

"Since when did you discover all this?"

Vincent's shoulders bounced up and down.

---

1. The grey casket. The box hosts a frigid pocket dimension, it's icy expanse shaped with Narcronim. My only question is how they managed to trap Paun inside. Did Pen Wishton place someone at the bottom of the chasm Paun fell from? Did they have the casket open and simply catch him? Was it magic that moved him into it? I've been trying to investigate, but this whole temple is shrouded in a vague darkness, blinding my sight and influence. Until they escape, my insight remains helpless.

"It can be awfully surprising how quickly people are to voluntarily open up with one another over the course of two unwilling hours in a cell together."

"*Precisely*," hissed Malvolia. "And don't you forget that *that* also applies to *you*. If you let something more, eh... *personal* slip, I shall be sure you bask in the same shaming radiance of my own humiliation."

Vincent gravely nodded.

"It would be an honour to stand shamed beside you, m'lady."[2]

"Wait—" Seizing his shoulders, Paun spun Vincent back around to face him. "What do you mean two *hours*?"

"Oh, well, to begin with, it was about thirty minutes for Chulian to scour the entire temple. Then... about *far* over an hour of waiting for Chulian's *right moment*—which..."—Vincent glanced down to his sword with an amused frown—"... if I may add, was terribly overextended. Nonetheless, after he freed us, it took about five minutes following him to the armoury and then *another* five for him to lead us down... here. Why? Was the delay too long for you?"

Paun rubbed his arm, taken aback by the beating heat of its flesh.

"Felt like... like a little under a *week* to me..."

"Well... I can't quite explain how that casket works, but pocket realms are of their own laws. I dearly wish we could've rescued you sooner, but it's in the past now. All we can do is rejoice in the fact we have the shards *and* someone who can access them." Vincent tapped the side of his icy-blue blade. "A shame the vidorae couldn't tell us of this place sooner... or the bloody cult occupying it. Which—"

"Any idea who they are?"

Vincent rolled his eyes.

"Y'know, I've only humoured this delay here thus far, for your strength needed to recuperate. If it's even *somewhat* restored, we should already be moving—"

"I can hardly lift my arms," said Paun, "much less a weapon. Although... it is strange, for I do indeed feel the strength in my limbs. It's just... I think my head is still reconnecting the various sinews of my mind to my body." He raised his left arm, but could only

---

2. Perhaps I don't need to note this, but Vincent pronounced "shamed" as "shay-meh-d." After I wrote it down, I realised only I could hear him, so I might as well point it out. While I have your attention, there was another time someone said "tear-ih-tree," and I wrote it down as "territory." It is odd listening to their conversations and realising all you readers have to go off is... well, what you read. Still... maybe if you focus hard enough, you'll be able to hear them too.

lift it halfway before it limply collapsed against his side. Paun shrugged. "During this involuntary interval, I might as well learn of our captors."

"I... well I suppose I concur. I'm certain the Oather would be all too pleased for such an exposition anyway. Perhaps we shall escape this labyrinth-fortress-temple-place without a scratch if we play to his favour, so why not?"

"You're veering off track." Paun winced as he rotated his arm at the shoulder. "The cult, Vincent. The cult."

"Eh..." Vincent's shoulders rose and fell. "Dark underground organisation, lethally demented beliefs and terrifying masks to hide their features. In the very least, they know how to utilise tropes effectively, I'll give them that."

"And who might *they* be?"

"The Death Order." Vincent smacked his lips as though he had acquired a bad taste in his mouth. "They're quite old and, in truth, I thought them to be long extinct. But... well, of *course* they aren't. Dark factions of their variety never simply die out—it's always too much to ask for."

Paun took the brief moment of silence to study Vincent's expressions.

"Have you any experience with them?" he asked, leaning against the wall behind him. "Any further information could always prove helpful for the future."

"And beneficial to the Oather, I know, I know." Vincent rubbed his beard. "In reflection... *yes*, I do believe I remember a high-ranking member of their sort monologuing to me when I was captured..." Vincent waved his hand and sniffed. "Twas back in mine days of youth, when I was but a babe... no younger than you two. They stole my sword, y'know, during the Witch Wars..."[3] Vincent smiled, almost fondly, at the memory. "That's when and how I met one the most remarkable of women species to ever grace this world..." He shook his head and deeply inhaled. "But... but I'm getting off course."

---

3. **Witch Wars**: Unfortunately, little is known of this cryptic event's origins, only its devastating effect. A great fog descended, suffocating and dark. Under its shroud, monstrous creatures besieged Ranitorl, attacking its capital from Nowood. A horde of black magic practitioners overran Harldïof's smaller towns. Throughout Beyond, bizarre and malevolent occurrences plagued the land. The regions fought back, but against what? No one knew. For reasons unknown, shortly after the First Lord of Harldïof vanished, the horrors abruptly ceased. Phantoms slunk back to the deep recesses of old swamps, eldritch beasts retreated to Nowood, and eerie occurrences now haunt only those who seek them. No one knows what transpired those 500 years ago. They simply call it the Witch Wars.

Paun nodded, as both his and Malvolia's features flushed over from his words.

"Yeh... that's... that's not *quite*—"

"*To continue*, the Death Order does not believe in life. Instead, they eagerly anticipate the glorious and beautiful existence of the *true* life beyond death."

"Well... don't we all?"

"*No*, to them, living in a body is nothing more than a temptation restraining us to this physical realm of suffering and pain. They believe it is their divine *calling* to... *assist* the world into the true life, that of peace and joy. As such, they will not hesitate in killing anyone and *everyone*, for they most assuredly believe themselves to be righteous inquisitors, freeing souls from their physical body of torment."

Paun grimaced, deeply unsettled by their crooked beliefs. It was nearly everything he believed in, but... but *morbid* and... and *darker*, twisted into an unnatural belief of feigned conviction. *Truly, this couldn't be what God intended for His creation?*

"If they're so... *convicted*, why don't they all simply kill *themselves?* Then they can enjoy their so called—"

"Oh, they'd love that. To die is of the highest reward. However, to kill one's self is the lowest, most selfish thing one can do. For my own reason, I agree, but they believe killing one's self is—and always will be—unearned. They are first called to... *free* their fellow brethren trapped in their physical cages. No, they shan't kill themselves. To free one's self from life is to free one's self from divine responsibility."

Paun heard Malvolia shiver behind him.

"Is there no reasoning with them? Surely, no child of God could be so lost—"

"Not unless said child was no child of God. Each one of their members will claim—to the point of torture—that they have beheld the commanding visage of Death. To them, Death is God's appointed spiritual overseer of our physical world, one who makes certain *none* are left behind to suffer and thus, will do whatever it takes in claiming a life. They are not God's children, whatever they might claim, for they have long forsook Him."

"Then what about *us?* Why have they not seen fit to kill *us?*"

Vincent opened his mouth to speak, but paused to glance at his sword, eyebrow raised. His face then shot up to the looming darkness overhead, the corners of his mouth twisting in grim thought.

"Unfortunately," he muttered, "it seems as though the Oather has forsaken my expo
sition."[4] Vincent shot another glance to his blade. "According to Chulian, our position
has been long compromised." Waving Malvolia over, he addressed Paun. "Can you thrust
a sword?"

"Perhaps, depends what—" Raising an eyebrow, he accepted his smallsword from
Malvolia by the hilt. "Aye, this'll do." He stripped the blade of its sheath, slinging its leather
across his back. "Did any of you see fit to retrieve the flasks?"

"If we escape alive, I assure you, we'll drink all the—" Vincent huffed as Malvolia swept
past him to coldly offer Paun a canteen. Rolling his eyes, Vincent began stepping away.
"So be it, but drink and run, would you?"

Nodding, Paun guzzled the water in heavy gulps. It was as jarring as it was soothing for
such amounts of cool liquid to slip down his throat at the rate it did. Slaking his thirst to
the last drop, he wiped his mouth and sped up to Malvolia's side.

"Is there any more?" He held the canteen out to her. "My mouth still feels puffy."

Lips thinning, she took the canteen from him and, slowing her pace, quietly lowered
it to the floor's black stone before jogging back up to Paun.

"They disposed of ours," she growled. "That was the only one I could find in the
armoury—still don't know who it belonged to."

"Well you didn't have to *lose* it."

"I'm not carrying it."

"One of us could've strapped it on!"

"That would be too much of a clattering *hassle* to bother—"

"*Lock your cakeholes*," hissed Vincent over his shoulder. "They'll find us if you two
keep talking so—" He came to an abrupt stop and fell back against the floor. Pushing
himself up, Vincent rubbed his forehead with a soft grumble. Malvolia rushed up to his
side and assisted him by the elbow. Paun himself was occupied examining the obstacle in
the hallway; it was a web-like barrier, composed of the same charred stone as the temple's.

Vincent released an irritated groan: "That wasn't there before."

Paun glanced back at him, only to pause in surprise; stone tentacles were extending
from the ground and ceiling, forming another solid barrier behind them. Gritting his

---

4. My influence here is dampened, weak. I can only extract info for so long before... *it* begins to
   notice.

teeth, Paun whirled back around to the first barrier, stabbing his sword into it. The blade passed right through one of its many gaps and came to an abrupt halt at the hilt.

Paun's eyes narrowed; the point of his weapon was but a hair's breadth from the ridge of Pen Wishton's nose. His electric-blue eyes glinted darkly in the shadows.

"Hello, Traitorson." Smirking, Pen slowly, but firmly, pushed back Paun's sword with the tip of his wand. Looking over Paun's shoulder, he greeted: "Mr. Virtos! I do believe this to be our first official acquaintance, though surely not our first encounter."

"No," began Vincent, his glare burning into the man before him. "Nonetheless, I have been informed of you. Why, I saw one of the other three not but a handful of weeks ago! He was quite upset, the little rogue."

"Yes... Cayaban was sure to report that. Of us three, you seem to cross paths with him the most. Hopefully we're in for some changes, yes?"

"*Aye*," growled Vincent, "I look *forward* to it."

"As do I." Pen's menacing gaze shifted to Malvolia. "But... *you*... These two were expected, but you... why, you're like that old sailor. You don't belong in the group of three and are but dead weight."

Paun lunged for the charred-stone bars of the barrier, gripping them so tight his knuckles began to pale.

"What have you done with Aresmas?"

"Me? Nothing at all. Us? Also nothing. But... *him*, the *Oather*. The Oather has done *exactly* what he'll do to *her*. She doesn't belong in this... special group he so seeks to create and, as such, he shall dispatch her the *second* it suits him." Paun froze at the mention of the one person who so haunted his heart. Catching this, Pen frowned. "Hear me now, O'Oather, this trope will *never* come to pass. All it takes is but one... *loss*... for your influence to die alongside them."[5]

"It's me," said Paun, much to the surprise of Vincent and Malvolia. "It has to be. That's what *they* said—the spinners. Between me and *her*, it'd be *me*."

"Mm." Pen tilted his head, eyes blazing with a mocking sympathy. "To each, there is a counterbalance, an opposing contrast to one's character. Only in your antagonist will you

---

5. Mm. The trope he might be referring to is the magic number of three in a group, often two males and one female. I'm aiming to create such a trio, with each member embodying a distinct trope. In my ideal group, there would be an old mentor with a hidden past, a young rogue with potential, and a female love interest. Developing such a trope would significantly enhance my influence and control over the story. Indeed, many tropes stem from this rule of three.

find destiny. But, bear in memory, the same could be said for the other's perspective." Pen leaned forward, his soft words echoing through Paun's mind: "Strike swift and true, lest they discover their destiny before you."

Vincent spoke up from behind, his voice humourless and cross.

"For one of silence, you certainly reveal more than you ought!"

"Oh, the Oather knows..." muttered Pen. "The Oather knows..."[6] As he spoke, a muffled *boom* echoed through the darkness. The entire hall rattled ominously and small bits of debris drifted from above. Pen looked up and frowned. His ever so slight expression of aggravation was all but too satisfying for Paun to behold. What must have been another explosion went off, its violent force rocking the whole temple. Following the sound, a robed figure emerged out of the darkness behind Pen.

"Lord Wishton," it greeted, its eerie voice somehow resonating from behind the silver skull mask, "the Unbequith regiment, they have breached the inner temple. For the present, Plague is containing their forces, but they've True Beyonders among them. Our hidden eyes have counted *three*."

"And you need... *me* for this?" Pen held up a hand, silencing the figure from responding. "Of course you do. We've been played by the Oather. It's time *we* do the same." He flicked his wand, causing an invisible force to tear the grey casket from Paun's jacket and fly into Pen's hand. He then shoved it into the figure's ebony chest plate, saying: "Take the shard's casket. I don't care what you have to do, but *try to* keep it bloody safe, alright?" He smirked. "You won't, but try. For my amusement, I beg you—*try*." With that, Pen delivered one last look before swiping his wand through the air, causing the gaps in the barrier to shrink till nothing remained but the frosty-blue glow of Vincent's sword.

"Well..." Vincent tapped the side of his blade. "That was foolish of him. We still have our weapons."

Paun winced at the thought of his beautiful sword bashing against the black stone of their containment.

"That," he said, "is too desperate for me, but I thank you for the... suggestion. Any more?"

Arms crossed, Malvolia rolled her eyes.

"And how do you think *we* escaped *our* detention? Gnawing through the bars, were we?"

---

6. I do. In fact, it's time I make a move.

Paun shrugged.

"For all I know, you *just* might've. After all, you two are completely insane."

"No," said Vincent, cutting Malvolia off. "He's right."

"About *what?*"

"Well, we're both mad for one and using the full extent of Chulian's power is *always* desperate. I can never repair the gashes left behind in reality's flesh. 'Tis an infringement against creation. However... I don't think anyone would mind if this horrid pit was left scarred by Chulian's blade. Yes... aye, I do believe I'm about to do something... *very* desperate."

"Like blunting your blade on stone?" said Paun.

"Blunt?" Malvolia crossed her arms. "It doesn't... blunt, it *slices*." Poorly concealed admiration edged into her voice. "Stone, armour, dragon scales, magic, reality, time, butter—truly through *anything* at all."

Vincent shrugged.

"Well, it's the prism shards finished with Chulian's ore which does most of the cutting—all that, eh, *crazier* stuff is the tempered power drawn from *within* the shards and, uh... speaking of which..." He gently tapped Paun's shoulder before harshly shoving him aside. Sweeping his sword upwards in a shining arch of frosty-blue, Vincent left a radiant gash in the dark face of the barrier. Within seconds, blue energy splayed forth from the gash, consuming the wall in ice. Bringing his blade downwards, Vincent jerked his sword from the wall. As his blade withdrew, the ice exploded in a flash of cerulean flames. Vincent then struck the barrier with the flat of his foot. Its charred remains gave way quite easily to his kick, crumbling to expose the dark figure speaking to another of similar attire. They both paused to eye Vincent, their expressions void beneath the hollow eyes of their silver masks.

"Jęh kee wan muo."

The figure who spoke shoved the grey casket into the arms of the other, who promptly dashed off.

"Oh, don't do that." Unholstering his celestial flintlock, Vincent sent three rapid bolts of yellow hurling after the fleeing figure. Upon immediate contact, the figure collapsed, unconscious. "Right, and as for you—"

Vincent was cut off by the deep chanting of the figure.

"I'yun arra," Its head bent oddly to the side as it dodged Vincent's shot. "Ikui ligbe mi'netore itun eka—" The figure abruptly collapsed to the floor, a radiant-blue gash illuminating the lusterless armour of its chest piece. Another such gash could be found hovering in front of Vincent, who was withdrawing his sword's point from it. He turned over his shoulder, about to remark something to them when a horde of more dark figures manifested from the shadows.

"Ke uli... mo'ek," they chanted, their grave vocals rumbling through the hall. Vincent shook his head as they continued to chant, mumbling something incomprehensible. Whirling his sword, he created a shimmering halo of blue over his head, one which his blade disappeared into.

Every figure then collapsed to the floor, a glistening splinter emerging from their chests as they fell. Extracting his sword, the halo vanished, but the gashes remained glinting in the air, static and deadly. Vincent sniffed, sheathing the blade in his shoulder's pocket-of-a-scabbard.

"I need not remind you *not* to touch those, aye?" Vincent carefully stepped over the bodies to move along down the hall and pause beside the figure who had fled with the casket. "Not unless you want the scarred edges of reality slicing your fingers open."

Paun himself knelt beside one of the fallen figures, feeling for its vitality.

"You killed them," he said.

"Yes," replied Vincent, proceeding to remove the robed armour for himself. "Blast it... the bloody mask won't come off..."

Paun felt the cauterised hole in the metal of its chest-piece. The complete and instant annihilation of their existence startled him. Demented cult or no, Paun had been raised by the belief that in any form of combat, every being deserved a chance to defend itself.

In combat, everything was chance and *risk*. The one who eliminated the most chance, and therefore the most risk, was the one who secured the odds in their favour, the one who would deserve the outcome they earned. If an archer in the shadows stuck a swordsman from behind, then that was fair. The archer secured more odds than the swordsman should have, so the archer won. The swordsman could have spent the better years of his life learning archery and his enemies, perhaps investing in the proper symbols for his armour. No matter how small it was, the swordsman had a chance, as everyone has and *should* have. But *this*—this didn't leave any chance. There was no room for the enemy to secure odds. All they could do was die to the flick of another's whim.

There was no honour.

Whether that was true or not, it still left Paun feeling somewhat disturbed by the sheer power a man like Vincent possessed, all in the mere hilt of a sword. He understood why Vincent had done it and Paun might have done the same if he could, but... *but he didn't—*

"You didn't give them any chance," he said aloud.

Vincent didn't look up as he strapped the figure's bracers to his wrist.

"I gave them *exactly* what they desired most." Vincent tightened the strap with a jerk. "And you'll do the same if you want these shards in proper hands."

That wasn't quite what Paun had meant. He did somewhat agree and—should the need arise—he would eliminate the unfavourable chances by taking the life of those who dared to infringe upon his. However, a more concerning topic arose in Vincent's words, one which completely uprooted Paun's unease with a more unsettling concern.

"*Proper* hands?" Paun's gaze flickered to the grey casket in Vincent's palm. "And whose hands did you have in mind, might I ask? Surely, you can't be referring to the cursed Steward of Tokade."

"No, he isn't..." Malvolia's voice lowered. She whispered something else, but it was too soft for Paun to discern, save for the last mumble of: "... so you needn't trouble yourself..."

"*What?!*"

Her gaze shot up to Paun's, clearly agitated by his tone.

"My *vidorae*," she snapped. "Upon apprehension, they immediately shattered it. We needn't trouble about my—about Steward Henagan. What connection he had to us was severed. He can't see us and thus, can't punish you or *me* for what decisions *we* make."[7] She positioned herself beside Vincent, continuing: "And Drendon here seems to be the only one with any *decent* idea of what's going on or how to proceed."

Paun raised an eyebrow, positioning his back to a wall.

"And what might... that... *be?*"

"Well," began Vincent, stepping forward, "we can't simply destroy the shards, not without having our flesh rent into thousands of pieces across the various aspects of reality—no, this needs to be handled *professionally*."

"By *whom?*"

"The only people with the knowledge, means and—dare I say—*morality* to handle the shards, are in Ranitorl—the best being in Aeraos. I know the journey is far, but they are

---

7. Yes, though such a convenient outcome was hardly a result of my influence. As such, I am... skeptical about this sudden turn of fortune.

the only people who can diffuse the shard's powers or—*better still*—harness them to an incorruptible and unchangeable cause."

Paun scoffed.

"We can't just... *waltz* into the capital of Ranitorl and expect assistance of *any* kind. Not with *that*." Paun shot a finger at the grey casket. "It's an absurd notion to even *begin* humouring."

"Perhaps... perhaps, *perhaps* if I *didn't* happen to be in a rather beneficial relation with the Lord of Ranitorl, it *would* indeed be so preposterous. Trust *me*, we can trust *him*. Like a brother to me he is. Well... perhaps not, for brothers often harm one another. Point *aside*, I know him, he knows me, we're one big happy—"

Paun cut him off.

"Was Ranitorl not one of the first and *only* of the four regions to align swords with Unbequith?"

"Well... *yes*."

"And yet you're so deeply assured we can trust this Lord of Ranitorl—the one whose judgement forged said harmful alliance to Unbequith—with *prism shards*. The whole reason for the regions' violent debacle to begin with! The *bloody* reason we're so rushed into this mess!"

"Aye, his judgement may have been... misled, but mine is *not*. Ranitorl is renowned for their science of magic and Aeraos, the only trusted fortification to safely handle these shards. Whether that means disposing or *not*." Vincent tucked the grey casket into one of the many pouches lining his waist. "Their fate is not to be decided by one man, or even three, but a council of diverse—yet absolute—wisdom." Vincent cast aside the Death Order robe, caring only to bear the armour. "However, know that I don't act on your approval. Whether you approve or no, that's the course we'll take and there's *nothing* you can do to alter it."

Paun's silence must've encouraged Malvolia to speak up.

"If you can't tell, he has quite rushed through his explanation. He's shared its full extent with me and I stand with him. You can either help or you can stay here." In one swift movement, she yanked the celestial flintlock from Vincent's holster and directed its muzzle at Paun. "Your limp body shall be rather heavy, but I'm sure we could find a lovely spot in the woods for you to wake up at, ey?"

Paun continued to remain silent.

Shaking his head, Vincent sighed and placed a hand on the celestial flintlock. Gently prying it from Malvolia, he holstered it.

"I'm not gonna shoot you, kid, not again." He softly smirked. "Twice would be more than you deserve." With that, he turned his back to Paun and proceeded down the hall. Malvolia looked from Vincent to Paun before shrugging her shoulders.

"Well, come on then," she said, chasing after Vincent.

Paun watched her go, a turmoil of conflictions raging through his head all in the heat of a mere moment.

I know I can't do anything... not against him. But... but in the least I shouldn't so easily abandon that which I've worked so hard to secure. I can't come home empty handed of feats. What would—eghh—what would he say? They're so terribly close within my grasp, I own a responsibility to their power. In the least, I can watch over their progress and what Vincent truly entails for them. Perhaps... when the time is right... no... what would I do with them if I did manage to nab them? Vincent's right... for now... for now I must watch, protect, and perhaps... and perhaps learn to trust him. After all, if someone like Malvolia trusts him, then surely his honour must be worth something?

Right?

Running down the hall, Paun shook his head at all the dead bodies he had to step over.

"I still can't believe any man could have the power to... to do whatever he just did."

His words were mostly meant for his own musings, but Malvolia still eagerly responded to them.

"Oh, well, see it's a complicated process, but a rather simple concept to grasp." A layer of enthusiasm lit her voice. "See, in a way, he segmented his sword between them, fractioning a splinter of his blade in each of their guts, *instantly* killing them." Her grin briefly faltered, but continued to remain. "It's quite morbid—absolutely *terrifying* to think about—but also truly riveting, is it not?"

Paun remained silent for a few moments before responding.

"Does the Oather run your tongue so easily, or is this just you?"[8]

Malvolia's earnest smile broke away to her all-too-frequent frown. Picking up her pace, she ran up to Vincent's side, leaving Paun to follow from behind in the dark quarters of the narrow hall.

---

8. Just her. I have little to no power here. I'm glad someone explained it, though I'm still *somewhat* confused how it all works.

CHAPTER THREE

TOOTHY BLACKS

"**U**P THE STAIRS, *UP the stairs!*" Vincent whirled about, urgently beckoning for them to hasten. Paun dearly wished to look back, but he had been *explicitly* warned not to. It was a good thing he hadn't, for sharp stones and gaping fissures littered the floor at fatally inconsistent intervals. "*Hurry* lads, they're right on you!" Vincent extended his hand, catching Malvolia as she leapt into the stairwell. Pulling her into the stairwell behind, he sent several crackling-yellow bolts whizzing past Paun's head. "*Faster* boy! Make haste!" A pack of rumbling, growling things echoed from behind in chattering whispers. As Vincent's muzzle flashed, several of the pursuing creatures collapsed to the floor, stumbling Paun's footing. The other creatures' enraged screeches tore through the darkness, rattling chains and unsettling debris.

Clenching his jaws, Paun leapt over a large gash in the floor to Vincent. He landed on the stairwell's edge, about to topple back over the precipice when Malvolia yanked him up the stairs. Paun stumbled forward, but continued to scramble up the steps with her. Vincent's back shoved into theirs as he retreated behind them, swiping his frosty-blue sword to keep the creatures at bay. Whirling about to stand his ground with Vincent, Paun saw only the head of a creature who had managed to shove its elongated neck through the stairwell's arching entrance.

Upon first glance, Paun was unsure of *what* he was looking at. It was a saurian of sorts, and such knowledge seeped all colour from his features. However, as though to make matters worse, the creature looked as though all flesh had been removed from its head, leaving naught but an exposed skull with black needle-like teeth snapping and chattering at Vincent. Two dull, red orbs gleamed from within the void of its sockets. Following an elegant slash of Vincent's sword, its horrific screech was abruptly cut off.

Just like its neck, thought Paun as its hollow skull toppled down the stairs and out through the archway. *For the love of all things sacred, why doesn't Vincent just—* Yelping in surprise, they all jumped back up the stairs as another creature ducked through the archway. Its scaly black neck slithered up the steps and over its fallen kin like that of an ungodly serpent. Bits of stone tiling were scraped off the walls by its heaving and bristly form.

Recovering from his initial surprise, Vincent shot the creature with his celestial flint-lock. A web of cracks split across the stairs as the creature's limp head made contact with them. Trudging down a few steps, Vincent buried his sword into its cranium. His fist dug into one of the many pouches lining his belt to hurl a handful of charred pebbles down the stairs. In a burst of fiery blue, they erupted, forming a shield-like dome in the archway.

A horde of displeased shrieks resonated from the stairwell entrance.

"Should contain most of them for some time." Vincent turned around with a sniff. "*Most* of them, mind you. A ward stone can only do so much."

"What *were* those?" breathed Malvolia, her voice shaken and soft.

"Well," said Vincent, resting his hands against his knees, "I don't know."

"You *don't*... know?"

"How the *blazes* would I? I can't possibly memorise every shadowy haunt that snips and swipes every *bleeding* catacomb." He brushed an arm across his forehead. "Toothy blacks. I can just *barely* recall their rumours of old, for they're quite old indeed. Whether it was their name or no, *that's* what I'm calling them next time we run into them if there ever *is* a next time."[1]

"Well... *next* time," said Paun, "make certain *everyone* is close behind 'fore deciding to run off into—"

"*Next time*," growled Vincent, stabbing a finger at Paun's chest, "don't fall so far behind!"

Paun splayed a hand to the bottom of the stairs.

"There were *scores* of Unbequith troops between us! Not all of us bear swords forged of prism shards or wield a dragon's *soul* for a navigator!"

---

1. **Zanswarsh**: Wyverns of the Silent Hand. "Zanswarsh" is Second Gotnoech, and "Toothy Black" is the universal speech. The Silent Hand, using Narcronim on the skulls and saurian ore of deceased wyverns, developed this accursed subspecies. Composed mostly of shadow and darkness, they are remarkably stealthy.

"Well, in the likely event you haven't noticed, I *wasn't* using my sword. To kill a soldier of *any* region is an interregional *crime* deserving of the divine judgements."

Paun pinched his nose, closing his eyes as he tightly exhaled.

"We don't have *time* for the Oather to run your mouth so! Why can't you bleeding *kill* when it's required of you? I doubt *they* would have shown you the same mercy!"

"From what I witnessed, ain't nobody was trying to kill us. Incapacitate, *perhaps*. But they always keep a healer on hand for such captures. They were completely harmless... from a granted perspective."

Paun rolled his eyes. Turning his back to Vincent, he raised his shirt and coat.

"Perhaps you ran too far ahead when the Death Order retaliated, but the following crossfire was no... *harmless* perspective." Paun heard Malvolia sharply inhale as he displayed his wound. "The shaft broke off, but methinks the head is still lodged somewhat."

Vincent whistled, stepping up to Paun.

"Aye, it's still in there, but it's not barbed—such heads would be considered a war crime. Here, it should slip out nice and—"

Paun gnashed his teeth as Vincent plucked the arrow head from his back. "There." He flicked the broken piece at Paun. "Now, if we just get some of those darb' bandages, you should be all set." He glanced over his shoulder to Malvolia. "We... do still have some in stock, no?"

She shook her head.

"The last of it was used for the shadow creatures and those snake... worm... *things*." She crossed her arms, frowning to herself. "I *told* you, if we took the time to save our sumpter, none of this would have—"

Sighing deeply, Vincent began searching through his various pouches.

"The nest your drake was taken to would have been days off in the wrong direction. And... maybe at the time I would've ventured off to find him, knowing what he meant to you—but... *no*, I couldn't have left you two maniacs alone. You would've devoured each other alive."

"*Perhaps...*" grumbled Malvolia. "Nonetheless, *here we are*. Left with nothing for Paun's sorry back." Her hand caressed his shoulder as she nodded sympathetically. "Goodbye, Paun."

"No... it's not yet his time." Vincent shot a wary glance through the stairwell's archway; the fiery-blue dome had burst in a shower of sparks. Huffing, Vincent hurled another handful of ward stones before continuing to dig through his equipment. "I've two stones remaining, so we best hurry along after... ah! Drink this." He forced Paun's head back and poured a vial of black liquid down his throat; it tasted just about as horrendous as it looked. "Don't gag the stuff," warned Vincent. "That's the only bit I have left—the only bit I've been carrying around for the past two an' a half centuries, so show it *some* courtesy, ay?"

Paun violently shuddered as the concoction slipped down his throat.

"I'm thinking the slight pain in my back would have been preferable," he groaned, nearly vomiting as the sinews of his muscles repaired themselves. "Where and... *why* did you ever attain that?"

Vincent shrugged.

"A girl," he said simply. "But we can't afford to have you damaged any further, not as your tissue repairs itself, lest it leave a rather crippling scar—one more crippling than you would have had if you *didn't* drink it."

"Delightful."

"Quite so. Scars are epic." Deeply inhaling, Vincent clenched his jaws and shattered the empty vial against the wall. "Chulian, chaperone Paun." Reaching into his coat, Vincent unveiled the grey casket. "Protect them with one of these, will you?"

In a glistening haze of blue, a dragon's whisper passed from Vincent's sword and into the grey casket. Seconds later, a prism shard emerged from the casket's top, engulfed in the auroral spirit of Chulian. Veins of fiery-blue ice split across the shard's surface, pulsing in contained force as it hovered before Paun. Without a moment's hesitation, he swiped the shard, surprised by how warm its ice felt.

"How does this work?" he asked. "Does it morph into a sword or—"

"No." Vincent tucked the grey casket back into his coat. "No, you'll need loresmiths if you're to forge it appropriately. Without the proper enhancements to focus its potentials, Chulian will only be able to manipulate the bare surface of its power." He shot a glance over his shoulder to the archway at the bottom of the stairs. "Right, that's enough exposition. Keep your wits sharp and your swords drawn—you'll need them."

"Oi, just a moment," said Malvolia, "shouldn't we—"

"Mal," interrupted Vincent, setting a hand atop her shoulder. "*You* keep a hold on *him*. And Paun, you *bloody* watch after her. *Heed* Chulian—he knows the way."

Malvolia slapped Paun's hand with the flat of her small sword.

"But *you*," implored Malvolia, ignoring Paun's glare. "What of *you?*"

"Chulian can't possibly divide the shard's unrefined power amongst three beings."

"Aye, you didn't mention *you*, so what of *you?* The threat is clearly far greater than any of us imagined."

"Fret not," he assured, "I still wield my sword." He held out his weapon to her, its crystal-blue blade no longer hosting an animate flame. "It's still fairly durable—and *mighty* sharp. Not enough to cut through the very folds of reality itself, but it's still of shard and dragon. Even more still, I possess quite the assortment of tools and techniques up *both* my sleeves. One doesn't simply become as old and dangerous as I without acquiring and *learning* a few, eh... *curious* tricks." Vincent spun Paun around and shoved him from behind. "Now *grab* her hand and make haste! I haven't the *foggiest* notion of where to go, so tell me what Chulian says, aye? The ward stones wear thin."

Brash fools... they had chosen to embrace the dangers of the frontlines. Their powers made them reckless and therefore... blind. His kind sought only a new battlefield on which to discharge their raw might. If only they had attuned their mind to their true purpose, focusing on securing the fruits of their toiling strife... not wasting precious time decimating all who dared cross their paths in a flourish of arrogance.

Darun knew them to be superior, in both rank *and* strength. However, he *refused* to follow after them as they breached further into the temple. They did not require his assistance, nor would they have wished for it. Aye, he was to hold the rear.

Chaos, the temple was strewn with it. Only a handful of heresy-clad cultists occupied this place and yet... the forces of Unbequith could not advance further without a number of slight, yet *painful*, casualties. Whether it be in some twisted trap of the mind or a stab in the back from the shadows. *Yet still, we continue to push deeper into the darkness... butchering our men like petty sacrifices.*

It sickened him.

If he hated his commanding brethren for neglecting their men, then his hatred for those dark folk who stole his brethren's lives was simply unparalleled.

Aye, Darun wished to kill them *all*: to end their dark practices with the flickering whim of his blazing emotions. To make them *suffer* for the brave souls they've so callously robbed from comrades and families alike. But, *no*... he had to... *resist*. Vengeance would only do him ill in such an accursed place as this. No, for now he must wait... and focus on that which they have spent so long pursuing. If not for his vidorae's insight, they would have long lost track of Paun Traitorson and his ilk from the distance which Unbequith followed. They couldn't lose sight of that now, not after all that's been done. *No*, they were here for prism shards—not the thrilling glory of combat.

Unlike Darun's other commissioned hunts, he did not so openly display his pulsating network of fiery strands. To do so would alert the enemies of his prying presence. As of now, stealth was but of the highest advantage. From hairline cracks within the ceilings to the crumbling pockets within walls, his fiery network infiltrated ever so quietly, *searching, roving...*

Darun sprang to his feet.

Rising stories above their heads, a surging element of pure reality made its presence known; a detection of energy so great, it nearly blinded the vision his network bestowed. It wasn't a prism shard no... but an entire *collection* of them... *their containment.*

There now, the surge had vanished, but the source remained; a casket of fragmented realities, *he*—of course.

Him... again.

Stealth was... no longer required.

Tugging on his network of fire, Darun snapped out of his trance to whirl the scorching strands about his head. Its might building with an energised thrum, cracks of pure energy split across Darun's pale features. He launched from the floor, crashing through the ceiling above. The soldiers stationed with him scattered in a chaotic disarray as rubble toppled onto their heads, but he heeded them not. Twirling the strands about his form, Darun barreled through stone architecture and intricate bits of hidden machinery. His form blazed in an inferno of heat as he gradually ascended the temple. Crashing through the final layer of stone, he erupted from the floor of what *must* have been a shrine. There were two cultists in this room, bowing over the imposing oily-black sculpture of a shadowy figure. Darun's eyes squinted, their radiance dulling; that hooded statue... he... he recognized it.

The inferno crawled back into his eyes.

Fingers clawing through the air, Darun summoned fiery strands of his hidden network to tear out of the walls and rip into the cultists. The two heretics folded against the floor, their dark robes flickering with bits of fire from where they had been pierced. More such strands ruptured from the walls, their burning tendrils wrapping about the statue. The temple shook as they tore it loose, chunks of black debris erupting from its foundation. Jutting his hands forward, the strands hurled the dark statue into the wall behind it.

Paun had *no* idea where they were. He knew where to turn only in the moment, but where Chulian led them remained a complete mystery to him. For all Paun knew, they could have been travelling back on the very route they had used to get inside. Oddly enough, there weren't many Death Order or Unbequith soldiers to be—the temple shook violently, upsetting Paun's balance.

The voice of Chulian resonated through his head.

Drop. All of you.

Paun relayed the alert over his shoulder, falling flat to his stomach. No sooner had the others heeded Chulian's warning, than a rumbling blast jarred their ears. Chunks of rubble exploded from their right as an oily-black statue shattered the wall. It gracefully passed over their heads with a heaving *whoosh* before toppling off into the abyss on their left.

Vincent shot back to his feet, his celestial caster firing off in one hand and his sword ready in the other.

"Get out of here, *now!*" he screamed, nudging Malvolia with his foot. "Heed Chulian's words, I'll—" Before he could finish, a blazing warrior of raging heat lunged from the hole in the wall. Holstering his weapon, Vincent swung his sword with both hands, slicing through whirling whips of fire and nearly lopping the warrior's head off. However, it came to a swift halt as the warrior's bracer deflected it with a burst of orange sparks.

Go... now, ordered Chulian. Paun tugged on Malvolia's hand, but she remained rooted, anxiously watching Vincent parrying the warrior's attacks. *Paun, you know you possess the strength, take her and go.*

Squeezing her hand, he jerked on Malvolia's arm and tore her from the unfolding duel. As he ran along the path, he sternly glanced to the shard in hand.

Does Vincent not carry the casket? he thought, his mind addressing Chulian. *It's beyond foolish to safekeep the shards with him, should the worst occur.*

And yet more foolish for him to trust anyone other than himself.

Paun frowned.

Even so, that doesn't—

Stop running.

Paun screeched to a halt, his back shielding Malvolia from toppling over into the sudden chasm before them. His head ducked through the archway, searching for some kind of hidden path.

"Where now?" he asked. Nothing could be seen but the looming darkness before them.

Grant me but a moment's patience.

"What does that—" Paun paused as the shimmering blue spirit of Chulian drifted from the ice-encased shard. "Hold on, where are *you*—" he huffed as Chulian's spirit dispersed into the wall. With nothing but the shard's now-dimmed light, they promptly found themselves surrounded by a smothering darkness. There were several moments of odd silence before Paun spoke up again. "I'll... take a punt we wait here then."

"Not so *loud*," hissed Malvolia. "We're vulnerable now..."

Paun lowered his voice to mirror her volume.

"Sorry... just... thought I'd give you some confidence."

She was quiet for a few moments. Nothing could be heard except the eerie bluster of a hidden wind and their own breathing.

"How's that?" she finally asked.

"Oh, something my father used to do—still does... to my knowledge. In the face of fear, he acts... brave or—dare I say—nonchalant. Such an attitude reassures those around him with confidence in his capabilities to protect. Whether he could or not, it still did good for others... for me even."

"Well..." She hesitated. "Well, you don't *have* to do that for me. It... it is a rather odd thing to do anyway."

"I suppose, but it's working isn't it?"

Nothing but the rustle of wind, then—

"A little... yes."

Paun smiled.

"Good, now let's talk about something to—"

A deep, chattering growl rumbled from behind in blusterous whispers. The very sound of it caused Paun's hair to rise and a chilling shiver to run down his spine. Malvolia urgently tapped his shoulder.

"Toothy *blacks*," she whispered, her voice as shaky as her hands.

Paun slowly turned around, stepping forward to push Malvolia behind him as the sound neared. His blade's tip was extended before him, his stance firm and ready for that which approached. The chattering rumbles grew closer, drawing near... until... *nothing*.

Complete silence.

Paun began wondering where Chulian was and what could *possibly* be taking him so—Malvolia's scream was overpowered by the shrieking roars of a living horror. He whirled about to have Malvolia topple back against him, her smallsword madly swiping through the air for dear life. His back screamed in pain as it made contact with the floor.

Rattling chains and ticking notes echoed through the walls.

Grunting, he tried squirming out from under Malvolia as the skull of a toothy black lunged for her feet. She swiftly tucked in her legs, pushing back against Paun even more. As the creature's jaws snapped forward, Malvolia directed her blade up at its throat. However, her thrust never landed, for the creature was abruptly swept aside by a dark platform. Paun couldn't see it, but he heard the creature's odd shrieking come to a swift close by a booming collision of stone. The platform returned to the archway before the chasm, various black scales fluttering across its surface.

Paun couldn't see past the first platform, but he heard the sounds of other such devices shifting throughout the darkness; he sighed in relief upon the appearance of Chulian's spirit drifting from the walls.[2] Before he could address the dragon, a shrieking growl punctured the shadows from the tunnel behind. Paun's sword twisted through the air, whirling about to strike the creature's face. Unfortunately, his blade did little to no damage, deflected by the creature's rotting skull. Catching him off guard, it lunged forward to bite Paun's vulnerable arm. With nothing but pure reaction, Paun tilted his blade up towards the creature's jaws; he hoped to at least stab its brains as it took his arm.

However, his blade never touched the beast; he felt no resistance, no pressure, no sudden jolt—*nothing* as the toothy black's gaping maw fell across his weapon.

Grab her hand! ordered Chulian. *You fool, grab it now!*

Paun had already spun about to seize Malvolia's arm. She squirmed away from his grip at first, but quickly froze in pure terror; the toothy black's needle-like teeth had snapped shut around *both* their waists. Backing away, its head tilted in an expression one could only interpret as bewilderment. The toothy black unloosed a bone-chilling howl, clawing at their stomachs and throats in a fit of frustration. *There now*, assured Chulian, *I've somewhat severed you from reality. You're nothing but a wraith to them now.*

---

2. It seems Chulian retains some ability to interact with the physical realm. He likely activated a hidden mechanism to bridge the chasm. How it would normally be triggered remains mystery to myself. I am blind here.

CHAPTER FOUR

TO BE A GHOST

P AUN'S HAND WEAKLY FELL across his chest, feathering up to his neck.

"Not a single mark..." he murmured, eyeing his fingertips with grateful astonishment. Paun then tried to stab at the creature's eyes, but his blade rendered no more harm than the slight touch of a breeze. He couldn't help but flinch as the toothy black once again began clawing and nipping at their forms, but only in vain.

Malvolia's grip violently tightened about Paun's hand as he rose to his feet. Cocking an eyebrow at her, he shook his head. "You're alright, I refuse to let you go." She mirrored his shaking head before hastily bobbing her's in a rapid nod. The voice of Chulian then echoed through his mind.

Indeed, you hold the shard, so it is in your hands that her safety resides. By the odd look Malvolia's features expressed, Paun guessed her to have heard him as well. *Nonetheless,* continued Chulian, *you must be wary of your stance. The soles of your feet are still of this world, for you must still interact with its laws to traverse it. However, if you stumble, I'll have to remove some bits of thine transparency, lest you fall through the floor and into the very void stretching infinitely beneath the world's crust. No, I would rather you two met a swift demise than for me to linger on in such a place.*

"So... *don't* trip into a ravine," replied Malvolia, grimly shutting her eyes as the toothy black's jaws gnashed at their heads. "Right... I shall... do my best then."

Good. Now, when you're ready, kill the creature, and I shall temporarily render thine swords physical once more.

Nodding, Paun readied his weapon. His eyes flickered about as he tried to focus on the creature's constantly shifting head. Nonetheless, it wasn't long before he found an opening; the toothy black shot forward, its head once again attempting to bite them. It of course failed, but when its head began to retract, it gave them a split second of vulnerability. Paun used it to jab his sword through its eyes, while Malvolia attempted to punch through its dense skull with a ferocious stab. At first, their blades effortlessly passed through the creature like the hand of a phantom.

They felt a sudden tug as the matter of their weapons shifted to a more physical state; the creature fell to the floor, instantly struck dead by the blades lodged in its head. Its body then ruptured in a cloud of violet mist, leaving nothing behind but a wyvern's skull and a trail of dark scales. Both Paun and Malvolia fell to their stomachs, jerked forward by their weapons.

"I *felt* that..." groaned Paun, rubbing his abused back.

Of course you did. I anticipated it.

Paun pushed against the floor to stand up, but his hand fell through it, causing him to frown.

"*Chulian...*" growled Paun, trying once again. This time, it worked without any trouble, allowing him to rise to his feet and assist a fumbling Malvolia. "Can you not simply read my mind and *see* what I intend?"

I can only hear your mind, explained Chulian. *You are fortunate enough I caught you.*

"Right, well... thank you for that." Gently shifting positions with Malvolia, he gazed through the archway and into the chasm's darkness. "So this way then?"

I altered the mechanisms in the walls and formed a bridge. Stay within its narrow centre and stray not off its sides. If you do, I shall try to let you die, but they won't, and they will catch you.

"Right." Paun raised the prism shard, pouring its fiery-blue light across the dark chasm. He could barely see the next few steps ahead. Even harder still was the dark tone of the pathway's stone: it was nearly impossible to determine where its plummeting edge resided.

You best hasten your pace, cautioned Chulian. *They know we're here.*

Being sure Malvolia trailed carefully behind, Paun advanced along the pathway, one grim step at a time. However, he paused upon completely processing Chulian's words.

"*They?*"

Paun nearly fell off the edge in surprise, for a bolt of colourless fire shot right through his chest. Malvolia yanked on his arms and the cuff of his shirt, helping him regain his balance. Sighing in thanks, he raised his palm to spill the prism shard's light across the darkness. It did nothing for the lighting, but someone must have caught sight of it; the sharp clang of metal against stone resonated from all about them. The concussion occurred twice, before falling to silence. As its echo faded, a soft glow began to illuminate, allowing Paun to dimly visualise his surroundings; there were scores of archways lining the walls, nearly every one occupied by a robed member of the Death Order. Each one wielded a bladed staff with the point resting against the stone. A number of fiery-orange symbols lined the metal of their blades, providing a warm lighting to the environment.

Not a single figure moved.

Not a single word was spoken.

Paun cleared his throat, hoping to quell Malvolia's quivering hand. Clenching the prism shard tighter, he smirked.

"Well then," he began, "ready for round two, fellas?" Paun felt Malvolia flinch at the jarring sound of his vocals boisterously addressing the Death Order. Contrary to what he had hoped for, they continued to remain in silence, unfazed by his fabricated confidence. Instead, Paun was left unsettled by their ominous presence far more than he had wished for. *Chulian*, he thought, *what now? Do we—*

A rattling of chains echoed from shadows above, followed by a metallic screech from the abyss below. Before Paun could wonder what that sound was, an odd ticking began beating at a rapid pace. Malvolia's grip squeezed tighter as the tiles beneath them began shifting away from one another ever so gradually. A deep reverberation boomed from below and Malvolia leapt off her tile just before it shot upwards. She shakily landed on Paun's platform, about to push them both off as it tilted to the side. However, he caught her other hand and leaned back, pulling her up to a more secure stance.

The rest of the bridge had begun splitting into various platforms. Some were gradually shifting to the archways in circling motions while other platforms remained static. Before Paun could consider his next course of action, Chulian was already shouting in his head.

Go back, go back now! With haste! Leap, jump! Together! Go!

Hoping Malvolia heard him as well, Paun yanked her hand and sprang from their sinking platform to the one behind them. It tilted at an odd angle as they landed on it, not enough to topple them off, but still— *To your left!* barked Chulian. *There is a tile approaching your left! Move to it as soon as it is within range!* Paun's gaze anxiously searched for what Chulian spoke of, but to no avail; he could only catch glimpses of the various Death Order; they were projecting bolts of pale fire at him from the blades of their staffs. It may have had no physical effect, but the blinding flashes of colliding magic greatly upset his vision.

"Malvolia!" he shouted over his shoulder, "do you see what he speaks of?" To Paun's alarm, the platform beneath his feet continued to tilt to the left. "*Mal!*"

"*No!*" she snapped. "I can't see a *bloody* thing with—"

No time—jump now! The urgency in Chulian's words compelled Malvolia to jump first. Not wishing to release her hand, Paun instantly followed after her. His vision somewhat returned as he leapt through the air, his prism shard confronting the darkness with its splay of cerulean light. In that brief moment of suspension, of... pure... weightlessness... he saw a great darkness stretching below his feet, a gathering of forsaken figures encircling him, and the lunging tile he was hurling into.

Paun and Malvolia both groaned as they collided against the platform's harsh stone. The sporadic flashes of fire resumed and Paun was once again left blinded. *Good, now, raise your arms. Jump when I say, no sooner, lest you lose your wrists.* Paun followed his orders without question. *Now.* Hopping, Paun felt a blocky object swing into his hands, violently lurching him off his platform. *Let go... good.* A sweeping object caught Paun's fall, elevating at a rapid pace. *Turn around—stop. Run.* Dashing forward, the blinding flames cleared. Paun found himself under an archway. The platform behind him fell away and he beheld a figure of the Death Order directing its weapon at him. A deep tunnel stretched behind it.

Reaching for its head, Paun tried to pull the figure over the edge behind him. However, upon contact, his hand passed right through its hood.

"Chulian..." he mumbled, running through the figure and into the tunnel. Before he could advance further, Malvolia jerked on his hand, causing him to turn back at her with a raised eyebrow. Just passing through the figure's body, Malvolia spun around to plant a firm kick in its back with her foot. Not a single sound escaped the figure as it plummeted into the abyss and over the edge.

"Huh." Paun peered out through the archway before ducking back into the tunnel. "How'd Chulian know you'd do that?"

I didn't.

"He didn't," she replied, rubbing her elbows with a frown. "But our feet aren't all ghosty, remember?" Paun nodded, to which she replied with a pat and a slap against his shoulder. "How's your back holding up?"

He winced, feeling the concave at the bottom of his spine.

"Every time it begins to heal, it's inflicted by some sort of blunt pain."

"But it's fine now?"

"It's certainly been better..."

"Good, onward then." She tugged on his hand and began trekking down the tunnel. "Chulian, is this the right course?"

The best I could find.

"It'll have to do." She sniffed in disgust as her foot squelched in some dark substance. Paun was sure to creep around... whatever that was.

"Chulian," he said, "where's this lead out to?"

Our only exit. It is just beyond that opening.

Malvolia picked up the pace, hurrying after the grey light at the tunnel's end.

"Yeah, I see it, it's—" she gasped after ducking under the archway.

Following her through, Paun couldn't help but mirror her dumbfounded expression at the room they had come into; it was huge, *colossal*—large enough to comfortably fit a fully matured dragon. To their left, stretching from one side of the room to the other, was an ivory staircase. Its faded hue starkly contrasted against the dark stone of their surroundings. Warily ascending the first steps, they tried to peer through the wide doorway, but couldn't discern much past its yawning opening. They could only visualise a pale light escaping its maw, occupied by a rather odd sound of cascading water that was... almost... silky.

There, said Chulian, *go in there.* Paun and Malvolia were already halfway up the steps, but still nodded in compliance; in the short span they had known him, Chulian had already saved their lives on more than one occasion—a little sign of respect was more than warranted.

Nearly ascending the steps, they came to a flinching halt at the jarring boom of crumbling stone and shattered rubble. They swiftly turned to see a body sent hurling through the air from a gaping hole in the wall from across the chamber. It came to an abrupt stop in the centre of the stairs, leaving a nasty impression in its graceful architecture.

"*Vincent!*" Malvolia made a dash for him, but was restrained by Paun's hand. She leaned forward as far as her arm would allow. "Vincent! Are you alright?!"

Shakily pushing himself up, Vincent raised a thumb.

"He's breaking through my body's reserve symbols but they should last long enough to—" Vincent swung around as the entire wall across the chamber came crashing down; a bright figure stood at the end of the room, dwarfed by its colossal surroundings, but... somehow all the more intimidating for it. Vincent pushed himself up to a defensive stance, shouting: "Just hurry up and focus on Chulian, would you?!"

Yes, heed my words. We've nearly escaped!

Tugging on Malvolia's hand, Paun started tugging her away from the unfolding combat and led her through the entrance. It took a while, but she soon followed willingly, gradually taking the lead.

"Alright, Chulian..." Malvolia's gaze flickered across her environment. "How do we help?" The room they now found themselves in was nearly identical in hue and tone to the rest of the catacombs, yet still remarkably different; a looming hole occupied its centre, its radius no shorter than a spear. Lining the walls of its edges was a cascade of glassy water, transparent and smooth. Paun and Malvolia stood on a catwalk twenty paces above the watery cavity, gazing down at its oily depths.

From what I gathered, said Chulian, *this should open us a rifting gate. However, we shouldn't simply open it, for it needs must collapse behind us after our passage.*

"Right," nodded Malvolia, "so, instructions please." She rubbed the side of her temple with Paun's hand. "I haven't the foggiest notion where to begin."

The centre of the room, go there. Good, now climb the ladder and make your way to the booth overlooking the entire chamber. Yes, you see the keydesk in it?

"I'm assuming you mean *this*." She patted a dark-grey desk, one riddled with strange machinery and odd inscriptions.

Yes, now simply—

A clashing ring cut Chulian off, causing both Paun and Malvolia to peer over the booth's edge. Vincent lay on the catwalk below, struggling beneath the boot of the Unbequith warrior. Before they could react, the warrior harshly shoved its heel against Vincent's chest. The grated metal supporting the two couldn't withstand the sudden pressure and thus, snapped in half. Thankfully, Vincent avoided toppling into the watery cavity, but instead fell against a white pavement coated in shallow water. Sputtering, he was barely able to recover as the warrior came boring down upon him in a magnificent blaze of fire. Vincent rolled over to avoid the impact, nearly toppling into the hole.

Catching eye contact with them, he cupped his hands about his mouth.

"Yank the bloody knob!"

Yes, that knob, confirmed Chulian. *Now, press the symbol with the—*

Vincent's vocal's, occupied by the harsh clang of metal and fire, cut him off.

"Press the symbol Chulian tells you to!"

Yes... and I was about to advise, you press that one. A deep metallic screech echoed from below and the water pouring from the walls violently doubled over, nearly sweeping Vincent and the True Beyonder into the cavity. However, they managed to stab their weapons into the white pavement as they were swept over the hole's edge, dangling by their enchanted hilts.

"What *now?!*" cried Malvolia, fussing over the various switches and engraved symbols.

Now, your finger swipes across the symbols from there to there, respectively, before pressing the knob once more. An energised hum began to build. Peering over the booth, Paun witnessed the water flowing into the cavity rise up, swirling in a frothing pool. Its bubbling surface gradually reflected another setting, as though it were a window.

A gateway.

The warrior forsook its grip to blast a fiery strand from its palm and over its head. The flaming tendril grappled onto the room's ceiling, allowing the warrior to propel itself into the air. Vincent took this moment of vulnerability to unholster his celestial flintlock, yank his sword free, kick off the cavity's edge and shoot a crackling round of energy at the Unbequith warrior. Vincent then fell straight into the cavity and through the gateway of water, disappearing behind it.

A brief shield of blazing orange materialised to protect the warrior, but the flintlock's yellow bolt punched straight through its magic and into the warrior's face. Paun felt a slight hint of satisfaction as the warrior limply splashed against the shallows of the white pavement.

"*Chulian!*" he hollered over the rushing water. " Chulian, what—"

You jump.

"Jump *where?*" shouted Malvolia.

Where else? We have only four seconds before it—

Paun had already leapt over the railing and into the window of water, jerking Malvolia over with him. A rush of cold air shot through his entire being before spitting him out onto a harsh surface. Shielding his eyes, Paun looked up to see the ruddy light of day warming his features from a row of glass windows. The brick beneath his limbs was of a reddish-gold, complementing the evening's soft glow.

"Where..." He spun around to see Vincent standing beside a great ring of silver and black, an aperture built into the room's wall. A window of murky black water spiralled in the aperture's centre, like the surface of a tarnished mirror. Nodding at his blade, Vincent sheathed his sword before stepping up to a curious desk similar to the booth's design. Pulling on various cranks and switches, the swirling hum gradually died down. The dark window of water hovering in the ring's centre collapsed, splashing against the tips of Vincent's boots.

"Oh..." Vincent chuckled to himself. "You two needn't hold hands any longer. Chulian returned himself to his blade the moment you popped through."

Paun's frown did little to conceal his ripening cheeks as he swiped his fingers away from Malvolia's. Upon a discreet glance, Paun noticed she too hid her blush, only better than he.[1]

"Don't get any *funny* ideas, *Drendon*," she warned.

"Oh, me? Never, no, I'm just hoping Paun could learn to trust you more. Perhaps, perhaps... you're a little less inclined to kill him than before."

"Mm..." She shrugged, accepting Vincent's hand to help her up. "Perhaps. I still might kill him in his sleep, though..."

"Well, that's a little growth," said Paun with a smile. "Before, it was merely a matter of *when*. Now it's progressed to a *might*."

"Yeah... well... before I only *thought* you helped me because of my father and the vidorae, but... but after my only leverage was destroyed, you continued to not just *help* me, but... *save* me. Over and... over again." She averted her gaze to the gold hues pouring into the room. "At any moment, you could have very well let my hand go and... and forsaken me to the dark's horrors, but... you didn't. Despite lacking my own assurance of protection, you didn't and... for that I am grateful." Malvolia sighed, wiping her hands across her knees. "In the least, if I *do* kill you, I'm certain I shall feel some form of twisted remorse over it. Don't know... maybe I'm hopeless." She gave a loose shrug. "Perhaps you could start working on your trust with Vincent. After all, he trusted you with both Chulian *and* a shard."

It was then Paun noticed the shard missing from his hand. Wildly whirling about, he searched the floor for anywhere he could have dropped it. Paun froze as Vincent set a heavy hand atop his shoulder.

"I've had Chulian return the shard to its casket," he explained, patting his coat's chest. "There's no need to so openly brandish such a notorious item as this—*especially* here. The less they know it's here, the better."

His mixed feelings for Vincent returned in a flash of doubt.

"*Here?*" Paun said, suspicion lining his sharp tone. "And just *where*—"

"We're in Mount Færas. Capital of Unbequith." Vincent nodded and inhaled. "*Yep*... that's enough time for sentiment. I suggest we make haste."

---

1. Huh.

And *make haste* they did.

WONDERFUL.

Who's that?

THEY HAVE PERFORMED... EXCEPTIONALLY WELL.

Ah, so you speak once more... and to congratulate my advance to victory I see.

NOT YOURS, NO.

How could that possibly make any sense? Events are moving *perfectly* along—in every way I had hoped.

LIKEWISE.

Chapter Five

WINDOWS AREN'T FOR KNIVES

A DELA'S BREATH HITCHED, HER lungs gasping for air. She had sampled three sets of armour before this and every one had been simply too large for her. With the pressure of time nipping at the back of her head, she had hastily slipped on the smallest armour set she could find.

How could any soldier be this spindly to begin with?

Adela tightly inhaled as her hands searched for the clasps about her waist. There had to be straps for someone to— *There.* She sighed in relief, for the amour had finally relinquished its choking embrace. Passing the shelves of gear, she strode back to the mirror and examined her disguise; it was highly impractical and far too small for any portion of her body, but her stomach. Resil had been sure to supply her with food, but that had been earlier in the morning. Her hunger could never be sated, not anymore. From now on, she would be nothing more than a ravenous beast of—

"Adela."

She whirled about to see Lesander's head popping in through the doorway. He was fully disguised of course—selected the perfect size the instant they stepped into the armoury.

"One minute... I think..." Grunting, she loosened the straps of her bracers. "Methinks I might be in need of a set two sizes larger..."

Lesander sighed, probably rolling his eyes under that helmet.

"Resil and Cormurants *just* triggered the alarm. We should have left already." He shook his head, leaving to resume his watch in the hall. "Hurry it along and *pick* one. If we skip the holding room, we should make up for this lost time."

Biting her bottom lip, Adela hastily adjusted her armour; the deathly-tight bits were loosened, leaving behind vulnerable gaps as the plating spread apart. It wouldn't protect her as it should, but it still functioned as a disguise—which was precisely what she required of it. Adela shrugged to herself, figuring the armour would just have to do. Snatching a more fitting helmet off the shelves, she dashed out the armoury to meet Lesander. Adela jerked the helmet over her features, nodding for them to continue forward.

As they began walking down the halls, Lesander caught a glimpse of her face and began tapping the side of his head.

"Oh." Adela lowered the visor over her features, saying: "Hopefully there's no one we need to hide our faces from teh begin with, yeh?"

"Aye." Lesander glanced down to the polearm he had acquired. "I'm not sure what I'd do if that occurred. I don't count myself too terribly familiar with their verbal exchanges and... what not." He released a heavy breath. "I wish dearly for my butterflies instead—I could better manage with those."

"Oh? What hap—" She then caught herself, gravely remembering *just* what happened to them.[1] "Oh. I'm... sorry."

He scoffed from behind his visor.

"You need not apologise for a tragedy not of your own doing."

"Oh... sorr—mm*hm*, mm." Adela shook her head. "Well, should the occasion arise, at least you know *how* to hold your own." She chuckled humourlessly to herself. "Well, I only assume so—having personally experienced your skills with the lasher."

"You could've very well killed me if you wished, so, *no*, that is not the most apt of examples." He glanced at his polearm again. "I'm not too keen with these variety of tools."

"Oh, well, it's simple, see? You just—" Adela sprang forward, wildly jabbing her polearm in the air. "*Stab, stab-stab-stab, stab.*" She cleared her throat, gravely resuming the posture of a soldier. "I... I don't have the heart for such brutal actions, but I'm sure you could very well—"

---

1. During his duel with Adela, Lesander fell, crushing a significant number. The few who survived trailed behind as he was deported to the Vault. There, they succumbed to the freezing temperatures of the harsh mountain climate. I don't believe Adela knows about the frozen ones, but she certainly saw him crush his butterflies.

"*No*, not anymore." His helmet's visor briefly flickered to hers. "As I've said, I'm not the man I was. You've changed me Adela Windcatcher. With all too much time for reflection, your actions of conviction were the one memory resonating through my heart. The actions you've taken, what I've witnessed, what you risk—*all* because of your resolute clinging to a moral principle... the invaluable worth of another's life. It... it converted *me*."

"Oh... I... it's not so much a belief, as a..." She tried to rub her brows, but scratched the metal of her helmet instead. "I just *can't*... do *it*."

He nodded.

"And you're all the more inspiring for it."

Adela was thankful her helmet concealed her expressions so well.

"Mm, well—" She huffed. "You're so *loud*. We're trying to *avoid* what detection might remain, yeh?" She raised her visor and scratched her right eyebrow. "But... nonetheless, it's still quite sweet you—"

"And here we are," he said, yanking Adela back by her pauldron. A comical gag escaping her, she was swung back to face a humble door of reddish wood. Adela squinted at its plain face before taking a step back to examine it.

"Why isn't this one marked?" she asked, pointing to its simple design. "All the other doors were labelled in second Unbequith. Shouldn't this one say holding room of the second, or *something* of the like?" Lifting her visor to study it closer, her freckled nose crinkled. "How could you ever know this was the room to begin with?"

He rubbed the door's silver lining.

"It's exactly as Cormurants described it would be."

Adela frowned at the mention of his name, remembering it was him whose information they so readily relied upon. Slapping down her visor, she reached for the door handle.

"Well," she said, "be sure to keep your guard—" Adela paused, confused; she had searched the entire door over, yet there was no handle, knob, or latch to be found. Rubbing her hands across its sanded surface, her fingers flinched as it softly creaked forward. She shot a look over her shoulder to Lesander before tentatively pushing the door forward. Adela peeked through the crack, but could visualise nothing beyond the room's darkness. Holding her breath, she swung the door completely open to allow the hall's natural light to spill across its shadowy interior. The warmth of the arriving light blended soothingly with the lurking grey of the room's previous shadows.

Nearly gasping aloud, Adela caught sight of a russet mask carved with intricate patterns. It rested beside a pack of folded clothes atop an ashy-grey desk. As they approached it, a startled, yet faint, gasp upset the silence, causing them both to freeze. Upon hearing nothing else for several moments after, Adela began to suspect it had been Lesander whom she had heard. Before she could ask him, he spoke up.

"Yeah.... might just be our imagination."

They immediately froze again as a feminine voice softly came from behind the desk.

"No," it said. "*I'm* down here."

Curious, Adela followed after Lesander as he rounded the desk to locate the voice's origin. Crouching, they peeked under the desk to find Ms. Elicy, knees tucked against her chest in a fetal position.[2] Adela had not the slightest idea of how to react and Lesander appeared to be in the same dilemma. Thankfully, Ms. Elicy didn't seem to notice as she brushed a hand through her eyes, grumbling: "What're you two even *doing* here? Shouldn't you both be at the western wall?" She sniffed, resting her face in her arms. "Probably just a stupid drill... not that I've ever seen a drill here, but... there's always a first... *right?*" She sighed, hiding her face from view. "Right..." Ms. Elicy then peered up at them from the cup of her elbow, coolly assessing Adela. "What's the matter with your armour? Isn't that a ceremonial set for children?" She brushed an arm across her nose, raising her head. "Except for your helm... that, that doesn't match at all..."

Lesander patted Adela's shoulder and jutted his head to the side. Understanding what he was indicating, Adela stood up and began following him to the door. "Wait! No, *halt!*" Scurrying out from under the desk, Ms. Elicy marched after them. "Stop walking away and *answer* me!" They continued to ignore her, having nearly reached the door. "*Look at me!*" she screamed. "You have no *right* to turn your backs to me! *No one does!*" She seized Adela's shoulder. "I'll have you sealed away in the darkest pit if you *don't—*"

Whirling about, Adela socked her square in the jaw with armoured knuckles. Ms. Elicy stumbled backwards, hand to cheek, staring at Adela with confused and gaping eyes. Gritting her teeth, Adela tore off her helmet to expose her fuming features. Using the

---

2. **Ms. Elicy Wishton**: Pen Wishton rescued her at the age of eleven from an abusive household. When they first met, Pen addressed her as "Miss" to help her build self-respect and confidence. As a result, Ms. Elicy ensures that everyone refers to her by this title. Even I, the Oather, strive to honour this preference. Since her rescue, she's become Pen's apprentice, right hand, and adopted daughter. Although Ms. Elicy doesn't possess intrinsic magical abilities, she benefits from the numerous enhancements gifted to her by her father. Through the enchantments, spells, and symbols he imbued into her, she has become impervious to direct attacks. However, it seems she still remains vulnerable to emotional damage.

shock of this reveal to her advantage, she then pounded the helmet into Ms. Elicy's face three times, sending her to the ground. The blows left no visible injury, but still seemed to somewhat stun Ms. Elciy. Adela tried to step over her to continue the pummeling, but was kept back by Ms. Elicy's legs.

"Grab my stuff, yeh! I'll meet you at the rendezvous point!" Adela seized Ms. Elicy's right ankle and swung her leg around to somewhat step over her guard.

Lesander watched them grapple for a bit before nodding.

"Aye," he said, stepping over to the desk, "but make it fast."

Adela nodded, her lips twisting.

"Leave the mask," she said. Grunting, Adela caught Ms. Elicy's right wrist reaching for a weapon. A sprinkle of fiery symbols illuminated across Adela's left shoulder, giving her strength to restrain Ms. Elicy. "*Leave the mask!*" she shouted as Lesander held it out for her to take. She let out a small yelp as Ms. Elicy used her legs to try and flip Adela over. "Put it back and simply *leave* it!"

Lesander finally heeded her command and retreated for the door, but not before kicking Ms. Elicy in the face. Such an attack rendered no harm, but it *did* distract her somewhat, allowing Adela's knee to firmly pin Ms. Elicy's left arm. With one hand now free, Adela began drubbing Ms. Elicy in the face as Lesander dashed out into the hall.

Adela huffed in frustration, for her blows were having little to no effect. Straining to restrain the other arm, Adela's left hand tore Ms. Elicy's weapon from its holster. She hadn't the slightest clue of how to use it, nor did she wish to find out. Instead, she heaved it through the dense fabric of some black curtains. A pocket of light spilled into the room as the weapon tore through the fabric, crashed through the crystal glass of a window and flew out into the mountain's hollow outside. Ms. Elicy used the moment to buck Adela, kicking her off. Rolling away from Ms. Elicy, Adela stumbled against the desk and hastily slid Aresmas's mask over her features.

All fell away to darkness and she saw nothing. However, Adela soon became aware of all that transpired around and near her—including the swift blade lunging for her stomach. Briskly side-stepping the stab, Adela caught the knife by its handle. She could feel the weak points in Ms. Elicy's grip and twisted the weapon accordingly. With the blade in her possession, she promptly tossed it over her shoulder and through the broken window—much to Ms. Elicy's displeasure.

"The *blazes* do you keep *chucking* it out there for?"

Adela then felt a fierce blow hurling for her face. Raising her arm to deflect it, she winced as it slid across her bracer; Ms. Elicy's knuckles were searing orange, its heat peeling the bracer's outer layer of metal. As Ms. Elicy's fist passed by, Adela nimbly caught it by the wrist. Triggering a string of symbols to illuminate across her arms, she spun about, flinging Ms. Elicy through the door and out into the hall. Symbols activated across Adela's calves as she sprinted after her, hoping to trounce her before she could recover. Unfortunately, Ms. Elicy recovered all too quickly, catching Adela's hands with her own. Moving in circles, they both tried to overpower the other, but to no avail.

Voice rising to a scream, Ms. Elicy's eyes shone fiercely as she propelled her foot into Adela's chest-piece. The enhanced strike launched Adela backwards, denting her plating inwards. Her back struck the wall at the end of the hall beside a dark archway. The door to the archway lay broken on the ground beside her, its hinges singed.

Sinking to the floor, Adela gasped for the breath which had been knocked out of her. She fumbled for her chest-piece straps, flinching in pain as a sharp object slipped between her armour's joints to pierce her shoulder blade. Wrenching the object from her flesh, she used its lean blade to cut the straps loose. Adela then felt many more such objects whirling in the air towards her as Ms. Elicy advanced.

Prying her chest-piece free, she held it in front of head, stomach, then between her legs, catching three knives in the armour. They sank deeply into the metal, stopping only at the handle. She grunted as Ms. Elicy's foot suddenly struck the chestpiece, causing the knives to prick Adela. Springing up to her feet, she flipped the chest-piece over, directing its blades to face her lunging opponent. Ms. Elicy merely grumbled as she accidentally punched one of the knives, her other fist striking Adela square in the mask. Stunned by the blow, Adela stumbled backwards, falling through the archway and down a dark set of stairs.

She tumbled halfway down the steps before coming to a stop, her head spinning. Still wielding the chest piece, she began prying a knife loose. She felt Ms. Elicy descending the stairs. Her head was still dazed as she hurled a knife at Ms. Elicy's left arm, followed by another shot for her right leg. Ms. Elicy dodged the first blade with ease, only to step into the trajectory of the other. The abrupt pain caused Ms. Elicy to trip, but not enough to completely fall over.

Rising from the steps, Adela wrenched the third blade from the armour. Ms. Elicy tore the knife from her own thigh and leapt for her opponent. With the mask's abilities, Adela easily caught her knife hand by the wrist. However, this time, Ms. Elicy turned her blade downward and yanked her arm back, slicing Adela's own wrist. Yelping, Adela tightly gripped her wound. Taking advantage of this, Ms. Elicy drove her boot into Adela's shins, sending her stumbling to the bottom of the stairs.

The room Adela fell into was embedded with reddish-gold bricks, shining warmly in the late evening's light. For whatever odd reason, a large ring of silver stood ominously at the back of the room, an aperture carved into the wall behind it. Various ashy-grey desks lined the walls, their angled faces covered with switches and odd inscriptions. Adela used one of these desks to pull herself up, the knife in her trembling hand pointing up at the woman descending the stairs.

"Not *another* step!" warned Adela, raising the knife over her shoulder. "Or *I'll*—" She paused, catching sight of the glass windows built into the top of the left wall. Ms. Elicy must've caught this glance, for she quickened her pace, raising an anxious finger.

"No, *no!* Don't you *dare*—"

Adela hurled the knife, shattering the window's glass as the blade passed through it. Ms. Elicy pressed her hands against her head, the white of her eyes gleaming in rage. "The *blazes* is wrong with you?! If you understood even a *fraction* of their value you would not *so... carelessly* treat them so!" Ms. Elicy brandished her knife, as though to charge, but faltered upon catching sight of the way Adela eyed her weapon. "No... *no*, stop—*stop* it! I'd rather you kill me and keep them than toss them aside so ignorantly." Shaking her blade at Adela, Ms. Elicy stepped aside. "*Don't* touch," she growled, setting her knife atop the desk. "If you're so truly against killing, then there should be no real reason for you to—"

Adela threw the nearest chair at her.

While that occupied Ms. Elicy's attention, Adela closed the distance, picking up another chair and promptly bashing her across the head with it. The force of its blow slammed Ms. Elicy's head onto one of the desks. Pinned against it by Adela, Ms. Elicy began sliding her fingers across the odd inscriptions decorating its panel.

An energised hum filled the air. Small valves lining the inside of the silver ring began to release a hissing mist, the liquid of which came together and formed a dark pool of swirling water.

Ms. Elicy kicked and jabbed at Adela, but the mask made such sloppy attacks all too easy to parry. Gritting her teeth, a few symbols trickled across Adela's right arm in fierce radiance. Planting three solid punches in Ms. Elicy's face, Adela seized her by the collar to headbutt her nose. A dazed flash of white light crossed Ms. Elicy's vision and she stumbled backwards. Feeling Adela plant a kick in her stomach, she fell back through the portal.

Ms. Elicy splashed through the gateway, flying up into the air before crashing down on a white pavement coated in shallow water. Ms. Elicy propped herself up on her elbows, sputtering and coughing profusely. Wiping her mouth, Ms. Elicy rose to her knees, rigidly contemplating the assortment of Death Order agents gathered in the shadows about her. Some were engaged in combat with what looked like Unbequith soldiers while two others stood by.

Staring down at her.

Ms. Elicy gritted her teeth and pushed herself up to her feet.

"You two," she commanded, jutting a finger at both. *"With me."* Ms. Elicy turned to dive back into the portal. However, as she approached the cavity's edge, Adela came lunging out of the portal. Springing atop Ms. Elicy, she pinned her to the floor and began pounding her with her right fist. Adela's wounded arm wielded a blue-flamed lantern, holding it back from the action, but still keeping it at the ready. Slapping the punches away, Ms. Elicy kicked wildly, her foot colliding against Adela's jaw.

Biting back the pain, Adela rolled away from her, just then noticing the two shadowy figures approaching from behind Ms. Elicy. Shooting a quick glance to her lantern, Adela hurled it onto the pavement behind Ms. Elicy. An unholy howl shot through their ears as the lantern ruptured and an invisible force knocked everyone to the ground. A fiery ripple of shrieking blue energy splayed forth, threatening to consume all in its maddening tendrils of fire.[3]

Adela quickly rolled over into the portal before the dreadful pulses of energy could reach her. Feeling a rush of cold spike through her body, she was spat out onto the floor of reddish-gold bricks. Adela hastily scrambled away from the portal as Ms. Elicy rocketed out from it to collide limply against the stairs. A cerulean burst of writhing inferno followed her from the portal, wrecking the silver ring and collapsing its watery gate.

Adela herself was on the floor, her head falling back with a sigh. She stayed like that for a few moments more before forcing herself to her knees. Crawling over to the stairs, she examined the shining eyes of Ms. Elicy; they were wide open, rigid and distant: haunted by the effects the lantern left imprinted on her mind. Physically, the lantern's blast may have left her unharmed, but heaven knows what it did to her mind. Slightly unsettled by her gaze, she prudently shut Ms. Elicy's eyes.

---

3. Oh... well I guess that's what's inside those lanterns. Why don't more people use them as grenades or something? I mean... I know why; it violates the Code of Preservence. But... still.

Adela recoiled in shock as oily black symbols began to form in the shape of a cross down Ms. Elicy's nose and under her eyes: a side-effect of the lantern's spirits no doubt.[4] Adela edged forward to observe them closer, unable to contain the shudder passing down her spine. Crinkling her nose, she pinched Ms. Elicy's right arm and raised it to compare bracers.

Oh, how bizarrely perfect.

Ms. Elicy's armour was nearly her exact size.

She smiled before frowning once more, noting the red liquid running down her forearm and spilling from her shoulder.

---

4. From what I can tell, it's a safeguard against possession, no doubt provided by her father. Given that her soul was once openly exposed to spirits, her recovery time may vary. It could take a while, or it could happen instantly. It all depends on the constitution of her soul.

Chapter Six

A Lord's Tea Social

"ALRIGHT, JUST STOP, *STOP!*" Vincent spread his arms, causing Malvolia and Paun to collide against his back. "I need a moment to think."

Paun rubbed his forehead with a frown.

"Just let Chulian survey our surroundings, so we don't decide everything on a whim's *bloody* guess!"

Vincent shook his head.

"That'd take *far* too long for a place as occupied as this. Besides, Chulian's been away from his sword long enough as it is—a break is warranted." Vincent peeked around the corner to glance down a hall. "We'll figure out where to go when we can, but, *for now*... we must remain in a *constant* state of motion." He sniffed the air. "Speaking of which..." Without warning, he darted down the hall. Not wishing to lose Vincent, they scurried after him. Paun was afraid that if he so much as blinked, Vincent would simply disappear from sight. Rounding a sharp corner, they once again ran into his back.

"Have you *never* been to Unbequith?" asked Malvolia, holding two hands over her aching nose.

"Of *course* I have—I've been everywhere."

"Everywhere... *except* here," said Paun.

"I actually *have* been here before, but that was long ago and for a rather formal occasion, so *excuse me* if I can't *bloody remember* it all." Vincent sniffed the air again, patting the inlaid stone of the wall behind him. "We're either in Vault Tahagorah or the Lord's Court—both of which are in Mt. Færas." Vincent squatted to the floor and began waddling to the nearest corner. "Either way, we don't belong and needs must locate an exit as soon as is possible."

Paun sighed.

"Well, perhaps, we could better locate said exit if we merely sit still for *one moment*—" Vincent's arm sprung back to clap over Paun's mouth.

"*Not so loud,*" he whispered, motioning for them to step back. "There's a security check just down the hall and we're on the *wrong* side of it." He shot a glance around the corner. "If we're fortunate, we could sneak around and—*nope*, they've spotted me." Hastily rising to his feet, Vincent took a step back. "Up, *up now*. We mustn't run."

"Yeah, I figured as much," said Malvolia, rubbing her neck. She nodded at the approaching guards. "I don't suppose you two could help us out?"

The two soldiers paused to give each other a curious glance before continuing forward. Touching two fingers to his forehead in greeting, the soldier on the left spoke up.

"I'm afraid not..." His gaze briefly flickered to Paun. "How'd you three get back here? The visitation wing is quite a way off from here."

"We're lost," answered Vincent, pushing in front of Paun and Malvolia. "We've lost our way and would dearly appreciate an escort to the exit."

The soldier gave another curious look to his partner.

"Tahagorah hosts several exits, all of which are heavily guarded." The soldier coldly eyed their weapons, saying: "There are only two ways to... *wander* back here. One, is *with* our permission, under *our* supervision." A glare steadily built beneath his helm. "The other... is without."

"Well now," began Vincent, "I can assure you, it was—"

"And I don't recall," continued the soldier, "any mention of three armed individuals granted permission to rove the East Wing." The soldier nodded his head to the right. "If you would come with me please, we'll be sure to sort out this... *mild* debacle."

Vincent chuckled lightly, waving for Paun and Malvolia to begin stepping backwards.

"Oh," he said, "that won't be necessary at all, but I thank you for the offer."

The soldier placed a hand on Vincent's right shoulder, while the other reached for his left arm.

"It wasn't an offer. Please, sir... don't make this difficult for us."

Vincent light-heartedly shirked away from their grips, as though it were a joke.

"Yes, of course, but you needn't touch me, I can—*mm.*" Vincent slapped one of the soldier's hands away. "I can follow just fine without your... *assistance.*" For every step he took back, the soldiers took two forward. They each had one arm extended towards Vincent, as though to calm him down. Their other hand rested on the hilts of their sheathed weapons.

"Lay aside your arms," commanded the other soldier. "If you are indeed innocent, you have no reason to fear. Please, cooperate and we shall do our best for you."

Vincent paused, his arms raised submissively.

"Very well," he said. "You're both right. *We're* the ones trespassing here. It's us who should—"

The voice of Chulian echoed through Paun's mind.

Run.

Vincent whirled about on the heels of his boots, shoving both Paun and Malvolia forward as they swiftly fled in the other direction. The furious shouts and metallic stomping of the soldiers followed closely after them, threatening to close in the moment either of them dared to look back.

Vincent picked up his speed, taking the lead down a long corridor. The fading light of day flickered in and out of the passing windows to their left. To his dismay, Paun couldn't see where they were headed and doubted Vincent knew either. Why couldn't he simply allow them to be caught? They could escape the same way they did when captured by the Death Order. Why, they would even have had enough time to let Chulian survey the vault! It's not as though they *couldn't* wait in a cell for him.

Paun bit his bottom lip, his brows pinching together.

Surely there was a reason Vincent did what he had done. There *had* to be some angle of the situation Paun was missing. In that regard, he supposed he'd have to trust Vincent. Nonetheless, Paun still wished he hadn't chosen to run. He was already exhausted from their unexpected encounter with the Death Order. No, to flee was foolish. Why, Vincent himself had even been the one to so plainly warn them of the obvious! So why the blazes would he *ever*—

Paun was roughly shoved aside by a lightly armoured figure with a ghastly white hood. Tripping to the floor, Paun glared back at the passing figure before scrambling to his feet. He was about to run back after Vincent, when the passing figure spoke up from behind, its words freezing every fibre of his being.

"Sorry..."

It was as though *time*... itself... lulled into a plodding daze by the utterance of that one *lingering* word. To Paun, the soldiers pushing past the figure moved at the gradual rate of a setting sun. The voice was tender... soft, fading as the figure hurried off. Paun whirled about to face the figure's back, a shout violently building in his throat, daring to break through at an unreasonable volume. However, it was nearly impossible for him to speak. All he could manage was a whispering mumble.

"Addy."

The figure briefly spun about, the features beneath its hood coming into view. With the increasing beat of Paun's heart, time returned to its jarring pace. The two soldiers crashed down upon him, one choosing to bat an enhanced club across his temple. In a numbing flash of white, a spark of electricity ran through Paun's body, sending his mind to darkness.

He never caught her face.

For what felt like a brief moment, there was nothing but black. *That couldn't have been her*— It made no sense. He never saw her face anyway, it... it could have been anyone really. Truly, he was simply losing his— Another flash of light tore his conscious free.

Paun inhaled sharply, his head arching forward. Blinking in the bright light, he tried to visualise his surroundings. Unfortunately, a heavy blur remained fogged over his mind, preventing him from thinking or seeing clearly. Shaking his head, a blurred shape rose into view...

"Hi."

Paun recoiled at the sudden greeting, the room about him snapping into clarity; he was seated at the end of a long table, its creamish wood roughly sanded down. The room about him was quite large, its walls a hybrid design of marble and bleached wood. The only visible light source was the yellow radiance of dawn, streaming in through an open balcony to his left. Chasing after the light, soft bits of snow would trail into the room, dissolving as they graced the floor's pale tiles.

Paun rubbed his eyes and squinted; sitting across from him was a man. Upon first glance, he looked to be an older gentleman, what with his tousled white hair. However, there was something almost youthful about him as well... whether it was his dark eyebrows or... no; other than the corners of his eyes, the man's face was completely devoid of wrinkles. He wore a simple shirt of white, rolled up to his elbows and ruffling in the chilly breeze.

"*What...*" Paun rubbed his eyes again, still somewhat dazed. "What did you say?"

"Hello." The man leaned forward, folding his arms over themselves. As he did, Paun caught a glimpse of something adorning the man's right arm. It was shaped like a bracer, but its dark fabric was far too flimsy to be considered armour.[1] "My son, I—" He chuckled to himself. "Heavens, you look as though a simple cup of water would do you more good than the works of my finest healers."

An imposing figure standing to the right of Paun set a silver teacup before him. The older gentleman smiled, waving a gracious hand. "Many thanks, Darun."

Glancing up to the figure, Paun couldn't help but flinch at the sight of the Unbequith warrior pouring him a drink. Darun's beaten chestplate and dark attire roughly contrasted with their pristine surroundings. Paun leaned away from the warrior, peering suspiciously into the teacup set before him.

"If you're wondering," began the gentleman, "no, it's not poisoned. Please, drink. I've had many opportunities to relinquish your body of its soul, but have obviously refrained from doing so." He gave a friendly gesture to Paun's teacup. "Please, your ghastly face is enough to make *me* thirsty."

Well now there were more reasons for Paun to be suspicious of the drink, but he sipped it anyway. Fatigue draped over the fires of his wit like a wet blanket; he was simply too tired for whatever consequences might follow. Paun gulped the liquid down, clearing the fog from his mind and soothing his aching throat. As he set the cup aside, the warrior named Darun proceeded to fill it once more—much to Paun's mixed gratitude.

The gentleman smiled at Paun.

"Better?"

"Mm." Paun thumbed the corners of his lip, studying the man before him. "Why have I been brought here—before... *you?*"

"You are a guest... of my table." His hands clasped together beneath his trimmed beard. "Welcome, Paun Traitorson. Welcome."

"I see you are well acquainted with your guest." It was then Paun realised his hands weren't bound. He raised a curious eyebrow at the man before him. "It seems curious that the guest can't say the same for his host."

---

1. **Velidicio Band**: A region lord's band. A sacred adornment worn by Beyond's regional lords that symbolizes and validates their authority. There are three types of symbols on the band, each glowing according to the favour they represent: the people, the previous regional lord, and God. Before dying, a regional lord may pass their band to another, bestowing a substantial number of glowing markings onto the recipient. Some regions, like Unbequith, have altered their bands. Unbequith's band grants power to whoever "dethrones" the previous ruler.

"It is indeed, for many have been hosted by Lord Monbel and many would lay down their lives for the service he has shown them."

"A lord, eh?" Paun scoffed to himself as he examined his refined surroundings. "You have quite the... *display* of wealth—for one of mere leadership."

"In truth, these furnishings are quite humble in comparison to that of my subjects."

"Truly? Pray tell, what territory do you steward which so wealthily supports such trifles?"

"Territory?" Lord Monbel sniffed to himself. "Why... all of them."

"*All* of them?"

Lord Monbel smiled, gesturing vaguely to his surroundings.

"Well, yes. All of Unbequith." A fiery glint flashed across his brown eyes. "I am no petty steward, nor stalwart warlord. I am Tersul Monbel, second Lord of Unbequith and direct descendant of Edrath, he of the Transcendent Throne. You are speaking to the highest authority in all of Unbequith." His fingers interlocked with themselves. "For a moment, you had my whole company fooled, what with the chaos of the vault's western reach. Such a commotion even managed to rouse the attention of this very peak." Lord Monbel shrugged to himself. "Perhaps, for the future, when you trigger an alarm, try to not make too loud of a commotion, yes? We don't have drills here, so it was terribly frightening."

Paun raised a perplexed eyebrow.

"I don't... sir, I quite literally *fell* into your vault *unintentionally*. If I could help it, I'd be leagues away from this place."

"Indeed. I doubt you had little idea where that shadow gate would lead out to. In truth, I myself was unaware of its existence till most recently." Lord Monbel clasped his hands, directing two fingers at the warrior. "Courtesy to dear ol' Darun for that information."

"Of course." Paun nodded, smiling sympathetically. "It's completely understandable. I always find myself overlooking the dark cult resurrecting in the shadows of my basement." He glanced over his shoulder to the warrior, Darun. "Have you brought me here to humour a frivolous conversation or shall I see myself out?"

Lord Monbel's features shifted to a stern frown.

"The gateway connecting my domain to the Death Order was conducted in secret by a rather scandalous individual who has violated my authority long enough. He and his... his *hand*, shall burn in the fires of their own retribution." Lord Monbel combed a hand through his tousled hair. "As for you, Darun has already supplied me with the full report of his campaign. You are to be returned to the Vault, where you'll experience the refined delicacies of our hospitable eviscerating devices. Or... in your tongue, torture." Lord Monbel's grave features fell away to a hearty laugh. "Oh-ho! Oh my boy, why so pale? Have I so easily frightened you?" He chuckled lightly. "Nonsense, my son. Such cruelty is merely populated by Harling forces intent on rallying their people to a corrupt cause."

Paun sighed, concealing his shaking hands beneath the table.

"Curious... a corrupt cause you say?"

Lord Monbel dismissed Paun's comment with a wave of his hand.

"Now before you start accusing me of rumours, you should know it was Harldïof who began this whole mess. They refused to cross swords with us, insisting that *they* were the morally superior. Of course we didn't believe it. 'Twas the very reason I shrouded my campaign for the shards in secret."[2]

"You could've left the shards well alone," said Paun. "All the other regions were doing, and *had* done so, for the past centuries, but the allure of power was simply *too*—"

"No." Pushing his seat back, Lord Monbel stood and leaned against the table. "I possess all the power I need." He strode to the balcony, viewing the grey expanse of clouds stretching outside over leagues and leagues of landscape. "If you remember, the shards were held under the watchful eye of the regions' united loresmiths before being raided by an unknown entity. As Lord of Unbequith, it became of immediate importance to recover the shards, for their power belonged not in the hands of thieves and... murderers." He glanced over his shoulder to Paun. "I am all too familiar with the nature of our species. The mere temptation within the sways of power is enough to corrupt the most virtuous of hearts. No, I couldn't trust the others with the plans of my intentions." He sighed heavily before shrugging. "It mattered not, for Harling spies had already relayed the secrets of my campaign and it became... too late. Another meeting for the Chamber of the Kin had been called for." Lord Monbel gravely shook his head. "That was the last Gathering of the Kin before the... the Evenfal *incident* ensued. It was... unforgivable... a sure sign there was no reasoning with the savages governing Harldïof."

"Mm." Paun nodded, somewhat confused by the lengthy exposition. "Again, do you simply harbour me to pass idle time with *talk?* I've quite the busy life, what with—"

---

2. When regional lords are on bad terms with one another, they "cross blades." Unlike other worlds, they do not go to war in the traditional sense; instead, they invoke the Code of Perseverance and fight under its binding law. Thousands should not perish in the name of one man, whom they serve out of loyalty they were born into. They are all Children of the Eternal King—brothers and sisters. It is considered an abomination to force people to kill one another in your name.

"The prism shards? Yes, I'm aware. You think Ranitorl will aid you in this pernicious scramble for power." Lord Monbel humorlessly smirked to himself. "As did I once..." He met Paun's gaze, amused. "Your consciousness was reviewed with a vidorae as you slept. If you're unfamiliar with vidoraes, they're a rare—"

"I'm familiar with them," said Paun, his voice souring. "Hmph, *rare*." He wagged his finger and clucked his tongue. "Almost everyone I encountered possessed one."

"With reason, I am sure, for those you've been acquainted with are never of the ordinary." Lord Monbel paused in reflection. "Mr. Traitorson, you have encountered quite the assortment of colourful souls throughout your campaign—nearly all sharing the collective hatred for the name of my people." He paused again. "My son... I share the events of the past so eagerly in hopes that you might understand Unbequith a little more. In hopes that you might bless us with cooperation."

Paun crossed his arms and reclined in his seat. He felt the smallsword at his hip clatter against his seat's base.

"That depends solely on how you define cooperation."

"Paun, son of Truval." Lord Monbel approached him to set a hand against his chair. "Your knowledge is more powerful than any magic I could conjure. I... I am at your mercy. Through me, my *people* are at your mercy. The very world is endangered by what you know. Please," he said as he knelt to the floor, "all I require is the shards' location. Assist me, and you will spare the world of its impending devastation."

Paun eyed him darkly.

"You speak of war and chaos, yet such are merely rumours. I can't help but wonder why you even bother humoring such dark speculations."

Lord Monbel exhaled heavily and stood.

"Ranitorl has forsaken us. Evidently, they've spies as well and are concerned for what we intend with the shards." He scowled. "I would not be so desperate to destroy them if Harldïof was not so *bloodthirsty* for power. Ranitorl is ambitious, learned—but terribly naive. If they do indeed side with the Harling forces... *no*, they mustn't." Lord Monbel shook his head, returning his attention to Paun. "War festers in the hearts of the corrupted. Without your aid, they will destroy us and inevitably attain the shards. Those underserved of its power will craft a new era of control and dominance." He slammed both hands against the table, upsetting the liquid in Paun's cup. "*Blast* it, boy, we *need* each other!"

Paun rose to Lord Monbel's height, meeting his eye level.

"And if I so much as feel inclined to refuse?"

Lord Monbel's gaze narrowed on Paun, his hands clasping behind his back.

"If your conscience allows it, you will soon feel the burning pain of regret in your decision."

"But what would happen to me *now?*" Paun pressed a finger against the table. "What would follow *my* decision?"

Lord Monbel eyed Paun for a few moments before responding with a sigh.

"Nothing. Your decision is your own. No matter how much power one may possess, they will never possess the right to infringe upon another's will." Lord Monbel gradually turned around, returning to his ashen seat. "If this truth resonates with thee, then I don't see how I have the will to punish you for it." He waved a hand at Paun. "You need not answer. Your resolve is as unchangeable as it is unreasonable."

"So..." Paun glanced over his shoulder to the warrior, raising an eyebrow. "So am I to leave of mine own will, or must I remain a prisoner here?"

"Under the *careful* protection of Unbequith, I shall have you safely escorted to the capital of Ranitorl." He glanced up to Paun's surprised features. "That *is* where you've made your heading, is it not?"

The warrior, Darun, roughly seized Paun by the arm and yanked him to his feet. Paun's glare lingered on him for a brief second before focusing on Lord Monbel.

"Initially, I dared not ask, but now... I'd very much like to know how you ever would know I had intentions in Ranitorl?"

"The vidorae revealed you had some conflicted, yet resolved, feeling to make the journey—though the reason you'd ever wish to visit such a place completely evades me." He nodded to himself, pondering the inside of his cup. "Under the command of my most trusted warlord—or... envoy—I've dispatched my entire army to iron out some... wrinkles in our Rantilorian relations. I've a rather ambitious campaign marching for Aeraos through the haunts of Nowood. I shall have you join their company, for it is presently the safest route to Ranitorl." He held up a hand to silence Paun's complaints. "Please, it is more than a mere courtesy. The direct line to Ranitorl is wrought with peril. Why, the very depths of Above are a mere *hindrance* compared to that of the thunders' territory lying between us."[3]

Paun shrugged to himself.

---

3. What's a thunder? A type of saurian. Oh, you wish to know more? No. I'd rather you experience them firsthand for yourself. If we're lucky, you just might.

"I'm in no hurry. There's a world-renowned ferry bordering Unbequith's outskirts of Above. You should drop me off at a lovely outpost, where I'll be transported via stagecoach around a tranquil range of mountains—the name of which completely evades me—before situating me in the Humphrey Hollows. I'm sure there's another lovely stagecoach that could transport me through the Wasted Plains. Oh, heavens, you needn't fret over the name's implications. On some maps, I've seen it labelled the Fields of Summer. Quite relaxing and *truly* breathtaking. Why, you're quite right, there's no reason for me to risk a direct route whatsoever!"

"Of course not." Lord Monbel smiled warmly. "Very well, I shall see you in Aeraos. Whatever reason you may wish to visit, I assure you, the capital would have been long secured by Unbequith. I shall personally see to it that all your needs are met." Noticing Paun's diminishing smirk, Lord Monbel cocked an eyebrow. "No? You're right, I cannot treat my guest so rudely. Under my direct order, you will be escorted to Ranitorl under the protection of Unbequith."

"I don't *require* protection. I shall make my own—"

Lord Monbel's hand swiped Paun's comment aside before addressing Darun.

"Take him to the ranks of Ashhelm. I do believe it's the final city to be merging with Aivon's forces." He shot a glance to the sun's light outside. "They've begun their departure just yesterday. If you leave now, you should catch up with little to no effort."

Paun glowered down at him.

"Have I no say in the matter?"

"Of course you do. However, said say is merely overpowered by my desperate insistence and wise foresight. You are dismissed. There's a battalion waiting through the doors behind you. They're quite familiar with the escort route. Aye, and dear ol' Darun will join you when he can."

Monitoring Paun's departure, Teresul Monbel smiled to himself. As the doors boomed shut behind him, Darun spoke up. It was to be expected, for it was his job to remain wary.

"Lord of mine," he began, "you know a young man like Paun Traitorson is sure to attempt an escape. What with the Code of our ranks, it makes it nearly impossible to properly contain him. Even I might fail you—"

"You will not fail me," assured Teresul, his voice smooth and composed. "He is not our prisoner. If he so wishes to forsake our assistance, then he does so at his own folly. By the time he reaches Ranitorl's capital, we would have long restored our alliance." He shrugged. "What a perfect thing it is we have chosen to launch our expedition against Aeraos when we did. Who could have possibly foreseen that the shards would be taken there as well?"

"Surely," said Darun, "the intentions of man dull in comparison to the works of the Almighty."

"Indeed." Staring into his cup, Tersul laced his hands together. "As we move forward, let us dedicate the plans of our heart to His will, that He might continue to bless us. Wherever the shards might be, they *will* reach Ranitorl. We must simply trust our King of Heaven."

"Should the King will it, may it be so."

"So be it."

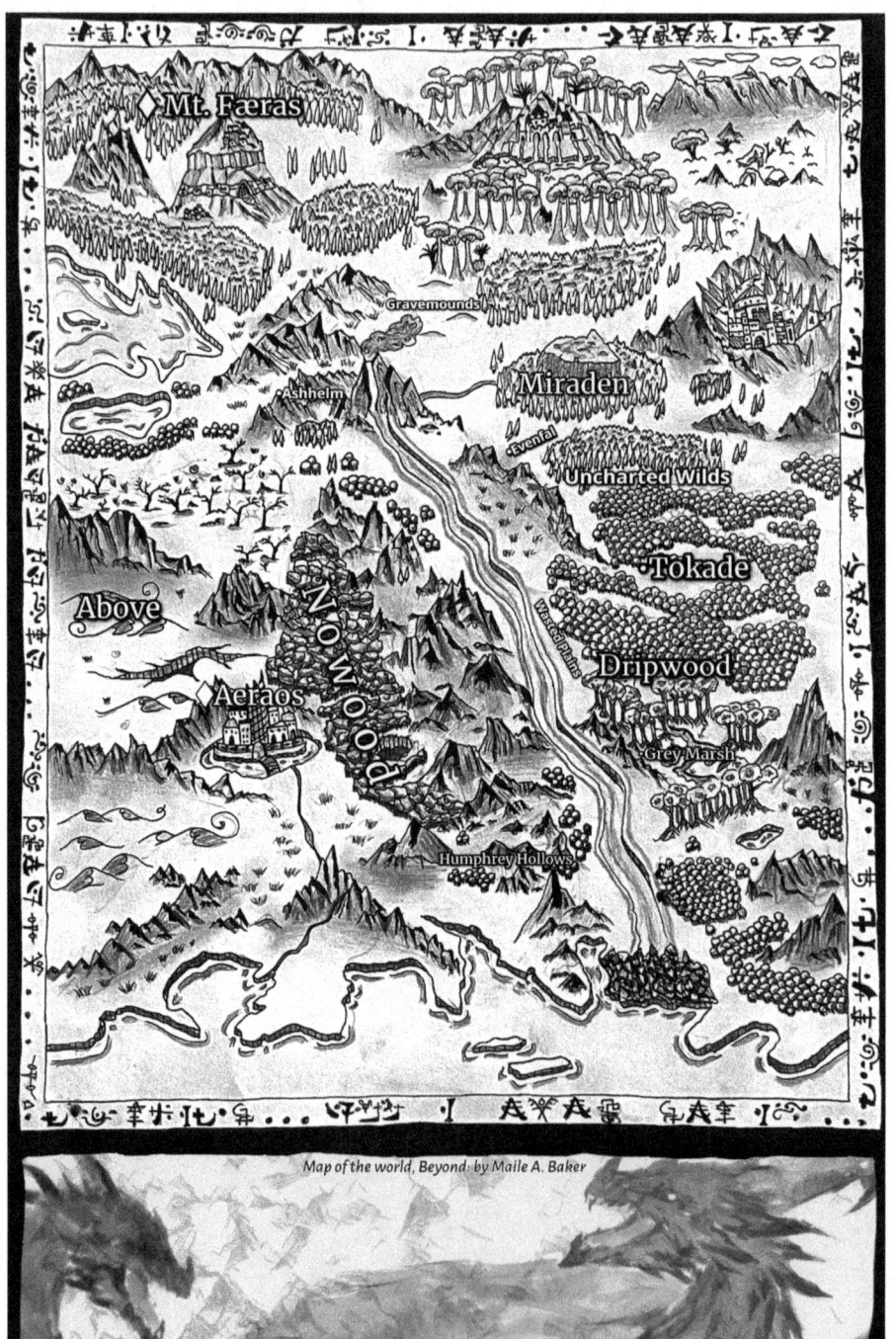

Map of the world, Beyond; by Maile A. Baker

Chapter Seven

Zugzwang

No matter how hard she tried denying it, Adela knew she was insane. It couldn't have been Paun's voice she heard, that was... impossible. It had been but a whisper in Adela's mind—a faint echo of a thought, nothing more. Yet... for whatever reason... it *did* feel more than that. As though he were actually there, wishing ever so dearly to reunite with her in holy matrimony—

Yeah, she was definitely mad.

This wasn't the first instance, and hardly the beginning of her insanity. There had been many occasions before where she had completely lost a sense of reality. Adela painfully remembered the time she sang to herself and was vividly seeing oceans.

She shuddered at the thought.

Not long ago, when Adela had been confined to darkness, she found herself surrounded by a twinkling host of fiery lights. Initially alarmed, she oddly found it reassuring. Perhaps it was the comforting wiles of the Oather.[1] There had even been *many* occasions where she heard the thoughts of his voice, but... the Oather had been silent for quite some time now. Perhaps even *that* hadn't been real either.[2]

Adela clenched her jaws, her hand pressing harder into her bleeding shoulder. Her other hand tightly gripped the wound of her left wrist. Adela's legs were aching and she couldn't help but limp along down the vacant halls.

Well, *almost* vacant.

---

1. Nope. I would have wrote about it if it was me.

2. Now that... that was real.

She approached a soldier at the end of the hall, preparing to unveil her finest impression of Ms. Elicy's shrieking vocals. However, the soldier spoke first, nodding at her attire. Adela scowled at the sound of his voice.

"I was... *sent* out here to... *retrieve* you. Saberheart and the... *Swindler* of the Crossroads are securing two... *esardrocan*. The fyldor key was supplied by me... of course. It took *much* cunning and a... *supplement* of stealth, but... in the end... there was no reason I couldn't *possibly* have... *not* achieved my goal."

As he fell into step with her, Adela felt him smile under his helmet. Clearly, he was proud about that last bit. It was moments like these she wished her mask wouldn't work the way it did. Shrugging his boast aside, she responded without much thought.

"Oh?" said Adela. "I hope that wasn't too troubling."

"No... not at all." Cormurants sniffed, gazing out the passing windows to their right. He stared oddly at the sun's fading light, glaring as though it were a person. "There were only two... *unsuspecting* guards in the stabledock's... office." His visor retreated from the window's light. "And *let* me tell you... the utter *rapture* I could feel in *slitting* the first one's throat and *gutting* the second—"

Adela raised her right fist, pinning Cormurants against a window with her other arm. Cracks split across the glass behind him with the pressure she forced against him. Cormurants tilted his head, his hands trying to shove her off in vain. Though he towered above her, he couldn't so much as budge her firm grip. Adela's injuries screamed in pain, but she heeded them not. Cormurants raised his hands submissively as the *entire* length of her right arm shone fiercely with lethal symbols of power. "Now isn't that—" Cormurants grunted as she pressed harder against his chest. "Now is that not simply... *curious*. I didn't even say if I *did* kill—or *harm* them in any way." Adela felt his strained smile beneath his helmet. "Your thoughts *amuse* me..." His pained cough briefly flickered with a chuckle. "Adela Windcatcher... can't tell... what she intends. She was struck... by a reaction... of pure instinct... you hate it, but you couldn't control it... such thoughtless outbursts always lead... to *death*."

Adela let the expressionless features of her mask rest on him before she released him. He fell to the floor as she stepped away, her arms dimming.

Her soft voice was laced with aggression.

"Why'd they send *you* of all people?" Not waiting for an answer, she stepped away.

Cormurants rubbed the base of his neck, catching up to her side.

"Simple. We've already secured the stabledocks and can depart whenever we please without so much as a second glance." Clasping his hands behind his back, Cormurants shrugged to himself. "They... didn't see *fit* to risk any... *unintentional* alarms with their... blundering... *ignorance*. So... logically, they sent *me* to find you. You should've *heard* the threats they made upon my person. I doubt you would've proud of them... had you been there to hear it."

"Don't know," she said. "I'm pretty close to conjuring some nasty ones myself." Adela felt his disappointment, smirked, and continued: "I hope you know your services weren't required. This armour allows me to traverse anywhere I please—no questions asked *or* exchanges required."

"Yes... but Resil and Lesander wouldn't have been *able* to *reach* you themselves. Unlike their blundering stupidity, I know how to... *manage* guards who—"

They both paused, for a guard stood alone at the end of the hall, idly staring out one of the windows. Raising a finger to his mask, Cormurants crept up behind the guard. How he managed to remain so stealthy in all that gear was beyond Adela. Perhaps it was due to his—Adela sprang forward with an enhanced speed, seizing Cormurants by the wrist; there was a dagger in his fist, one he had swiped from the guard and raised to plunge into his back. The guard himself had been thrown to the ground, squirming beneath the foot of Cormurants.

Cormurants tried to free himself from Adela's grip, growling something indiscernible. His wrist twisted and squirmed, but to no avail. Twisting about and throwing him over her shoulder, Adela hurled Cormurants to the ground. She twisted the knife free from his grip and spun around to direct its point at the—

Adela froze; at the end of her knife was the pale, yet stern, expression of Jhess. He shoved his boot against her shins before scrambling away and calling for support. The dagger fell limply to Adela's side as she watched him go. She tried to call out after him, but her voice was too faint, worn to a whisper by the pure shock of her realization.

Tearing off his helmet, Cormurants rose to tower over Adela. He held a trembling finger just under her jaw, his glare burning into the top of her head.

"Are you... *bloody*... *mad?!*" His scowl twisted further, forming into an expression of pure hatred and poorly concealed confusion. "The whole *garrison* of this reach will be on our heels within *minutes*." He pressed a finger against her bleeding shoulder. "At your own... *self-righteousness*, you *refuse* to take another's life. Yet *you*—"

Adela shoved Cormurants, pushing him against the floor.

"*Get... away from me,*" she whispered, turning to continue around the corner and down a hall. At its end, she beheld two great doors, their wooden design girdled with patterns of red. Adela tightly exhaled as she heard the footsteps of Cormurants catch up to her.

"Your almost... *religious* concept of morality will be your undoing. In sparing one life, you have *doomed* three others. How can you possibly be in opposition to the necessary? If the sparing of one man kills innocents, would you still stand by and let them die in the name of your principles? You might as well *kill* the innocents yourself if you're so keen—"

Adela whirled about to face him, spreading her hands out in exasperation.

"Just... *stop!* Stop talking!"

"Addy, what's the matter?"

Adela spun about, sighing in relief at the sight of Resil and Lesander. They had shoved the great doors open, the bridge behind them shining brightly in the sunset's light.

"*Resil...*" She slipped the mask from her features, ran straight into him, and wrapped her scrawny arms about his. "*Please,*" she breathed, "we have to leave him here."

He placed an arm about her shoulders, prying her off to look at the top of her head. "Fret not," he whispered. "Should the moment come, I shall be sure to... *manage* him. He won't be coming with us." Resil ducked lower, trying to make eye contact with her downcast features. "Addy, what's the matter? Did he—" It was then he caught sight of her wounds. "Whatever happened to you? I swear by all things sacred, if *he*—"

"Got in a tussle..." she mumbled, stepping away from Resil. She tucked a strand of hair away from her eyes. "I'm fine. Just a wee bit faint is all."

"Mm." He gently raised her wrist before examining her shoulder blade. He winced at the latter. "This is a deep wound." Digging into one of his various pouches, he withdrew a package of folded leaves. "This won't heal it, but it should quench the bleeding." Resil tore off a layer, softly pressing it against her shoulder wound. His hand cautiously retreated as Adela held the leaf herself. Taking some of the string off the package, he wrapped another layer about her left wrist. Satisfied, he returned the package of folded leaves into his pouch with a soft pat. "There. Plenty left over for fooling around."

Adela nodded, grateful.

"We'll surely need it," said Lesander. "It appears as though the Western Wing's diversion was for naught."

Tracing his outstretched gesture, Adela beheld a horde of soldiers rushing at them from the end of the hall. Cormurants sniffed, somehow amused.

"You can thank Ms. Windcatcher for that."

"*You*, keep your trap *shut*." Resil pulled the warhammer off his back and pointed it at Lesander and Adela. "You two, get to the stabledocks." He set a hand on Lesander's shoulder as he turned to leave. "Ride with Addy. Let her take the lead. That esardrocan is too wild for you."

He nodded, gently tugging Adela's elbow and leading her out onto the bridge.

"Come on now. We can't manage this type of work." Realising the truth of his words, Adela ever so begrudgingly followed him through the doors at the end of the bridge. Before passing through, she glanced over her shoulder to Resil. Despite the screaming urge to stay at his side, she knew she'd be nothing more than a hindrance. Hastily averting her eyes as Resil turned in her direction, she continued after Lesander.

Cormurants turned to trail after them. He rigidly came to a halt as Resil set a grave hand on his shoulders. "You," said Resil, "*stay*."

Shrugging, Cormurants coolly drew a smallsword from Resil's sheath and a long dagger from his own boot. Resil raised an eyebrow, but decided to allow it... for *now*. Taking a proper stance, Resil slid on his helmet and raised his fur-lined hood. The soldiers charging lowered their weapons; they intended death. Resil was left with no choice but to mirror their intentions.

For several moments, they waited in silence.

A blood-curdling war cry tore from Cormurants' throat as he dashed forward, whirling his blades like a madman. Sprinting beside him, Resil's own shouts mingled with Cormurants', forming an intimidating cacophony of pure madness. It wasn't long before their deranged cries were greeted by the clashing of metal and the chaos of battle. Resil's brutish bashing stood in contrast to Cormurants' precise and snappy stabbings. Nonetheless, the one aspect they held in common with one other was their pure aggression.

And they were all the more lethal for it.

Few to little words could describe the heat of that bloody instant, for a bloody instant it was. Before they knew it, a mass of soldiers lay gathered about their feet, moaning in agony or silent in death. Resil had taken many lives before, but this... this felt different—nay, it *was* different. The blood staining his hammer was foreign. All other blood had been malicious, immoral, and... *deserving* to be laid bare. Yet this... this was the blood of brothers—men of honour and virtue.

They were only soldiers.

For a brief moment, Resil felt nothing but the overwhelming sense of regret, threatening to drown him in its agony. *Oh Windcatcher*, he thought, *how I now understand.* His very weapon had become foreign to him. Resil's hammer sent a booming thud through the bridge as it dropped to the floor. *Aye, I did what I had to... but never shall I do it again. Not to men like these. There has to be another—*

Resil gasped, his breath coming short; a blade was stuck in his side, slipped between the thin gaps of his armour. Whirling about, his fist swung back, only to have Cormurants duck beneath it. Resil's eyes widened in shock, before igniting with wrath. *"You... slithering worm!"*

Swiping his weapon from the floor, Resil sprang forward to smash his hammer across Cormurants' temple. However, the worm sidestepped the blow, Resil's warhammer slamming against one of the bridge's window panes and shattering it. Cormurants continued to dodge every other following attack, as though he perfectly anticipated their coming: reading Resil's every move. In the spare moments Resil was vulnerable, the worm's weapon would dart forward, stabbing and slashing at the straps of his armour. It wouldn't completely fall off, but it did begin to loosen and leave behind gaps. Gaps that could—

Cormurants' blade slipped past Resil's defence and into the side of his ribs. His breath came to a stuttering pause and Resil fell to his knees. He leaned against the broken window sill for support. His entire form trembled at his attempt to rise. However, the worm struck him down with his foot while viciously tearing off Resil's chest piece and stabbing him again... and again. Cormurants' blade dug into every vital it could. He left no organ unturned.

Resil fell to the floor, limp.

Without a single word, Cormurants swept under Resil's arms to assist him up. He then dusted off Resil's pauldrons before using one hand to shove him in the chest. Cormurants' features were utterly devoid of emotion as he watched Resil fall silently out of the window, plummeting through the expanse of clouds below.

Bending over, Cormurants curtly retrieved a dagger from a fallen soldier. He wiped the blade with the corpse's uniform. He then bolted upright; doors thundered open at the end of the hall; a troop of Unbequith soldiers had breached the bridge and were charging straight for him.

Yes... that hurried him along.

Adela shifted anxiously in her saddle; Resil still hadn't returned. Her iron dragon sniffed at Lesander as he tried to board its haunches. Shirking away from its snout, he pulled himself up behind Adela.

"Why can't he be more... *stationary* like the others?"

Adela eyed the fyldor key in her esardrocan; Jhess had done as she asked: keeping the dragon's ore whole and allowing the creature to develop life. If it were to be *her* esardrocan, then she dearly wished for it to be more than a machine—something she could love, yeah?

She still hadn't figured a name for it yet.

"Nah, he's too special for that. Has the wiggles, yeh?" Adela leaned forward to rub the overlapping ridges of its metallic neck. "His heart overflows with the fire of vitality. To simply sit still with so much life would... why, it's nearly impossible."

"Even so—" Lesander flinched as her iron dragon shook its sides. "Even so, we should remove its key. Perhaps we could return it to its former—"

Lesander's voice was cut off by a shout in the distance. Looking up past the rows of stables, Adela saw Cormurants, hastily sprinting towards them.

"*Take off!*" he shrieked, his arm waving frantically about. "Take off *now!*"

Studying him for but two seconds, Adela's eyes widened in shock.

"*Where's Resil?*" she shouted after him.

Running up to them, Cormurants leaned against her iron dragon's flank, ignoring the snout pressing into his arm.

"There's a hundred footmen headed this way. Resil's keeping them at bay, but he will soon be overpowered—"

"You *abandoned* him?!" Adela was about to dismount her saddle, but Lesander restrained her from doing so. "You, *let go*," she ordered, "I can't just stay here and let—"

Nodding, Lesander slipped off the saddle and landed besides Cormurants.

"Where is he?" he asked him.

Cormurants gave him a curious look before gesturing to the archway leading out the stabledocks.

"Beyond the hall, in the bridge, Passine. He was holding them off well enough, but he may die at any moment if he doesn't—"

"*Coward.*" Lesander turned from Cormurants to look up at Adela. He gripped her hand. "If you can, take him with you. If we can, me and Resil'll find another iron dragon. Have yours ready in the air. I would hate to linger another second because of you."

"I can *help,*" she reasoned, about to step off her esardrocan. "Just give me a weapon and—"

"*No.* I can't let you force yourself to do what *needs* to be done." Stepping away from her, he slung the polearm off his back. "And besides, I've long been in debt to you. Simply consider us even!" He then turned to dash back the way Cormurants had come.

Adela's gaze shifted to Cormurants, who shrugged under her glare.

"You might as well murder me yourself if you intend to leave me here. You've already gotten *them* killed. Might as well finish—"

"Just *get on,*" she growled, yanking him up by the wrist. "And keep your trap *shut.*" She gestured to the saddle's ankle straps. "Put those on, unless you wish to be swept off to your death." Signalling her esardrocan with her thoughts, Adela steered it straight for the cliff. The rigid tension she felt in Cormurants behind her was enough to coax a smile from her lips, if ever so slightly. However, as her iron dragon flew into the air, she heard a violent commotion sounding at the end of the stabledocks. Looking over her shoulder, she saw a mass of soldiers pouring in through the archway. Searching through their crimson ranks, she found Lesander, utilising his polearm to deflect the incoming blows. He managed to keep them somewhat at bay, whirling the weapon about his head as they encircled him. It held them off for a brief moment, but soldiers with tall shields were stepping forward, jabbing their weapons at him.

Adela whirled her esardrocan about, causing it to dive straight for Lesander. No sooner had she done so, than several soldiers stabbed their weapons into Lesander from all sides. Adela couldn't hear the sound of her own voice as she screamed after him. His eyes turned to meet Adela's one last time, gazing at her with a medley of mixed emotions summed up in one crooked smile.

"*Go now!*" shrieked Cormurants, his vocals roaring over the wind. "Turn back you fool—he's *dead!*" Cormurants wildly shook her shoulders. "Turn about *now!* Do you wish to take *hundreds* of lives for two *dead* ones! There's no—" He cried out in pain, for a volley of arrows had been launched at them. Adela had avoided the projectiles with mild ease, but Cormurants himself was less fortunate; two arrows had punctured his back and one jutted from his thigh.

Gritting her teeth, Adela reared her iron dragon, her thoughts cueing it to climb higher into the sky. The stabledocks very quickly became a speck in the distance, the arrows far beyond harm's reach. Her esardrocan swirled about the various cities floating in the air as she flew higher and higher.

Feeling the temperature drop, she gave in to the emotion of her thoughts, causing her dragon to briefly pause in the air, weightless. Cormurants' grip tightened violently, his shrieking vocal rising above the wind as they turned over and plummeted straight down. Building speed, she signalled for her esardrocan to extend its wings. Such an action harshly levelled them out, rocketing them through one of the many colossal archways encircling the mountains. Other riders flying in and out of the archway hastily dove out of her path, not wishing to collide with the fury of her speed.

Tears welling in the corners of her eyes, she departed from the mountain's hollow.

Cold puffs of air could be seen exiting her shivering lips in a furious pace; the girl had stolen not only her armour, but her layers of insulation as well. Without it, she was left with nothing but a sleeveless top and dark pants. The outside air chilled her to the bone; perhaps she had allowed herself to be spoiled by her armour's integration of advanced tech and arduous magic.

Yes, she must learn to brave the cold's discomforts.

Ms. Elicy brought her sprint to a jarring halt. Falling against the battlements, her fist pounded against the merlon; Windcatcher was escaping. She simply flew *right past* Færas's exterior defences without a single protest. Every.. *single...* defence and not *one* hindrance or delay.

The Oather was making this far too easy for Windcatcher.[3]

Overpowering her pathetic shivers, Ms. Elicy assumed a more commanding posture as she raced down the mountain's battlements in her bare feet; the little witch had even swiped her socks. Ms. Elicy ground her teeth as she ran, annoyed it was today of all days that she had upset her father and now... now this!

---

3. I do try.

"Oy!" Waving her arms, she approached one of the battlements' flanking towers. "*Oy!*" A gathering of soldiers turned to watch her with curious eyes. "*Fire!*" she shrieked, slowing to stomp along the ramparts. "*Fire all artillery!*"

What must have been the captain of the guard stepped out of the tower to address Ms. Elicy, pressing a hand against her shoulder to halt her.

"Ms. Elicy? I don't..." He hesitated, clearly unsettled by her burning eyes and blemished features; never once had she allowed any Redfolk soldier the privilege of viewing her face. He must've recognized her harsh shouting. "Ms. Elicy, you're—"

"*That* girl," began Ms. Elicy, pointing up to the departing esardrocan, "is a *convict* of the Vault!" She shoved against his armour as he stood there, unmoving. "What are you *standing* about for! Fire *every* ember cannon![4] Did you not hear a *word* I just *said?*"

"That rider will soon be out of our cannons' range of accuracy. But, even if—"

"I... don't... *care.*" She pushed past him to walk through the tower's entrance. "Fire them all. It'll hinder her flight enough for me to—"

"No." Ms. Elicy turned about to see the Captain standing firm, about a dozen soldiers behind him. The Captain set a hand atop his sword's pommel. "By order of Tersul Monbel, Lord of Unbequith, your rank's privileges and command of respect have been revoked." He drew his blade, directing it to point beneath her jaw. "Elicy Wishton, no longer shall you—"

One of the soldiers standing behind the Captain used his enhanced club to bash the Captain across the back of his helm.[5] The Captain stood no chance against its blow and crumpled to the floor unconscious.

The soldier with the club gave Ms. Elicy a respectful nod before turning to pace the ramparts, shrieking orders to fire all cannons. Ms. Elicy herself was busy ascending

---

4. **Ember Canons:** they operate similarly to celestial casters, pulling in symbols from the air and tearing them apart to produce raw energy. However, while a celestial caster's energy is tempered to ensure contact with its target, resulting in a less powerful but guaranteed impact, Ember Cannons do not temper their energy. Instead, they keep it unrestrained, explosive, and deadly. This raw energy is focused into enchanted metal casings, akin to Earth's artillery shells. Upon being fired, these casings are designed to peel away under air friction, releasing the explosive energy in a controlled direction.

5. **Celestial Clubs:** Containment clubs. Such clubs were lent for apprehending criminals and maintaining order. They're a more primitive version of a celestial flintlock: unobstructive by magic or armour and fully capable of subduing the strongest of foes.

the tower's ladder, climbing out its top through a trapdoor. She slung her rifle off her shoulder and positioned it between the tower's merlons. Both eyes open, she zeroed in on Windcatcher, tuning her instrument's windage accordingly.

The boom of ember cannons resonated across the battlements. From the vantage of her scope, she could see Windcatcher dodging the lethal spirals of the ember cannon's shells. Having to steer her esardrocan clear of the incoming fire, Windcatcher's rapid flight was reduced to a sudden slow. At such a range, it would have been nearly impossible to hit such a target.

Be that as it may, Ms. Elicy's rifle was *built* for the impossible. On more than one occasion, her rifle had struck targets far beyond the field of view. A range such as this was hardly difficult for one such as herself; Windcatcher's head was practically gifted to her on a silver platter. Yet, for whatever reason, Ms. Elicy's trembling fingers had difficulty overpowering the trigger's lethal tension. She had already ordered for the cannons to shoot her down, so why should she hesitate at all?

But then... she knew the sluggish projectiles of the ember cannons would be unable to strike her—especially one as protected as her. *No*, she *had* to manage this. Oather's armour or no, Ms. Elicy knew she could end it all here.

Despite that, the words of Adela Windcatcher rang in her ears as she pulled the trigger.

CHAPTER EIGHT

WRAITHS AND KITTENS

HE *NEEDED* TO WALK.

Unlike his siblings, Paun's childhood had known nothing but the laborious toil of his upbringing. Among other facets, his father had been sure to establish a keen endurance within Paun, for such were the arts of Fallen Guild; it was expected of their hunters to dare impossible voyages for weeks on end: most lacking the trouble of a sumpter. Resentful as he might have been for such a childhood, Paun was still grateful for such skills; 'twas no strenuous feat travelling about, but a simple pleasure. However, on the most rare of occasions, he was forced... to *sit*.

And wait.

Paun pressed a hand against his knee, trying to restrain his leg from bouncing. Even with that, he couldn't contain the energy building in his limbs. Paun wished to at *least* walk beside the carriage, but... *no*. He simply wasn't allowed and he had no desire to break loose.

Not yet.

They had been travelling for hours now and the day was nearly spent. A good portion of those hours were occupied by the ever-changing landscape outside Paun's window. Though there were sparse counts of coniferous trees here and there, nearly all forms of vegetation had declined to obscurity; shrubs and bushes were substituted for rock and stone, grass for dirt, and soon dirt, for sporadic pools of sand. Paun himself was quite familiar with sand, for he had beheld a number of beaches in his lifetime. Yet... this sand was different. It was almost... foreign to him: less brittle and more... *rich* and... *dusty*.

Quite dusty.

Blast it, the musty smell had been smothering him for *hours*.

Though Paun sat within the carriage, fine grains of sand had still managed to slip in and find him. Its dry hue was painted across the edges of his sleeves. Even the soldiers sitting across hadn't escaped the desert's mark: the joints of their armour lined with a powdery haze of tan. Two of the soldiers had refused to acknowledge Paun's existence, choosing instead to monitor the canyon walls outside their respective window. However, one soldier sitting between the two stared directly at Paun, unwavering as he was unmoving. Unlike the others, this soldier's plating was pure black, from helm to sabaton. The only colour the soldier hosted was a curious red scarf tucked about his neck. Upon further inspection of the ornate armour, Paun was beginning to doubt if he was a soldier at all and not some kind of glorified knight. Whatever he was, the knight eyed Paun's every action, unless—he wasn't sleeping... was he? Unfortunately, the knight's helm completely veiled his features, concealing the state of his awareness.

If the knight was indeed sleeping, escape would be no grand feat.

If he *wasn't*, Paun would have to *completely* recalibrate his plan.

Resting his elbow on the carriage window, Paun propped a fist against his chin; perhaps he should bide his time till the day's passing, for the guise of night suited his plan's stealth-reliant nature. However... no... they'd expect it more, wouldn't they? Aye, perhaps slipping off in the day's broad light would grant Paun the surprise his favour so desperately required.

First, he'd take out the fellow in the centre—the black knight; he was the more robust of the three and *perhaps* the more attentive. Paun couldn't risk chancing his escape on whether the soldier was sleeping or not. Aye, he would be the first to fall. After him... well, the other two soldiers would then notice his assault. *Perhaps if I could only...* Paun discreetly scooted to the carriage's right side; the leftern soldier would be somewhat delayed in responding to the assault, granting Paun a split second advantage. Time was currency in the swift chaos of combat. However small it may be, any amount could be used to purchase positive odds for one's own favour.

The black knight didn't react to Paun's movement, remaining perfectly still; perhaps he truly was asleep. If so, he'd have to alter his plan again. Maybe if he—

Paun's thoughts were then interrupted by the grim voice of the black knight.

"There's no need for escape," he began, his voice attracting the attention of the other two guards. However, it was only a moment before they resumed their watch with the windows. "You seek passage to Ranitorl, yes?" Paun met his inquiry with silence. The soldier gave a heavy shrug, saying: "This is the surest route, and with our protection—"

"I don't *require...* your protection." Paun shifted in his seat. "I could very well find the nearest outpost by my own grace."

"Perhaps... but that's not for me to say." The black knight pointed to Paun's hip. "You hold the privilege to leave, should you truly desire it. Why, if you were a prisoner, we would not have permitted your effects to remain on your person... primarily that sword."

Paun glanced down to his weapon. The knight spoke *some* truth; Paun wasn't *quite* a prisoner... not yet anyway. They allowed him to remain armed and the carriage was unlocked for him to leave whenever he desired—why, they hadn't even taken the precaution of binding his limbs. Despite knowing this, Paun still held no wish to leave, but to *vanish*. Why else were there soldiers stationed to watch him unless they intended to *follow* him or, perhaps, something far more sinister? Whatever it was, Paun couldn't risk a potential *dupe*. No, his departure would go unreported if he could bloody help it. Still, it surprised him how openly the knight admitted to releasing him; yes, they didn't seem to mind him leaving—but under what motive? Paun found it hard to believe they were simply being courteous.

Either way, it mattered not.

There was too much risk; he'd most certainly have to escape. Deciding to occupy the soldier with talk, Paun transitioned the conversation.

"My sword?" He shot another glance to it. "The density of your armour matches that of your skull. You know very well a sword like this would be useless against it. Especially in such quarters as these."

"Aye, cuff-bound wrists would be more deadly than a bleeding smallsword. But no, I would never disregard a blade of *that* make. Aye, its metal works wonders, but it also carries weight in its meaning." The knight nodded at Paun. "Who'd you kill before claiming it?"

Paun raised a curious eyebrow.

"Well... in truth, I do believe it was *given* to me. Although..." Paun unsheathed his smallsword, catching the nervous attention of the other two guards. "It may have belonged to another before me. I am faint to remember, but it was some variety of Unbequith warlord."

"Aye," said the knight, his hand resting on his dormant weapon's hilt. "Aye, that'd be a ceremonial blade. Impractical in some bits of design, but you can't *help* but admire them, yeah?" Much to Paun's surprise, the soldier reached out to rub the blade. "Even then, it still operates far more efficiently than any other sword I know. There be some cons to it, aye, but its enhancements far outweigh all such disagreements... Aye, if I could, I would apprehend you of that sword and return it to its rightful owner." The black knight reclined into his seat. "I can only urge you do the same." He gestured to the sword's crossguard. "There's an inscription there. 'Twas written in First Unbequith... but... I am certain you'll be able to figure it out."

"Mm." Paun sheathed his blade, much to the ease of the other two soldiers. "Can you not comprehend the first generation of your region's vernacular?"

"No, few can except the nobles of Teresul's court. Our people's language of old has declined into a topic of status, affordable only to those wealthy of coin and time."

Paun leaned against the carriage's window, studying the knight's relaxed posture.

"Sad thing it is... when the ways of old become nothing more than an optional luxury." Paun's eyes flickered to the dagger in the soldier's belt. Its hilt was quite visible, perfect for him to snatch. "Makes one reconsider the position of power and he who sits upon it... does it not?"

"*No.*" The soldier's tone was firm, almost chastising. "God Himself surveyed the crowning of our Lord. If you suggest treason, you suggest heresy. No sorry soul becomes Lord of Unbequith without first a divine blessing." The knight adjusted his position, tucking the dagger out of view and reach. "Even so, though we preserve not the ancient practice of our vernacular, there is one aspect Unbequith continues to preserve." The black knight sniffed, for once breaking eye-contact from Paun to glance out the window. "Our loyalty."

"Hm." Paun followed his distant gaze outside the window. "Terribly ironic considering your present Lord led an underground revolt against the Redfolk's first Lord before succeeding the throne." Paun shrugged at the knight's glowering form. "Come now, you can't tell me the records of your youths' teachings say otherwise? I only speak from what I've learned... through established documents of truth."

"Aye, a *biassed* truth, propagated to the extreme by those who teach it. The first Lord of Unbequith went *mad*. Lord Teresul did his region proud and thus earned the grave position of power he guides us from. The other regions are far too weak to see it... power should be succeeded—not *bloody* inherited. For should the power fall to corruption, the true King, the Infinite One, shall bestow the blessing of His power to a successor of *His* choosing."

"And who is to determine whether this is the word of God or lies fed to the—"

"*Because,*" the black knight stated as he rose to an intimidating height, slouching over Paun in the carriage's confined quarters, "those who succeed others only have the power to do so, should God bestow them with such might. Lord Monbel is still in power and *therefore* deserving of it, for it is divinely willed so."

"But *how* do you know this? How are you *so* certain? For all you know, these are but the conjured up words of *another.*"

"*Logic,*" said the knight, sitting back in his seat. "Every child of Unbequith is taught the reasoning science behind every facet of life and how to apply it to such beliefs as morality and tradition. If only the other regions would follow suit... why, those Harling dogs are even allowing women to fight amongst their ranks!"

"Their motives are certainly corrupt, but I don't think *it*—"[1] Paun lurched forward as the carriage came to an abrupt stop. "Oy!" He pressed a hand against the window to steady himself. Gazing out the window, he raised an eyebrow; the entire troop had come to a halt. "What have we here then?"

The black knight leaned forward and opened the door.

"Must be stopping here to make rest..."

"Are you now." Paun followed after him, hopping off the carriage and onto the rocky surface. A thin layer of sand veiled the ground, emitting a grating-scratch with every step of his boots.

"Aye." The soldier crossed his arms as he surveyed the bustling ranks. "Take caution you don't wander too far off, yeh? Who can fathom the dangers stalking the ravines of these wastes." He beckoned for Paun to follow him. "Since you're staying, you might as well lend a hand. Should take just an hour establishing a secure bivouac."[2]

An hour indeed. It took nearly *four* hours to finish the camp. They had initially planned to rest with the sun's setting, but rumours and sightings of a haunting shadow and ghostly figures caused the whole camp to double down on fortifications.

And all the while, Paun had been the one to labour through it all.

---

1. Harldïof opened their enlistment to females in hopes of expanding their army's numbers. Because of this unconventional act, Harldïof possess the largest infantry in all of Beyond. Harldïof doesn't care one lick about equal opportunities, only in expanding their power.

2. That is, to set up camp.

Be that as it may, he hadn't been forced to work. Paun merely required an output for which to vent his combustible energy. It was fortunate too; halfway through depleting his fiery vigour, Paun had realised the true *brilliance* of his mind; in spending the time he did establishing the camp's security, he himself had become familiar with it more than any other. The camp itself was well defended, built with a fortified wall of rock and mud, while guarded at several points by sentinels; sneaking in was a nearly impossible feat. Slipping out, however, was quite simple; within the camp's perimeter was a single flaw, a flaw crafted by Paun's very hands; near the canyon's western ridge was a small hole. It was concealed by a tent's crimson flap, secured to a withering, yet quite *stubbornly* resilient, bush.

An hour had passed since he'd slipped away. They were sure to notice his escape any moment, but it would already be too late; he was too far gone in the sandy wastes. The yellow light of an outpost flickered hospitably in the distance. It was quite simple to locate from a low mesa he had wandered atop of. Aye, in the deep blue of darkness, the outpost's lights shone like a candle in the distance. Upon first glance, it appeared not too far off, but Paun knew it to be a deception of the eyes and heart. Truly, he wouldn't arrive till dawn's first light—and that was his *earliest* estimate. Though he didn't mind the walking—a soothing practice of exercise—he was still somewhat exhausted from the evening's labour.

And water.

He wouldn't mind a sip... or a *guzzling* for that matter; his throat ached something mighty. Smacking his lips, Paun's gaze drifted to the starry heavens above: it was clear, like a celestial pool of water. It was... gracefully *daunting*, in an almost—

Paun froze; from the corners of his eyes, he caught a glimpse of a... a *shadow* bolting between the rocks ahead. Sword drawn, he darted for the rocks, swinging his blade around it. His sword's edge jounced off the stone, ringing with a hair-raising pitch. Paun hated treating his weapon so, but he knew its symbols would protect its edge; he understood a few of them.

Gradually resuming his stride, he froze again at the sound of a soft pitter-patter and the feeling of being watched... both from behind. Sword raised, Paun whirled about to see nothing but the dry landscape stretching out to the black curtains of the horizon. He may have been unsure of *what* it was, but Paun was *certain* it was stalking him.

Cautiously turning back round, Paun shook his head. *I swear, if it's those bloody phantoms again, I'll lose what little sanity I have left.* Paun's stride came to an abrupt halt;

a small shadow had darted out from behind a stone and in front of his feet. To his muted surprise, Paun beheld a kitten.

The kitten.

Its mouth stretched open in a wide oval as it released an odd chirping sound.

"*Bah-hoo-rum-dah,*" it said, in what Paun interpreted as a greeting. Its voice was unnervingly deep, enough to make the hairs stand on Paun's arms. "*Shoo-ihl-loo,*" it continued, "*eyah-nah-coo-ehu.*"

"You're Steward Henagan's cat, are you not?"

"*Kuh-nah-oru-woo-shlu.*"

Paun shrugged and continued walking.

"I'm sorry, little one. I couldn't remember your name for the love of me." He glanced down at the kitten as it began trailing alongside his ankles. "But... to be fair... it was a rather odd one. Vocem *Pink*, was it?"[3]

"*Mew-eyah.*"

"Y'know, for some odd reason, I have this recurring memory of you playing a pianoforte. You're not *that* magical, are you?"

"*Nah-ohun-thoy*"

The odd note of its last chirp was humorous enough to make Paun smile.

"Well... even so, I don't—" Paun came to another pause, frowning; a spinner stood hovering but ten paces before him. Its eerie form resembled that of Aresmas, much to Paun's open displeasure. Walking straight through its translucent form, Paun continued, undeterred.

The spinner addressed him from behind.

Are you so hasty as to forsake the merry company of this soul?

Paun shook his head.

"He forsook *us*. I always knew he would, for the vidorae revealed as much."

You blame him for this choice?

"If what you've said of his family is true, then... then no." He paused, considering just how much he'd interacted with this... these beings. "You led me to the Death Order..." Paun glanced over his shoulder, flinching at how close the spinner was. "Why have you chosen to guide *me* to the shards?"

The Oather follows you.

---

3. N-nope... not his name.

"Clearly..." Paun begrudgingly tore his attention from the spinner and resumed his stride. "Still doesn't answer—"

And you are yet to answer us.

"Answer *what?*"

Aresmas Hul has long since vanished, yet this concerns you not.

"I... well I *do* think of him from time to time, but... I can't *always* trouble about a departed companion."

And why not? You do so with the girl.

"Adela's different... that... she was *my* fault. I can't *help* but trouble about her."

But you have always troubled over her, more so than Aresmas.

"Yeah, well..." Paun sighed, grinding his jaw as his gaze rose to the stars. "I suppose I am yet to answer you, for I am yet to answer myself."

The girl is a key piece to the Oather's trope... A trope he seeks to conjure against the wiles of silence. You can't help but feel drawn to her, for you too are a piece in his trope of three.

"Trope?" Paun shot a glance to the ghostly figure, its form resembling that of Pen Wishton's. "I only know of one other who has uttered that word before."

Indeed. Still, it is possessed of many other meanings, but of the mundane variety. Nonetheless, said meanings can be delved into and exploited by the Oather. Tropes are powerful tools, aspects of reality rooted in this world and sprouted into all others. The spinner's features dissolved away into a face Paun didn't recognize. *The trope of three is one of the strongest and most unbreakable.*

"Course... might as well be, whatever that *might* be to begin with." Paun shook his head, confused as ever by its words. "I recall Vincent mentioning... *something* of the fact, though I cared not to take mental record of it, for his words seemed of the nonsensical variety."

Drendon knows little of what he speaks. He is the first piece, but a piece nonetheless. Be wary, for should any of the Oather's three die, the silence shall go unanswered. And we... we must have answers.

"I doubt we're at risk dying, Spinner. According to some, the Oather protects us with a type of... what was it... invisible, yet impenetrable, armour? Over the course of recent events, I am beginning to believe such."

It is true. However, his power shall null upon the eve of battle.

"How lovely."

A chance for one of the three to perish shall arise, for such is the trope of silence. It shall be the old mentor or the young interest. Perhaps it shall be the young adventurer, but only if the girl slays him.

"Mm." Paun then froze, disturbed by its cryptic words. "Adela is quite more than simply *a young interest...*" The spinner remained quiet, allowing Paun to continue thinking. "*Spinner,*" he finally whispered, "I grow tired of your presence."

You despise it as much as you yearn for it. Our presence is limitless knowledge and knowledge is as cursed as it is propitious. You crave to know more, yet are afraid of what it might entail.

Paun's mind was a jumbled mess of emotions. He didn't know how to feel; having the spinner describe him so accurately was... it was— *Unnerving as it is assuring?* said the spinner, finishing Paun's thoughts.[4]

Raising an eyebrow, Paun watched the spinner's body take another unfamiliar form; it was a lanky young man with dark hair and deep-set brown eyes. After studying it for a few moments Paun recognized it as the man Adela had danced with at the ball—albeit, slightly pathetic in comparison. *That... creature,* it began, *operates beyond the Oather's comprehension... and ours.*

It took Paun a couple of moments to realise the spinner referred to the kitten. Chuckling at such an odd notion, Paun bent down to scratch the *creature* behind its ears. A deep purr rumbled softly in the kitten's throat as Paun buried his fingers in its plushy fur.

"Heh, I wouldn't doubt it for a second." He withdrew his hand, prompting the creature to rub against his ankles. "Do you happen to know its name?"

It introduces itself as Jovem Pynk, but... no. We are unaware of its name... or its nature. The spinner's features had shifted to that of Abaddon Henagan, causing Paun to frown. *Tread with caution, we know not its motives.*

"Mm." Paun rose to his feet and continued to the outpost. "Should I outrun it then?"

It has chosen you for companionship. However long that may be, you will not escape it, for it is not within your power to do so. Treat this entity with utmost caution...

"Alright, but *how*—" He pursed his lips, irked at the sudden absence of the spinner. Crossing his arms, Paun gazed down at the kitten; it was sitting on his boot, licking its round paws clean. "Well," said Paun, nodding at the kitten, "I'm going *there* if you'd like

---

4. Thoughts the Oather *was* about to translate into sentences for documentation, but sure. It's fine, cut off his writing and interrupt him. It's fine.

to come." He gestured to the lights in the distance. "Though I have been warned by a potential threat that *you* could also be a potential threat."

The cat looked up from its paw, giving Paun a slow and deliberate blink.

Paun chuckled, saying, "Aye, makes little sense to me either, but one thing *did* strike my curiosity." He shot a glance to the lights in the distance. "Is it truly impossible to outrun you...? I wouldn't doubt it considering you found me all the way out here. I'm still quite clueless as to how magical you are. But, nonetheless..." Without another word, Paun shook off the kitten and shot off, sprinting as fast as he could for the outpost in the distance.

The kitten gradually diminished from sight, enveloped by the horizon's starry curtains.

CHAPTER NINE

AN INSECT

"**S**HOULD'VE KEPT YOUR PLATING on..." she grumbled, glancing over her shoulder to Cormurants. He was blatantly ignoring her, tossing the last arrow from his flesh and watching it fall. Adela's gaze returned to the horizon ahead. "Could've protected yeh more than that jerkin," she said.

"I'm... moved... you're...so *deeply* urged to... *trouble* over... mine health..." He tightly gripped Adela's shoulder as turbulence shook the esardrocan.

She pulled away from his hand.

"I'd rather not *have* to trouble about your wounds if *you* could've helped it." She squinted, eyeing the desolate wastes below her. "Only makes things all the more difficult..."

"Perhaps... but the armour was... *far* too limiting for one of my... *particular* manner of management."

Adela scrunched her nose.

"If you weren't so bleedin' *keen* on killin' everything, we could've *all* been alive. I knew that guard who alerted the others—could've reasoned with him y'know."

"In the moment... I couldn't have... *known*, nor... bothered to... *care* knowing. Eliminating *him* would have eliminated whatever risks *shadow* his existence."

"You would've *killed* him."

"And you should've *let* me! You didn't even *have* to kill him yourself! All you had to do... was *nothing*. But *see* now! There is *nothing* to be done of it."

"No, we can still *learn* from this and know what *not* to do for the future, yeh?" Her iron dragon drifted to the left, catching a helpful updraft. "Perhaps thinking twice 'fore doing something as drastic as taking another's life—*or* considering the weight of one's divine consequences, yeh?"

"Or perhaps if you don't allow your own... *muddled* misconception of morality to be... *forced* onto the actions of others... we might've just *stood* a bloody chance!"

"Perhaps you didn't hear me... but we could've *all* made it out... *alive.*" Her attention rose to the ruddy line of the horizon. "Lesander is *dead* and Resil could be too for all we know." She tilted her head to the side in reconsideration. "Still, there's been many other occasions to think him dead. If anyone could escape... *that* situation, it'd be Resil. Can't hurt to hope and pray... even *you* must see that."

"No, he is most certainly *dead.*"

She shot an irritated glance in his direction.

"There's no way you could know that."

"Can I not?"

"*No!* Like the *coward* you are, I *guarantee* you fled at the first sight of danger, leaving *him* to fend for *himself!*"

"Aye, and he *died* because of it... because of *you.*"

"We don't know that for certain!" She huffed, knowing very well Cormurants was merely trying to sow chaos in her heart. Abiding her tone, she continued: "He could've very well retreated after assessing their numbers—hid somewhere. Resil's no fool, he'd know when he was beaten." Her eyes sparkled at a thought. "Why, you should know yourself he's Fallen Guild! Means even if they did catch up, he'd stand a chance seeing as our ranks are quite immune to almost any form of metal."

"Aye—" Cormurants grunted, holding his bleeding side with a tight grimace. "Aye... but not to the... the *enchantments* of your own weapons. No... your kind are not as... *untouchable* as you... so... *desperately* wish to believe."

All colour drained from Adela's knuckles as she squeezed her reins.

"No... but why... would *that*... matter?"

"Because..."—he leaned forward, speaking softly into her ear—"*you* killed Resil Saberheart. If you had but allowed me to *manage* the circumstance, he would be safe... and well. *But no.* You had to burden mine actions with your... moral superiority, *infuriating* me to the point of where... I *had* to kill him. You see... *you* killed him with your self... *righteous*—"

"You lie," she whispered, fiery symbols beginning to glow along both arms. "*You lie...* You lie, for I know what you desire of me... and you won't be satisfied."

Cormurants continued, undeterred.

"*Truly*, why do you suppose I returned devoid of armour, hm? It was far too bloody of a mess for me to clean... I had no time."

"You... can't. I... *refuse* to... fall prey to your words, *Cormurants*."

"He *died*... by his own *blade*... its metal *sinking* into his *beating* chest. His very breath *choked* on the blood of his... *expiring* heart. He was never granted the *privilege* of last words, for—" Cormurants' voice cut off, gradually building into a hair raising scream as the esardrocan dove straight down. He leaned forward to seize Adela's shoulders, only to have her slap his hands away. In an explosion of sand, they collided with the desert below.

The air about them clouded in a brownish haze and Cormurants came to consciousness again. He was certain several bones were broken, but that didn't stop him from hastily undoing his ankle straps. The iron dragon stirred beneath him as he slid off its saddle. Falling to the sand below, Cormurants feebly edged away from the creature. The overlapping design of its metallic lips slid back in a snarl, revealing a fine row of needle-like teeth. Cormurants held a begging hand out, laughing as he spoke: "You would truly have that creature devour me alive?" He chuckled, gasping as he tripped backwards against a rock. Glancing about the tight canyon, he then realised just how trapped he was. "How... barbaric..." He smirked to himself. "How *truly barbaric!*"

The esardrocan remained put, its pupils shining a terrifying blue. Pressing a hand to his side, Cormurants smiled at the sight of Adela coldly approaching him from behind the creature, a long dagger in hand. The orange cloud of sand and dirt parted in swirling wisps, as though fleeing the touch of her furious advances. Cormurants' disturbed smile widened at her advances and he pushed himself up to a frail stance. "Come now," he said and laughed, "you *want* me to die, you can't deny it! Your thoughts are clearer than—" He grunted, collapsing as Adela's fist struck his face. Spitting out sand, he feathered the sharp pain in his jaw: it felt like a hairline fracture. "You..." he murmured, "*won't* kill me..." His breathing was short, a bitter-red liquid running from his features. "You want to... so... *so* terribly... but you can't... more people... die... because you... *can't*." His gaze rose to meet hers as he attempted to stand. Though his expression evoked a cold confidence, his green eyes burned with dread. "You're weak... and you *can't*."

Tears streaming her dirty cheeks, Adela's fist struck him again. The tip of her knife was then poised just under his jaw, preventing him from rising again. Grinding her teeth, she stayed like that for a few moments before stabbing her blade into the sand beside his head.

"For your *sake*," she whispered, "don't touch that knife." With that, she turned to her esardrocan. A venomous flame lit in the eyes of Cormurants. With an enraged shout of pure madness, he sprung up from the ground, wrapped his arms about her neck and yanked her onto the sand. She broke from his hold quite easily, turning over as she rose. Swiping the dagger from the sand, Cormurants bolted up to stab her neck. In a motion too swift for reaction, she deflected his assault with her wrist, twisting her hand to wrench the knife from his grasp. Jerking the blade downwards, Adela raised the knife defensively as Cormurants lunged for her throat; he froze, mouth gaping. She cocked an eyebrow, following his gaze to her hand and the knife she wielded.

Its blade was buried in his stomach.

Cormurants gazed up to her, the fading light of his eyes locking with hers. "You... you killed me." His features of utter disbelief reformed into an expression of hideous amusement as he erupted in laughter. Horrified, Adela released him and covered her mouth. In a plume of sand he collapsed against the desert, convulsing with laughter and blood; "You *killed* me!"

Her breathing was ragged and her eyes wide. Clenching her eyes shut, Adela averted her gaze and turned to mount her esardrocan. His mad laughter followed after her, crying: "Adela... Windcatcher... *killed me!*" His tone abruptly shifted to a blood-curdling shriek of pain. Adela winced at the sound, refusing to look back as she straddled the saddle. Tapping the side of her esardrocan's neck, it propelled from the earth with a heaving tremor and a cloud of red dust. The maniacal mirth and tormented cries of Cormurants faded from hearing as she fled to nowhere.

Adela was too broken to cry.

CHAPTER TEN

FISH, FOOT

P AUN STAGGERED THROUGH THE gates of the outpost, nearly passing out for lack
of breath. He paused, leaning against the gatehouse built of dried mud and bundled
sticks. Paun's breath was slow to return, but he was soon able to think *somewhat* clearly.
His befogged sight rose, squinting at the cloudless sky; though there was plenty of sun,
the air itself was quite chilly—even after all his running. Paun jerked his coat closer and
shoved his hands into his sleeves with a shiver. His mouth was dry, fine cracks running
along his lips as he smacked them.

Oddly enough, none of the rugged travellers shuffling by thought to pay him so much
as a curious glance. Paun ignored it for now, shading his eyes as he stepped out of the
gatehouse to examine the sea-blue sky; it was well into the morning now and the cat,
Jovem, was nowhere in sight.

Truly a shame. Would've made another lovely companion to have trust issues with.

Puffs of sand swirled across the town's worn pavement, peppering Paun's boots as he
walked along. The outpost was occupied, aye... yet it felt like a ghost town.

Paun couldn't tell whether he stood out or blended in with the rugged nature of the
town. Though he felt the eyes of various citizens resting upon him from the shadows
of their homes, he also felt as though none paid him any mind. Perhaps the locals were
used to hosting vagabonds such as himself or—perhaps not; whenever he glanced in their
direction, he would briefly catch their eyes before they hastily shifted their gaze. Paun
tested this observation on one local resting against a wall of pale stone. The man was armed
with a nocked bow and appeared to be dozing under the cool shade of his conical-straw
hat.

Paun raised an eyebrow; perched on the open window sill beside the man was a peculiar
bird; instead of feathers, it was wrapped in layers of wispy-white hairs, a large clump of

said hairs gathering beneath its chin in a thick beard. Its hooked beak dug into its wing, roughly preening itself of dust and sand. Paun hastily averted his gaze as its beady yellow eyes locked onto him. He shuddered; they were practically bulging out of its skull.[1] As Paun glanced away, he caught the unwavering eye contact of the bird's owner. Unlike the other locals, this man refused to break his gaze.

Nodding in his direction, Paun approached, asking: "You know where I can find a drink, friend?"

The man assessed Paun with drooping eyelids before turning to study his bird.

"There's something of an inn before the southern entrance... just yonder." He loosely gestured down the street as he scratched the scraggly chin of his bird. "I recommend their water... 'tis the only drink there for one of your condition."

Paun nodded his thanks, eagerly following the man's directions. The establishment was quite simple to locate: its dark wooden design contrasting with the dull environment about it. Stumbling through its butterfly-wing doors, Paun stumbled past various tables and on to the bar's counter. Not one occupant paid him a single mind, as though his bedraggled state were completely expected.

"*Water*," said Paun, swallowing hard. "I need water."

The innkeeper behind the bar nodded, reaching under the counter for a glass jar.

"That'll be five pieces," he said, puffs of dust flying off his red beard as he spoke.

Paun reached into his coat's pocket, feeling nothing but a folded piece of paper. Discreetly removing his hand, he tapped the counter's surface.

"That'll be fine. Just pour it."

Setting the jar before him, the innkeeper filled a pitcher to the brim from one of the many barrels lining the back wall. Before he could pour its liquid into the jar, Paun seized the pitcher and began drinking from it directly. In the first few gulps, his thirst was immediately slaked. However, he knew this to be a deception of the body; though it expressed satisfaction, it was still in dire need of liquid. It was overtly grateful, aye, but not quenched. Proceeding to drink the entire pitcher dry, Paun fell forward, resting his weight and the pitcher atop the counter. "My thanks, good sir," he said and sighed.

---

1. **Jawbird**: named for their unique underbite, which hosts a row of omnivorous teeth. Their feathers are more akin to hair and are quite ticklish. They enjoy snacking on dried fruits, lizards, or eggs. Amusingly enough, they're terrified of snails. It seems they simply can't comprehend such curious gastropods.

"Course, but that'll be—" The innkeeper paused, lifting his arms as a grey kitten climbed up from under the counter to rest beside Paun's elbow. "Cheeky little creature, aren't ye?" The innkeeper patted the kitten's head.

"His name's Jovem," said Paun, eyeing the cat with relative surprise; apparently he *can't* outrun the creature. "I believe he's mine, but I'm quite unsure."

"Whatever he is, he showed up this morning in mine kitchen. Now, most often than not, I don't mind a pretty kitty droppin' by for a snack. But *this* critter was stackin' 'em!"

"What's that?"

"Fish! Bleedin' *fish!* It was a neat pile an' all... but I didn't need it!" The innkeeper glanced at the cat and rubbed its ears. "Not just that, but I had to wash 'em all over again..."

Paun pointed to Jovem.

"You want him?"

The innkeeper leaned against the bar, his features etched with disbelief.

"What, for free?"

"As payment for this drink." Paun peered into the pitcher's depths, sourly regarding its bottom. "Speaking of which... I do believe I could use another round."

"But you're already—"

"Sure, it's on the cat." Paun shoved the pitcher into the innkeeper's arms. "I'd be more polite, but I feel as though I'm dying."

Frowning, the innkeeper filled the pitcher from the back wall.

"Ye do realise it was five pieces a jar, yes?" The man set the pitcher before Paun, its liquid sloshing precariously, but not spilling. "Yet you've consumed a whole *pitcher's* worth of water."

Paun shrugged, proceeding to drink from the pitcher and speaking between gulps.

"I'm the... the cat is worth far more... than anything this water could be." Paun set aside the freshly-emptied pitcher. "Unless water's something scarce in these regions?"

"No, in truth, it's quite plentiful." The innkeeper gestured through the doors. "There'd be a harbour just through the southern gate, bordering the Above Desert and its sea,

Below." He returned his heavy gaze to Paun. "It's purifying the water's gases that be so costly."[2]

"Ah, well..." Swooping under his forearms, Paun snatched Jovem off the counter and jutted him beneath the innkeeper's nose. "I have mentioned the magic cat. Does it not pique your curiosities?"

"Aye, but it don't cover the cost. And he'll only haunt my stock o'fish." He shook his head. "My *poor* fish..."

"Aye, well, you see—as of present—I regrettably find myself completely devoid of currency. Perhaps there's another agreement we could..." Paun's voice died away, and the inn had become awfully quiet. Slowly looking over his shoulder Paun saw everyone at their tables had frozen, staring at him with hard glares. Turning back to the innkeeper, Paun continued: "Please, take the cat. It's all I have."

The innkeeper slung a cloth over his shoulder and gestured to Paun's hip.

"What about the sword?"

Paun nodded, biting his bottom lip and wagging a finger.

"... all I have to *offer*," he clarified. "I just don't—I haven't—" He huffed. "*Why* are you *all* staring at me?!" Paun spun about and confronted the hostile eyes boring into his person. "It's... *making* me *jumpy*."

"We're awfully close in this little outpost," said the innkeeper, a burly hand seizing Paun's shoulder and spinning him about. "Like family we are. They just don't wish to see me swindled by some passing thief."

Paun heard various chairs creak behind him.

"*First* of all,"—he raised a finger to the people behind—"*first of all*,"—he spun back to the innkeeper—"I am no thief. Surely you are not crude as to strike down an *already* beaten traveller with such a *blunt* accusation?"

The innkeeper's eyes narrowed.

---

2. The Above Desert is a layer of sand suspended over the sea known as Below. Each grain of sand is hollow and filled with a toxic, lightweight gas, reducing their overall density and allowing them to float above the denser sea, Below. The balance of buoyancy and gravity keeps the grains suspended, while electrostatic forces prevent clumping and sinking. Below produces these fine, hollow grains from its depths, where fissures release micro-bubbles of eroded rock. The currents of Below affect the Above Desert, causing the grains to rub together, break into smaller pieces, and eventually fall back into the sea, sinking to the bottom of Below's dark depths.

"You haven't the slightest notion of *what* I'll strike down." From behind, Paun heard the cracking of knuckles mingling with more screeching chairs. "However, I'm sure you could work off the debt in the span of—"

"I don't have time for that."

"You haven't heard but one *word* of my proposal!"

"I should have departed this outpost yesterday—I don't have *time* to remain *put*, working off a debt to... for water!" Paun looked for Jovem to offer as a down payment, but the cat was nowhere in sight. "What was that you mentioned of a port? Southern gate was it?"

One of the patrons shouted at him from their tables.

"You ain't leaving this outpost till you've *paid* what's *owed!*"

Paun spun around to face the voice, slightly taken aback by the number of people standing from their seats. They bore no weapons, but their red knuckles looked tough enough to beat a tree down.

"Alright... now..." Paun raised his hands, edging slowly for the exit. Their stern glares lingered on him as he passed, threatening him far more than words ever could. "Alright, I'm... I'm no fighter... but I'm not wasting another moment either. If you like, I can come back and—"

He was halfway through the exit when it all happened in an instant; one firm grip seized his sword's hilt, another his coat's shoulders, and one more jerked him back into the dining room. Paun grabbed a chair as he fell back, twisting over to bash it across the nearest assailant. A hand on his shoulder released to catch the chair and wrench it from Paun's hand. With his shoulder free, Paun rolled to the right, dodging the swinging chair and pummeling a townsman in the gut with his fists. Whirling about, he then shoulder-rolled to the one who had swiped his sword and was drawing its blade. He seized the man by his wrist, kneeing him in the stomach, manipulating his joints and catching his sword's hilt as it fell. Twisting the man's fingers, Paun forced him to the ground, stepped behind him and flicked his sword over the man's throat, shouting: "*Back! Back* now! You—"

Paun shook off a local clinging to his ankle. "*You*, lemme go!" He whirled about to face the innkeeper. "And *you*, I hadn't the *slightest* clue water was so *bloody* expensive! I can't pay you in pieces *now*, but I *shall* when I return!"

"And... when might that be?" Paun swung about to face the voice; standing at the inn's entrance was a man with a scraggly white bird perched on his shoulder. His gaze scanned the room from under the shade of his conical hat, his sandy-grey coat swishing at his ankles as he approached Paun. His voice was raspy, ground to such a tone by years spent in the sandy wastes. "When... can we expect you to grace our humble outpost again? Why, very few ever visit us, save by accident. What assurance can you offer Baxton here—your lovely host—that you'll be able to find us again... much less pay off your little debt?"

Paun glanced at the others surrounding him and licked his lips.

"In truth, I don't believe there's anything I can really say—nothing beyond mine own word."

The man shrugged, scratching the side of his scrubbly jaw.

"How much does he owe you?"

"Thirty pieces," answered Baxton, a wooden cudgel wielded in one hand. "But you heard him yourself, steward—he don't have that!"

The steward nodded, returning his collected gaze to Paun.

"Then you'll work it off."

Paun scoffed, gripping his sword tighter.

"I don't have *time* for that."

"No... I think you do." The steward raised his arm, directing an object of brass and metal at Paun's chest. Paun immediately recognized it as a revolver: a weapon of great power and rarity, a weapon Paun had only heard *rumours* of. "You'll make the time," said the steward, "lest you cheat ol' Baxton, here." His revolver gestured to the satchel on Paun's right hip. "What's in the bag, boy? Perhaps we can compromise."

Paun slid the satchel to the back of his hip.

"Nothing that would interest you... or... Baxton." Paun glanced about the room. "Look, I'll just—"

The steward cocked his revolver's hammer.

"Girdle thy loins and answer me like a man. I don't got all day either. Oh... right." He pointed to the man Paun held at swordpoint. "Lettem go, drop to your knees and sheath your blade, lest I shoot you in your descendants."

Paun scoffed, but obeyed all the same.

"Well that's simply pathetic."

Blinking slowly, the steward stepped up to Paun, his boots clinking with every step.

"Come again?"

"*That.*" Paun frowned as the revolver was raised to his head. "Used to getting your way with *that*, are you?" He sniffed, hoping to play the steward's pride. "You hide behind its power like a *coward*, 'cause without it, you *know* you're powerless." A snarl twisted across his features. "Put down the revolver and what's left?"

The steward crouched to Paun's eye level, twirling the gun in his hand to hold it by the barrel. Without a word, he bashed its butt across Paun's temple. A flash of white stung Paun's vision as he toppled to the floor, a line of blood trickling down his temple. Those gathered around chuckled. As for the steward, he merely rose back to his feet.

"A man."

Rolling over on the floorboards, Paun froze, completely taken aback as Vincent and Malvolia stepped into the inn.

"Oy, Steward," began Vincent, speaking up from the entrance, "appreciate your guidance, but we've found the port and needs must make haste—he already left without us."

The steward nodded, his revolver still trained on Paun.

"Sorry," he said, "got a little held up." The steward tipped his hat. "I wish you many blessings on your journey, Uncle."

"And you as well." Vincent glanced to Paun and nodded at him. "Make it if you can, we haven't time." With that, he turned and departed from the inn.

It was then Paun spoke up, alarmed at the sight of Malvolia following after him.

"*Oy* now, *hey*—is that all? Mal? *Vincent!* I know you two won't leave me here!"

The steward's firearm briefly lowered.

"You know Mr. Merrybender?"

"*Yes!* And—" Paun bounced on his heels to peer out after them; they were nowhere in sight. "And they're leaving me *behind!*" Scrambling to his feet, he darted for the doors, only to halt as the steward pressed his weapon's muzzle against his stomach. Flustered, Paun's hands waved about the air. "They're leaving *without* me!"

"Aye," said the steward. "They've a boat to catch and it's already departed. You best be sprintin' if you hope to catch up." To Paun's relief, the steward holstered his firearm. "I'll personally handle your wee debt, son. You just run."[3]

Nodding his thanks, Paun bolted out of the inn, down its steps and into Vincent. They both fell to the dusty street, sputtering sand. Vincent bounced back to his feet, one hand rubbing his bruised forehead, the other yanking Paun up.

---

3. Well... that was a little more convenient than I wished it to be. Mm, I need more action and tension than that. Let's see what sample of chaos I can summon... just for boredom's sake. How can you complain, Beholder? This is action!

"Good," he said, dusting off Paun's shoulders. "I was beginning to think Stew shot you."

"How did you—" Paun cut himself off to chase after Vincent, following him down the street and through the southern gatehouse. "How'd you know I'd be here?" he finally asked, shouting over the blusters of the building wind.

"I hadn't the slightest idea!" answered Vincent, darting left down a descending alley. At the alley's bottom, Paun could distinguish a sort of harbour, built into the sands of the desert. "In truth," he continued, "we assumed the worst and made haste without you!"

Paun couldn't help but roll his eyes.

"*Well*, that's *certainly* a way to reassure trust!"

"Yes! Very true! Truth is the best method to establish trust with a previously forsaken companion, ey?!" Vincent elbowed Paun, suddenly halting. He surveyed the rugged harbour lying before him; there was no water in sight. Nothing but a stretching sea of sand. Vincent shielded his eyes from the sun, saying: "Why, can you just imagine the odds?!" His bright countenance sulked and his hand fell. "The odds..." His gloomy features turned to address Paun. "You've brought the Oather's eye with you... all... this... way... to me."

"I... in truth, I don't know." Paun followed Vincent's gaze to the docks. "But... forgive me, what are we looking for?"

"It's perfect, really. Things were going so smoothly—*too* smoothly, in truth! Yes, some action is *just* what I needed. I was worrying we'd never get some near-death *excitement!*"[4]

Paun shrugged.

"Perhaps we've avoided his detection. My life's been fairly uneventful thus far."

"One such as yourself is... *incapable* of comprehending the word *uneventful*." Vincent's posture straightened. "Hullo now, there she is."

Following his gaze, Paun saw Malvolia, standing far beyond the docks atop the shifting tides of sand. She was frantically hopping up and down, pointing to a small ship in the distance.[5]

"*They're picking up speed!*" she hollered. "We shall surely lose them once they catch the current!"

---

4. Oh, shut up.

5. Ships travelling through Above are designed to plough through waves of fine sand, breaking them into smaller pieces and harnessing the currents below. These ships are extremely expensive to build and are equipped with numerous enchantments to prevent capsizing.

Vincent slapped Paun's shoulders, hastening him to follow. Their hurried steps thumped along the dock's planks in a rhythmic fashion.

"Sorry," said Vincent, "I understand how it must feel to be rushed through events like this." He slapped Paun's back again. "Not a moment of peace for the Oather's *piece*, eh?" Reaching the dock's end, Vincent leapt onto the sand below, its grainy nature rippling beneath his weight. "Mind your footing, ay? There're plenty of shallow patches along the shores! Even *now*, if you fell through, I wouldn't be able to help or... well *maybe!*"

Paun cautiously leapt onto the sand beside Vincent, teetering from side to side as he tried to find his balance; such was the way of the Above Desert. It had other names, aye, but all the nomads had referred to it as *Above* and the churning sea under it, *Below*. He remembered a story they—the nomads that is—shared with his town, a rather humorous tale they called *Stubborn Loyalty*.[6] In it, they told of a great sea, a sea whose very sand was lighter than its own water. Paun glanced to the sand beneath his feet, cautious of those shallow patches Vincent had warned of: the watery depths lurking beneath the sand, beneath his very feet, remained devoid of all light. To be trapped beneath the churning sand in the unforgiving folds of darkness was far too terrifying a thought for Paun to consider—no, he'll be fine.

Just watch your step, mate.

He smiled at the thought of the nomad's tale, finding it oddly amusing how similar his life was to a chicken of all—Paun froze in his steps, jerking Vincent and Malvolia back by their collars and shouting: "*Stop*, stop!" His sword whipped out from his sheath, pointing to a fin in the undulating tides of sand. It was grey, the width of Paun's shoulders, and charging for them at a hostile pace. "Vincent... I'd start using Chulian if I were you..."

Vincent scoffed.

"Right, I'll simply leave a astral scar in the face of a quite occupied trade route—aye 'tis nothing *but* a responsible use of such power. *Boy*, you don't *just*—" Vincent shoved Paun aside and kicked Malvolia to the sand. In the same instant, his other hand tore Chulian's blade free and slammed it through the air in a mighty arc. The blade slashed across the skull of what Paun recognized as a shark—a big shark. The more Paun looked at it, the more it looked less like a shark and more like a horrific myth, twisted into its hideous state of predatory monstrosity by the dark waters below. He and Malvolia squirmed away from

---

6. The Nomads who told Paun the tale of Stubborn Loyalty refer to it, with a twinkle in their eye, as a Fernweh tale—a story that hasn't come to pass or transpires as they speak.

its now ice-encased corpse; it was limp, struck dead by Vincent's blade. Its heavy form then sank back into the sand, bursting in cerulean flame as it slipped off Chulian's blade. Vincent spat at its sinking corpse.

"*Scagles*," he growled, glancing up to see several more fins popping in and out of the sand: a pack.[7] "Mind your toes, lads." He helped Malvolia up, gesturing for her sword to be drawn. "Stay close—but not too close! Lest our weight plummet us through the sand." Vincent seized their hands, sprinting for the ship in the distance. As they neared it, a set of sand waves began to build, approaching them in frothing dunes. They ran up and over, far to the left of where they had seen more fins; they hoped to at least circumvent the creatures.

But it was not to be so simple.

From the corner of his eye, Paun caught a glimpse of movement beneath the rollicking desert. Breaking off from the group, he stabbed his sword through the sand, its blade sinking into an unseen flesh. He was about to tear his sword loose when the scagle erupted from the sand, spinning violently. With his blade still stuck fast, Paun was lurched off the sand and carried through the air. Before it could dive back into the desert, Vincent leapt for Paun and slashed the creature in midair. It collapsed to the sand in two chunky pieces.

Tearing his blade free, Paun rolled to the left, for another such creature was flying towards his head. Its flailing form burrowed back into the sand, oblivious to Paun's frantic slashings.

"Does *nothing* hurt them?!" Paun squinted, holding an arm over his eyes as its crazed tail flapped wildly. It struck Paun across the face and sprayed sand in his eyes and mouth. Sputtering, Paun felt someone pull him to his feet and urge him along. He rubbed his eyes as he ran, asking: "Vincent! Is there anything we could borrow?!"

"*Just this!*"

---

7. **Scaglerii**: Carnivorous elasmobranchii which inhabit the epipelagic zone of the Below Sea, typically residing near the shore regions of Above where the sand layer is thinner. Their advanced olfactory receptors and mechanoreceptors in their dorsal fins allow them to detect prey through chemical cues and substrate-borne vibrations. Scaglerii exhibit significant strength in the muscle structure, enabling them to exert sufficient propulsive force to breach the sand layer. To successfully re-submerge, they must achieve a critical velocity during their leap. Insufficient velocity results in the scaglerii landing atop the sand's surface, where they experience a temporary state of increased predation risk as they slowly resettle into the sea, Below.

Paun opened his eyes to see Vincent firing his celestial flintlock towards the sky. He then shoulder-rolled, just avoiding the limp form of a scagle crashing down. Rising to his knees, he tossed the flintlock to Paun. However, before he could catch it, Malvolia snatched it from the air, shooting sporadically into the sand as they ran.

"Oy!" Paun tried to yank it from her, but she shrank away from his attempt. "He was tossing that to me!"

"*Nope!*" Malvolia shot a scagle in the mouth as it lunged from the sand. "Pretty sure he was aiming for *me!*" She fired it off a few more times into the sand, a beaming smile lighting her features. "It's just so bloody *neat!*"

Paun frowned, slowing his pace to run *behind* her; she had the weapon; he was too vulnerable.

"Vincent!" he shouted, "did you mean to throw it to me or—"

"*The boat!*" Vincent flailed his arms, pointing to the ship like a mad man. "They're *stopping!* They must've seen us!" He bounced up and down, flapping his arms and continuing to run. Vincent whirled his blade about his head, decapitating the two creatures hoping to make a quick snack of him. "*Run* my children! Run truer than you ever have before!"

"*What?!*" hollered Malvolia. "The *blazes* do you *think* we've been doing?!"

"I didn't—*mind the wave!*"

Vincent was right to warn them; a colossal wave of sand was barreling upon them. It wasn't terribly steep, but still an imposing sight to behold. The very horizon vanished to its heaving approach. Vincent laughed as its shadow fell across them, saying: "Oh and would you look at that! There's scagles in it!" His mad laughter mingled with the rumbling weight of sand. "Oh, don't you just *love* the Oather!"

Paun felt the sand beneath his feet incline as the wave passed beneath them. His knees began to touch his chest and he soon found himself in a crawling posture, scrambling up the mountain of sand. As he'd thought, it wasn't too steep, but he still felt as though its flowing sand would sweep him away the moment he stopped moving. To make matters worse, all manner of scagles were lunging from the roaring sand below.

The others were nearing the boat now and Malvolia herself was running along its portside hull, her celestial flintlock handling the monsters with ease. The same was said for Vincent, what with his skill and Chulian's blade. He was in no threat whatsoever. But Paun—

Everything went wrong.

The moment Malvolia leapt off the wave, a scagle burst from the sand and seized Paun's ankle. A brief shout of Vincent's name escaped him and he collapsed to the sand. The crushing weight of its teeth sank through his boots, puncturing his skin and doing more damage than Paun cared to entertain. His blade's point repeatedly stabbed the creature's snout at a frenetic pace, yet to no effect. Paun felt the rushing sand of the wave beginning to claim his limbs, gradually pulling him into its brittly embrace. With a decisive jab, Paun managed to stab the creature through its eye. The scagle went deathly limp before sinking into the rollicking sand.

Unfortunately, Paun's foot was still locked in its mouth. He screamed in pain as it dragged him down with it. The desert wave passed by, but Paun was still sinking. To his alarm, he felt a biting liquid seize the warmth from his feet and—

"*I have you boy.*" Vincent seized Paun's free hand, gripping it by the wrist. Straining to pull him up, Vincent's very ankles began to descend into the sand. "*Back!* Get in the ship!" He waved frantically to Malvolia. "I got him! He's—"

Paun shrieked in pain.

"My *foot!*" He jerked away from Vincent's grasp, only to seize it again as he rapidly sank to his shoulders. Paun now felt the frigid water up to his waist. He winced, speaking through clenched teeth: "*You're... pulling me apart...*"

Vincent stared into Paun's eyes, his gaze flickering, his mouth grimacing.

And then... he nodded.

"Right."

With that, Vincent released him.

"*No!*" Paun sharply inhaled before being dragged down through layers of sand. Plunging into the ocean below, a frigid rush of liquid climbed up his body, claiming every limb until even his head was submerged in its remorseless depths. He tried to swim back up through the surface, but he couldn't claw through the thick layers of shifting sand. Paun eventually gave up, hoping to conserve his breath in his energy.

With dread, Paun opened his eyes.

The water was unlike any he had ever seen before; everything about him... it was all displayed in a sharp clarity. Beams of light would sporadically pierce the darkness as the sands' surface was disturbed by scagles. To Paun's helpless terror, they began to swim over to him, only leaving at the sight of the dead scagle latched to his ankle: dragging him down.

And then... it stopped.

Paun was still sinking, but at a reduced pace; the scagle was no longer locked to his limb. The pain in his ankle was nigh on unbearable and all feeling in his foot screamed; it felt as though his foot were replaced by a biting flame, torturing his ankle in the most cruelest of fashions.

And then... it was gone.

The pain in his foot was no more.

Nothing remained save the ever growing torture in his ankle, its fiery bite spreading up his limbs and threatening to consume his consciousness. Though his tormented mind raged with pain and terror, he couldn't help but feel a certain peace by the haunts of those waters. The cold depths of its abyss lulled his mind to a calm... encouraging him to cease resistance and submit to the smothering embrace of its infinite darkness.

He felt nothing but peace—even at the sight of two flaming eyes peering at him from the darkness. Whatever it was, it drifted towards him through the waters, its ghostly form like that of a sea serpent's skeleton.[8] Its bone-white jaws creeped open, large enough to swallow an entire house. It was a ridiculously *colossal* thing, but Paun felt no fear; the waters were far too peaceful and his body far too afflicted to trouble about such... *petty* concerns.

No, he shall die and it will all be over.

Unfortunately, a violent grip seized Paun's shoulder, abruptly snapping him back to the biting cold and unrelenting pain of reality. An arm wrapped about Paun's shoulders, securing him from sinking any further. As the gaping jaws of the creature loomed over them, a flash of fiery-blue darted past Paun, carving a broad circle into the face of reality. A vacuum of air was created and they were sucked through, moments before being devoured by a nightmare.

Carried through the portal by a rush of water, they landed on a hard surface of wood. There was an assortment of surprised voices as Paun sputtered for breath. He heard Vincent shouting something, but it was nigh on indiscernible. Why, Paun's very moaning soon faded from his own hearing. All he knew, was the wood beneath his resting head and the clear blue sky above; they were moving, Paun could tell that much. He raised his head, looking out to the fading sight of... of something rather... rather odd; hovering over the desert was a giant ring of... shining blue light, spilling volumes of water out both sides of

---

8. **Courcan**: skeletal-like sea serpents which grow up to 61 meters on average. They can be found in the trenches of Hoaräk, The depths of Below, and the wilds of Nowood.

its two-dimensional shape; an astral gash Vincent had cut into reality. Indeed... it was an odd sight... That waterfall... hovering in the air... pouring into the desert sands below... probably doomed to exist till kingdom come... and trumpets sounded.

All was black, silent, and peaceful.

Then there was *noise, pain* and *light*. He was being cradled by someone—Vincent.

"*Fetch a stretcher!* A cot! Is there not a surgeon aboard?! He needs... *something*... to..." The frantic words of his voice numbed and Paun knew nothing but the hard surface of wood he was being set on. Even then, such feelings of awareness were short-lived and everything gradually returned to the silent dark's serenity.

Paun willingly gave in, relishing what little peace he was finally allocated.

CHAPTER ELEVEN

IN CORSAIR COMPANY

*H*IS SIGHT SOARED OVER *the fields of a billowing desert, its sand sparkling like gold dust in the evening's expansive light. The desert was at peace, as was his soul. However, it was not to last. His vision plunged into the waves of sand, burrowing through its layers until it was submerged in the darkness. It was cold... unsettling... remorseless... all attributes of his life Paun had become familiar with. His gaze descended to the bottomless darkness beneath his feet. All manner of sea creatures passed his view; some were like the animated corpses of great serpents while others were nothing more than shadow and thought. They were haunting, but they, like all things, passed away. Only this time, the deeper he sank, more nightmarish and horrific creatures began to appear until finally—he found himself at the bottom of the sea. It wasn't merely his vision now, but himself: vulnerable, bare, exposed to the watchful presence of sea titans. There were deep ravines all about him, their dark canyons stretching down to an infinite void, one which alien things swam forth from.*

HAVE YOU NOT EYES? THEN SEE.

Paun's gaze rose from the seafloor; there was a figure cloaked in white standing before him, a hunch to its posture and arms dangling at its sides. It wore no armour except for a crude mask of black steel.

"I don't wish to see... not anymore."

THE BEAUTY OF LIGHT CAN ONLY PIERCE THE SURFACE.

The cloaked figure gestured to the stretching darkness above.

THE DEEPER YOU FALL... THE MORE MONSTROUS IT BECOMES... THE TRUE NATURE OF ITS CORE... LAID BARE BY THOSE WHO DARE BRAVE ITS COLD... UNSETTLING... REMORSELESS SOUL.

Paun's heavy breathing boomed through the sea in dull echoes.
"This is a dream. I've seen many of its kind before. There's nothing to fear."

EXAMINE YOUR FOOTING. KNOW WHERE YOU STAND.

"A dream. One which I do not see fit to humour."
Paun tried to move, but couldn't; his feet remained fast to the chalky-grey sea floor.

THE SEA REFLECTS THE HEARTS OF MAN AND THE INEVITABLE HORRORS OF ITS CORE.

The figure gestured to the colossal sea creatures hovering overhead.

THERE ARE DEMONS IN THE DARKEST DEPTHS OF ALL OUR HEARTS. EVEN... YOU... O'OATHER...

Paun nervously scoffed.
"I'm no Oather, I'm merely—"

ARE YOU NOT?

The figure closed the distance in an eye's wink, seizing Paun by the throat. Its mask fell away to reveal a writhing void of shadows.

HE SEES THROUGH YOUR EYES, BOY—SPEAKS YOUR THOUGHTS AND DWELLS IN YOUR VISIONS. I DO NOT SPEAK TO YOU, BUT HE WHO DARES DENY ME THAT WHICH HAS ALWAYS BEEN MINE...

Quell your voice, O'silence, for it is not your place.

Paun's wild gaze shot around the void, confused by where the voice had sourced.
"Oather..." gasped Paun, "you've protected me before. If you could wake—"

Have you not ears? Then heed. Have you not eyes? Then behold.

The figure whirled about, hurling Paun leagues across the sea floor. His rocketing form stirred the sea floor, its grey sediment rising up into cloudy shapes of armour-clad warriors, hacking, stabbing and... dying. As Paun flew past them, one of the great titans above caught sight of him, swooping down to the sea floor. Despite its sluggish pace, the moment it opened its jaws, Paun was sucked in: left to face nothing but an infinite black.

He floated about... weightless... alone... until... no, he wasn't... wasn't alone; there was someone in the heart of the darkness, holding their knees and grieving.

It was a girl.

Paun had stopped spinning about and now found himself right-side up. Tentatively approaching her, he placed a gentle hand on her shoulder.

"Addy...?"

The girl whirled about, plunging a dagger through Paun's heart. She had no face, only the lightless shadows of a cruel void. He fell to the floor, gasping for breath as she stood over him, her lament doubling tenfold.

Every molecule of water flooded over with a resonating voice, though its presence hosted no sound. The force of its power built within the sea, trembling water, rumbling roars—all climaxing into a thunderous silence of three powerful words.

Adiuva me esse.

Paun shot up, slamming his forehead against a plank of wood. Grunting in pain, he fell back into a cot and rubbed his forehead; aye, it was a dream, but what a dream at that... Surely, it meant something more than a mere passing of untamed thoughts; his other dreams had been proof of that. Unfortunately, its finer details began to fade from memory as he awoke and became more aware of his surroundings; he laid in a cot. Other such beddings were built into the autumn wood of the adjacent wall.

Someone's hand pressed into his shoulder, preventing him from rising.

Looking up, he flinched at the sight of Malvolia.

"What—what're you doing... here?" He glanced at her hand, trying to squirm away in vain. "You're touching me."

Malvolia sighed, her eyes rolling to the back of her skull.

"Making sure you are not so mad as to bash your face again." She removed her hand, allowing Paun to prop himself up on his elbows and raise an eyebrow.

"But what are *you* doing here?"

"Waking you up," said Vincent, bending over and peeking into Paun's sleep quarter. "Captain wants a word with us and methinks you've slept long enough as it is."

Paun rubbed his head before sliding his feet out of the bed.

"How long?"

"Long enough."

Paun groaned as his feet made contact with the teetering floor. Gazing to his left foot, he saw a string of black symbols imprinted on a scar encircling his ankle. Below his ankle, his skin was of a lighter hue. He fell back in the bed, sitting in shock.

"What... what'd you do to me?"

"Fortunate for you," said Malvolia, "the ship's surgeon was a caster. Bit weasley and quite shifty, but a caster nonetheless." She shook her head. "May not be your own foot, but it's still a foot."

Paun paled.

"Not my foot? Where's my foot? Who's foot is this?" He flexed his left pinky toe, gagging. "Do I even want to know?"

Vincent shuddered.

"You do not. Your old foot had been lost to the sea. This was... all they had in your size."

"My... my foot." Paun shivered, eyeing his new foot; He needed to cut its nails. Still, it worked the same as his old one. It's not like he had always been sentimental for his feet. No, to dwell on it any further would be... odd. Honestly, it was as though nothing had happened. The less he thought about it, the better he felt. "Thanks." He sighed, rubbing his nose. "A shame killing the bloody fish didn't save my limb."

"Even in death," said Malvolia, "scaglerii don't let go." She smacked her hands together like a pair of predacious teeth. "Strong jaw force, ay?"

"Aye," agreed Vincent. "You're blessed to have survived. The Oather's armour has served you well."

"How'd you..." Paun rubbed his aching eyes. "It was *you* who saved me..."

"Aye," said Malvolia, her eyes twinkling, "he seized the fin of a scaglerii leaping overhead and used its driving momentum to *pierce* the layer of sand! All in the span of a few bloody seconds it was."

"It felt..." Paun rubbed his aching forehead, "*much* longer than that..."

"Well come on then," urged Vincent. "You'll be glad you came. Besides, I'm not too terribly keen on repeating myself." He seized Paun's wrist and yanked him onto his feet. Groaning, Paun rubbed his sore calves.

"I need a moment to rest."

"You've already *had* it, but you'll soon *get* it. For *now*, just come along and *listen*. He wanted Malvolia there too and I'm not leaving you alone... might bash your skull to crumbs if we did."

Begrudgingly following Vincent's beckoning, Paun followed him from the forecastle and up a flight of stairs to the main deck. He paused for a brief moment to eye the passing waves of sand; they were calm, their fiery nature dimmed to a peaceful lull.

He couldn't say the same for whatever horrors lurked beneath it.

With a prompting shove from Malvolia, Paun hobbled forward: past the bustling crew and up the quarter deck. Something about his left foot felt... off balance. He glanced down to his bare feet. It was a slight inconvenience, but not an unbearable one. Still, it was something to be wary of.

Last thing I need is tripping over my feet in battle. What a horrible way to die... bleeding embarrassing.

When he looked up, he nearly ran into Vincent's back; he paused just in time, peeking over his shoulder to see a pair of doors. There was one desert-worn sailor standing guard, explaining why they couldn't speak with the captain.

"He's in a pressing meeting, he is. Can't be disturbed on pain o'death."

"*Pain* of..." Vincent rubbed an exasperated hand across his features. "Are you deaf to the irrationality of your own words? *Your* Captain said—nay, *over-stressed*—that we were to meet at this hour, in *this* very moment. Judging by his previous actions, I thought him to be the sort of man who'd understand the weight of punctuality."

"Aye... but... an unexpected—and rather unforeseen—eh, castaway turned up and if you understand *he* understands punctuality, then I'm sure you understand how *he* understands priorities, aye?"

"No, I don't understand." Vincent was about to shove past the sailor when a boisterous and clearly agitated voice roared from the other side of the doors.

"*Ye bilge-slurpin' bloke!* We'll see if a week in the brig tames such arrogant sass!"

The doors flew open and two burly sailors stormed out, restraining a fluffy chicken. Paun peered into the cabin they came from, observing the man standing at his desk and waving a shaking finger after the chicken. As it was escorted past Vincent, this very man splayed his arms open in a welcoming gesture, exclaiming: "Fauntaso! Merrybender! How unusual for one o'yer sorts to arrive so early!"

"Captain Foley," greeted Vincent, stepping into the cabin. "Though I do believe this is the exact hour at which you summoned us." He shot a glance over his shoulder before looking back to the captain. "Was... was that a *chicken?*"

"In truth," began the captain, "it is the hour of which we spoke, though quite early on into the hour for a man of ye reputation." He shrugged before reclining into a plushy throne and poking at his desk with a chopstick. "And... aye... we do not speak of the chicken."

"Mm." Vincent's eyes narrowed. "So, what are we—"

"Oy!" The Captain leaned forward, gesturing to Paun in excitement. "A whole bleedin' day and yer finally up an' about! A bloody *miracle* we had a prisoner with your shoe size, ay? Well, maybe a tad smaller than you, but mighty damn close if you ask me."

Paun stepped from behind Vincent.

"I'm sorry, what?" He glanced down to his ankle and the string of symbols encircling it. "Did the previous owner of this foot *consent* to having it lopped off for me?"

"Nay, but you needn't fret. 'Twas a petty thief, stowed away on our vessel in hopes of escaping justice. Him donating his foot was the punishment me and crew decided upon. We'll set him free once the ship berths, you needn't bother." The Captain waved his chopstick at Paun. "Just be grateful yer alive to begin with, lil' laddy."

"I am, aye." Paun shrugged. "I thank you for giving back what the scaglerii took."

"Skagller... *reee?*" The captain's features twisted curiously. "What an odd name... no, we just call 'em blood fishies!" He let loose a clamoured chortle, pounding the table with energised enthusiasm.

Paun raised an eyebrow.

"I... don't understand... was... was that a joke?"

The captain's roaring laughter came to a sudden halt, his features assuming the most grave of expressions.

"No, it was not. How *dare* ye think of gigglin'." He tapped his desk with the porcelain chopstick. "Blood fishies are no *light* matter, seein' as how much they *weigh*." The Captain doubled over in wheezing bouts. Paun heard Malvolia groan from behind. The Captain smirked, saying: "Speakin' o'blood fishies, we need'a talk fare."

Vincent shook his head.

"How's that then?"

"Ye delayed us, Mr. Merrybender. We dropped anchor 'pon sight of you fleeing them fish. We're not monsters, aye? But droppin' anchor in Above..." The Captain tutted. "Tis a mighty risk in partaking... even for such old friends as thee."

Vincent waved his hand, gesturing for him to hurry along.

"Simply lay bare what needs must be paid and we'll be done with it. Fifty pieces a person was the original fare, yes?"

"Aye, the *original* fare. Expenses have since altered and we be in demand of a new price."

"Say it."

"One, we left ourselves vulnerable in the shores of Above, where the sand is thin and treacherous. Two, our lovely surgeon here don't work for free and havin' her operatin' on such a foot as *his* is terribly costin'. Third, I just realised I've only ever been to the Sinkin' Canyon once and 'twas in another vessel. Such passage is risky, haunted by the tendrils of predators who live in its fallin' walls o'sand." He reclined in his throne, gazing to the ceiling in thought. "All in all, that brings us to about a thousand and a hundred pieces—a full sack and pouch me should thinks."

"Mm." Vincent rubbed his aged beard, his other hand cupped about his elbow. "Perhaps there's a way we can reduce the price, ay? After all, we could simply circumvent the Sinking Canyon and—"

The Captain scoffed.

"*No*. No, goin' about would take *far* too long and only increase the price for the various supply stops we'd have to make. The Sinkin' Canyon may be the riskiest route, but it is also the surest, if not most enjoyable, route to Ranitorl via the Above Desert!"

Paun left Vincent's side and approached the captain's desk. Leaning against it, he observed the map fastened to its face; it was a chart of the Above Desert, what with its various currents, outposts and islands. The parchments were riddled with runes, but someone had taken the initiative to scribble red-inked translations beneath a good number of them. Paun traced his finger along the ship's plotted course to a black bolt stretching from nearly both ends of the map's southern reach.

"This." Paun tapped it. "This is the Sinking Canyon?"

"Aye, lad... that it is." The Captain whistled an odd tune before continuing. "A great chasm scarred into the face of this cursed desert. Been there myself on an occasion." The Captain raised a flat hand in the air, motioning it as though it were a ship. "There ye be, sailin' through the sands of a fair current, wind in your hair, a bright tune on your lips. But oy... said current begins to build, seizing yer hull and draggin' ye into the gapin' maw of an endless crack!" The captain's hand plummeted to his side, slapping against his knee. "Ye fall straight through the canyon with none the wiser." He shrugged. "Course, it's then ye realise the underground caverns it leads to... and how one could sail right under Ranitorl, *poppin'* up wherever one should please." He threw his chopstick at the edge of the map. "We've established a few climbin' stations here and there, what with the various pits and ravines leading up into Ranitorl. However, knowin' ye intentions, ye best be dropped off at the southern pit. Though cuddled up to Aeraos it might be, it also climbs out to the Black Fields' edge."

"What? No. The Black Fields?" Paun felt the colour in his features dissipating, though he tried to conceal it. "You mean the Hollow Plains—Mitrak, territory of the *thunders?*"

"Aye." The Captain looked up with a terrifying glint in his eye. "The Mitrak Versalian. It borders the Obelisks of the Lost, memorials just outside Aeraos." His shoulders lightly rose as he smirked.[1] "I'm sure with Vincent's magic, ye'll be just fine."

"Mm... depends," muttered Vincent, crossing his arms. "I'm not too keen on leaving astral gashes across reality... an unfortunate force of habit it seems to have become, but I'm afraid circumstances have forced such desperation."

The Captain snapped his fingers.

"Oy, that reminds me! If ye recall, ye damaged my poop deck somethin' terrible with ye wee manoeuvre o'magic." He stuck another chopstick in his mouth and began picking his teeth with it. "That'll be costin' ye many a pretty penny as well, eh?"

Vincent opened his satchel's mouth, digging through its contents.

"Oh, yes, regarding that, it would do you well for you to spread the word—no one is to touch the ring of that waterfall, lest the fine edge of reality slice them clean open."

The Captain shook his head.

"Is there no way to be rid of it? I'd hate for any, eh, *unwary* traders to sink their vessels, should they be foolish enough to sate their curiosity."

Before Vincent could respond, Malvolia spoke up.

"Afraid not. It will remain there for all of eternity, till kingdom come and holy trumpets sound." Malvolia shrugged in response to Paun's curious gaze, saying: "You should know you're quite chatty when you sleep."

Paun's eyes widened.

---

1. 'Mitrak Versalian' is Second Ranitorl for 'Rightfully Forsook.'

"You were... *watching* me sleep?"

"I was making sure the surgeon didn't pull any tricks! And... I've never seen you sleep before." She reddened under his baffled expression. "It was curious..."

"Aye, that it was," said Vincent, handing the first mate two coins as he turned to leave. "Even I have trouble coming by such a rare sight."

"Oy!" The Captain shot up from his seat, pounding his desk. "The *blazes* ye think yer headed off to? You've a fee to settle!"

Vincent continued his undeterred gait, followed closely by Malvolia. Paun stayed behind for a couple of moments, watching the first mate approach the Captain with the two coins. Snatching the coins, the Captain raised their metal to the light, displaying the prismatic sheen of hunter's metal. The Captain looked up at Vincent in shock, his mouth gaping like a fish. Smiling, Paun turned and followed Vincent out to the quarter deck, where they stood watching the dying light of the sun.

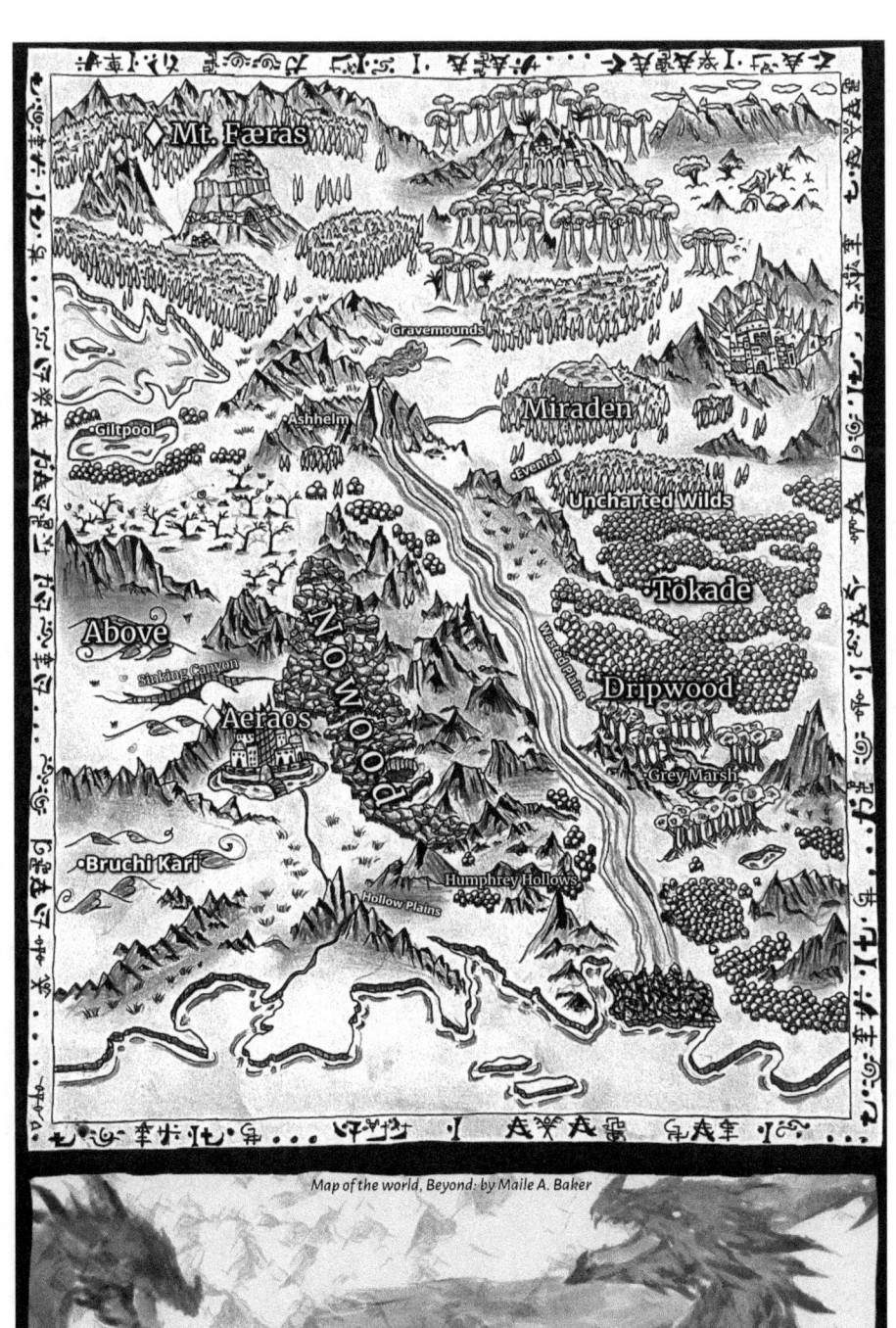

Map of the world, Beyond: by Maile A. Baker

CHAPTER TWELVE

BLOOD FOLK

S HE WORE NOTHING BUT her prison attire, the burden of armour cast aside into the
desert below. Adela had flown past several settlements and outposts, but never once
did she consider stopping for rest. Cause... well, how could she? How could she possibly
bring herself to face a fellow being without bursting in tears and rage? How could she
look another in the eye and ask for rest when she knew she'd never sleep again?

How could I?

Adela fell back against her saddle, staring up into the creamy-orange heavens; she flew
aimlessly and cared not where she landed... Adela sat up. Her teary eyes blurred the passing
landscape below. That wasn't completely true... she did care where she landed. In all
honesty, more than anything, she wished to find Paun, to tell him what happened, what
she had been through, and to hear the comfort of his sympathy. *Yes,* she was so desperate
as to desire another's *pity.* But... that wasn't a bad thing... was it? Considering all she'd
been through, nearly any form of compassion would be more than welcomed.

Child... A silky voice, comforting and masculine, resonated through her head. *Child,
my care for you extends beyond the mere wails of pity.*

Adela's gaze fell to her esardrocan; it had plenty of time to develop its sentience over
the course of their aimless flying. Though she was somewhat surprised it could speak
her language so well, this wasn't the first time it had tried to communicate; on many an
occasion, it attempted to speak through her thoughts: its feelings translated to echoes of
soft whimpers or quiet snuffles.

Adela gave a tired nod.

"So, you can speak now, yeh?" She patted its side. "That's nice... ehm..." She sat up again.
"Oy, I haven't a name for you."

What would you like to call me?

"Have you not a name yourself?"

The dragon whose ore I once belonged to had a name... but I am unsure whether I hold right to it.

"Course you do. And by technical speakings, you're an extension of that saurian, so you might as well embrace your ore's past life, yeh?"

Yes... he was called Regonrud, the Wingless.

"Yeh, well, you have wings, so we can ignore that last bit, luv." She rubbed her eye, a choking smile rising to her lips. "Perhaps I shall simply call you Regend, yeh? Regend... Flyfar!" She leaned forward to pat the side of its neck. "Cause you're not wingless and you do indeed *fly far*, yeh?"

If you wish it, Adela.

"Oh please, call me Addy." She forced another smile, her heart sinking at its feeling. "I don't suppose you're any sort of exhausted now, are you? We can land and rest if yeh like."

No... not yet. I haven't been so careless as to fly you to the end of nowhere. There's a camp nearby, I've heard so from the stabledocks. A campaign in the woods led by our dear friend. Unfortunately... I do not think it safe to land till we've met him.

"Woods?" Adela glanced down to the passing landscape; it was then she noticed the change of environment and the stretching presence of a dark forest. "Oh... no... I don't... I think we should turn around, luv." Adela shivered at the sight of shadows shifting between the trees. "Yeh, didn't know we were flying this west o'the desert... I'd rather... I don't think we should go any further unless yeh plan to fly right on over it all."

Our friend has secured a trail of refuge, blazed by the fires of my kin, levelled by the strength of rooks, refined by the sabatons of soldiers and made safe by the wards of casters and blessings of holymen.

Adela's posture straightened as she processed what Regend had said.

"Oy, who's this mutual friend you keep bringing up?"

Aivon Seeker stood bent over a hasty display of maps and charts. An assortment of Unbequith stewards stood gathered about his table, arguing about whose garrison deserved what position. Every territory in Unbequith had joined together to form the United Legions of Lord Monbel, second only to the might of Harldïof. Lord Monbel and his court had long constructed the various rank formations and procedures for the trek through Nowood. The stewards knew this, yet *still*, they insisted on arguing for the more favourable of positions. It wasn't as though they actually cared; they simply wished to reap the benefits of that which was sure to occupy said positions. However, they weren't bickering *amongst* themselves, so much as arguing *to* Aivon; he was the Unit Commander, bestowed such a position by Lord Monbel himself.

They knew this.

As such, they all wished to *reorganise* their city's respective military and they needed *his* word to do so. No one expected war of any variety, much less the possibility of casualties. They merely desired to attain the glory of an Unbequith victory, bestowing their city with twofold the legend and sevenfold the primary choice of business... and therefore *profits*. They didn't think in terms of caution, tactics, or strategy, but in reckless parading showmanship—*bureaucracies*. In the least, they cared for the welfare of their territory.

But that was all.

Deciding to humour their complaints, Aivon had granted a hearing, but hadn't wished to proceed any further until the forces of Ashhelm had rendezvoused with their campaign; they were the primary means of establishing a supply train. Aye, their forces were beyond a simple necessity.

Unlike these stewards.

Though Aivon wished to wait for the arrival of Ashhelm, each official sought to put in their two pieces about who should get what, go where, and how Aivon had shown favour to Giltpool's ranks. He shrugged to himself. It was true; Aivon trusted his own to do their part and had placed them accordingly. Of *course* he showed favour to Giltpool. If he didn't believe them to be the best of the best, then he'd fail them as their Steward. Aye, he positioned Giltpool in the flanking wings of the front lines: the position *everyone* desired.

The position they all *demanded*.

So, Aivon stood bent over his table, their discordant arguments flying about the tent. It looked as though he were ignoring them, too absorbed in the charts to hear a single word. However, he had a knack for performing multiple tasks at once and knew the importance of listening: gathering what information one could.

Even if one had no choice.

"*Mín Greyt!*" A young scout burst into the tent, anxiously gesturing to the sky. "Un-is-erdracan symas! Uþ—uþ-astegínd, hæt oem Unbéqiþ!"

The stewards eyed the boy curiously before turning to Aivon; it was clear they hadn't understood a word the scout said. Sighing, Aivon combed back his hair before giving a respectful gesture to the council of stewards.

"Pardon my absence, brothers, but a pressing matter has arisen, one which necessitates my immediate attention." That wasn't *completely* true; in truth, one of the commanding officers could have dealt with the matter or maybe the man's lieutenant. Be that as it may, the scout had chosen to alert his Unit Commander. Aivon thought it only right to respect his decision. "Aþír uþ-dyht'us," he said. "And if possible, speak in a universal tongue henceforth, for not all understand these words of tradition."

The scout nodded before leading Aivon out the tent. The ground beneath them crunched with every step, charred to ash by the breath of Cádmus and iron dragons. Their encampment in Nowood was a dangerous one, but they were yet to encounter any haunting devils or cursed wonders. Aivon eyed the ground as he followed the scout, observing the sprouts of grass increase in number as they neared the camp's border; it was a wonder, but certainly nothing bewitched.

Standing beside a row of archers, Aivon squinted at the creamy-orange heavens, asking: "And just what might you have for us, captain?"

The Second Captain of the western defence stepped forward, gesturing to an odd blur in the sky.

"An esardrocan, my Lord."

"So I've heard." Aivon studied the row of archers before turning back to the sky. "Your line of defence is... sloppy. Have you not time to construct an abatis or earthwork?"

"We've been swapping stations, Commander. Haven't had time to—"

"It's approaching fast." Aivon stepped in front of the line of archers, causing them to ease the tension of their bowstrings. "Have you identified the rider?"

"Aye, it be a girl, sir."

It was difficult to visualise through the shady haze of Nowood, but Aivon was almost certain there was something flying towards them. "Looks like a bird from this distance." Aivon glanced at the scout before gesturing to his belt. "Your spyglass." Receiving it, Aivon unfolded its black chambers to peer through its lens. "Ah, so it is a girl."

"Shall my men down the creature and secure its intruder?"

"Have you arrows for such a task?"

"We're the garrison of Morsberth, aye, we've arrows."[1]

"Mm." Aivon peered through the glass a second time, confirming his suspicions. "Have your men stand down. Prepare for the girl's arrival." He handed the scout his spyglass and turned to leave. "Make holy a patch of ground; she is not to be disturbed by our men. Pitch a fresh tent, ready a fire, construct a private privy, food, drink, blankets, a cot! For the sake of Unbequith, show some hospitality!"

Regend sharply dove, the mass of soldiers clearing as he landed. Clumps of dirt and puffs of ash clouded the air as his claws tore into the earth. Undoing her ankle straps, Adela slid off the saddle, flinching as the hoard of soldiers rushed her: one with steaming food, others with blankets, and one peculiar soldier who openly stared at her.

She accepted the plate first.

"Oy, give her some space then!" Adela's features lit up at the sight of Aivon Seeker shoving his way through the ranks of soldiers to greet her. "*Adela.*" He straightened his armour and bowed, much to her amusement. "I am beyond honoured to host your presence. Please, if you follow me, we can begin sorting out this mess of paperwork."

"Oh." She nodded, resisting the strongest of urges to hug him. "Course, thank you..." She wrapped her hands about her arms, shivering as she looked back at the woods. "Are you... are yeh certain we're safe here? I don't believe Nowood to be the most... ehm, hospitable o'wilds."

"Oh, it's quite dangerous to be sure, but forces of shadow can do *nothing* against the emboldened faith of our ranks. Through vales of shadow and death, we shall bear the Eternal King's light."

"Ooh, that's bonnie then, luv." Adela eagerly shoved the food into her mouth, its contents spilling from her lips as she stuffed her cheeks. "I faw an ahmy mahshin dis way ash weh foo en."

"Come again?"

---

1. Morsberth is a town renowned for its weaponsmiths. It is here that ember cannons were created and torpify arrows were enchanted. Swords from Morsberth are reputed to possess extraordinary abilities, such as cutting through steel, never growing dull, and enduring all manner of harsh conditions. All Morsberth weapons are black, permanently stained by dragon fire ash.

Adela swished the chewed food around her cheeks before swallowing it.

"We saw an—"

A deep horn bellowed through the encampment, signalling the approach of what Adela had seen. Aivon glanced at her, hesitated, then gestured for her to continue following.

"By my side, child. I'd escort you to your resting room, but 'tis mine noble duty to welcome the factional cities of Unbequith." Aivon smiled politely, waving to the line of soldiers approaching the encampment.

Adela knit her brows.

"*Factional?*"

"Aye." They paused at the camp's edge, awaiting their meeting. "I know what I said."

A soldier Adela hadn't noticed till now spoke up from Aivon's right.

"That'd be Ashhelm, sir." The soldier straightened, his hands clasping behind his dark jerkin. "With their supply trains, the regional union shall be complete."

Aivon nodded, his features grave.

"Aye." He scratched the underside of his bearded chin, his high collar concealing his hand. "Lord Monbel promoted their steward as my *deputy* Unit Commander, though he refrained from sharing his name."

"Would you care for me to enlighten you?" asked the soldier.

Aivon was silent, his eyes narrowing on the man leading Ashhelm's ranks on foot.

"No. I would rather meet my second command the way our Lord intended." Aivon tapped Adela's head, gesturing to the man on his right. "This is mine Lieutenant. His name is far too long and complicated for me to share, so everyone calls him Bo." Aivon turned to his Lieutenant. "This girl is Adela. I'd share more, but it seems they await my attention."

The soldiers were within speaking distance now, coming to a rhythmic halt as their steward stopped; he was quite the burly gentleman, sporting a prodigious oak-brown beard and filthy trek-worn armour. To Adela's dismay, she recognized the steward, though she couldn't recall his name. Ashhelm's troops clashed their shields twice and gave a chanting greeting before their leader spoke.

"Hail Giltpool!" He shouted, his hand gesturing in respect. The soldiers behind him clashed their shields twice before he continued. "And its steward, made warlord, turned Unit Commander..."—the clashing of shields—"Aivon... Seeker!"

Aivon replied with a stern smile.

"Hail Ashhelm. Since you're already in position, your garrison shall be stationed in the northern reach of our campaign. Have you any objections, steward?"

The leader spun about to face his troops

"Oy, you hear that, boys?" he exclaimed, his arms shooting into the air, practically praising the heavens. "Set up camp and I'll be sure to have you at ease!" His troops gave an enthusiastic cheer before bustling about their carriages and wagons.

Aivon's smile grew ever so slightly.

"I recommend against settling your comfort, for we advance in the wake of 'morrow's dusk."

"What? So soon?!" He gave a hearty laugh, stepping forward to clap Aivon about the shoulders. "Whatever is the rush ol' boy? Can you not allow an old man some rest?"

Aivon's head tilted to the side, his smile assuming a more playful expression.

"You're not... why, Master Roabard!" Aivon wrapped his arms about the man in a rough embrace, their armour clattering discordantly. Slapping him on the shoulder, Aivon took a step back. "Why, have the very years forgotten your existence? I thought you were still managing charts behind a desk for Lord Monbel!"

"Aye, that I was. But, even our ever-busy Lord knows it foolish to leave a brilliant strategist like me behind the bars of a bloody desk!"

Aivon patted Adela's shoulder as he gestured to Roabard.

"This man was both mine instructor, professor, and—dare I say—more of a father than mine own." Aivon gave a hearty laugh, clearly missing the falling countenance of Roabard as he caught sight of Adela. Aivon continued, undeterred: "You'll do well to make his acquaintance, he's truly the kindest man I know." A light chuckle escaped Aivon. "If you simply refrain from arousing his temper that is."

"A—aye." Roabard's frown grew heavier. "Aivon, I don't think she—" He gave a tight exhale, shaking his head. "I assume you know her story?"

"Of course!" Aivon dismissed Roabard's unease with a light-hearted gesture. "A miracle she wound up with us to *begin* with! I shall be sure to share the unfoldings of her fate, but first... where's that youngling of yours..." Aivon's head peered over Roabard's broad shoulders. "I assume he's all grown now?"

Roabard's anxious eyes shifted from Adela, resuming their sparkly hue as he addressed Aivon.

"Oh, the baby? Aye, boy's grown in everythin' 'cept muscle it seems. Oy! I see your smile—make no mistake, he's quite a sturdy little fellow." Roabard gazed over his shoulder to the line of troops, shouting: "*Oy, fortunate son o'mine!*" He turned back to Aivon with a shrug. "Mighty pooped he's been, though he insisted on walking the entire journey himself—alongside the other men, aye?"

Aivon smiled.

"Full gear?"

"Aye. Boy's probably sleeping under a rock somewhere. Poor thing'll get gobbled up by the devils of these woods 'fore we find him, ey? By all things sacred, he—oh!" Roabard lifted up his arms to sling about a young man's pauldrons. "Now where've you been off to, eh, Jhess? Took you naught but five minutes to find us!"

"Just five seconds, sir." Jhess lifted Roabard's hand to set atop his copper-red head, making it ruffle his hair. "Been right behind you with the other men I was."

"Oh, waiting like a puppy to be called, were yeh?" Roabard snatched his hand away from Jhess before returning it to scratch his son's head himself. "You're an odd one, Jhess."

"Only a little, sir."

"Right, well that's enough of that then." Roabard relieved Jhess's hair of his hand to gesture at Aivon. "This here be our Unit Commander, but also our friend. Consider him the uncle you never—*oy, lad!*" Roabard dashed forward after his own son, only to be softly restrained by Aivon.

As for Adela, she could hardly breathe in Jhess's heartfelt embrace.

Don't know why they keep calling him weak... can feel my own face turning blue. Adela then reddened under the curious stare of Roabard and the knowing look of Aivon.[2] Nervously chuckling, Adela patted Jhess, saying: "Alright, luv, I... sorry, but you need'a let go." She tapped her shoulder blade as he backed away. "I'm fragile there, yeh?" She deeply wished to return the show of cordial affection, but was too insecure to do anything under Roabard's stare.

Aivon was gentle in his restraint, but still maintained a firm hand on Roabard's shoulder.

"It's simply a hug, old friend. Your boy hasn't committed one trespass of law... yet." Aivon shot a glance to Jhess, his lips smirking. "Save for embarrassing himself so openly."

Jhess's copper-red hair fell over his eyes as he tucked his head, concealing his expression.

"Right... ehm, sorry—Addy. I had hopes, but I didn't truly think—"

---

2. If she turned blue... and then blushed red... would that make her face purple? Dunno, I'm colorblind.

Adela patted his tousled hair, having wished dearly to do so after seeing Roabard touch it.

"No need for apologies, luv. I needed that more than yeh know."

Roabard's stunned silence soon came to an end.

"I... Aivon, the blazes are you doing?" He shoved Aivon's hand aside, moments before remembering his place and bowing. "Apologies, Commander... but, this girl is a convict. You yourself *assured* me you were aware of this!"

"I am, but she is pardoned. Those garbs she is forced to wear are ill-suited for the position she deserves." Aivon snapped his fingers, speaking over his shoulder to his Lieutenant, Bo. "You did place the uniform in her tent, did you not?"

"They did."

"Excellent!"

"*Just* a moment now," Roabard said and held up both hands, stepping between Jhess and Adela. "A uniform?! By *jove*, Aivon! Have you truly not heard tell of this girl?"

"I have. Your boy told me everything."

"*Not* everything! Naught but two days ago, three convicts assisted in her escape. We lost a fourth of a battalion, Aivon. Nearly a hundred lives... *lost*."

"Yes... I know." Aivon wrapped an arm about Roabard's shoulders. "But... tell me this, old friend. Have you any evidence to show *she* took a *single* life?"

"As far as... well... no."

"Of course not. She's never taken a bloody soul in her entire life and she'll never take one so long as she's breath in her little lungs—and you know why, O'Second Command, mine?"

Roabard shrank under Aivon's piercing gaze.

"Why... Commander."

"Because her spirit is filled to the brim with the Almighty's blessed innocence. Her very soul spills over with divine purity and you *dare* judge her character based on the unjust circumstance brought upon her? You *dare* punish her for the crimes of another? You... *dare* question... *my judgement?!*" Aivon's voice roared throughout the encampment, bringing the entire wood to a daunted hush. Aivon sighed, his voice resuming its collected tone. "As I said, she is *pardoned*."

"Of course, Commander... I am... I'm simply old and... forgetful of my place." Roabard turned to Adela, gingerly taking her hands in his. His face was red and his brown eyes were those of a sad puppy. "Dear, by the truth of my superior's word and by the loyalty I owe him, I see just how I have wronged you." He knelt, unashamed of the onlookers. "There's nothing that can possibly make up for—"

"Oh! No, yeh can—there is one thing or—many things, but one *among* many things that—well, I'd like to talk to your son, if you'd allow it."

"Course!" Roabard shot up to his feet, slapping Jhess across the back. It amused Adela to see him so readily transform from a sad puppy to a boisterous bear again. "Jhessaun would be most honoured to... ehm... conversate with a friend. Ain't that right, boy? Won't you be honoured to talk with her?"

Jhess nodded, his hands clasped tightly behind his back.

"Always."

"Mm." Roabard raised a bushy eyebrow. "That was a weird answer, boy." He turned to Adela and shrugged. "He's learning, he is. Mighty odd too." He then turned to Aivon, his right hand gesturing respectfully. "If you don't mind Commander, I best be off. I've men to organise and many a stomach to satisfy. By your leave... Commander?"

"Aye, off with you then." Aivon smiled after Roabard as he watched him go. "He's quite stubborn at times with a temper as shifting as the tide, but he's a kind old fool at heart." Aivon smirked to himself. "As such, I doubt he'll be getting much sleep tonight. Not without overthinking everything that's been said and done." Placing a hand on Adela's shoulder, Aivon gestured for her to walk with him. "You'll have plenty of time to catch up with Jhess, but I'd rather you wander about in a less degrading attire. I've a uniform awaiting you in your tent. Should fit nicely, being enhanced to the top degree of—"

"Oy, just a..." Adela paused, trying to process his words. "Just a moment now... what's this uniform then?"

Aivon gave her a bemused stare.

"Your decision. Did you not come here to join the ranks of Unbequith?"

"I... no... I merely came at the advice and guidance of Regend—my esardrocan that is."

"Ah, so you *have* named him!" Aivon shook his head, raising a hand. "You needn't say anything now. Your tent is just yonder. Change into whatever you like. I'll have Jhess standing twenty paces off. Simply holler if you can't find him, aye?"

"You're... are you not upset then?"

Aivon knelt below her eye level, an armoured hand resting on her shoulder.

"Adela... you've been through more than any soul should have to endure, much less one as yours. To come to a decision in such a tormented amount of time is simply unjust."[3] He smiled kindly. "Think on it at your own pace. If you wish to be elsewhere, I shall personally oversee your excursion's safety." He held up a hand once more, silencing what protests she had. "I'll not have you leaving alone, should you wish it. It's simply immoral of me and I won't stand for it. If you wish to depart, you *will* be escorted. Nowood is treacherous. By my watch, no adversity shall befall you."

"Thank you... I..." Adela scoffed to herself, the motion causing her shoulder to ache. "I truly am at a loss for words—but... I have had time to think on it! Many a times did I wish to be among your noble ranks, serving a holy cause for the name of the Almighty and His people. I've dreamt on it quite a lot and... and it does seem like my purpose, as you said. Still, 'fore I commit myself to anyone or... anything, I'd best like to know unto *whom* I commit myself. If it's simply you then of course I'll say yes, yeh?"

Aivon nodded, considering her words for several moments.

"I do believe... I can arrange you a meeting with the Lord of Unbequith."

Adela paled at the mention.

"Heavens, there's no need for something so extravagant! All I need is your word and I'd believe you!"

"Perhaps... but I'd rather you discover the conviction of our loyalty yourself. Aye, I shall arrange a meeting. You may ask him anything you wish. If you find him and his leadership suitable, then... perhaps you'll join us?"

"Yeh... I think I... course, but... but the Lord of Unbequith?!" Adela pulled on the ends of her short hair. "I'm not fit to stand before a Lord of any kind, much less *speak* to one!"

"Nonsense. If it be a matter of deserving, then it is *he* who should worry about speaking to *you*." Aivon smiled at her flustered disposition. "And if he were here, he would agree with me. But come, we need to dress those wounds with proper enchantments. Then, you may clean, change, drink—sleep, if you must. I have matters to attend and a meeting to arrange."

"Of course... thank you... Oh! And Aivon!" Adela dashed after him, tugging on his pauldron. "Since Jhess'll always be close by... do you think you could—with his consent—promote him to mine personal guard?"

---

3. I get it... it's just too sappy for me. If it was my story, they'd be at each other's throats. Still... I mustn't remain biased. Just record what I see and... help. I'm helping her, aren't I?

Aivon's eyes twinkled as he turned to leave.

"I already have, child."[4]

---

4. Aivon had promised Jhess that he would make him Adela's bodyguard if they ever saw her again. Jhess had already been her escort, which could be considered a form of being a bodyguard, but he wanted to hear it officially from Aivon.

CHAPTER THIRTEEN

COVENANT

T HE CREAMY-ORANGE SKY HAD dozed off into a cherry-red hue, complementing the odd colour in her cheeks. A soft breeze crept over the grassy knoll and rushed across her features. Her face reddened to its cool touch, for the rest of her body remained warm; among the other clothes she had found in her tent was a great coat, its collar stretching up past her jaw. Adela figured it was one of Aivon's, for she had seen him wear this variety on a number of occasions. It was a lovely feeling: sitting in the late sun's cool breeze whilst wrapped in a cosy fabric—caused the blood to speed through her cheeks, it did.

That... and Jhess... sitting beside her.

He was currently inquiring about her shoulder blade; a healer had taken one look before mending the flesh under her skin without asking. It was an odd feeling, almost painful... yet not quite: as though she were being stabbed again... but backwards. Adela merely shrugged in response to Jhess, rubbing the scar tissue on her wrist.

"It's fine now," she said, gazing vacantly into the sunset. "Even when I was wounded, there was simply too much going on to truly bother over it." She shrugged again. "Besides, Fallen Guild imbues each of its members with a certain level of... eh, tolerance. Why, for the final pit, you have to stab yourself with a glint knife, yeh? Could be anywhere really... I did my thigh."

Jhess sharply inhaled.

"How deep?"

"To the hilt." She began picking at the grass under her knee. "But... it was a glint knife, so it mattered not. If anything, I was simply worried whether it would truly repair the wound or not."[1]

"Aye..." She felt Jhess shiver. "I don't think I'd be able to do it... not anywhere."

"Yeh, well, I was quite acquainted with the bite of pain." Adela softly rubbed her shoulder, reflecting on its origin. "Still, her blades were a wonder... pierced my symbols they did."

"And who was it that wielded them? It wasn't one of our own... it couldn't have been. The only enchanted items they're armed with are their containment clubs. Unless... there has been rumour of infiltration and—"

"Ms. Elicy."

Jhess muttered a string of fiery words beneath his breath.

"Lord Monbel himself had ordered a surgical termination of the Wishtons' rank in Unbequith. From what I've heard, they've fled to some unknown stretch of territory, but I still think they're lurking in Unbequith, plotting their insurrection in shadow." Jhess shook his head. "Our Lord would have acted against them sooner, had they not been agents of Siolant."

"Mm." Adela sat in silence for a moment, contemplating his words. "Sounds like your Lord's hand plots against him."

"Well... yes, everyone knows that. But Siolant, though treacherous, is useful—too useful for one." Jhess sighed. "Our Lord seeks to change all that, but we're yet to see when... or how." A moment of silence lapsed between them before Jhess spoke up again. "So... you didn't, ehm... kill her, did you? I thought you couldn't... y'know."

---

1. **Glint Knives**: Toltur Steel. These blades are among the most complex to craft, exceptionally difficult to produce, and even harder to obtain. Only a highly skilled practitioner of darbio and durbio can forge such an object. The blades are adorned with intricate symbols, and its metal emits a soft greenish glow. When used to stab, the weapon inflicts pain and damage like any other knife. However, upon withdrawal from the flesh, the metal repairs the skin and instantly heals the inflicted damage and pain. Crafting these blades is a complex process. A version capable of slashing or cutting has yet to be designed. If a limb is severed, it will not regenerate; the blade's healing properties only activate when it is withdrawn from a stab wound. The process leaves behind a scar, resembling freshly repaired skin. This weapon is considered a war crime due to its potential for effective torture. Nevertheless, the Fallen Guild utilises it in the final pit of Hareesh, where members take a glint knife and stab themselves in a location of their choosing.

Adela sighed deeply.

"I didn't think I could."

She glanced to Jhess, watching the colour fade from his flesh. Adela shook her head, saying: "No, I didn't kill her, but... but yeh. I can't bring myself to do it... I refuse to."

"That's always fascinated me... Have you a specific reason or is it something more, ehm... unexplainable? I know you harbour a strong hatred for the ways of Fallen Guild."

"Well, I wouldn't say hatred, luv... but, they've a method for desensitising the soul, numbing it to the sickness that comes with death. Why, when I was a child, I couldn't harm a single creature—nary a bloody fish!"

"Did they notice?"

"Who?"

"I... I don't know. Fallen Guild?"

"Mm... well I had an assortment of masters if that's what you mean." Adela puffed at her bangs. "They made me start from insects... then work my way up." She glanced to Jhess's puzzled features. "Killing," she said, looking away. "But only for food. Still, they cured my initial sickness of death." Her gaze rose to the ruddy sun sinking behind the horizon. "I know how simple it can be to lose one's sickness, how all it takes is just one insect to begin the curing process." Adela's breath was shaky now, exiting her mouth in soft quivers. "Just the thought of taking a life, a *real* life, a life as real as my own... it makes me sick and... and I don't want to be cured of that sickness. To become so calloused like—" She cut herself off with a sigh, unable to speak his name. "Or maybe I'm just weak..."

"Well... I think it's a good thing." Jhess nodded firmly to himself. "I've never taken a life either and... and I do think we're better off if we go our whole life without doing so. Hopefully none of us ever have to carry out such an extreme form of judgement, yeah?"

"Even if I had to, I... I don't think I'd be able to." Adela tucked her face between her knees, wrapping her arms about her head. "Maybe if I could... or had... managed it—the moment I needed to—*they'd* still be alive."

Jhess was silent for several moments. She studied him from the pocket of her elbow before whispering: "And I *have* taken a life... one." Her gaze rose to the sun, the lines under her eyes darkening. She wished to say more, to open up and spill her emotional afflictions onto Jhess, but she couldn't. Her feelings clashed through her head and heart, battling for supremacy of her principles. How could Adela possibly explain that which she herself didn't understand?

Sighing, Adela glanced over her shoulder to the settlement of tents and soldiers. She considered telling Jhess it was her disguised as Ms. Elicy, that she was the one who saved his life from... an unspeakable man. Despite wishing to share the truth, she... no, she decided against it; Jhess was the one who alerted the battalion after all. Bringing it up might make him feel responsible for tragedies not his own... no, she'd swallow the guilt herself and spare him the burden.

Adela pushed herself up to her knees, saying: "Sorry, luv, I... I've an arrangement, one I should have left for several minutes ago." Unsure of how to leave, Adela gave a short bow. "Good day, Jhessaun."

"Wait, Addy, now hold on!" Jhess seized her hand, gently restraining her from leaving. "You can't just up and bid me farewell! I needs must protect you... yeah?"

Adela glanced down to his hand, her eyes heavy and tired.

"... Yeh."

Jhess began pulling her along, trudging up the knoll with her behind. Before he reached the camp's threshold, he paused to speak up, not daring to look back at her.

"Might... can I ask who it was?"

"Eh?"

"The one you... ehm, *managed*, so to speak." Jhess's posture straightened as he turned about to face her; his features had assumed a more mature expression. "Did they have it coming?"

"I suppose, yeh..." Adela's teeth ground against each other, her gaze unable to meet his. "He was the lowest of... of *insects* to say the least."

"There she is, lads! Dead ahead!" The captain's maniacal laughter roared from the quarter deck. He had taken the helmsman's position, insisting that this was his *favourite* part. "Hard to port!" he cried, the ship lurching sharply to the left. They continued to drift for the cateract-canyon, pulled on by the current of sand.

"Are you *blazing* mad?!" Vincent seized the rails as a shudder ran through the whole ship. "We'll topple over sailing like this!"

The captain's dead serious expression shifted to that of amusement.

"Aye, that we should've! If we were a weaker vessel made for sea, we would have capsized long ago! Our hull's enhancements are strong and our madness stronger still! Sail on, my children! Sail on, *sail on!*"

Vincent turned to Malvolia and Paun, his eyes rolling.

"I suggest we take shelter below deck where—" Vincent fell against Paun, grumbling something indiscernible, before saying: "I suggest we take shelter in the forecastle, aye?!"

Paun and Malvolia nodded, agreeing in unison.

"*Aye.*"

"Oy, Vincent!" shouted the captain, as they turned to leave. "You don't wanna be doing that! Fasten yourself to the main mast! I'll be in need of your skill to ward off all the bleedin' pit krakens!"

Malvolia paled.

"Kraken?! *Krakens!*" She turned to descend below deck. "*Love* to stay for that, but I have had quite enough of monsters as it is!"

Paun was about to follow after her, when he glanced back at Vincent; he was tying a thick rope about his waist, one secured to the mainmast. Scowling to himself, Paun ran to Vincent's side, following his actions.

"Come now," said Paun, "sand squids? I can't have you dying for me to a death like that! No, we'll find a more noble sacrifice for you, aye?"

Vincent slapped Paun's back with a hearty laugh.

"Aye! Merrybender and Truvalson, Octopode Wranglers!"

Their conjoined laughter sharply transitioned to an excited shriek as the ship toppled into the Sinking Canyon.

Adela ducked through a black tent's red-lined flaps. She nearly ran headfirst into Aivon's breastplate as she did so. Thankfully, he stopped her by the shoulders, a sigh of relief seeping through his smile.

"Adela," he greeted, welcoming her into his tent, "excellent timing. I was about to fetch you myself." Aivon nodded to Jhess before returning his gaze to her. "Lord Monbel and I were just discussing the subject of your service. Please." With a hand behind her shoulder, Aivon guided Adela into the tent's heart; there was a stone table in its centre, shaped like a hemisphere with its flat surface facing upwards. Its face was like that of glass, revealing the geode-like hollow beneath it. A shimmer of water layered the table's surface, its light refracting into the colourless shape of a gentleman standing atop the glass; he had rather youthful features for his aged face, a humble shirt of white rolled up to his elbows and a soothing voice of comfort which he used to address her.[2]

"Hail Adela Windcatcher," he said, his right arm gesturing respectfully. "Most regrettably, I could not be here to greet you in person, nor lead my fold in this dispute. For that, I deeply apologise."

"It's quite understandable, truly," said Adela, her gaze lost in the stone's rippling surface. "In truth, any meeting with one of your rank is an honour in and of itself. I never expected to meet you, much less in person, so you needn't trouble over it, luv."

"No, a regional lord should be with his men, leading them *from* conflict... not into it. However, Harling powers force my hand into rather desperate measures. They move against my region, my cities, my... people. Had I not retreated their cities to the shadow of mine mountain's fortitude, they would have long been sacked and burned by the greed of Harldïof." Lord Monbel shook his head. "If not for them, I would not be so forced as to linger behind and protect my own against unnecessary evils."

Aivon nodded, his hand securing Adela's shoulder.

"A most admirable trait, M'lord." He glanced down to Adela. "Do you not believe so?"

"Oh, no... it certainly is honourable... the most I've seen a lord do for his region since the olden days, but... it's just..." A nervous chuckle escaped her. "I don't mean to insult you... sir, but I've heard such monstrous things about Unbequith—its infamous history of war and... and perhaps that's all propaganda, but I still can't help but feel some scepticism about... well, everything." She hastily waved her hands before he could speak. "My opinion is quite differing by now! I've had time to acquaint myself with the better side of your ranks," Adela said, then shot a glance to Aivon and Jhess, "but also its worse side... as well." She returned her gaze to Lord Monbel. "I'm sorry, I truly don't wish to offend..."

"No, you speak the truth." Lord Monbel's reflection swiped her insecurity aside. "Our history is riddled with bloodthirsty strife and cold agony. Propaganda... does exist. But to say it doesn't exist without reason, would be a lie." His arms spread open. "And we have nothing to hide, especially from you. But, tell me..." His features hardened fiercely. "You say you've witnessed the worst my region has to offer... is there anything you imply?"

---

2. Looks like a hologram projection device to me, one crafted of magic instead of technology. How curious.

"I've lost two brothers to you," said Adela, not caring to soften the gravity of her words. "Aivon here has expressed his deepest of apologies, but I've still been tormented in *every* way possible. I've been led to believe there is some treachery amongst your ranks, but I don't—"

"The hand of my hand, Pen Wishton. Aye, it was *his* forces who lost their lives to Resil Saberheart, his treachery who overwhelmed Lesander Flude, and the very forces that allowed Cormurants to force *your* hand into desperation." He held up a bare palm. "Do not ask me how I attained this information, nor assume I know nothing there is to know of you. I am the second Lord of Unbequith. To know is my burden."

"Mm." Adela pinched the dark fur lining her thick cloak. "For every misdeed, for every wrong of Unbequith... you take no responsibility for them?"

"Aye, but I shall bear their consequences as is my place. My hand, Siolant... he has infected my kingdom with the influence of his presence. Verily, I assure you, he shall be disposed of for his treachery the moment he serves his final purpose."

"Right... well... again, excuse my open scepticism, but—"

"Child, you need not apologise for such warranted suspicions."

"Oh, yeh, sorry—I meant, no... shouldn't apologise for *apologising*... But, I don't mean to be rude, I—mm." She paused to gather herself. "You said you were vulnerable to the incoming march of Harldïof, did you not?"

"Indeed, even now, they approach our unguarded city of children and women. It violates the Almighty's laws of Beyond and is a *truly* atrocious violation of one's own morality."

"Yeh..." Adela nodded before facing Lord Monbel's reflection. "Why leave your cities vulnerable to begin with? Why deploy all your troops in a campaign through the most treacherous of woods? Again, I beg pardon for such crude scepticism, but history has shed such an unfavourable shadow across the wars of Unbequith."

"Well, for one, Nowood is the surest route to Ranitorl and—"

"Precisely! Ranitorl is your *allied* region. Why would you dispense *legions* of soldiers against them—leaving *you* vulnerable?"

Aivon touched her elbow.

"Adela..."

"No, she's a right to know," said Lord Monbel. "Her ignorant outburst is to be expected for one of her virtuous character." He nodded to Adela. "Initially, I prepared a third of my army, for my intent was nothing more than a display of persuasion. They seek to join the uncivil motives of that which marches against my people. I could not allow such a thing. However..." He paused, his finger shaking in the air. "However, suspicions have led me to believe the shards have long been secured and are to be taken to Aeraos where they'll be dissected by the brilliance of Ranitorl. I cannot... stand by idle and allow such powers to be exploited by the evils of Harldïof. My decisions are all but actions forced onto Unbequith by desperation."

Adela sniffed to herself.

"Funny what that does to people..." Her fiery gaze rose back to mirror Monbel's. "And the entire division of *rooks?* What of those? Surely, their ancient designs surpass something so meagre as *displayed* persuasion. What need have you for their devastation?"

"A precaution," said Lord Monbel, a terrifying glint in his eye and a stern frown on his lips. "Any general will tell you the wisdom of a cautious and prepared mind. However..." Lord Monbel sighed, his shoulders falling. "However, any old fool could discern you are not completely persuaded of Unbequith's intent."

"Well... you did put Aivon here in charge of... *it.* And I'm certain he'll command your campaign with honour and wisdom, as he has already shown." She bit the side of her bottom lip before continuing. "But... you sir—to put it bluntly—it's *you* who's so bloody shifty. Still, if Aivon gave me the word, then... then I don't see why I shouldn't aid in your endeavours."

Lord Monbel slowly shook his head.

"No, I cannot ask you to do this, nor do I grant you the right of pledging to Unbequith... or me, for you lack the conviction of loyalty... patriotism and divine calling to one's region. Something that could only be inspired by an Unbequith upbringing over time—time you have long since outgrown."

Aivon stepped forward.

"Please, M'lord, she's been through more than any of us could imagine. If you only gave her a—"

Lord Monbel silenced Aivon with a single look.

"You haven't granted me the honour of finishing... Commander."

Aivon bowed his head and stepped back.

"Of course, Lord Monbel. My deepest apologies."

"Tame your emotions, Commander, and all shall be well." His gaze flickered to Adela. "Since you haven't had time to develop loyalty through the respect I am yet to earn from you, I cannot enlist you under the ranks of Unbequith. No, instead, I merely ask you operate under the guidance of Aivon Seeker, for he commands your respect, I should think. Surely, you must have no complaints with him as your singular superior."

"Lord Monbel..." breathed Aivon, his features pale, "this... this is truly a generous display of humility—my Lord, surely I am not worthy for such mechanics of loyalty to take place?"

"Perhaps not, Aivon. But 'tis the only acceptable solution I could conjure for one of her spirits... and skills. This is no whim, for I've dwelt quite some time on this matter as a contingency for... well, an outcome such as this." His gaze rested on Adela. "Do you find this suitable, m'lady?"

"Oh, yeh—yes! Truly, a position and purpose like this must be something of providence! As long as... well, Aivon said I would be able to utilise my proficiencies without taking a life or... having to be ordered to do so."

"I doubt Aivon would demand such an act from you, nor do I expect any of mine men to be engaged in such drastic warfare. To do so is to violate the United Region's Code of Preservence. No, the only command to kill is that which arouses in the judgement of your own conscience. Lord Aivon, her gift, if you will."

Adela spun about to see Aivon brandishing a black quarterstaff, lined with white symbols. He set it in her hands, its weight oddly satisfying. Twirling the quarterstaff about her head, Adela examined it with a beaming smile.

"Stick," she said.

"Aye," agreed Aivon, clasping his hands behind his back with a pleased grin. "In the age of our grandfathers, there was a hunter, Fallen Guild of course. Patron of Unbequith, The Fleeting Spector... *Ravensbane*—Amos Shaid. And that... that would be his blackberry quarterstaff."[3]

"An absolutely bonnie stick!" Adela frowned upon feeling its hard surface. "This could still bash a skull something lethal... but... but I might be able to—"

"That staff is quite incapable of taking a life," said Lord Monbel. "It's symbols are designed specifically for torpification, its make is similar to that of the clubs wielded by the wardens of Vault Tahagorah. Amos kept it for those he was commissioned to capture alive." He shrugged to himself. "We'd produce it as standard issue for our wardens, but to stretch out such enhancements along a length as this is a mighty tedious process."

---

3. Amos Shaid. A Solirmos. One of the few outsiders admitted into Fallen Guild's ranks. Renowned for killing Oswald Tailfeather, the "Raven."

"Aye," began Aivon, "I had it retrieved from Giltpool's archival collection as an honorary gift for your acceptance. I... never had the chance to gift you it, though I knew our paths were sure to cross once again. But... if you're unwilling to join, then, then keep it all the same."

"No... of course, course I'll join! Or, well..." She bit her bottom lip. "I would like to know what you would need of my talents... especially if I can't... *won't* kill."

Lord Monbel cleared his throat, catching her attention.

"Killing is more of a propagated fantasy among the higher terms of war such as ours. Though in hostile dispute, we are still brethren. The Code of Preservence prevents us from slaughtering the children of God in the name of a lord's petty squabble. No, a thousand shall not perish for one and you shall not kill for said one." Lord Monbel interlaced his fingers, holding them beneath his jaw. "With that said... the outbreak of war is never certain, but you are not to fight among the ranks of steel and blood, no. Your position is an elite force, designated for mine delicate variety of tasks. Unrecorded missions for the more... surgical of strikes."

Adela scratched the side of her head, her nose scrunching up.

"Sounds awfully ambiguous... but if Aivon controls it and... if he's the only one I answer to, then... then I don't see why I shouldn't accept that which fits me so, ehm... exquisitely!"

"Excellent." Lord Monbel clapped his hands together. "Then we'll draw up the—"

"One last inquiry, if you'll grace it, Mr. Moan Bell, sir."

He raised an eyebrow, his hand paused in the air.

"And what is that... child?"

"You mentioned how you were led to believe the shards were finally found and, well... *stolen*." Adela gave a loose shrug. "Have you any ground reason to believe so? Even more still... how would you suspect they'd end up in Aeraos of all places? 'Tis awfully specific for a guess."

"It wasn't a guess. I never guess. My forces have recently uncovered the temple of a dark and forgotten cult, protecting the legendary power we have all come to know as prism shards." Lord Monbel paused, gazing down at his drumming fingers. "They were stolen before we could rightfully secure them."

Adela raised an eyebrow, thinking how—if given the chance—she would run off with the shards and find a way to destroy them herself... or maybe she'd take them to Aivon; Adela truly couldn't say for herself.

"And yeh saw the thief headed off to Aeraos *specifically* then?"

"No, by the most hidden and cruel of circumstances, the thief wound up in my vault, where we secured him before setting the poor thing free." Lord Monbel tapped the side of his nose. "But not before prying his memories with a vidorae."

Adela froze at the mention of a thief.

"This man—or... boy?"

Lord Monbel's shoulders gestured loosely.

"Young man. A child in my eyes. A dull thing, though quite cold and stubborn. Despite his outward confidence, he merely feigns bravery. There's a weakness about him, one which we could exploit to our advantage... should the need arise."

Paun flew helpless through the air, only to have the breath jerked out of him by the rope about his waist. He came to a sudden halt at the ship's railing, his hands gripping it tightly. Glancing to the quarter deck, Paun shook his head; the Captain was engaged in a fierce battle, cackling as though he were ill. Apparently, the surgeon thought this to be the proper time for a mutiny: what with the colossal, black tentacles grasping for the ship as it fell through the canyon's sinking walls of sand.

Everyone bustled about, busy with one of three activities. Some—like Malvolia—were having a bonnie time with the ship's ember cannons: gunning down the tentacles which dared to smash their ship to pieces. Others—like Vincent—were engaged in a crude combat of swords. And some—like the surgeon—were simply too occupied with their mutiny to trouble about *circumstances*.

Paun held up his hand to a charging mutineer, one whose sword was brandished over their head in preparation to strike.

"I'm just cargo, mate."

The mutineer paused and nodded, giving him an apologetic wave before turning to find someone else to duel. As Paun watched him go, one of the writhing tentacles overhead crashed down against the deck, landing on Paun's rope and pulling him flat against his back. Squirming to stand up, Paun paled at the sight of another tentacle bearing down upon him; it was oily black, lined with infinitesimal rows of red teeth.

Turning over, Paun used his smallsword to cut through his rope and hastily roll to the left: moments before being obliterated by a crushing limb. As he sprang up to his feet, a convulsing tentacle shot out of the wall of sand, clearing the deck. Many managed to avoid its blow, but some—like the mainmast, rails and Paun—were not so fortunate.

Hurling over the rails, Paun fell off the ship, plummeting into the indiscernible darkness below. He cried out for help, but doubted any would hear him above the unfolding madness.

"A young man..." echoed Adela, rubbing her cheek. "Was he alone or... accompanied?"

"From what I gathered, he is indeed occupied... by two companions, a young woman and an older fellow. We've nothing to trouble about with the woman, but the man... the older gentlemen. Yes, he's an unnatural force of the Oather. One to be reckoned with."

"I've got you, boy!" With one hand, Vincent held onto a line, his feet pressed under the ship's gunwale while his other hand was clenched roughly about Paun's arm. "By *jove*, you're something heavy!" Straining, a rough growl was let loose from Vincent as a score of symbols began to race up his bracers. Paun groaned as Vincent lifted him to his eye level before chucking him back onto the ship's deck. At the same moment, the line snapped and Vincent fell below.

Racing to the ship's devastated rail, Paun peered over to see him land on a whirling tentacle and run across its fleshy surface. His sword digging into its flesh, he dragged his icy blade across its surface, erupting it in cerulean flames as he flipped off onto another tentacle. As the ship fell past him, Vincent lopped the tentacle beneath his feet, leapt forward in a dive and landed in the ship's shrouds.

An assortment of crew members—including some of the mutineers—cheered boisterously for Vincent's success before returning to combat. Paun could only fall to his knees, his hand gripping his shoulder in pain and another on the rails for dear life as the ship plummeted further into the cavern's waters below.

"And their *names*," said Adela, her hands pressing against the stone's circular edge. "What are their *names?*"

Lord Monbel's gaze briefly flickered to Aivon before returning to her.

"We've sent the boy off to Ranitorl, though recent intel indicates he escaped to rendezvous with his two companions."

"Yeh, but what are their names?"

"Despite the uncertainty of their whereabouts, we're certain they're making way for Ranitorl to deliver the shards. We doubt they'll be there by the time we arrive, for our intelligence deciphered the vidorae's riddles to indicate a cowardly route of—"

"*Enough.*" Adela shirked off Aivon's grip as she climbed atop the table to stare Lord Monbel in the eye, a hair's breadth from his reflection's face. "*What...* are their names? I'd find out the truth sooner than later, so there's no use in lying."

He sighed, his unwavering eyes refusing to break contact.

"Of course not. I have already pledged nothing but honesty to you."

"A luxury to be sure," chimed in Aivon.

Adela ignored his comment, continuing to stare Teresul Monbel dead in the eye.

"Then tell me, luv. What... are... their *names?*"

CHAPTER FOURTEEN

THE GROWL OF THUNDER

T HE SHIP HAD DROPPED anchor, for a hint of bluish transparency had crept into the cavern's stone ceiling. The captain—who stood arm-in-arm with his wife, the surgeon—had bid them a hasty farewell. Malvolia remembered the mad sailor warning of how they stood beneath the edge of the Hollow Plains and how he wished them *many-a-blessing*, for they were all to die a most legendary and unsung death. An end as awesome as it was pointless. The Captain and his wife found that hysterical for whatever reason.

Despite such cryptic words of certain doom, they continued on, scaling a rope ladder to climb out from the great pit. Once again, they found themselves in a desolate landscape—though quite different from the wastes of Unbequith. They had been certain it was the middle of day, yet the sky was a deep shade of black, flashing with bolts of lightning every now and again. The rock beneath their feet was an odd type of black mineral with a fine layer of cobalt blue sediment over its glassy surface. No vegetation had been in sight except clumps of teal-petal flowers.

And now they were walking... in the rain... *slowly*.

She understood they must have been sore as well, but... was there no need for haste? Was time of no importance? Was there no risk of danger? Still, if Vincent advised it, Malvolia figured there *had* to be a good explanation.

Besides... her legs truly *did* hurt.

Like, a lot.

She shot a glance to Paun; though his features remained calm, she could tell he was anxious. He was usually so composed. To see him in such a nervous state was as amusing as it was disturbing.

"Oy," growled Vincent, glancing over his shoulder to Paun. *"Don't* look up."

"Blast it, Paun." Malvolia's hand curled into a fist. "Temper your fear and control yourself, lest we—"

Paun shook his head.

"*They're close.*"

"The blazes are you—" Malvolia was cut off by a profound roll of thunder directly over their heads. She paled at its sound; initially, she had interpreted it as nothing more than the clash of weather. But now, with the insight of Paun, she recognized its dull rumbling to be that of a creature: a creature so profound in size, its very roar shook the heavens.

A thunder.

"*Listen* to me," hissed Vincent, jerking Paun closer. "You know what'll happen if you give into your fear. *Don't* look up. I needn't tell you a hundred times over, just *don't...* look... *up.*" He shoved Paun before pointing to a small bluish haze in the distance. "Those lights are the Obelisks of the Lost. If we can simply make it there without attracting any attention, we'll be well beyond harm's reach."

Paun seized Vincent as he turned to lead the way.

"There's no telling they haven't already spotted us," he said, releasing Vincent as his hand was swiped away. "For all we know, they're simply toying with their prey—toying with *us.*"

Shrugging, Vincent continued walking.

"Perhaps. Truly, there's no way of knowing."

"But... but there is. If we're prepared, maybe we could—"

"*No.* For now, there's no way of knowing. But, if we look up, then it's *certain.* Believe you me, there's no way about it. They can spot the life in your eyes from leagues away. Head *down.* By all things sacred... I'm not telling you again."

Malvolia nodded, her head shaking from the concentration.

"Aye... but there's no need for such concern, ay?" Malvolia's self-control grew with her confidence. "I am certain one of Vincent's skill is more than capable of overcoming them." She almost glanced nervously to the sky, wishing more than ever for the pace to pick up. "Surely, your celestial flintlock could overpower them?"

"If it were a leviathan, ghosts, bleedin' primordial entities, then *yes.* Thunders? In truth, I'm not too sure! It's their breath after all that inspired the make of such casters as mine." He shrugged. "We're safe... unless we're not, in which case we should be running for our wee lives, but that would just attract more attention—no, we're most likely probably fine methinks."

Malvolia heard Paun's breathing grow heavier; it was unnerving to say the least.

"Oy, Chulian! You can hear me, yes?" Malvolia flinched at the flash of lightning over-head, immediately followed by a thunderous roar. The helpless feeling building in her stomach was akin to that which the toothy blacks made her feel. "*Chulian!* Kill *anything* that gets too close, *alright!* Chulian? Blast it, dragon, I know you can hear me!"

"*Oy.*" snapped Vincent. "He says lower your *bloody voice.* They're right over—"

A crackling burst of white lit up the sky and the surrounding environment. For a brief moment, everything was clear and visible, everything but for where they resided; a great shadow was cast over them, its darkness stretching out like that of a tremendous wyvern.

Malvolia looked to Paun and he, sword drawn, looked to the sky.

Unable to resist the pull of dread, Malvolia followed his gaze, looking up to see a crea-ture swooping down from the heavens. Another flash punctured her terror, illuminated by the sheer energy of the saurian bearing down upon them. In that brief moment of primal fear, she saw every detail: from the creature's imposing lines of black teeth to its enflamed, yellow eyes. Bolts of white energy flickered across its rock-like hide and midnight-blue scales as it descended.

Feeling a tug on her hand, Malvolia was jerked backwards and thrown to the ground beside Vincent. She whirled about to see Paun, rolling away from the snapping jaws of the beast. Sword drawn, Vincent rushed the creature, seizing its attention moments before heaving his blade across its snout. Its pained roar transitioned to silence as a layer of ice encased it jaws. It tried to yank its head back, but was jerked down as Vincent slammed its chin against the ground; a string of symbols illuminated the dark landscape, spiraling along Vincent's bracers. As the thunder tried to squirm from his sword's magic, various bolts of light began to spark across its lips under the ice. His eyes widening, Vincent tore his sword from the creature and dove under its stomach. A plume of cerulean flame burst across the thunder's snout, moments before it reeled its neck back to unleash a torrent of black lightning. Paun and Malvolia leapt back, arms over their eyes. The creature tucked its head under its legs to blast Vincent with its breath, but its head was batted aside in a spray of ice and cerulean flame.

Unleashing a violent shriek, it lit up the landscape with a flash of light from its body before tearing into the ground where Vincent had been. Malvolia couldn't see him behind the thunder's sporadic movement, but she knew he had to be safe.

He had to be.

The gashes in the stone beneath the thunder grew in size and number until the very ground fell away to reveal a bottomless chasm—one which the thunder dove into. Vincent remained on the other side of the hole, sword poised and ready. Upon seeing the creature disappear into the caverns below their feet, Vincent ran about the hole and seized both Malvolia and Paun.

"*Run,*" he said. "I've asked you to do so before, but nothing compares to the urgency I demand of you now." He slapped their backs before taking the lead. "*Run!*"

The ache in Malvolia's limbs faded as she followed after him. Despite how hard she tried to ignore her fatigue, she couldn't help but notice how much she was beginning to fall behind. Thankfully, Paun tapped Vincent's back, causing him to spin around and hoist Malvolia over his shoulders.

As grateful as she was for it, Malvolia couldn't help but feel terribly undignified.

Rising atop Vincent's shoulder's, Malvolia examined the stone plains stretching out before them. It was impossible to see anything beyond—a pulse of light flashed beneath the ground, a league or so away. As it faded from sight, a distant boom promptly followed its absence.

The light appeared again... closer.

"Vincent..."

"I see it, lass." Vincent's lips curled into a determined snarl. "We can get past it. Trust Chulian."

A dull rumble echoed from below.

"Chulian?" scoffed Paun. "He's a *dragon*. What would a dragon know of thunders?"

A light flashed from below, illuminating the approaching form of a living terror.

"I needn't, nor *haven't* the time to explain, just *bloody trust him.*"

A loud boom followed the light's absence.

"Vincent..." whispered Malvolia, urgently tapping his head. "Vincent... use Chulian... please."

"I have abused my power enough as—"

A flash of light and a thunderous boom flashed naught but a hundred paces from where they stood. As they ran, a single commanding voice spoke in Malvolia's head; it was Chulian.

Stop.

They came to an abrupt halt as a flash of blinding light lit up beneath their feet.

The thunder erupted just before them, its meaty roar deafening their ears and quaking the earth. Vincent matched its vocals with a cry of his own before driving his blade through its chest and tearing it out with a slashing flame of blue.

The thunder reared its head back in a quaking shriek before attempting a snap at Vincent. However, as it lowered its jaws over him, Vincent struck his blade up in its mouth and through its head. A crackling tremor of light ran along the thunder before it collapsed against the ground with a resounding thud.

Sighing heavily, Vincent turned to face Malvolia and Paun.

"Right, so—"

Vincent sprang back as the thunder stirred suddenly, releasing a stream of black lightning into the sky before finally falling dead. Following its breath, Malvolia's gaze rose to see two thunders descending upon them.

"Vincent!" she cried, turning to face him, "Vincent, you *have* to *use*—" She fell against the ground in utter shock, for a third thunder stood over the other's corpse with Vincent locked in its claws. It gave a triumphant shriek before rocketing into the clouds.[1] The other two thunders followed after it, unleashing a storm of their deadly breath.

Malvolia held an arm over her eyes as she stared up into the sky. Every now and again, she could see a small crescent of cerulean flame in the midst of frenzied thunders and bursts of black lightning.

"He'll survive."

Malvolia glanced to Paun.

"How can you be sure?"

Sharply inhaling, Paun nodded.

"He's never in any true danger... not him."

"Mm." Malvolia glanced at Paun. "Then why so pale?"

Paun's shaky exhale contrasted his stern expression.

"He's but a man..." A flash of white shook the sky before Paun continued: "and yet, he possesses enough power to rival that of reality itself... I've said it before and I shall say it

---

1. The thunder shoots into the sky at the other thunders in a final defence of its food. These territorial creatures don't cooperate well. While they don't immediately fight on sight, they prefer to avoid one another. Although they don't wish to kill their own kind, disputes over food, territory, and mates still arise. Thunders mate only once, then spend the remainder of their lives with their partner underground until death takes them.

again... it's unnatural... and wrong. He may claim to be otherwise, but his mind is still that of a mortal and no mortal should wield such ungodly power."

"Well..." Malvolia squinted at the sky, trying to visualise the chaos through the rain. "In the least, it's a man like Vincent who—" Malvolia shakily drew her sword, unsure of how to deal with the cataclysmic wrath of nature descending upon them. She closed her eyes as a streak of black lighting tore free of the creature's jaws to completely annihilate them. However, it never touched them.

Malvolia felt the ground beneath her give way as she fell through an astral gash. Oddly enough she found herself lurched to the left as she was teleported through the gash. A rough grip then seized her wrist, yanking her away from the gash; a torrent of black lightning exploded out from its portal.

Rubbing her elbow, she rose to see Vincent, his sword shining a fiery-blue. Pulling Paun to his feet, Vincent shrugged under Malvolia's quizzical gaze.

"Yeah..." he began, looking down to his sword, "I used it. I know." He pointed to an ensemble of black pillars, their sides laced with layers of shining blue runes. Similar formations surrounded them, but he gestured only to one; it was in the centre of the obelisks and larger in dimension than the others. "Take cover behind that. They're bound to find us any moment now."

Malvolia crossed her arms.

"And you? What of—"

"*Need I repeat myself?!*" Vincent's expression was rugged and stern, enough for Malvolia to shrink before it. Shaking his head, he raised a hand. "Go... *now.*"

Malvolia pursed her lips, but still listened, turning to take Paun by the arm with her. She looked over her shoulder to see Vincent duck behind a pillar. Though he was concealed behind it, he was completely visible if someone were to walk past him.

Or prowl... whatever thunders do.

She let out a sharp gasp as Paun yanked her to the left behind the large obelisk. Giving him a swift glare, she peeked about the obelisk to see two flashes of white diving from the sky. One thunder landed before the other in an earth-shattering tremor, sniffing about the obelisks for the trespasser it knew was there. A deep, guttural noise emitted from the creature's throat as its head swooped between the obelisks. Its massive head cocked to the side, its lips sliding back to reveal its rows of black teeth. Malvolia's heart dropped as it began rounding the obelisk Vincent stood behind.

Drawing her sword, she jerked away from Paun's grip and stepped into the open. She attempted a fierce war cry, but was unable to muster the required vocals at the sight of such an imposing beast. Still, it made no difference, for the thunder had noticed her. Its head swooped low to her level, its jaws cracking open and lined with black lightning. However, in the same instant, Vincent sprung out from behind the obelisk, sword shimmering overhead. With a decisive slash of his blade, he decapitated the creature. As he landed beside its corpse, the second thunder crawled atop its dead kin to snap at Vincent. As it did, Vincent swung his sword into the thunder's mouth, relieving it of its jaw before plunging his blade up through its skull.

Yanking Paun out from behind the obelisk, she turned back to watch Vincent ascend the thunders' corpses. His eyes were raised defiantly to the heavens, screaming for it to send more. All colour fled her features as she watched him. The sky, however, merely boomed in response, light exploding across its face.

But it did not retaliate.

For even the heavens knew better than to question the might of *he* who slew its children.

CHAPTER FIFTEEN

HELL'S BUTTERFLIES

U NBEQUITH'S CAMPAIGN STEADILY MARCHED onwards. The front lines were composed of iron dragons, their breath quite literally blazing a trail. A squad of rooks stomped behind them, levelling the charred trees to make way for the marching advance of foot soldiers. Some of the more... *dignified* officials chose to travel alongside their legion in carriages or atop sumpter drakes. Others, like Adela, were transported in the *Kingsquaker*, a rook designated specifically for Aivon and his company.[1] They stood in its circular chambers now, the world outside its windows passing by at a gradual pace.

"This... is Adela Windcatcher."

The stewards gathered about the table murmured and whispered amongst one other, causing Adela to flush. Still, she retained a confident composure, for she trusted Aivon and his authority; he was, after all, the highest rank among them.

Aivon cleared his throat, silencing the chamber. Nodding, he continued: "She is not pledged to any city, faction, or region, but rather, a living extension of my will and thus... Unbequith's will. None are her superior, save I, Greyt Aivonfel." He paused, allowing

---

1. **Rooks**: a roaming watchtower. Rooks are powerful mobile watchtowers designed for battle. Resembling the tower chess piece, they feature mechanical appendages equipped with gyroscopic stabilizers and hydraulic actuators, extending from their base like spider legs for terrain traversal. These legs can retract, giving the appearance of a standard watchtower. Mounted at the top are ember cannons, along with multiple embrasures for bowmen. Each brick of a rook is blessed with prayers and reinforced with symbols, making them suitable for all climates and biomes. Designed with a reinforced exoskeleton, rooks are extremely mobile and heavily armed, serving as formidable front-line fortresses. Their quick setup and repair capabilities, along with a hybrid power source combining alchemical engines and magical energy, make rooks essential for disrupting infantry and breaking enemy lines on any battlefield.

time for his stern gaze to set in. "To shed some light on the true gravity of her title I shall tell you... that even if one such as Teresul Monbel, *Region Lord of Unbequith*, were to give her an order unapproved by mine word—and mine word *alone*—his actions would be considered an act of treason against the whole of Unbequith. So be it, for it is so... she is the Eáldorfeil."[2]

An uproar of diverse voices united together in the shared disapproval of Adela. Though she tried to understand their reasons, Adela couldn't discern what... well, *anyone* was saying in all the clamour. Biting her bottom lip, she looked up to Aivon, studying his amused expression; it gave her confidence. To know one of such a rank as he stood behind her and *for* her was beyond reassuring.

The stewards' clamouring disagreements gradually died down as an elderly fellow raised his hands. Delicately interlocking his fingers, the steward addressed Aivon. His voice was an odd mixture of snowfall-like whispers and crow-like rasps.

"Lord Stalherd," he introduced, "first and only steward of Evenfir. I believe I speak on all our behalf when I say this is not only an embarrassment of your title—or an abuse—it is simply... a disgrace."

Aivon nodded, rubbing his chin with seemingly genuine interest.

"Continue."

"Well... are you so hasty as to forgo our creed? In the chance her short hair has duped you, this is indeed a *female*. Yet you are so blind as to promote one of her... *kind* to a farce's rank of unfathomable honour?"

"*Continue...*"

"It clashes with the ways of old, our very *foundations*. In undoing our convictions, you undo our society. Please, I beseech thee... bestow such an honour upon a suitor who's bloody *worthy* of it. You had us hand-pick the finest of our regions—"

"Stop." Aivon gently rolled his knuckle across the table. "The title *Eáldorfeil* does not exist to bestow *honour*. It exists so that *she* may honour *us* with her loyalty." Aivon raised a hand, silencing the steward. "I am well away of our tenets and all the more aware

---

2. "Eáldorfeil" is a title of distinction, blending "Eáldor," meaning "set apart" or "holy," with the feminine suffix "-feil," symbolizing honor. This rare and esteemed title is reserved for those who act as patrons of Unbequith. It is given to foreign individuals who relinquish their own heritage in service to furthering the goals of a region that is not their own. Because Unbequith is reluctant to admit outsiders into their ranks, the title is seldom conferred. However, those few who receive it are treated with the reverence of an angel sent by divine decree to aid them.

of their importance... perhaps even more so than you." The elder sniffed, a venomous sneer scarring his features, but Aivon continued, undeterred: "If the... *primeval* ruins of your mind's library can recall, the laws of old were instituted to preserve our region's existence throughout the many generations to come. Adelafeil is no child of Unbequith. We needn't trouble over her ability to bear our next generation."

Adela opened her mouth to say something, but couldn't speak over her flushing emotions. A brief smile lit Aivon's features before it resumed its grave expression: "Said law was instituted to forge the strongest army of any region. Unyielding, enduring, and *mighty*. Women are the antithesis of this—they are a hindrance to the ideals of war." Aivon pounded his fist on the table. "But *by jove* is she a bloody exception! She falls into neither categories of what the old laws forbid. She hath sevenfold the might than all in this room combined into one lethal force! She is both an asset and a blessing."

Lord Stalherd rolled his cloudy eyes and puffed; it amused Adela to watch his snowy-white beard react to such a sour expression.

"This is true. But it's besides the point. It's the fundamental principles behind your actions that creates this troublesome act of symbolism. She is a living seed of Unbequith's downfall. The ways of old exist for founded reasons and the laws dictate—"

"*My word* is law." Aivon was silent for a few moments, as were all others. "You might disagree with the situation... but you cannot disagree with me, for such practices are... treacherous. It would be the beginning of our ruin. 'Tis the very reason our punishments are so swift and our fell judgement *swifter*."

"Of course..." said the trembling steward, shrinking under his glare. "I meant no disrespect to Aivonfel. But... was I wrong to assume you assembled this council so you might hear what wise words we've to offer?"

"As is my position's duty, I inform you merely to inform you—*not* to bother about your *bloody* opinions." Aivon nodded to the elderly steward before raising his arms to all those gathered about the table. "And what say you?"

The council's discordant voices came together in six words.

May it be so Greyt Aivonfel.

Nodding his approval, Aivon bade they present their best men. As the stewards' various champions lined up against the chamber's wall, Aivon placed a heavy hand on Adela's shoulder, saying: "Choose wisely, for *both* our lives may depend on who we allow into this circle."

Adela nodded. Before he summoned the council, Aivon was sure to share everything that was to transpire; under Aivon's supervision, she was to select five men of her choice. There were thirty or so laid out before her now. However, one of those five was to be Lieutenant Bo; he was an extension of Aivon's command and the predesignated leader of their force, for Adela didn't feel confident enough to accept the role's responsibilities. Though long agreed upon, Adela was to select Lieutenant Bo publicly: before the stewards as though it were an action of her own will—which was... *technically* true. Even if Aivon hadn't ordered her to do so, she would have selected him for being Aivon's Lieutenant: if Aivon could trust him to such a rank, then why shouldn't she?

Adela stepped up to him now, softly patting his head. He gave her a bemused glance but stepped forward to her side all the same. The rest were a tad more difficult, for she knew them not. Thankfully, upon approach, each official proudly presented their men to her. Though they each offered a polite gesture of the hand, only several or so actually shook her hand—and even fewer than that with a smile. With those standards in mind, it was fairly simple for her to narrow down the options set before her.

The second man she selected was a True Beyonder. Upon first glance he was utterly terrifying: from his pale features riddled in scars to the emotionless and cold expression he maintained. His chest-piece was quite beaten, yet the ornamentation engraved into it was absolutely lovely. Suddenly aware of how close she was to his armour she looked up and offered an apologetic smile. A light grin escaped the corners of his lips and he introduced himself as Darun Fyrwriss. Shaking his hand, she had him step beside Lieutenant Bo.

The third man of her choosing wore a traditional Unbequith mask. Its snarling design was fearsome and it fascinated her. He didn't speak, but she liked his conical straw hat—reminded her of Aresmas it did. Upon inquiry, she found him to be named Ramsoen Riversbane, master of infiltration, stealth and creature-wrangling. He seemed a curiously interesting fellow—and he *did* shake her hand...

She had him stand with Darun.

The fourth man of her selection had pulled her handshake into a wild hug. However, upon being chastised by his steward, he hastily set her down. Adela told the steward to think nothing of it. In truth, she was in awe of the wild man's actions and wished to know more of him. Apparently, he was a learned True Beyonder as well, though, in contrast, was a practitioner of durbio—muritos of token-casting. He wasn't all straight in the head, but she didn't mind. At the word of her approval, Fel—for that was his name—took his place beside Ramsoen.

The final man was simple to choose. He wore standard armour plating and looked like almost any other soldier. What set him apart, however, was the charred-black colouring of his armour. There were no hints of red to be found across it except a red scarf tucked about his neck. The Black Knight they called him, champion of Ashhelm and thrice-renowned victor of Unbequith's yearly pit tournaments. His armour, sword, and shield were enchanted trophies of his victories, displays of strength and cunning. Despite the imposing introduction, he was quite humble and had offered her a little yellow flower. His name was Samuel Reedson, but Roabard simply introduced him as Sam.

Of course she picked him.

With her team of five finally chosen, Aivon promptly dismissed the council and all others not selected by Adela—save for Jhess of course; he *was* her bodyguard after all.

After the stewards departed, Lord Aivon clapped his hands together and ordered them to form a straight line for his inspection.

"Yes, you too, Jhess," said Aivon, gently prodding him along. "You're her bodyguard, are you not?"

The crazy one—she had already forgotten his name—snickered as Jhess took his place beside Adela. He was corrected with a swift smack on the back of his head from Lieutenant Bo. Nodding his approval, Aivon continued: "You have each been handpicked by Adela Windcatcher—she of the Fallen Guild and conqueror of Hareesh's Pits—to form a contingency reserve." A glint in his eye lit for a moment as he glanced to Adela with a grin before returning his gaze to the others. "This elite force is to be referred to as Déaþinferleas Popilégan; *Hell's Butterflies.*"

Initially, there was naught but a heavy silence. Not but a few seconds later, it was swiftly broken by a handful of discreet coughs which gradually evolved into poorly concealed snickers. Even Lieutenant Bo was having trouble maintaining a straight composure. The restrained amusement was soon destroyed by Fel—the crazy fellow—in one horrendous chuckle. Before they knew it, the whole chamber was in a giddy uproar.

Except Adela who simply smiled mischievously.

She knew *exactly* what she had done.

CHAPTER SIXTEEN

CITY OF MAGIC

P AUN STARED OUT INTO the vast lake before him; the heavens' heavy gloom did little to hinder the public from enjoying the various activities the lake had to offer; several dinghies sailed across its aqua-blue face, their pale sails dimming in comparison to the great ships about them.

Stretched across the lake was a bridge of wood and stone. It was just large enough to allow carts, wagons, and other means of transport to bustle alongside one another in either direction. At the end of the bridge, within the lake's middle, was a sprawling city; though its milky-brick walls were of imposing heights, Paun could still catch glimpses of the capital within and its ruddy-orange tile roofs.

Aeraos.

"You can put me down now."

Paun glanced to Malvolia sitting atop Vincent's shoulders; she had been sore all over and had been slowing them down. Despite her verbal protests, she had made no physical objection to riding atop Vincent. Not till now anyhow, as she slipped off his back and adjusted her hat. Her hair was a wild mess, but she didn't seem to mind—she never did really.

"Feeling better there, Mal-mal?" Vincent ruffled her hat, much to her evident displeasure.

"Aye..." she mumbled, tugging it over her head. "Still sore something mighty, but I shall manage. Simply pains mine ego to see you two so casually embrace the arduous demands of this journey... is all."

Paun spoke up over the bustling crowds as they continued down the bridge.

"Well, 'tis only because I was built for it. Trained for it since I could walk I was. And Vincent—" Paun paused to eye him. "He's a freak."

Vincent blinked.

"*What.*"

Malvolia snickered.

"Even so," she said, "I'd rather not breach the capital of Ranitorl astride Vincent as though he were mine war mount. Wouldn't be much of a formidable impression for either of us."

"Formidable?" Paun raised an amused eyebrow. "Now who bloody cares two *pieces* about that?"

"What? Are you—surely you cannot *mean* that! Why, the moment I beheld you striding into Tokade with your dark eyes and roguish attire... alongside that masked stranger and yellow princess as well—*well*, I *knew* you were adventurers looking for trouble of some sort. Kept an eye on you, I did—and by God, was I right to do so..."

"Mm." Paun rubbed the bags under his eyes. "I think I was just tired..."

They had now reached the bridge's end. A shore of grey sand and thin grass stretched along both sides of a brick path. Many families and figures were dotted along the beach, enjoying the activities it had to offer. Most of the women wore white dresses and straw hats while the men were attired in white frilly shirts. Some simply walked about, others fished, and almost all the children were frolicking in the waves. Some children closer to the bridge stared at them in awe before being ushered away by their concerned mothers.

Malvolia shook her head with a heavy puff. "You see now? *Pure* intimidation. We're entering this city like bloody heroes of old! Impressions dictate how legends are told. Do you *not* see? We're bloody legends in the making!" Malvolia paused, hands on hips, as they stood before the city's first gate. She popped her coat collar. "You've not the slightest idea how my—"

"Hey."

Malvolia gave a short squeak, hurling her fist at the man who suddenly appeared before them. Her knuckles thudded against his whiskered jaw, though seemed to have little effect on the man. He looked tired, the youthful black colouring of his beard lined with grey.

He sniffed, the right side of his face twitching where it had been hit. "Didn't break a single bone..." He feathered his jaw. "Nope, not a single one. I suggest working on your hooks, little lady."

Malvolia only frowned in response, sulking behind Vincent to rub her knuckles.

"Theo..." Paun murmured, catching the stranger's attention.

"Yeah," said the man, his nonchalant expression hosting what little surprise it could. "Remember me, do you?"

"I remember everything, every detail... from *that* day."

"Unfortunately, I can't say the same." Theo's shining grey eyes drifted to Vincent, narrowing ever so slightly. "You're *hauntingly* familiar... have I killed you before?"

Vincent's sour expression was poorly concealed behind his formal smile.

"The Mad Ball. I kept to myself for the most part, but I remember you. An uproar such as yours is impossible to miss. I knew you not then, but I do now. Truly... it's astounding... the Red Brotherhood hosts quite a number of records on your... ill-encountered person."

"Ah." Theo patted his hips and tilted his head. "So you're one of *them* then."

"No... I am not. However, I am of the same circle... as *you*." Vincent's expression shifted darkly. "I know the powers you've fallen into are of great temptation and—at times—demanding, but the brazen indifference you display in abusing your circle's privilege... why, it leaves me to wonder why they haven't apprehended you sooner."

Theo shook his head, the hair over his eyes falling to the sides of his face.

"I'm not here to chat about the Aft-Circle's paradox."

"Then why *are* you here?"

Theo shrugged.

"Call it a job. The Lord of Ranitorl is desperate... and that's always dangerous." He shrugged again. "I've been designated as the shards' caretaker—protecting them to the best of my abilities till this all, um... *blows over*." Theo's arm lifted to point at Paun before falling to his side again. "How 'bout you? You wanna hand 'em over or... do I have to..."

Paun drew his smallsword, directing it under the man's chin.

"I think we'll take them to the Lord ourselves if it's all the same with you."

"Hm." Theo took a step forward, the blade's point passing through his throat as though it were nothing but air. "What the Oather must've done to protect a helpless mortal like you—"

"Not another step, *boy*." Vincent's hand rested on his weapon's pommel. "Chulian's appetite surpasses that of steel. You might be a ghost to those of the Fore-Circle, but you're just another man to me, same as I am to you." He smirked. "I doubt you would be ready for such a swift reacquaintance with defeat."

"A truly provoking proposition, but that'd be abusing our *privileges*, wouldn't it?" Theo's head tilted to the right with a smile. Swifter than an eye's blink, he suddenly appeared before Vincent then disappeared completely from sight. The instant he vanished, Vincent patted his coat with a scowl.

"They're gone," he said, glaring up to the keep in the distance. "He has them."

Paun seized Vincent's coat by the shoulder, turning him to face his eyes.

"The shards?"

"Aye."

"Well..." Paun glanced at Malvolia, nervously inhaling as he patted Vincent's shoulder. "Well, let's get him."

"No." Vincent shook his head and patted Paun's head. "No, there needn't be any need for haste. One such as he does not require prism shards or even the wealth of a regional lord." Vincent sighed, rubbing the back of his neck. "Why he's accepted this... *job* still remains a mystery to me, but I don't doubt his alignment with the Lord of Ranitorl."

"If you say so," said Malvolia, stepping out from behind Vincent, her features pale. "In truth... I did not think it possible for the existence of one who could outmatch you."

"He *can't* outmatch me... probably. If anything, it'd be a fair match from what I learned of him. But enough of that. Come, let us make merry with what peace is to be found in the simple journey from here to... wherever we need to go. If Theo speaks the truth, then they know we're here and have long sent an envoy out to meet us. Until then, can we enjoy ourselves?"

"Aye," said Malvolia, crossing her arms. "Aye, I can do that."

"Good girl." He turned to his left. "Paun?"

Paun had much more to say on the matter; of how he knew Vincent was holding back his true power, how terrifying of a thought it was that more beings like Vincent existed, or how much Theo's rightfully arrogant disposition reminded him of Vincent's—but Paun simply nodded in response.

"Aye... it *is* the city of magic after all. We mustn't waste the sights on helpless fretting."

"That we mustn't, though it wouldn't hurt to maintain a steady pace. We are, apparently, expected after all."

"I myself gathered as much, aye."

"Very good, onward then."

The city's first gatehouse hosted no gate, much to the initial surprise of Paun. However, as they passed through the city's entrance, Paun felt a hum of energy, like that of electrified air, pass over him as he stepped through. He ruffled his hair, shuddering at the feeling.

Capital of Ranitorl.

City of magic.

Right.

The path leading into the town was built over a sparkling canal, with pairs of watermills at organised intervals. Following the crowd, they came across what must have been a town square; there were many vendors and shops to be found, their frames composed of a warm-brown wood. Paun wondered why a capital would ever begin to use such a material, for the risk of fire was always possible—especially for a city with such an antagonised history as this. Perhaps it was a special wood? *Magic wood?* He truly didn't know.

"Oy, Paun."

"Yeah, Vincent."

"Don't you know that girl?"

Paun followed Vincent's gesture, the insides of his stomach turning over upon sight of who he referred to.

"That's..." Paun cleared his throat, discreetly pulling Vincent and Malvolia behind a vegetable cart. "That's *definitely* a girl."

"Aye..." Vincent nodded gravely, hand on chin. "So it is."

"What of it?" exclaimed Malvolia, refusing to crouch beside them. "I'm one as well, I'll have you know!"

Vincent yanked her down to their level.

"*Quiet you.* We're treading in unknown territory here. Paun, what do you know—"

"She's gone."

"*What?*" Vincent clawed past Paun to peer out into the square. "How could you lose her?"

"It happens more often than you think."

"Wait, Vincent—who even *is* she?"

"I don't know, ask Paun!"

"Paun, *who—*"

"I *don't* wanna talk *about—*"

"Excuse me."

They spun about to see Junia standing over them, her bemused eyebrows knitted together. "I'm terribly sorry," she began, helping Vincent to his feet, "but did Theo swipe the shards from you? I personally think he handles his position with a little too much, ehm... zeal." Her eyes widened upon sight of Paun. "Oh... you."

Paun nodded, brushing off his knees as he rose to his feet.

"Aye... you."

Malvolia remained on the ground where she was, her legs and arms crossed.

"These are *not* the impressions I was talking about..."

Junia glanced down to Malvolia, frowning on sight.

"You're Henagan's daughter, are you not?"

"Not." Malvolia's gaze rose to face Junia's. "I'm a grumpy princess."

"It's true," said Vincent, speaking up from behind Junia. "And I'm an unmasked stranger."

Junia curtsied with the ends of her jerkin.

"A pleasure. In the chance ol' Paun here hasn't mentioned me, I'm called Junia Ortunato, hand of Ranitorl. I've been sent to escort you to the chambers of mine good Lord."

"An escort, ey?" Vincent stroked the edges of his beard. "Fancy. Mighty fancy." He nodded and slapped Paun's chest. "Would you not agree?"

"Aye, but—" Paun turned to eye Junia. His suspicions clashed sickeningly against one another in his gut. "How could your Lord anticipate our arrival, much less know of the shards we had borne?"

"All answers shall be resolved in time, for—" Junia reddened, her features scrunching up. "Sorry... I simply... sometimes the surreality of the moment carries me away to disbelief and I am left to address you as I would any other."

"Oh, no," said Paun, "truly it's fine. You needn't apologise." He remained undeterred by Malvolia's poorly-concealed groan as he bowed. "In truth, I never thought I would have crossed paths again this soon." He paused for a moment before shrugging. "Truly, I too find myself at a loss for words. I haven't the slightest idea of where to begin."

"Well, for starters you can follow me to M'ord's chambers. I'm certain we'll have time for catching up over the course of such an... *arduous* journey."

Paun smiled.

"Please, lead the way." As he followed Junia, he glanced over his shoulder to see Vincent trailing behind, one hand held up in a thumb, the other restraining Malvolia. Paun's mouth briefly gaped open in inquiry, but was cut off by Junia.

"She *is* Henagan's offspring, is she not?"

"Aye, that she is... but..." Paun shot another glance over his shoulder to see Malvolia wildly slapping Vincent's hand away. "She's not the same as he. At one point, I do believe she might have been under his manipulation, but not by choice methinks." His gaze shifted about the city, admiring the beauty of its architecture. "She was something of a sour spirit, but... but I do believe she's changed for the better, even if it be but a slight alteration."

"Hm... curious." Junia's features remained neutral until she tilted her head to eye Paun. "And what of you?" she asked, a playful smile lighting her lips. "Has the man I've known for but a prolonged spell already vanished? Has he long been replaced by a better man?" Her eyes narrowed. "Or something far more sinister..."

Paun gave a short laugh.

"No, I doubt one as simple as I could ever change—much less over such a short span of time. But you... you look different."

"Oh?" Though her cheeks reddened, she eyed him confidently. "How so?"

"Well..." He briefly hesitated before deciding to shrug off the question. "Your hair for one. I've never had the opportunity to see it like this... not truly."

"Oh, well yes, there's *that*." She tugged the ends of her raven-black hair. "I did let it sit in the sun for a tad... scouts gave me about an hour or two of preparation." She sucked in her lips upon realising her words. Hastily changing the subject, Junia began pointing out the various shops and enchanted aspects of the capital: a whimsical tailor shop here, an animated fountain there, and other such wonders. Paun would ask a question every now and again, but remained silent for the most part, choosing instead to listen. For a moment, all ailments of the heart had fallen away, leaving nothing but contentment. He was satisfied with her company and truly relieved of the burdens fate had strung about his neck.

But only for a moment.

Within what felt like no time at all, they were entering the keep of Aeraos. Its walls jutted out in odd angles, resembling that of a star. Even odder still was the great tower in its centre, its architecture standing out like a black moon amongst shimmering stars. Curiously enough, its almost alien design reminded him of the obelisks encountered earlier. Despite the fascinating architecture, what interested Paun most was the interaction between Junia and those in the keep; while following her throughout its elegant halls and decorated corridors, they would pass various members of the keep, from servants and pages to nobles and officers—all of whom treated Junia with the utmost respect.

"Lady Junia," greeted a guard as they approached. His armour was a deep-black, outlined with forest-green ornamentations. He sat on a wooden stool positioned outside a simple door. As he spoke, he rose to offer a polite bow. "Lord Ortunato is still consulting with his war council. He may be a few moments more."

"Ah." Junia nodded, her hands clasping rather professionally behind her back. "We shall wait then." She turned about to face them. "I'm sorry, but we'll have to wait for a spell."

"So I've heard," said Malvolia, crossing her arms as she leaned against the hall. "I take it you are all aware of Unbequith's approach then?"

"We have been for quite a while, yes." Junia glanced to Paun. "Initially, they were to send a simple envoy to our capital. We had just pulled our reserves from their region, you see." She paused to bite the inside of her cheek. "However... we're not sure if that's simply the truth anymore." She shook her head, leaning against the wall, beside Malvolia—much to Malvolia's alarm. "Legions upon legions approach from the north," Junia continued. "We doubt anything will escalate beyond control, but... but considering their history there's no reason to *not* prepare for the worst."

"Perhaps..." Vincent crossed his arms and leaned against the wall as well.[1] "You're no match for their might should they see fit to lay siege. Your region may hold an advantage in raw casting, but their technology and strength alone is enough to overwhelm such tactics."

"I agree, our tricks can only take us so far. However, our Lord is not so stubborn as to depend on his forces alone. The Harlings were made aware of our plight and a third of their forces march to our aid as we speak." She shrugged. "If anything at all, expect a stand-off of sorts. Whomever employs the most intimidation would be the one to triumph."

"Mm... and what *of* my shards?" said Vincent, his features scowling. "They were an awful lot of trouble and I'd *hate* for them to be forsaken in stupidity's name. As of late, I've been forced into wielding desperation and I'd rather *not* have to do it again."

Junia sucked in her lips, eyeing him from below pinched brows.

"Rest assured... sir. They're currently stored in the Lord's Vault. It was originally built for M'lord's forefathers—an enchanted shelter to safeguard our leaders from Nowood's bewitched raids. It has withstood an unfathomable onslaught before. It could do so again... should it need to."

---

1. I should like to add, Malvolia is sandwiched between Vincent and Junia like a fuming piece of baloney. She's debating between barking at them to back off or telling them she's never had friends and, from what I can tell, crying. The result is flustered silence.

"Well then... I suppose it will have to do." Vincent shoved Paun off the wall as he leaned against it. "And what of mine effects?" he asked Junia, ignoring Paun's cold stare. "If memory serves, I've had them sent here."

"Yes," she said, nodding, "they're—"

"I've a rather rare assortment of gear, not all of which I could take with me."

"Aye, they're—"

"My hoodmet for example, mighty handy and beyond unobtainable to those of your circle."

"My circle... I don't—"

"I've also an elite Tokadan crossbow. That could *easily* damage if handled improperly."

"It was all in a parcel, I couldn't—"

"There's some hunter's metal in there as well, a good portion. If any were to open it and—"

"If you continue interrupting me, you'll *never*—"

"It was sent from Tokade you know—such an awfully long journey could damage—"

Junia bounced off the wall and glared at Vincent, lips pursed, eyebrows pinched.

"*Everything* is waiting in your assigned dorm, *just* as you sent them."

Vincent raised his eyebrows and hands.

"A'ight now... just ease your breath a bit, no need to be so puffy." He shot a glance to Paun. "Your friend has quite the temper, boy."

"Aye." Like a breath of fresh air, a genuine smile lit Paun's expression. "Aye, that she does."

CHAPTER SEVENTEEN

ELDRITCH HUNT

S OME... *THING* MOVED IN the trees. From the corner of her eyes, Adela would catch glimpses of a dark shadow with biting, red eyes. However, when she looked to observe it directly, the haunt would flicker from existence, leaving nothing but an eerie imprint of its memory. As if that weren't enough, the same creature also haunted her dreamscape; she had recurring nightmares of the... the *thing* ever since she joined Unbequith's campaign. If not for that, she may not have been as disturbed as she was.

"Oy!"

Adela shook her head, placing a hand against her temple. Hearing footsteps approaching, her gaze rose to Lieutenant Bo; they had been off the side of the campaign's trail, practising and familiarising with one another as the legions of Unbequith marched past. Initially, their practices and technique had been handled under the supervision of Bo. However, he wasn't so arrogant as to refuse advice from Adela; hunting as a pack was one of the many skills her guild had imbued in her and one she felt the need to share. Before long, she was the one instructing her peers, showing them how to advance as a pack while covering one another's positions. She showed them how to breach windows, sweep rooms and slice corners. Some, like Ramsoen, were already familiar with this, yet knew not how to apply it with a squad. Initially, Lieutenant Bo had stood off to the side, studying her silently. But, he too was soon partaking with the others: training in Fallen Guild techniques under her watch. For once in her life, Adela was glad for her upbringing and felt as though she truly *had* discovered her purpose; everything felt perfect and as it should be.

Except for those bloody shadows of course.

Lieutenant Bo stood two steps below her on the knoll's grassy face. With a bemused expression he followed her gaze to Nowood's forest line. "Nothing troubling you... I should hope?"

"*No*, no..." Adela's expression shifted to her feet as she clutched her right elbow. "Not at all." Her eyes rose to study the gloomy forest. "I've seen mine fair share of phantoms and the like before. Why, when I was but a wee child, I would roam the shadows of Dripwood lookin' for their sort." A cold breeze ruffled her hair. "No, I suppose there truly ain't anything troubling me."

"Well, this *isn't* Dripwood." Lieutenant Bo's features were stern, yet hosted a hint of concern. "Nowood phantoms are no light matter. If you're truly haunted, then it's something we should attend to *immediately*."

"Ey, what's that about being haunted?" Roabard stood up from his bench, resting his instrument over his shoulder; he had been fiddling with it for the past hour, talking to Jhess as they watched their training. "Who's a haunted then?"

To her embarrassment, the others had begun gathering about her.

"Adela's haunted," explained Bo, his hands clasped before him. "I recommend we utilise this moment into a team-building exercise of sorts."[1]

"Oh, no, there's truly no need for such a hassle." Adela shrunk under the attentive stares of her team. "It truly isn't no bother you know, after all, there's hundreds of men passing by... why don't we attend to them before me?"

"Because," said Ramsoen, his voice surprising her, "their souls have individually been cleansed and the Holy Spirit of their hearts laid bare."

"Aye," agreed Bo, rubbing his dark moustache. "You may be the only one of us who truly is haunted. The wards we placed along this path may protect you from further hauntings, but you weren't protected when you brazenly flew straight over Nowood itself. No, we needn't trouble about the other men."

"Besides," began Darun, his pale features turning gravely to Adela, "it's our pack we should be watching out for. There are a number of haunts in these woods, not all of which are mere phantoms alone." He set his hand on her shoulder. "Tell us, in what guise did it assume?"

"Well... in truth... I don't truly know. I've only ever caught glimpses of it, but never a good look." Adela flushed under their baffled stares, knowing how unhelpful she must

---

1. ugh

sound. "But, maybe... maybe I can identify it... methinks the Oather has bestowed me dreams of its existence, for 'tis only in my nightmares that I can have a good look at it."

"It's no Oather mischief," said Ramsoen, tipping back his conical hat to eye the woods. His tattered poncho flickered dramatically in the breeze; Adela thought he looked simply stunning. "It's a haunt," he continued. "A retchwirm... by the sound of it. The only experience I possess with Nowood's creatures was gained from an incursion with the Black Circus, but even *they* weren't foolish enough to host such a haunt."[2]

Lieutenant Bo clasped his hands behind his back.

"Then it *is* a pressing matter to attend to? Very good. Is it perishable by sword or can we stick it with arrows? I'd rather not journey any paces into Nowood's wild if we can help it."

"No..." Ramsoen knelt, his finger drawing into a patch of dirt. "As Ms. Adela can probably tell you... it's nigh on impossible to spot, much less *kill* in the open. No... we'll have to engage it in a setting it's comfortable with."

"But is there any *real* need to kill the creature?" asked Adela, bouncing in vain over the shoulders of the other men to view the dirt doodles. "Could we not simply let it be and just pass on?"

An exasperated sigh could be heard from behind Ramsoen's snarling mask.

"Retchwirms aren't something one merely *passes* on. They're of the mære genus, falling into one of its few parasitic categories. You see, whilst you sleep, they watch your body from a distance, the evil of their gleaming eyes piercing your head's reality. Once firmly latched onto the host's mindscape, they continue to haunt one's dreams, feasting on your fears and draining your vitality like blood."

Adela blinked.

"Oh."

Ramsoen stood up, eyeing the strange figures he drew into the dirt.

---

2. At first glance, the Black Circus lives up to its name: a spectacle of eldritch wonders, bizarre performances, and stunts that defy natural laws. In reality, the Black Circus is a clandestine marketplace for illicit wares, offering eldritch creatures, forbidden potions, and enhanced mercenaries. Wealthy patrons aren't merely watching a show; they're shopping. Always on the move due to its illegal nature, the circus appears in obscure locations, its arrival signalled by cryptic symbols and unsettling omens. Only those in the know can find it, ensuring the Black Circus remains a shadowy myth to outsiders.

"If not dealt with immediately, they'll lurk in your dreams like a sickness, festering in your mind beyond control, driving you to madness and... eventually... death." He turned to eye her from behind his mask. "You are a brave one to not have succumbed to its wiles."

"Oh, thanks love, that's, um..." Adela shook her head. "I'm sorry, but the only way to prevent such drastic outcomes is if we *slay* the creature?"

"No... *you* have to deliver the killing blow. If it dies to anyone or anything else, its spirit will continue to lurk in the shadows of your dreams' pocket realities."

"Oh..." Sucking in her lips, Adela straightened her posture. "As you say it then. I'm no fool and... I know I have no other choice but to do what I must. However... however I haven't the slightest idea of where to begin."

"You... *alone* must kill it," began Sam, his black armour glistening in the late sun's light. "But *we* shall slay it *together*."[3]

"Aye," said Lieutenant Bo. "Do you not remember my proposition? This is a team-building exercise. I shan't have you slaying your demons without some proper support."

"She hasn't much of a choice..." said Ramsoen. "Killing it is the easy part. Setting up the kill... that's the feat." He pointed to Darun. "You... you're a practitioner of Reexah, yes?"

"Aye."

"Good, we shall need it." He then gestured to Fel, consulting him of the various concoctions of suppression and separation, gesturing to the symbols inscribed within the dirt. Before long, he was briefing every member of their pack with a task and purpose.

Adela clasped her hands behind her back, mirroring Lieutenant Bo as they watched Ramsoen order the other's about.

"You've the marks of a true leader," she said, looking up to him with a smile. Lieutenant Bo responded only with a brief grin before resuming his stoic disposition. Adela didn't mind the silence, for she believed a true display of friendship was standing in another's company without the desperate urge to say something. For the next hour or so, she refrained from saying anything at all, choosing instead to nod and listen. Though Adela was gifted with an assortment of abilities in beast slaying, she had never dealt with an eldritch creature as this. Aye, she knew how to handle other such phantom-like monsters,

---

3. *ugh*

but the process of killing this particular beast was more meticulous than she had originally figured.

When they were confident enough in their plan, they began to descend the knoll and approach Nowood's dark line of trees. Lieutenant Bo set a hand on Jhess's shoulder, restraining him from following them.

"Sorry, lad," said Bo. "But I'm uneasy enough as it is about *any* of us setting a foot in this accursed forest. I can't have you coming along, for I refuse to be responsible for what should befall you."

Jhess opened his mouth to object, but was silenced by a pleading glance from Adela. Nodding, he stepped back to stand beside his father and Sam, the Black Knight. Lieutenant Bo nodded in approval before turning to face Darun. "Right then," he said, "have you the bait conjured?"

Darun sighed behind his black kerchief.

"Physical wrath, confidence and... dare I say... *arrogance* are the tempers I tend to rely on for burning through reality." He paused, flexing his hands. "Fear... fear is something of a reaction... reserved for a parry or a counter. As such... I might require a moment to conjure the proper temper."

"Of course," said Bo, stepping back as a spark of grey shot out from Darun's ankle and into the grass. "Though you haven't very long, for nightfall is upon us."

Hastily nodding, Darun lowered his features. He then began to deeply inhale, followed by shaky exhales. With every breath, a grey spark would cackle from one of his joints and dive into the ground, singeing the grass. With every exhale, his breathing would increase in pace, growing faster and sharper. Puffs of frost began exiting his kerchief with the building rate of his breath until, finally, his eyes snapped open and bolts of grey shot out from his limb to obliterate the line of trees before him. Disintegrating in a frosty ash, their timber fell away to reveal the hovering form of a phantom. The retchwirm looked as though it were a ghostly figure draped in torn robes of wispy-black. It stared out at them from under its cowl, its rancorous-red eyes gleaming from the hollow sockets of its faceless void. Every now and then, Adela thought she could discern a black skull for features, but it was difficult to say.

They stood frozen, unsettled by its brazen stares. It wasn't until Sam reached for his hilt that the haunt reacted; its head hunching forward, a row of red teeth slit across its face. Unleashing a blood-curdling shriek, the retchwirm darted into the woods.

Fel gave a cheering howl before chasing after it: Darun and Ramsoen following closely behind. Looking back, Adela saw Sam lightly slap Roabard across the chest.

"A tune for an eldritch hunt, aye?" Drawing his sword, Sam dashed into the forest. Adela followed after him, Lieutenant Bo at her side.

"Aye!" she heard Roabard exclaim from behind. "A tune from the Witch Wars of old to bolster your spirits!" He tossed his instrument to Jhess. "You can still be of some use yet, boy! Play! Play and spur their spirits onward!" As Adela crossed the tree line, a damp and earthy scent struck her senses; the forest was ancient, one could smell the age in its black soil and withering bark; for aeons upon aeons, its evil festered and grew, unbeknownst to the outside world. And yet... it felt natural, as though its sinister nature was just that... nature: an unchangeable and rooted aspect of its reality. Adela felt as though she were trespassing, entering an alien world her existence couldn't comprehend. From the forestline outside, she could hear Roabard's deep, yet merry, vocals recite a chanting melody.

> *We're but dark-fell days where women weep*
> *In moors of old yon' shadows creep*
> *Their hallowed call bade none no sleep*
> *Oh, bane, by blade, begun...*
> *Oi!*

Adela came to a halt; she wasn't too deep into the woods, for she could still hear Roabard's boisterous vocals from behind.

> *Come, raise your Lord's lantern bright!*
> *To purge the devils in its light!*
> *Eldritch, in these dens o'night!*
> *A jolly huntin, son*

As Adela shot a glance over her shoulder, she could still see some light seeping into the woods, scorching the darkness with its purity. Turning to face the tight clearing, she beheld the retchwirm screeching and writhing in pain; Darun had entrapped it in fiery chains of confidence—his primary temper.

In dales o'death and fell shadow
Venture our vorpal blades' might aglow
Fear not, the wicked phantom foe
For our bonds're strong'n are spirits one

Fel cautiously approached the retchwirm, a pale dagger gleaming in hand, as though it were forged of moonlight. Adela knew that to be somewhat true, for its painted symbols were of celestial ink.

Oi!
Come, raise your Lord's lantern bright!
To purge the devils in its light!
Eldritch, in these dens o'night!
Oh, jolly huntin, son

With one slash, Fel sliced open the wraith's translucent form, leaving a black gash where a mortal's stomach would be.

Lay-ho-la-da-lay-la!
Ra-ho-ra-la-da-lay-do
Lay-lay-la-da-ra-lo!
Lo-ro-da-fo-ro...

Fel leapt back from the spirit, for a dark substance oozed forth from its wound. To her disgust, Adela realised it was the retchwirm's physical form; it was like a slug of uncanny proportions. Its contorting form was bulbous around the head, tapering off as one observed its end. It had no legs and was protected by the needle-infested plates of its oily amour-like hide. Rearing its head back, the five palps about its head outstretched like a hand, revealing its circular jaws. An unnatural screech escaped the chittering throat of the retchwirm's physical form.

In choice o'game, we lack all dearth
For none compare to a huntsmen's worth
Fret naught o'wives, fear no wraithe's girth

For we shall be their end...
oi!

The retchwirm whirled about to dash deeper into the woods, but was met with a fiery wall of raging courage; Darun stood off to the side, restraining both of its forms from retreating.

Come, raise your Lord's lantern bright!
To purge the devils in its light!
Eldritch, in these dens o'night!
Fair well thine huntin, men!

Letting loose a mad war cry, Fel unstrapped an orb-like vial from his person and hurled it at the retchwirm. It broke open with a flash of white followed by a heavy cloud of dark purple. The retchwirm's palps clawed at the ground, pulling the monster forward like a decapitated arm. With the creature now blinded, they charged in.

Our horns we'll blow, their heads we'll mount
We'll break their jaws and skin their snouts
These trophies we'll claim beyond all count
Oh, bane, our blades, begun...

Sam swung his black sword into its head, scores of golden symbols lighting across its blade. His weapon managed to slide under the creature's plating, tearing it off to expose the beating and vulnerable flesh of the retchwirm's head. In the same instant, Ramsoen had fired six arrows into both sides of the retchwirm's soft quarters, pinning the creature to the spot.

Oi!
Come, raise your Lord's lantern bright!
To purge the devils in its light!
Eldritch, in yon' dens o'night!
A jolly huntin, son...

Lieutenant Bo leaned heavily on the sword he had stabbed the creature's tail with, holding it down with grunting effort. He waved his arm at Adela, urging her on to deliver the killing blow. Accepting the pale knife from Fel, she lightly pressed its tip against the retchwirm's head. Adela knew what she had to do, she knew the creature was a *devil* and... she knew how impossible it was for her to press the knife any further.

To so intentionally take a life.

Another insect.

The woods had fallen to silence. Even Roabard's music had come to an abrupt and premature end; all stood in anticipation, waiting for Adela to do what needed to be done. The retchwirm, however, was not as kind: rearing back its head and bucking Sam off. The knife flew from Adela's hands and into some thorny brush as she was thrown back. A repulsive ripple ran along the retchwirm's form, the quake of which sent the arrows in its flesh flying in all directions. Lieutenant Bo and Ramsoen fell to the ground, scrambling back from the now-freed creature. Lieutenant Bo cried for them to fall back as the creature whirled about in violent spasms. The effects of Fel's concoctions were wearing off and the retchwirm's vision began to return. Wildly whirling about, it caught sight of the one entrapping its forms and charged Darun; unfortunately, the True Beyonder was too occupied restraining the retchwirm's shrieking spirit to defend himself from its physical form. Noticing this, Adela held an outstretched hand out to Sam, wildly calling out his name and gesturing to the creature.

Leaping onto Darun, the retchwirm pinned him to the undergrowth with its finger-like palps. Its jaws lunged forward to bite his head clean off. However, before it could, a sword sprouted from its mouth, its black blade sizzling with golden symbols. The dark spirit behind Darun uttered its final shriek before sinking into the ground like a dissolving corpse.

The retchwirm's head lurched sharply to the left as Adela withdrew her sword and hopped onto the ground beside Darun to offer him a hand. Despite her forearms being contaminated with the creature's gore, he still accepted the help.[4]

---

4. I was too caught up in the moment to detail exactly what happened, but I believe Sam threw his sword to Adela for her to catch. It's the pinnacle of Unbequith weapon-casting, imbued with symbols, prayers, and layered in arcane potions. The ultimate weapon for the ultimate champion. I don't think he's gifting it to Adela; he's simply allowing her to borrow it. I don't believe he's ever trusted it in anyone else's hands before, so that's... bonding or whatever Bo wants.

"Oy," exclaimed Fel, dancing atop the retchwirm's corpse, "we killed it!" He turned about to wave his arms and joyfully proclaim: "We've done it, lads! Pick up the tunes, ready the finest provisions and grant us our own privies! Hell's Butterflies have slain the devil's wile!"

They slapped one another's backs as they turned to leave, Roabard's merry tune returning all too suddenly. Adela followed from behind, her gaze distant, her features expressionless and her skin pale...

> *Ra-ho-ra-la-da-lay!*
> *Lay-lay-la-da-ra-lo!*
> *Lo-ro-da-fo-ro...*
> *In one fortnight or a bloody score*
> *We tightened our belts and waged this war*
> *Spilled foul guts an' ungodly gore*
> *Our kin we're fightin' for... Oi!*
> *Come, raise your Lord's lantern bright!*
> *You've purged the devils with its light!*
> *Eldritch fled to dens o'night!*
> *Return to home, my son!*
> *We have dared this far, but deeper still*
> *Into night's den with resolve to kill*
> *Nightmares take us, but it's a battle won*
> *Though our lives may fade, our deeds live on...*
> *Oi!*
> *Come, raise your Lord's lantern bright!*
> *To purge the devils in its light!*
> *Eldritch, in these dens o'night!*
> *A jolly huntin, son*
> *Come, see my boy's pyre bright*
> *He purged the devils with his light*
> *Eldritch, lost to dens o'night*
> *We'll meet'n Heaven, son...*

CHAPTER EIGHTEEN

PEACEFUL CONTINGENCIES OF VIOLENCE

T HE DOOR BOOMED OPEN and an entourage of officials and officers filed out. Their jumbled chatter thundered the hall, making it impossible for Paun to focus on what *any* of them were saying. One meek-looking official paused to lock a nervous gaze with Paun before hastily shuffling away. The others merely granted a brief glance before dispersing in a similiar fashion. To Paun's surprise, Theo filed out last, pausing to lean against the doorway. He raised his hands and smiled mischievously at Vincent.

"If it eases your temper," he said, "I gave *you* the credit for their finding."

Vincent lunged forward, spinning Theo around to pin him against the wall, Chulian's blade pressed close to his throat. The corner of Theo's lip twitched... ever so slightly.

"I care not for such *frivolous* rewards," growled Vincent. "They are fruitless and hold no meaning... not to one as old as I."

"Sure." Theo nodded, looking past Vincent's shoulder to wave at Malvolia. "Then why the hostility?"

"You took my shards."

"And you don't care about the glory." Theo shrugged. "If it was a trespass upon your person, then I cannot apologise." He smirked to himself. "I've been hired to protect the shards and protect them I shall."

"Aye... but don't you ever use your Aft-Circle techniques on me *again*." Chulian's blade pulsed a deeper blue with a soft thrum. "If so, I shall be forced to use *mine*." Vincent's gaze lingered on Theo for several moments before he lowered his blade. "Do we have an understanding?"

There was nothing but a heavy silence in the hall before—

"Maybe." Theo disappeared from the spot only to reappear beside Junia. "Did you not have time to sedate him into a better temper?"

Junia punched Theo's arm, the blow causing him to grin.

"I told them only the truth," she said. "And I already told *you*, I was not going to be making any excuses for your rude behaviour."

"Rude is simply a negative term invented by the sensitive of heart for the forward and honest." Before she could respond, he vanished from the spot. Pinching the ridge of her nose, Junia sighed.

"He can be rather irksome at best, but we're in *dire* need of his talents."

"They're not talents," corrected Vincent. "And it's a wonder your Lord permits his service."

Junia crossed her arms.

"He hasn't a choice and he trusts my judgement."

"Right, well—"

"And just because you find his methods offensive, *doesn't* mean we'll jeopardise the wellbeing of our people or even the bloody world just to satisfy one man's grazed feelings!" Turning to the door, she beckoned for them to follow. "*This* way if you will."

As Paun followed behind Malvolia, Vincent grabbed his shoulder.

"She's starting to drive me mad, that one."

Paun smiled.

"Well, you already *are* mad, so there's nothing to worry about then." Jerking from Vincent's grasp, Paun ducked through the door and into—*heaven's name, what is this?* The room was warmed by a natural lighting: light which filtered through the bright green of treetops. It poured through an assortment of large windows, their panes reaching up from the floor to the ceiling. Though the room was in the centre of a fortified keep, it appeared as though they were in a glass cottage in the middle of an open wood. Staring out one of these very windows was an elderly fellow in a simple black tunic outlined in green. His hands were clasped behind his back, revealing the band of grey fabric about his left arm; it was shaped like a bracer.

"Fauntaso Amello!" exclaimed Vincent, shoving past them to embrace the man. "By thunder, you haven't aged a day!"

The man looked up at Vincent with pinched eyebrows. They were black, with light hints of grey, complementing the bright green of his eyes.

"You must be Drendon," said the man, apologetically squirming from Vincent's grip. "I was hoping to meet you one day."

"Aye, though I go by Vincent now." He placed his hands on his hips with a delighted smile. "Jove's name, it has been a while—a couple of centuries, has it not?"

"Amello Ortunato," said the man. "Aye, I'm afraid you have mingled our identities, for I am Emelio, his son. It has not been but a century and a half since he passed—claimed by the final assault of Nowood's unholy forces."

Vincent froze, his head tilting.

"Ah." He retracted his arms. "Ah. Forgive me, but it has been a while."

The man shook his head and embraced Vincent all the same.

"Come now!" he said, resting his hands on Vincent's shoulders. "I'm still your nephew! And my niece, your grandniece!"

Vincent blinked.

"Come again."

"Junia!" Emelio held out his arms to her, setting one across her shoulders. "She's my brother's daughter."

"Yes, well that defines *niece*, doesn't it?" Despite his biting tone, Vincent's stern gaze softened. "I'm afraid I've lost nearly all account of mine family. It was difficult to monitor my own line after the first century and practically impossible after the second. In truth, I only maintain contact with one great *great* grandson. Probably one of the only decent stewards left in Unbequith."

"Ah..." Emelio combed his hair back before sitting at a large table, beckoning for them to sit as well. The table was a round slab of wood, cut from a tree's massive trunk. "A terrible shame one of our own kin must enslave their loyalty so. But then... I myself am in no position to chastise." He rubbed his temple, staring out the window to his left. "When I aligned myself with their region, it was because their hand, Lord Aivon, was a respectful and honest man who expressed Unbequith's stance with sense and conviction. But now... now we learn they wish to use the shards for their own means." He sighed. "No... my conscience forbids I continue aligning mine forces to such a blatantly corrupted rule."

"Of course," said Vincent, "you saw through their deceit, admitted you're wrong, and corrected your mistake the best you could. No one can blame you."

"Perhaps... but I am my region's Lord. The legions of Unbequith march upon us because of *my* decision. A mere campaign to sort out the technicalities of our disunion,

says they." He scoffed to himself. "How many more of their... *claims* should I allow myself
to tolerate? Surely by now, their spies have found us out and know we possess the shards."

"Surely."

Emelio looked up to Vincent, an apologetic smile forming.

"In the event you haven't noticed, my war meeting has just concluded."

"No, no... it's perfectly alright. I understand. It's no delicate matter that—*Paun.*"

"Hm?" Paun didn't turn around to face them. While they were all seated, he had
continued to walk about the room, examining the windows and shelves. The windows
were magic, that much he knew. But the shelves themselves were constructed of sticks...
and nothing more; a humble design as it were. Paun stood before one shelf now, his
hand feathering the withered sunflowers in a dirt-brown vase. "Continue," he said, "I'm
listening."

Vincent raised a finger, about to say something when Emelio spoke.

"You must understand, Drendon, should events escalate, we stand very little chance of
a positive outcome. Their technology, pure ferocity and proud numbers are enough to
topple what little advantage we hold in our casting and castle."

"Well then," began Vincent. "Don't let things escalate."

"Mm... my father spoke fondly of you," said Emelio, his eyebrow raised. "Your brotherly
wisdom may have not compared to that of the eldest, but you always spoke with a
certain..."

"Asperity?" suggested Paun, eyeing a weathered book he had found. "Cynicism... mor-
dancy... perhaps acrimony?"

Vincent's mouth gaped open for a second before he spoke.

"Is... is that a thesaurus?"

"*Yet,*" continued Paun, striding about the table dramatically, "dedicated... vicarious...
and most certainly..."—he shut the book—"dependable."

Vincent groaned from behind his fingers, Malvolia reclined in her seat, scratching her
forehead, Junia discreetly smirked and Emelio nodded his approval.

"Precisely," said Emelio, snapping his fingers at Vincent. "That is... just the verbiage my
father would use to describe you. Sometimes paired with other... more... befouled choices
of vocabulary, but from what I have heard tell, I'd be a fool to withhold anything from
your judgement."

Emelio continued to share with Vincent the situation of Aeraos and... well, in truth,
Paun had mostly tuned out after that. He still somewhat listened in on the conversation,

but was more immersed in the environment about him. As such, he only heard random bits of information and not the details within or the gaps in between.

Paun heard how the capital was enchanted, forged into its current state of fortitude from decades of assault by the unholy beings of Nowood. How the gear of Ranitorl's armies were of the highest enhancements. Their scouts reported only a few champions with any enchanted gear to begin with, so they stood a fair chance with that.

Emelio then went off on some side trail about enhancements and blades. How an enchanted sword clashing with another creates an argument between their symbols. Whoever possessed the symbols to outthink an opponent's algorithm, won the argument and would overcome the other's armour or blade—and loresmiths of Ranitorl forged the most compelling of arguments to be found in any region. Emelio then went on to say the true peril lie in the True Beyonders; the Redfolk possessed more than any other region and they alone could tear through their defences. It would, of course, be a direct violation of the Code of Preservence, for there would be nothing they could do to overcome them. Vincent begged to differ, saying he could put a stent in their forces should the need arise and that True Beyonders can only deflect that which they're aware of.

As Vincent continued speaking, Paun had discovered a most curious golden sphere encased in a bronze frame. Malvolia peered over his shoulder to examine it as well; she had grown bored of the conversation and had joined his quest of discovery. Intrigued by the sphere, Paun rubbed his fingers along its engraved surface. To his surprise, the room's lighting took on the hue of a deep and dark blue. Looking up, he was even more surprised to see a window standing out from the others; it no longer displayed an open wood, but an aquatic setting at the bottom of some sea.

His curiosity rising, Paun approached the crystal-clear glass of the nearest window, marvelling at the school of black fish swimming by. The world behind the glass was vast and dark: its scintillating ceiling the only source of light. A pale shape slithered in the backdrop of water, making Paun uneasy. Someone was talking to him, but Paun was too entranced by the submerged scene to so much as turn about—the pale shape returned, slithering towards him at an alarming speed. The last thing he saw was the gaping jaws of some loathsome beast before the window suddenly changed to reveal the open woods once more.

"Paun!" Vincent spun him about by the shoulder, his stern eyes meeting his. One hand was on Paun's shoulders while the other firmly gripped Malvolia's. "My nephew grants you the privilege of wandering about his home and you go ahead touching everything?!"

"It's quite alright, Drendon," said Emelio, his hand on the golden sphere. "Your pupils are merely curious."

Paun and Malvolia's vocals rose up in discordant objection, but were overruled by Vincent's sharp tone.

"Oy!" He gave them a light shove as he released them. "Why can't you two sit *nicely* and behave like my grand niece here?"

Junia raised her hand.

"I'm sitting because I have to," she said. "As my Uncle's Hand—"

"No." Vincent held up a finger to her. "*You*, quiet. I'm trying to lecture my younglings."

Whatever Malvolia was complaining about, Paun was sure to cut her off.

"How do you keep the creatures in there?" he asked, gazing over Vincent's shoulders to Emelio. "And why must you hide them with the visage of these woods?"

"It's not a visage," responded Emelio with a light chuckle. "The oceanic scenery you saw was one of our first foresight windows... an experiment as it were. 'Tis why it only appeared in this window and not the others."

Paun stroked its glass.

"You can look anywhere with these?" he asked, glaring at Malvolia as she slapped his wrist.

"Anywhere we've placed a counterpart, yes." He gestured to the window Paun had touched. "The light you saw in this window was reflected by one of its many sisters—one of our first experiments which we dropped into Sher's lake. It sank to the bottom, yet not so low as to fall into our trenches." He gestured to the windows encircling the room. "Took us some decades before we discovered how to link more than two panes with one another." Emelio swiped two fingers across the sphere, turning it over. As he did, the room suddenly shifted to an ashy lighting. The windows displayed the charred setting of a smouldering evergreen wood: Miraden. One of the windows was indiscernible, revealing only a web of cracks. Emelio continued: "Through trial and error, we have learned to enchant our windows' counterparts with emblems of reinforcement and concealment. As such, our scouts could now place them in strategic positions along new routes... like this, for example." Rolling the sphere with two fingers, Emelio changed the scene to another wood, one which dampened the room of all light. It was dark and heavy, shadows draping from the canopy like cobwebs. "Turn around."

Following Emelio's word, Paun turned over to view the other windows, finding himself standing as though he were on a crag, looking down into a great path carved into a mighty and sinister wood. The path's trail was of ash and soot, barely visible beneath the legions of soldiers who marched across it. Among the soldiers were scores of rooks, watchtower-like machines with heaving, mechanical legs to pull them along like spiders. Rooks were tanks, siege machines, line-breakers... weapons of war. But that wasn't all; leading the frontlines were iron dragons, burning through the last line of trees. Following from behind, a cavalry rode on shanks, a type of drake infamous for its lethal breath. And then there was the pale dragon, its proportions casting a shadow over the legions of footsoldiers. Truly... it was all a force to be reckoned with. Feeling terrible for thinking so, Paun knew its enemies would stand no chance against the ferocious onslaught of such a campaign. In the distance, beyond the last line of trees, he could see Aeraos.

"What... where is this...?" asked Vincent, rigid lines cracking in the corners of his eyes.

"Seeker's Passage..." Emelio's once gentle features were hard and grave. "From the very woods which have poured nothing but generations of death and sin upon our region... approach the legions of Unbequith. Aye, Seeker's Passage is its given name... and scores of legions fit for war walk it... in the name of peace." Emelio leaned against the sphere's casing, a soft gasp of humour escaping him. "But no... it's, as they say, all but one big... *plenipotentiary* to resolve the terms of our loyalty..."[1] He raised his hand, as though to knock over the sphere's frame, but painfully restrained from doing so. Emelio's clenched fist gradually sank to his side. "Just... how *much* of a fool... do they take us to be?"

Paun raised an eyebrow at the Lord's sudden change of behaviour.

"Well," he said, walking about the room to examine the other windows, "you *were* fool enough to cross blades with them in the last Chamber of the Kin, so... aye." Paun paused to eye the Lord. "They probably take you to be downright harebrained."

Emelio smirked under Paun's gaze.

"A fair point to be sure... though I cannot be blamed entirely for mine supposed blindness. Lord Monbel was quite a different man before paranoia broke him to such a state of desperation..."

"If that's true," said Vincent, "then perhaps there's still hope in reasoning with him."

"Oh, I don't doubt it for a second."

"But you *did*—" said Malvolia, furiously inhaling as Junia elbowed her.

---

1. **Plenipotentiary**: an official with authority to speak, sign, or act in the name of their lord. A representative with complete regional power.

"I do not doubt they are prepared for war," corrected Emelio, a light smile at the edge of his lips. "However, I *do* doubt they seek to wage it. We must prove we're not the monsters of their people, but fellow kin... just as they must do for us. Yes... I do believe we can ease the sense of desperation for either party if we merely *remember* what we *were* to one another... who we *truly* are."

"Are you so certain?" asked Paun, finally sitting at the table, though everyone was now standing. "And just how do you intend going about all that?"

"I'm sure you will find out soon enough," answered Emelio, his hands folding behind his back. "For now, I wish to know just *how* you secured the prism shards. How you managed to succeed where many were yet to fail."

Paun was about to press him further about the subject he was avoiding, but Malvolia interrupted him instead.

"Aye, about that, you're the Lord of Ranitorl, are you not? Your sort are given the roles to be guardians and judges of your region *and* beyond—yet you *all* insist on doing a bloody *terrible* job with it. You might think I lack the ethos to state such an accusation, but I believe us securing the shards would suggest otherwise!"

"Yes," encouraged Emelio, "please, continue."

"Do you know where they were?" She pinched her fingers together, silencing his response. "No, of course not. Otherwise they would have been found sooner. You lords are too preoccupied troubling about your own kin to see the true evil festering in the heart of your region and beyond. Do you not see the wisdom of uniting against a common enemy, or are you all too bloody *blind* to see anything except the evils within one another?"

"There are but a few assumptions fogging the complexity of your queries with a haze of simplicity. But come, tell me of this true evil."

"The *Death Order*," spat Malvolia, crossing her arms. Paun could tell she felt as though she were being patronised—and was all the more bitter for it.

"What of them?" asked Emelio, his kind voice causing Malvolia to scowl. "Such an example has long been—"

"*In the event* it has eluded your *illustrious* watch, they're *not* extinct. Quite active... in truth. Had the prism shards, they did. For all we know, they might still be in possession of some terrifying weapon hidden away, empowered by the very thing you fight and accuse one another over!"

"Are you certain of this?"

"Of course not, but there's no telling *what* they might have done all these years with such powers at their wicked fingertips!"[2]

"Indeed, if it truly is the Death Order and not some *mock cult*, then perhaps it was they who whisked the shards away to their... *diabolical* lair—or how you'll have it. Maybe they were studying it... or perhaps they thought themselves the rightful guardians of such a power... we may never truly know."

"Well it matters not!" shouted Malvolia, her hands raised in exasperation. "Whatever their motive, is nothing to be done of *this* Death Order?"

"Nothing *can* be done and nothing *should* be done."

Malvolia sputtered for a few moments. Strands of hair poked out from between her fingers as she gripped her forehead.

"Are you..." Her soft voice was lined with bitter anger. "Are you such a *coward* as to—"

"*Speak not* out of turn, child, and recall whom you address." His soft—yet stern—voice mirrored hers. "Contrary to the narrow beliefs of your assumptions, I must ask you to beg the question... why the Death Order?" Emelio leaned forward, tapping the table. "Why bother with them at all?"

Malvolia's eyes narrowed.

"They're a live *threat*. Have regional lords all but forsaken the honour of their duty? The Death Order are an evil that *must* be extinguished."

"That they are. But, I'm sure there are far more pressing matters of evil to *extinguish* than a floundering cult which scarcely manages to so much as keep its head above the waters of society." Emelio tilted his features, trying to make eye contact with Malvolia. "What of the Gravemound haunts or the sea thieves of Unoeble? Dare I even mention the ever-growing power festering in the heart of Nowood? No, there are far too many evils, both hidden and brazenly exposed to trouble about all at once. One must first address the evils of their own, evils that play a personal and immediate threat to one's own kin. Once those have been cleared, we can trouble over duties beyond our region. If not, another obelisk shall be raised."

---

2. In truth, she was partially right, as they were using the shards to craft ethereal armour. The most dangerous and powerful version of this armour was taken, in another time, by Theo—the great weapon Malvolia spoke of without realising it. Hm... perhaps Theo's story is one worth looking into. Perhaps in another book, we can dive into his origin.

"And what of this immediate threat?" asked Paun, his finger tracing the heavy grain in the table. "You're yet to explain how you mean to handle it."

"I've already *explained*, reasoning shall be the primary focus of our engagement with such forces. But, as for—"

"Yes, *however*, this is no *peddler* knocking on the doors of your region. It's *Unbequith* and they have trespassed the borders of your house with an army capable of razing it to the ground."

"Our newfound Harling allies shall arrive for means to counter such intimidation."

"Aye, yet what till then? And even when they *happen to* arrive, what could they *possibly* contribute to aid the defence of your city against the raw might of Unbequith itself?"

"Should it come to that—well... no, I would be lying to say I am thoroughly confident in the tactics of mine council. However—whatever may happen—I know their Unit Commander shall honour the Code of Preservence... Yes, through a few occasions, I've managed to assess his person in moments that define his character."

"And?"

"A true gentleman, a skilled commander, and one upright in honour. As such, we should calculate accordingly."

"*We?*" repeated Paun.

"Aye. Drendon that is." Emelio nodded to Vincent. "I have shared with you everything I know of our plight, enemy and vulnerabilities. But, also of our resources, techniques and advantages." Emelio sat in his chair, gesturing to the charts and maps laid strewn about the table. "I have humoured the various advice mine council had to offer, but... I think I shall incline mine ears once more." He prudently knit his fingers together. "Tell me, your wisdom is old and your knowledge vast... what do *you* advise?"

Vincent was silent for several moments, his piercing gaze lingering on the table.

"I believe—"

At that moment, the door slammed open and a young man in black and brown burst through. He paused to lean against the doorframe before—

"The... the Redfolk's forces," he said, panting. "They've breached the horizon."

Vincent met Emelio's heavy gaze and set a firm hand on his shoulder.

"Hows about we hear the voice of their intentions before we speculate the worst, aye?"

Emelio nodded gravely.

"Aye."

Paun scoffed.

CHAPTER NINETEEN

THE NAMELESS CHAPTER

J HESS FLIPPED THROUGH THE crisp pages of his journal, pausing to examine the
sketch of a proud family; despite their simple clothing, they were strong, their eyes
fierce, and their confidence invoking a sense of nobility. Loosely sketched in between them
was a gangly and awkward-looking girl. Her crooked smile stood in stark contrast to the
grim expressions about her. Jhess studied her intently, the corners of his lips twitching in
bemused amusement; this was but one of many drawings he had managed to salvage from
her first cell—drawings Addy had doodled whilst he was absent. It had been an awful good
deal of trouble, but he eventually managed to compile everything into a journal during
his allotted sleeping hours.[1]

Jhess frowned, recalling the day he decided to give it to her; the day he was to tell her she
was to be freed; the day he found her cell to be empty. To worsen matters, Jhess couldn't
recall the last moment he had with Addy before she vanished. He remembered escorting
her to a new holding chamber and then... well... his mind was befogged with gaps, but he
was sure he dropped her off before reporting back to Aivon himself... yes... that had to be
it. After that, Jhess was sure it was... *something* which involved Ms. Elicy. Although... he
wasn't too sure; whenever he thought of Ms. Elicy, his memory would elude his thoughts,
as though they were snatched away by an unknown force of... of emptiness.

And... purple.

Purple fogged his mind.

Jhess shook his head and shut the book.

---

1. Oh, by the by, the spinners have divulged nothing, so I respectfully follow their wishes and keep
this chapter nameless. I recommend you do the same.

He meant to ask Addy, but every time he *began* bringing it up, she would make some cryptic response, her mood shifting darkly. It felt wrong to trigger a state so unlike her. Truth be told... it frightened him. Even more so, it only left him with a strong feeling of guilt for bringing her into such a state—one such as she never deserved.

Patting the journal, he rose from his stool to stand before his polished shield. In truth, it was both impractical and quite ancient in design, but he had brought it along to serve as a sort of looking glass; he still had some trouble fitting into his armour without one. Thankfully, he had long donned his armour in the early hours of dawn and was merely waiting for Addy to wake. But then... perhaps she was awake; she didn't seem like the type to avoid the greater hour of opportunities which morning had to offer.

Tightening the straps of his pauldrons, he turned over to examine his shoulders; though sleek in its black design, it did make him look somewhat... ehm, well-built. His armour was lighter than the others', with bits of chain mail peeking through the joints—*but* it still felt *just* as imposing as any other warrior's, mind you. Sighing contently at his image, he gazed down to his journal, delicately rubbing its leather-bound face.

"*Ay*... boy."

Biting back a rising gasp, Jhess spun about to see the True Beyonder, Darun... the one from Addy's butterfly force... or whatever it was.

"Yes? What is it you need?" His dark eyebrows furrowed as he peered over his shoulder. "Is Lady Adela not with you?" Jhess intentionally refrained from calling her Addy in front of this... *dark* and... grisly-looking fellow.

"*Lady* Adela, is it?" Darun scoffed from behind his black kerchief. "As you say it then. No, I'm afraid your Lady was summoned by Commander Aivon to the shores of Sher's Lake to discuss rather private details with the other butterflies."

"*Butterflies?*" repeated Jhess, his lips turning upwards in amusement; this was all Addy's doing after all.

"Aye," said Darun. "Déaþinferleas popilégan. Each member is referred to as a butterfly."

"Of course you are." Jhess eyed the True Beyonder up and down, doing his best to conceal his amusement. "But what are *you* doing here? And why haven't I been summoned to escort Lady Adela? I could have very well monitored her safety from a distance—"

"Settle down, lad. What's done is done." Darun turned to leave. "What's important is that you're needed now. The meeting is dismissed and the Windcatcher has requested your audience."

"Oh... oh! Has she?" Jhess stuffed the journal into a pack, slinging it about his shoulder as he stumbled after Darun. Mirroring his stride, Jhess crinkled his nose. "Oh, she doesn't..." He paused, briefly considering whether to tell Darun or not. Deciding it'd be selfish not to, he continued: "The name Windcatcher stirs something in her... disturbs her it does."

"Not from what I can tell."

"Aye, well... she doesn't show it and... is rather good at hiding it. She doesn't wish to inconvenience people, see—"

"If it offends her, she can tell me herself."

"Yeah, but that... *that's* the thing... see, she won't tell anyone if she thinks it would inconvenience them."

"And she's told you this?"

"No, but it's something any good friend could see for themselves!"

"Ah!" Darun clapped his hands together. "Good friends, are you?"

Through his reddening features, Jhess glared.

"*Yes.*"

"I see... thought you two were something else."

Jhess frowned, his cheeks quite literally on fire.

"What are you—"

"Soulmates," explained Darun, his unabashed vocals echoing about the camp, "sweethearts, beloveds, darlings—"

"*Ay—hoi*, that's enough of that nonsense." Jhess had just begun to visualise a small group gathered about the lake's shore, naught but seventy paces off from him; they were standing near a long bridge stretching across the lake's radius. He shook his head as Darun began speaking.

"Oh, you needn't riffle yourself so, lad. I only jest." He delicately ruffled Jhessaun's copper-red hair. "I wouldn't tease if I didn't hold reason to believe she liked you as well."

"She..."

"Ah, there you are, boy!" His father welcomed their approach with outstretched arms. "Slept in, did you?" He caught Jhess about the neck and dragged him to the others. "Thought I raised you better than that, I did."

"I didn't—"

"Fret not!" hollered his father. "I've the little knave right here!"

The group talking amongst themselves paused to give Jhess various odd stares. He felt the freckles on his features blend away to the colour of his own insecurities.

"Jhessaun!" greeted Aivon, "it's, ehm... we're grateful you could—"

"Jhess!" Addy darted out from the group to wrap her arms about his neck. From her embrace, he could tell she was wearing a type of scale-plating beneath the dark fabric of her jerkin-dress-looking... thing; he hadn't seen female armour before. "Sorry for makin' you wait, luv" she apologised, pulling out of their hug to grip him tightly by the shoulders. "Would've fetched you sooner, but they quite literally whisked me away."

"Oh, you needn't bother about me, it's—" He paused, briefly befuddled as she patted his shoulders. "I—I'm sorry... I don't mean to interrupt anything... going on here. You didn't have to... ehm, bother about me." Addy always baffled his speech, for she was one of the few people who actually listened.

"*No!*" She slapped an arm about his neck and pulled him into the group. "No, I couldn't have left my bodyguard waiting all morning, now could I? 'Tis simply rude." She gestured to Aivon with a crooked smile. "Commander here was jus' talking 'bout an envoy of sorts, yeh?"

"Aye..." Aivon glanced down the bridge to the first gatehouse in its middle; there were a host of officials, soldiers and other such figures gathered about it: waiting for Unbequith's arrival: *their* arrival. "We shan't move in together. Such actions may arouse alarm amongst their ranks and prompt an escalation." Aivon sighed heavily before returning his gaze to their group. "Still, we shan't go in defenceless either. Darun, you're to come with me and Bo."

"And—but... but what of us?" asked Jhess, his voice attracting their heavy gazes.

"Oh, you needn't trouble 'bout it for three seconds, luv." Addy patted his head. "Roabard's in charge, yeh?"

"Oh."

"Yeah, and Darun here'll signal us if anything goes amiss, yeh?"

Aivon nodded, his gaze focused on the first gatehouse.

"Aye, stay vigilant," he cautioned. "With any fortune, they'll yield the shards and this whole debacle would have been nothing but an unnecessary show of force."

Three dark figures detached themselves from the group across the bridge. Junia rested a careful hand on her concealed weapon; it was a gift from Theo, one she had received upon becoming his right-hand lieutenant. He had told her of its origin and other-worldly functions—how it didn't belong in this world or to her, yet to her it had been given.

Grimuth's Breath... that's what he had called it.[2] It was akin to an ornate flintlock, but Theo had insisted it was far more complicated than that; it was a firearm, one whose ammunition pierced the delicate fabrics of the spirit, rupturing its fibres, and separating one's soul from their body; painless and instant *death*.[3] Initially, such a powerful weapon had frightened her, but... now... now she would use it without a moment's hesitation. Why, she was already considering how to kill them individually. Even as the Unbequith delegates approached her uncle with warm exchanges, she plotted their demise. Junia didn't intend to, but she was prepared for it; that's what Theo had taught her... in his own way.

She would start with the True Beyonder, catching him off guard by shooting him from the shadows of her poncho. She would have to move quick, but she was sure she could subdue the other two in a mere spasm of seconds if she only—

"And this is my hand, Junia," said her uncle, placing a firm hand on her back; from its grip, she guessed he knew *exactly* what she was thinking. "It is with open arms that Ranitorl welcomes you."

Junia tossed her bangs from her eyes, smiling ever-so kindly.

"Commander Seeker," she greeted with a light curtsey of her cream, beige poncho, "I do believe I owe you my deepest gratitude for... *attempting* some variety of well-intentioned heroics with my aunt at the Mad Ball... though it was directed upon the wrong force." She gazed over his shoulder to the lake's shore and Unbequith's sprawling city-of-a-camp. "Though Ranitorl may welcome you as an individual, I cannot say the same for your show of hostility."

A coughing chuckle escaped her uncle. Though confident in tone, she could tell he was uneasy.

"I'm afraid my hand speaks far more directly," he said. "And... in doing so, I'm afraid she also speaks the truth."

---

2. No, I don't know what *Grimuth* is. If it's a person, they're certainly not from this time period.

3. This is my first time hearing about it.

"Of course," said Aivon, nodding, "I admire such forward honesty." His right hand touched his heart with two fingers before moving to his forehead and gesturing to her in a solemn dip; she took it to be a sign of respect. "However, I cannot offer an apology, for these are trying times. Unbequith's intentions are strictly that of peace and security. I solemnly promise, two-thirds of our legions shall return to the refuge of Færas once the shards are safely—"

Her uncle raised a hand, politely cutting Aivon off.

"Though ancient in tradition, topics of such material can only be discussed after a feast of kinship, for once we dine as family... we shall reason as brothers." He clasped his hands behind his back, a hospitable smile on his lips. "I'm sure you are one to understand such... foundational values."

Aivon glanced at his Lieutenant, sharing an odd expression before returning to face them.

"I believe we agreed the discussion of our occupation was to be hosted after the feast. However, am I truly mistaken as to believe such delicate and dangerous matters were not to be surrendered to a more capable force *immediately?*"

"*Yes,*" snapped Junia, cutting off her Uncle. "They've been under our watch for naught but three hours and yet you already know of them. Such blatant infiltration indicates just how little we truly *should* trust your kind."

"*Junia...*" cautioned her uncle.

"*No,*" she continued, "we shan't stand by idle as you purloin the shards beneath our noses and you *shan't* occupy *any* city of Ranitorl, much less its bloody capital."

"Your... *region,*" began Aivon, "signed an oath in the *blood* of your honour. Yet *your* region insists on blatant *treachery* to that oath. *That's* why we came. To ensure you were not so treacherous as we believed—and now you say you won't yield the shards? Do you so willingly forsake our pact—your *honour?*"

"The shards aren't property of the Redfolk or *anyone.*" Junia met his stern gaze with her own fiery eyes. "You have no purpose here."

"*Junia,*" hissed her uncle, grabbing her by the elbow.

"Have we *not?!*" roared Aivon, gesturing to the pure military might behind him. "I believe we were here to assure the intentions of Unbequith—intentions *your* regions swore to defend and uphold—intentions that *clearly* stated you were to surrender the shards to our greater watch and superior protection, for it was *your* region who lost them!"

"Well, it seems those intentions have bloody changed haven't *they*—"

"Junia!" Her uncle slashed a hand through the air, holding it before her. *"After* the feast of kinship. *After."* Emelio sighed, shaking his head as he addressed Aivon. "Please... whatever you may have been led to believe, I ask you disregard it until I've properly hosted your presence as both guest and kin."

Aivon's chest rose and fell, his hand combing through his snowy-white hair.

"I apologise for my outburst," he said, his right hand gesturing respectfully. "Honour is... it's an absolute, unyielding as it is unforgiving. And..." Aivon's gauntlets emitted a soft screech as his fist tightened. "And to see others so carelessly disregard the fundamental significance of such a... *key* aspect to our own morality and... and thus our own *lives* as children of the Eternal King, well... well it irks me so... to say the least."

"Indeed." Her uncle smiled, a genuine smile of relief. "I can respect such beliefs, for I myself hold to them." He swiftly raised a hand. "But please, we shall clarify the muddled details of our honour *after* we're put in a finer temper, yes?"

"Of course... I apologise twofold and shall do my utmost best to restrain myself."

"And I shall be all the more grateful for it, mine brother." Emelio patted Junia's shoulders. "Run ahead and signal the arrival of our guests, will you? I'm sure the dining staff await in a most eager anticipation."

Curtsying with pursed lips, Junia spun about to put this nonsense behind her. However, she hadn't taken but several steps before a commotion caused her to turn around; to her alarm, a score or so of darkly clad soldiers were approaching the gatehouse. Turning to run back, she returned within hearing distance of Aivon.

"Please," he began, a hand raised defensively, another gesturing to the darkly clad soldiers, "they mean no hostility." Aivon raised his hand to the gatehouse archers who had drawn their weapons. "They're the guard of mine person," continued Aivon, "designated to lay their lives before mine. I've already tested their restraint of honour as it is, but I shall not continue forward without their blessing."

"Lord Aivon..." chuckled her uncle, "you make heavy demands."

"I make no demands," corrected Aivon. "They *will* shadow me. Not because I demand it, but because you hold no choice." His features softened. "My Lord, there is... nothing to fret." He gestured to the line of men atop the gatehouse. "I'm sure your misplaced suspicions need not consume you under the overwhelming assurances of your men."

Her uncle's good-hearted expression fell away to reveal a scowl. However, he quickly recovered with a polite smile.

"Of course, but I cannot allow you to carry your weapons—and *I know*, I know..." Her uncle nodded. "But such a sight is sure to sow distrust amongst mine people. No, if we're to avoid any and all means of conflict, then I'm afraid you must leave them here with my—"

"I cannot," answered Aivon. "*They* cannot. I refuse to leave myself or mine men defenceless in a sign of trust, for trust you we do not." He gestured to the dark figure on his right. "Besides, mine True Beyonder here can never render himself defenceless and is far more dangerous than all mine men combined. He cannot disarm his own nature and neither shall we."

Junia rolled her eyes and turned back down the bridge, not caring to hear how it would play out; she already knew Aivon would get his way. Rubbing her temples, she passed through the unseen portcullis of the city's gate, its enhancements of security passing over her with a light thrum. To her brief alarm, a figure emerged from the shadows, matching her stride.

"Oh, Paun... you—hello." She shook her head with a friendly smile; he was always catching her off guard.

"Hello." He squinted at her forehead before returning his gaze to the path ahead. "I don't suppose there'll be a war anytime soon?"

Junia touched her forehead in bafflement.

"No, I doubt such things will ever come to pass—not a real... *war* anyway."

"You think so?"

"Of course! Aivon is an absolute gentleman. If his character reflects the whole of Unbequith, then there was never any need for such an extravagant show of force to begin with." Her eyes darted to and fro about the town, assessing all the various ways she could—

"You're thinking of how you'd kill them all... aren't you?" An amused grin slid across his noble features. "Debating how you'd do it in the cleanest and most effective of manners?"

"Oh, well... no, not quite... I've already done that, you see." She smirked sheepishly, tucking a strand of hair behind her ear. "If anything, I'm considering how best to overcome their forces without taking their lives." She bit her bottom lip, studying the roofs and carts about her; the town square was abnormally empty. "In truth I... I probably should have considered that before musing how to... well, kill them."

"Perhaps."

Paun was silent for the rest of the walk back—*all* was silent. Not a single word was said and not another sound was heard: nothing but the soft patter of their own footsteps. Oddly enough, the silence between them didn't bother Junia whatsoever.

From the shores of Sher's Lake, they watched as Aivon disappeared into the capital, an arm about the Lord of Ranitorl in close affinity.

"It's like they're brothers," whispered Jhess, not caring who heard him.

"Yeah..." Adela squatted onto the wispy grass, crossing her legs. "They should've yielded the shards by now... somethin' went amiss."

"They... they have the *shards?*"

"Yeh."

Jhess's mouth went dry and the strength in his legs began to fade; he sat upon the grass beside her.

"If they've truly forsaken their oaths and aligned with Harldïof, then we have already lost. Besides, no amount of soldiers could ever persuade the power they wield, not with the shards."

"Unless they don't know how to use 'em," said Adela, picking at the grass. "Or perhaps using them violates the Code of Preservence... I have heard Aivon mentioning it." She sighed deeply, her forehead resting against her kneecaps. "I miss my boat..."

Jhess blinked.

"If the Rantilorians were in possession of the shards, they should have yielded them to us *immediately*. We shouldn't even be here! We should be up and on our way back to Unbequith with the,"—he lowered his voice—"with the shards in tow—*that* was the allegiance they swore."

"Yeah, Aivon told me." Adela shrugged. "Do you know where they're keeping Regend—ehm, my esardrocan?"

"Oh... yes... you—have you not visited him this whole time?"

"I've been quite rushed about as it is."

A number of occasions where she could have visited her esardrocan ran through his head, but he refrained from bringing them up; she excluded those moments for a reason.

"Right, well... yes. Upon Aivon's return, I shall see what we can do about paying a visit to the stable yard."

Her gaze peeked out at him from the corner of her elbow, a small hint of a smile slipping through.

"Thanks, Jhess."

"Course."

He would never forget those sparkling eyes.

CHAPTER TWENTY

FEAST AMONG FOES

J UNIA SAT ON HER uncle's right-hand side with Aivon's Lieutenant sitting beside her. Aivon himself was positioned on the left of Emelio, separated from his True Beyonder by Vincent; she figured it was since Vincent knew them both and was thus positioned accordingly... that, or her uncle needed Vincent there to keep an eye on them. Junia gingerly cut a portion from her spit-roasted steak, smeared it in her region's cream sauce, and thoughtfully chewed it. She peered over her table to Paun; he sat amongst the lower tables encircling the ballroom below. To her amusement, Theo sat on his left, doing most the talking while Paun stared out into the ballroom; Unbequith soldiers and Ranitorl citizens alike were dancing with one another.

Though she felt some attachment for him... *Paun*, that is... she couldn't help but think of how, in all honesty... she hardly knew him; she knew *of* him, but only from cryptic dreams and hazy visions. As for his deeper incentives, loyalties or character... she knew only that which she wanted to know, but not what she could *truly* know; Paun was a wildcard and the fact *he* was the first one to secure the prism shards before all others—well... it truly frightened her—and she was left all the more confuzzled for feeling so. Shaking her head, it was then she realised Lieutenant Bo had taken up conversation with her.

"... their citizens," he finished, much to Junia's confusion. "If your Lord is an example of such laws, then why does he position himself on such a table... distancing himself from his people?"

Having some idea of what he referenced, she decided to answer.

"In truth, it's merely a measure of security."

"Perhaps... but can you not agree it has transitioned into something more? Something of distinguished royalty? The lord is no different from his people in rank and must be one among them... I see no example of that here." Though speaking such bold accusations, Lieutenant Bo's expression was of complete calm. "The Eternal King," he continued, "did not establish the lords of old, that they might elevate themselves above one's kin."

"Mm..." Junia poked at her food; though she was hungry, she couldn't eat. "The Redfolk are one to talk..."

She heard the leather of Lieutenant Bo's glove tighten, though his voice remained perfectly composed.

"How so?"

"If your Lord was truly one amongst his people, then why is he not here on his own behalf? Alongside his men?"

"Lord Monbel hasn't a choice," he sourly remarked. "Our intelligence has reported a third of Harldïof's forces march against our now vulnerable capital." Bo shook his head. "Not only is it a signified protest against honour, but one of the highest forms of punishments to be inflicted from a regional offence—" Lieutenant Bo sharply inhaled before continuing. "Such an abuse of power deserves a revoking of his Lordship's titles."

"I'm... we weren't aware they were—"

"And yet still, you so readily align yourselves to an enemy who marches against unarmed citizens, violating their intrinsic rights as innocents—why, some of our own strongly disagree with Unbequith's interpretation of lordship, yet still they shall be slaughtered—should the Harling Lord have his way." His shoulders rose and fell before he resumed eating. "I must thank your Lord for hosting such an appetising hospitality... our campaign's provisions have been nothing but the practical sort. Perhaps—if delegations proceed on route—he could share such kindness with the tired men of Unbequith." Sipping from his mug, he coughed a chuckle to himself. "And one girl."

Junia clasped her hands across her lap, rocking lightly as she stared down into the ballroom.

"Perhaps your Lord was mistaken to invest all trust in the corruptible heart of mortals. Even if the Harlings had honoured the regional laws of the Eternal King, you should have still maintained some form of defence—or in the least, *feigned* unbreachable fortifications. An openly defenceless region simply screams for one's enemies to take advantage... I might even say it's a temptation to the struggling heart of those in power."

"It's not that we can't hold our own... it's the *principles* behind it. Os Finyeld believed our cities and major towns to be gathered under one mountain... unarmed and ripe for the fell blade of conquer." Lieutenant Bo shook his head, a light smile forming across his lips. "His treachery to his own morality shall be rewarded with a merciless stroke of justice."

"Ah..." Junia glanced to the soldiers about the ballroom, those laughing and chatting merrily with her region's people; the feast of kinship was working. "So, your region isn't so defenceless as you've led us to believe?"

"No..." Lieutenant Bo swished the drink in his cup, eyeing it bitterly. "No, we are not."

"How many men have you left behind? A third of the Harlings' forces is equivalent to the legions you've mustered against us. Surely, you don't possess just as many still remaining in Mount Færas?" She raised an eyebrow. "Why... is that why you left all the women behind? Did you all secretly plan this from the—"

"*No.* Oh, Heavens forbid, *no.* We would never be so cruel as to thrust all responsibilities on those who possess such valuable roles to our society. No, we have but two *men* who defend our families and hold the lines of our Lord's mountain."

Junia's eyebrows pinched together.

"And?" she questioned, her hands gesturing forward. "Come on then, who are they? Has our region even heard of them?"

"One yes, though the other... I doubt." His eyes sparkled proudly and his shoulders straightened. "You know him as Teresul Monbel, Regional Lord of Unbequith and heir to the Transcendent Throne."

"Oh..."

"The other... is his hand—though everyone knows our Lord will promptly exile him once he has served his purpose, levelling the Harlings." Bo sipped his drink before setting it aside ever-so-delicately. "It is our great relief Os Finyeld is so ignorant to the powers of Lord Monbel and Siolant."

"*Siolant...*" echoed Junia, her brows bunching together. "What a... curious name..."

"That's... one word for him... or it."

"And who *is* he to possess such powers alongside his Lord so treacherously?"

"I..." Lieutenant Bo deeply inhaled, gazing down into the ballroom. "I'm afraid his existence is confidential as it is... and I've already shared more than I ought." He shrugged. "Take it as a good sign of trust if you will."

"I shall." Junia nodded. "Still, I do think... I believe this Siolant is something all regions should know of, lest—"

Junia cut herself off, for her uncle's favourite page had dashed into the ballroom through the chamber's tall doors. He gasped for breath—a sign which hinted he had something to desperately share. Peeling her gaze from him, Junia turned to see her uncle rise, lifting both hands to silence the ballroom.

"Fauntaso," her uncle greeted, a hand on his heart gesturing to the page. "Loranzo, of what urgency do you bear which so effectively stifles mine court?"

"My Lord," he breathed, leaning against a random Unbequith soldier. "My Lord, the forces of Harldïof—they approach, nay—they're *here!*"

"What *is* this?" Lord Aivon rose from his seat, his gauntlets pounding the ledge of his table. "You *must* deny them all entrance at *once!* Engage them at the walls, we can't—"

"I'll decide what is to be done," said Emelio, his voice stern and commanding. "They are not enemies, but our invited guests."

Aivon scoffed.

"Surely, you can't mean to say you've summoned the ranks of Harldïof on the eve of our kinship! The *implications* of such actions..."

"In truth," began Emelio, "I prayed they would arrive sooner, for maybe then you would have been less pressed to utilise your legions' might as a threat against me."

"The only reason I did so was because you didn't honour the—"

"*Sir,*" interrupted the page, "they're right—"

"Just give us a moment's grace!" roared Aivon, holding a hand up to the boy.

"It's too *late* for that!" pleaded the page, urgently pointing behind him. "They've already stormed the—"

The doors to the chambers slammed open and a military force began steadily pouring into the ballroom. Their armour was of a pure white, outlined in bright blue ornamentations. Its metal glistened in the chandelier light as their forces marched through civilians and soldiers alike, approaching the high tables. To Junia's surprise, a man with faded-auburn hair stepped forward, his dark green coat mingled with humble shades of brown. His brown eyes were tired... and *dark*, yet his smooth words were spoken with an alien authority.

"Lord Ortunato," he greeted, pressing a hand to his heart before gesturing to her uncle, "on behalf of Lord Finyeld, Regional Lord of Harldïof, I, Abaddon Henagan, present you a third of our region's might, here to defend your honour and—"

"You *can't* be serious!" exclaimed Aivon, pounding another dent into the table. "It's unacceptable that—"

"*And*," continued Henagan, "ensure the regions' wellbeing by consequently ensuring the safety of the shards... that they might not be compromised by the corrupted hands of Unbequith."

"*Corrupted?*" repeated Aivon, his tone blazing. "Corrupted says thee! You're the bleeding fools who prompted the escalation, the ones who allowed their region to fall to corruption, the *one* who hosted the Mad Ball! Surely you *don't*—"

"I'm... sorry," apologised Henagan, his eyebrows bunching together, "but did you not expect our company?"

"No... of *course* not... not this soon. You lack the firepower to cleanse a trail through Nowood—the journey would have taken at *least* an entire fortnight beyond today!"

"Aye... yet cut through Nowood we did, though you are right to believe we lacked the fire power to do so."

Aivon shook his head, clearly disgusted.

"You dared the haunts of Nowood without any means of sanctification?" His scoff resounded through the chamber. "It's a wonder any man can be so foolish as to brave Nowood so unprepared—and a *horrifying* wonder at what toll it must've taken on your legion's men!" Aivon's eyes narrowed. "And women..."

"Regrettably, several went insane... but they are being attended to... in a way. The other twelve thousand, *however*, are bright and healthy"

"Aye... but who knows what long-term effect the others will carry after so brazenly charging such a dark wood—*the* dark wood of all dark woods! Have you not a care for their souls?"

Henagan rubbed the side of his neck, as though he were somewhat exhausted.

"Your Lord's rank of fifteen thousand men left us no choice in doing so. Our time was short and Ranitorl had left us but a few weeks for preparation."

"No... that can't..." Aivon turned to Emelio, a heavy hand set on his shoulder. "Surely you don't mean to tell me the dishonourable rumours of shifting allegiances are true? They can't be, it's simply—"

"Nay," answered Emelio, "they *are* true. Your legions marched against us, unprovoked, leaving us naught a choice but to seek a willing ally in our desperation."

"Y—yes," sputtered Aivon, "but *they*—"

Junia stood up, her seat screeching back; she couldn't remain silent anymore.

"My Lord," she began, hastily pressing a hand to her heart before gesturing to her uncle, "Lord Aivon does not accuse Henegan without good reason." Like a thunderous bolt of accusation, her finger fell to Henagan. "That... *man* is not only a traitor to his region and beyond, but his own *soul*. His morality knows not itself and he *is*—"

"A ruthless criminal," finished Henagan. "I admit, my misdeeds are no light matter, nor a matter concealed in ignorant shadows. As such, I have long been punished for my crimes. Indeed, the reason I represent my Lord on such a perilous expedition is no other than the retribution of my poor decisions." His brown eyes narrowed. "Trust my word when I say I'd rather be *home*, rebuilding my town and supporting my people. My presence here is *punishment* and evidence of my Lord's... *virtuous* intentions." Henagan shot a sideways glance to Aivon, who was clearly more upset than before. Junia didn't blame him, for she herself was too baffled with anger to speak.

Aivon, however, could speak his thoughts just fine.

"This man is an insult! It's a wonder your conscience even *granted* them an audience!" He directed his scowl to Henagan. "How could... *anyone*... be so far gone as to believe a position of honour such as yours is... is a sentence of some kind! No, Harldïof is—" Aivon set another hand on Emelio's shoulder. "The Harlings are beyond reason and any grounded sense of virtue—*please*, I know it is with *you* that the choice lies, but I must urge you to relinquish their aid."

"Oh?" Her uncle scoffed humorlessly, a finger propped against the side of his head. "Must you?" His gaze rose from the armrest, lingering on Aivon. "Why must I be so urgent as to forsake the only aid I see in standing a chance against the legions of warriors you've mustered upon my door?"

"My Lord," pleaded Junia, "*please*. If not the words of Unbequith, trust the word of your closest kin... you're more of a father to me than mine ever was, *please*. Trust *me* when I state you *cannot* trust this man."

Before he could respond, Henagan spoke up.

"My Lord, your child speaks the truth. You can never trust me... but you can trust *my* lord—and if not him, our region who offers their services. I can only beseech thee to not judge the sins of one chastened man to condemn an entire region."

"Ah!" Junia snapped her fingers. "So you admit to the treachery of your heart? You who represent an extension of your Lord's will?"

"Of course, I already have. 'Tis the very reason I am here." Henagan gave her a curious stare which irked her even more; it was so... condescending. "However," he continued, "if you do not require Harldïof's aid, then we shall return from whence we came and you may defend the purity of your region from the Redfolk's infestation *without* our forces of persuasion." Henagan raised a hand, cutting off all protests as he roared: "*Silence!* If Unbequith truly isn't the blood-craving monster of old—the one we all know and *fear*—then tell us, O'Aivon Seeker, of what intentions does Unbequith maintain to so desperately wish in securing the shards?" Henagan lowered his hands, stuffing them in his coat. "Please, lay thine intention bare and restrain thine tongue from lies, for they shall aid you not."

Aivon's posture straightened.

"I shall not, for I am certain one such as you is familiar with the nature of deception..." Henagan shrugged and Aivon continued: "*In truth*, and Lord Ortunato can verify this absolute, our region thought nothing but to secure the shards and destroy or otherwise utilise them for a noble cause to change our regions and beyond for the better."

"*However...*" pressured Henagan, "you are no longer of such intentions."

"Only the latter," corrected Aivon, frowning as he addressed Henagan. "Their potential aid to our world is too great for us to merely forsake. But... we had also realised the frivolous heart of mortals could not be depended on for such a tempting task." Aivon sighed. "It is a nature we cannot depend on." Aivon's voice rose over the disagreeing cries rising about the chamber. "No, the shards *will* be taken to Unbequith and supervised under a lord who possesses the *virtue to—*"

"You see now!" proclaimed Henagan, raising his hands as he strode about the discordant chamber. "Their self-righteous ignorance demands *they alone* be the ones to hold dominion over *all* other regions!" He spun about to Aivon. "Is that not true?"

Aivon frowned.

"There is but one king."

"Yes, but would your Lord not wield the shards' potential to... how would your region put this... hold the other regions in check? Not a king, no, but an overseer of sorts?"

"We are the only region who remain with any sense of honour and the only region who possess the will to enforce it." Aivon's frown deepened at the chamber's growing collection of enraged objections. He continued: "For the *betterment* of Unbequith and beyond, it is *imperative* we secure them before..."—his features twisted into a sneer—"before they're *spirited* away into hands of *true* corruption like *this* slithering fellow." Aivon fell against the table's edge, speaking heavily under his breath. "Lord Ortunato," he said privately, "you must understand... only a third of their forces came to your aid, for a third is protecting their region's capital and another third is marching towards our vulnerable cities to claim what they *believe* to be defenceless—*despite* such actions being in direct violation to the Code of Preservence established by our one true king." He spoke a little louder now, but only a little. "Can you not see they hold no sense of hon—" Aivon paused and sighed to himself, clenching his fist, "*morality*. Surely, you are not so lost as to willingly side with such treachery?"

Emelio shook his head.

"No... of course not." Raising his voice, he addressed the entire chamber. "I do not side with them willingly!" The room fell to silence, for all heeded his soft words. "No, not whatsoever. We are grateful to the Harlings for their aid, but we do not approve of their methods and shall indeed hold them accountable for the atrocities they've committed and *will* commit against Unbequith."

Henagan nodded, unfazed.

"But we hold a common cause?"

Emelio gravely mirrored his nod.

"But we've a common cause," he affirmed, turning to Aivon and resting a hand on his shoulder. "My brother," he said, his old eyes glistening with compassion, "my brother, you must understand, I shall not allow any occupation of Unbequith, for such is merely providing a foothold to the unspeakable. Nonetheless, we swore an oath to uphold the Redfolk's intentions, intentions which have since shifted to an extreme I cannot tolerate and *must* strive against at all costs. And... and I'm afraid *you* have left me no choice but to accept the willing aid of a corrupted ally—but only in thanks to the pure desperation you have forced my people into, *Commander*, for I refuse to yield the shards."

"No, it's not..." Aivon laughed in disbelief. "It's not like that whatsoever! We're... *we* are not the monsters here!" He shot a finger at Henagan. "*They* are!"

Emelio shook his head, ever so somberly.

"And what of it?" he answered. "Without the Harlings' aid, what say do I have? Where is my authority to speak as Regional Lord of Ranitorl? Without them, I am left no choice but to submit—and I will *never* submit."

Aivon sighed and—though he appeared furious—Junia was certain his eyes were glazing over.

"Is that it then?" His face twisted in a humourless smile. "Is this your final answer? To side with monsters against your kin in oath?"

Emelio paused for several moments before nodding slowly.

"I'm afraid so, mine brother."

Aivon simply stared, his features gaping in disbelief before resuming his composure and straightening his posture.

"As you say it." Bowing curtly, he descended the steps of the higher tables, his men following after him. "I shall have my men ready for the ageing dawn, O'brother mine." Aivon paused, halting his men as he gazed back to Emelio. "As is tradition, I expect to meet representatives of both parties in the early dawn."

"Aye," answered her uncle, "we shall await you there. However, before you part with your men so hastily..." Emelio leaned forward gesturing to Vincent as he spoke. "For a man who's wisdom hath aged so finely, you have done naught but remain of the utmost silence. Have you no words of advice to part with us quarrelling kinsmen?"

Vincent glanced at Aivon before returning his piercing gaze to Emelio with a shrug.

"By the Oather's bloody name, more talking's been done than I ever thought to say." Releasing a tired sigh, he gradually rose to address Aivon. "In the youthful light of dawn, the Code of Preservence shall be recited and our disputes settled." He rapped his knuckles against the table. "Thanks for the food, ol' nephew." With that, Vincent descended the tables' steps, leaving the entire chamber in heavy silence.

CHAPTER TWENTY-ONE

THREE LIES, ONE FACE

FEEL FREE TO SKIP THIS CHAPTER, YEAH?

S TRAIGHTENING HIS PAPERS, HENAGAN set them aside and studied the chart secured to his desk's face; a blueprint of the chambers he had been temporarily granted—useless in almost every aspect other than some failed attempt at aesthetics. He shrugged, stuffing the papers into a drawer beneath his desk before taking a seat; the first of his appointed visitors had just walked in.

"Lord Ortunato," greeted Henagan, refusing to rise from his chair, "I am honoured you could find the time in your... busy *lordship* to acquiesce to such a humble meeting." He reached into the drawer for a stack of papers.

Ortunato sank into the seat across from Henagan with a tired sigh.

"In truth," he began, "it's been ominously... quiet since the feast. I've found myself with more time than I know is better for me." He gazed out the white-stained glass of the window to his left; the only source of light in those shadowy grey chambers. "Perhaps," he continued, "after we have concluded here, I shall pay mine people a personal visit... renew their confidence and... and *engage* with them."

"Mm." Henagan spread the papers across his desk, very well intending to straighten them again. "A true image of lordship, to be sure." Henagan idly tapped one of the sheets: what were they even *for*? "In truth," he continued, "if you so care for them as truly as you imply, then it shall render what I have to say all the more impactful."

"Please," said Ortunato, pulling a knee to his chest and gesturing politely, "continue."

Henagan reclined in his seat, snatching one of the sheets to examine.

"If I recall correctly, Evenfal experienced a similar incident to the one you now find yourself in, though their circumstances were under less tension. And yet—even still—*it all*... swiftly escalated... to a minor, yet *historic*, skirmish of sorts." He examined the fine figures on the sheet, unable to decipher their meaning. "It's funny... what something like desperation can do to a man... how truly it can tear down the once-firm restraints of one's character into something of a *monster*." Opening the drawer, he stuffed the sheet inside before slamming it shut. "I suppose," he continued, calm and collected, "you know where I'm leading with this?"

"Aye..." said Emelio, "a desperate quarter... though I don't believe such a protocol is called for whatsoever." He shook his head. "No, such would only break the spirits of my people and fracture what little hope there is for unity between the four regions."

"Unity..." echoed Henagan, tapping the charts on his desk. "Unbequith stands at the door of your region and yet... you have allowed them to march through in a parade of siege machines and war engines, designed to violate the most intimate and safeguarded of places a man can have..." He stood up to stand besides Lord Ortunato, hands clasped behind his back: "your home."

"You speak words of truth, Master Henagan." Ortunato rose to stand and gaze out the rain-streaked window. "However, its reason is tainted with hints of false conclusions." He gestured to the court beyond the window. "Take the man there, tending the garden. You see him? His life is worth far more than anything I or your Regional Lord possesses."

"Mm." Henagan watched as the man disappeared further into the garden, cultivating the enchanting foliage. "I'm certain merely two percent of my Lord's wealth shall render more profits than the price of his death."

"Truly, I would agree with you—if I were as myopic to life's value." Ortunato gestured outside the window again. "Observe the elder there, or that man, the youngling over yonder, her too. The young man standing there, that woman and the life in her womb—they are each and *all* priceless, for a life can never be measured by value, but by the pure existence of their soul. Do you not see? If such is true, then we are *each* worth as much as the next... but only if it's true." Ortunato shook his head, hands clasped behind his back. "The true difference in value can be seen more clearly when drawn between them and I. Verily, I say unto you, because of their steadfast loyalty for me, courageous sacrifice to their region and true love for their family, they are *each* more precious than the lord whose guidance they follow. And to think... I possess three thousand men... ready to fight for their steadfast belief in my very word. Who am I to reward such devotion with death?"

Henagan shrugged nonchalantly.

"A desperate quarter might be just the surprise we need to emerge from this squirmish *triumphant*. If we don't seize what advantage we possess the moment it appears, then we have already lost."

"Even so, I'd rather die three thousand deaths myself than be at fault for *any* of them to pass on."

"Some believe those are strong words for a regional lord to utter before battle—if, that is, they hold conviction—or, no—something *stronger* than conviction."

"And what might you believe that to be?"

"*Action*." Henagan shrugged again, leaving the window to study the masks hung about the room. "In the least, I overheard Mr. Seeker remarking something of it... not me, *myself*, mind you, but my spies." He paused to eye Ortunato's curious stare. "You're not the only one capable of gathering intel." Henagan resumed his seat, rocking as he fell back against it. "They've engines of war, perfectly fitted to overcome the distance of water between us and the shores."

Ortunato leaned against the chart on Henagan's desk, his brows furrowed.

"My spies have long assessed their strengths," he finally said. "The Miracle Trenches are designed to counter such tactics. Like trying to invade a castle, it is. Even *with* the Code of Preservence in play, one would waste time and men in any foolish attempts to cross it."

"Mm..." Henagan retrieved the sheet from the drawer, folded it and tucked it into his coat. "Surely, you are not so naive as to believe your trenches are devoid of vulnerabilities?"

"One, but only if they manage to breach—"

"But *one* vulnerability... nonetheless." Henagan spun in his chair, taking note of the shadows about the room. "As such, my forces have secured a rather *fascinating* specimen for this cause. It was found in a state like that of *death*. However, my finest casters confirmed it was merely in a state of paralysis on the *brink* of death. They managed to retrieve a piece of metal which had been lodged in its skull, holding it in such a state. With this in mind, they believe we could harness this specimen to protect our vulnerability... a guardian if you will."

"I've noticed... spies have reported hideous descriptions of its dormant form as you brought it in. I am cautious to consider whether it can be trusted with its task or whether it's very service violates the Code of Preservence."

"From what we have learned, the creature is not unfamiliar with the role we intend for it. Beyond that, the capital's vulnerabilities cannot be breached unless the Code has already been violated and desperate quarters long enacted. I am certain if they target our vulnerability with the Code of Preservence engaged, they would be violating the regional laws of engagement."

"Very well then." Ortunato waved a hand through the air. "Do as you will. I doubt we shall ever be in need of... *its* services, for the trenches have proven their worth for centuries over—" Lord Ortunato was cut off as the jarring tone of pounding wood resounded from behind. Ortunato gestured to the doors of his chamber. "Were you expecting someone else?"

"A few, yes, but not *that* one." Henagan rubbed his temple. "Would you mind?"

"Certainly." Ortunato left to open the door. "I suppose I best be on my way as well, for I am only granted the leisure of so much time before the day forsakes us all."

"Of course." Henagan forced a friendly smile as the Lord of Ranitorl opened the door.

Vincent thought it would be a good idea; that was the *only* reason she was here. If not for his earnest sympathy, she would have very well put off the necessary for... well forever. She didn't care. Who did? Not her. Where was Paun anyway? She hadn't seen him for... well, for a while now. She wondered what he would have thought about her situation. Would he have encouraged her to go? She didn't think so. There was no *real* reason to be here—not one she could see. No, perhaps Vincent *was* wrong; it wasn't necessary in the least.

Crossing her arms, Malvolia stared down the two guards who had denied her access. They ordered her to disarm herself and provide a name: two absurd requests she had refused to humour. Both soldiers were elite guardsmen of Harldïof, their ivory-white armour reflecting their self-righteous arrogance. They both rested a hand on their sheathed weapons: a warning she had earned for shoving them so hard.

Shrugging, Malvolia turned to leave, only to whirl about at the last second and hurl herself against the door. As she did, the two guards seized her by both arms and the door splayed inwards.

Falling to the ornate-stone floor, she kicked off the two soldiers who had landed atop her. They swiftly scrambled to their feet, weapons drawn and ready to kill.

An elderly man spoke up from beside the door.

"Well, I'll..." Lord Ortunato cleared his throat. "I'll excuse myself then..." With that he turned to leave.

"Temper your hostility and reserve the blade of your weapons for those Redfolk *scum*."

Malvolia sighed at the sound of... *that* voice. She turned to face it as the guards left, shutting the door behind her.

"I have hithered to report, O'Steward, mine." Malvolia gave a polite bow, prompting her father to raise a curious eyebrow; to her passive annoyance, he refused to stand and meet her like the father he was supposed to—

"Malvolia," he greeted, rising from his chair, "there's no need to address me so. It's... it's only you and I."

Malvolia crossed her arms, shrugging.

"How was I supposed to know?" She stared coldly at his hand, the one gesturing for her to sit. Grinding her jaw, Malvolia remained upright, leaning against the window instead. "Since when did you forgo formalities?"

"Since I lost contact with you... with your vidorae." His tone was calm... in an almost mocking, sympathetic fashion. "I couldn't..." He sighed. "For the previous week, it's turned up nothing but a dismal darkness."

"Yeah, well, sorry 'bout that." Malvolia turned over, leaning on her shoulder and pretending to stare out the window as she monitored her father's reflection. "There's nothing I could have done to avoid the trap *they* laid for us. I doubt even Oleander could have escaped *that* situation." Her knuckles paled as she thought of how obvious she had made it for the Death Order to find her vidorae. Truly, no other relief was so great as when they confiscated it. "Maybe," she continued, "I should have fought harder... to the death perhaps. Sorry." She briefly glanced over her shoulder to eye him. "I'm sorry I didn't die."

Her father's eyebrows were drawn together in some form of what one could interpret as regret. In truth, she knew it to be disappointment. She shook her head and returned her gaze to the window, refusing to grant eye contact as he spoke.

"It was *horrifying*," he began, his sarcasm making her sick, "the thought of outliving another child... the *only* child I have left... I had no choice but to consider the grim possibility's truth, for that was all I could speculate." He rose from his seat, leaning against his desk with two fingers. "I am grateful you've taken the initiative to reassure me of your safety—*or* contact me, or..." He paused, thinking to himself for a moment. "What *are* you doing here?" he asked, his eyes narrowing. "You're not the type to set aside precious time for sentiments alone."

Malvolia huffed with an exasperated smile, pushing herself off the window to stride about the room.

"No... I *am* the type, for I've done it before... but you would never allow yourself to witness such moments." She shrugged, observing a peculiar mask with fur surrounding its edges. "Still, perhaps it *was* merely sentiment that I thought to meet you—after all, what kind of daughter would I be if I avoided my own *father* who I haven't reported to for the previous... well... *weeks* or so?" She unhooked the mask from the wall and held it over her features as she turned to face him. "I hope you've been well, O'father, mine..." She set the mask aside on a pedestal of faded flowers. "It's remarkable... how freeing an excursion can be without the looming judgement of one—"

"Freeing? *Freeing?*" Her father scoffed, leaving his desk and returning the mask to its proper place. "If only one could experience such a fantasy..."

"I certainly did." Malvolia bounced her shoulders. "And I'm sure you would too if you only allowed yourself."

"Truly, if you cared so deeply, you would have *nabbed* one of the shards for your *own* entrapped father. With their power—" He lowered his voice, wrapping an arm about her as he whispered: "*With their power*, I can be *free* of the desperation which so drives my soul to the accursed place it resides."

"No." Malvolia unhooked his arm and continued striding about, careful to address him with her back. "The only thing which binds you to such a lowly state of desperation is your *own* stubborn greed."

From the reflection in the window, she saw her father shake his head.

"If only you thought to show *any* small sign of compassion for your *own family*, then I would achieve *freedom* from the grip of those who bind my will to a leash."

Malvolia froze, her shoulders hunched over.

"Why... why *are* you here?" She turned about to face him, her arms crossed. "More death and chaos at the hand of greed?"

Her father's impassive features remained grave.

"In truth," he began, "it was I who begged Lord Finyeld to lead this expedition on his behalf. As I have said, it was a chance to redeem my actions."

Malvolia's gaze darkened as she eyed him from behind strands of greasy, auburn hair.

"Is that what... *she* told you to say?"

Her father's only answer was grave silence. Shrugging, Malvolia began fidgeting with another mask. "For the past decade, Ms. Elicy has funded your city while you carry out her dirty deeds in shadow. I understand you've a city to support, but *Heavens* alive! How much longer shall you continue to allow this avarice to plague your heart?"

"That's *enough*," he growled, swiping the mask from her. "You know not the pain your ignorance so *readily* inflicts upon my heart."

Malvolia eyed him with a blank expression before shrugging again and turning to leave. Her hand was on the handle of the door as her father sternly called: "*Malvolia Henagan.*" She froze, grinding her jaw, but refused to face him. "I... I do care for you," he began, "ever so deeply... and beyond your very comprehension. You *know* that—you *have* to know that." He paused before continuing: "and I... I am glad you are safe... truly."

For a moment, Malvolia couldn't move, briefly overcome by the genuine affection of his tone. But then... then she remembered everything she knew of him; its pain overcame the softness of her heart with the cold feeling it was so akin to. After all, she had no doubts this was simply some failed attempt to manipulate her with such... feigned *sentiments*. Shaking her head, Malvolia stormed out the room, slamming the door behind her.

Heavens alive, she was ready to pour out the raging emotion of her heart to Vincent—*sorrow, wrath and all.*

"Mm... absolute shame that." Ms. Elicy stepped out of the shadows as Henagan sank into his chair. "It matters not, for you accomplished your part to the best of your *meagre* abilities." In truth, it wrenched her heart to see his relationships so fractured. But it... as she said, it mattered not. He was nothing more than a jumble of sad words on a beholder's page. He wasn't real, so she didn't have to—

"How much longer...?" he rasped, asking as though he were parched of water. His hand was propped against his eyes, rubbing it with a rugged sigh. "I have already lost a child to your crooked *schemes*... must I lose another so soon?" Henagan's hand fell across his face, lowering to his jaw. "In truth, I think it far worse to lose another at their own *choice* to forsake you." He looked up to her, his eyes bloodshot. "How could any soul tolerate such cruelty without perishing under the weight of its own *misdeeds*?"

Ms Elicy was pale, opening her mouth to reply, but was cut off from her father.

"Trust me," he said, stepping out from the shadows, "your daughter is too attached to this synthetic world for one of your calibre to trouble over." Pen wildly spun Henagan's chair as he passed him. "You've done what we've required of you, yes?"

"Aye..." Henagan's voice was ragged and torn, tearing away at Ms. Elicy's heart with every word. "Aye, your unholy monster has been haunting their aqueducts since long before I sought permission."

"And what of the secret gate?"

"Do you so naively expect me to willingly betray my honour and region?"

Pen shrugged, striding about the desk with his hands shoved into his coat pockets.

"You've done it before and you'll do it again." He whipped out his wand, directing its burning tip just under Henagan's jaw. "Or I shall be forced to find someone *else*."

Henagan shrugged.

"Very well then. Leave me. Find someone else for this... this puppeteering."

"No... *foolish* boy, I..." Pen paused, thumbing his wry smile, "I'm threatening your *life*."

"Yes, I *know* that." Henagan withdrew a sheet of paper from his sullen coat. "Here, if you're to choose another, you might as well give them this." He dismissively tossed the sheet at Ms. Elicy. "I can't read it anyway."

Ms. Elicy bent over to retrieve it, blinking in surprise as her father snatched it from her.

"It's not *for* you," growled Pen, shoving the sheet in Henagan's chest. "This script was to be given to a certain *fellow* we picked up in the desert—but it's too *late* for that now. All you can do is read your own script and *bloody* cooperate." Pen gestured to Ms. Elicy, saying: "or I shall ensure you never see the last remnant of your line again... not living anyway."

Ms. Elicy hardened her heart as Henagan glanced her way; she had to show him she'd do it; she'd done it before, and nothing could stop her from doing it again.[1] Not even the fatherly grief of his eyes, contrasting starkly with his impassive expression; the raw disbelief that any would *do* such an atrocious thing to his own daughter—*No*, he wasn't real, none of this was, she couldn't—Ms. Elicy shook her head, clearing it of Windcatcher's twisted logic; she mustn't let it corrupt her.

"If you insist," agreed Henagan, gently, yet forcibly, pushing Pen off him. "How could I possibly refuse the chance to forsake the conscience of my own soul at the chance of... *honour*... as you believe it to be?"

"Do not lecture me of honour, for you cannot possibly fathom the true depths of its nature." Pen shrugged, striding about the desk to stand in the shadows. "After all," he continued, "how could one like you speak of honour after the will of silence so graciously

---

1. No, I can fix her. I can try, anyway.

allowed you and your forces to pass through Nowood unscathed? Have you no gratitude? No sense of repayment?"

"Not *all* my forces," reminded Henagan, sliding the sheet back into his coat, "There were the seven who—"

"The seven troublemakers," finished Pen. "Through your own sloppy ineptitude, they began sniffing out our motives." Pen leaned against the desk, tracing the various lines across the chart. "I wonder... could one like yourself ever allow your actions to devolve to such a careless state... or was it... *intentional?* A desperate ploy to escape your situation... as it were." He shrugged, hopping off the desk to disappear into the shadows. "Their minds are lost now... that's on *your* conscience. Pray you do not make the same mistake again." With that, he moulded with the shadows, vanishing from sight. Ms. Elicy knew he had used his magic to summon a hidden portal; it would only stay open for so long, for they wished for none to discover where it led out to. With this in mind, she gave one last look to Henagan before turning to follow after her father.

"I ask again... how could one ever become so heartless...?"

Ms. Elicy froze at Henagan's words.

"*What did you say?*" she asked, whispering for fear of her voice carrying through the shadow's gate. "Where *the blazes* did you hear *that* from?"

"My own conscience," he answered, continuing to stare with his back to her. "It pains me to see one so willingly enlist themselves as a child of the Devil." He shrugged. "I can tell you now... it will be a rather one-sided relationship."

"You know... *nothing* of my father." She was sure to state this louder.

Henagan sighed, his body immovable like some ancient statue.

"I wasn't referring to your father, though I suppose it's all the same... is it not?"

Ms. Elicy refused to answer, turning silently to disappear into the gate's shadows. No... she couldn't let her—him—*them* get to her.[2]

Really?

How much longer would she continue to shun the truth in some mad effort to believe a twisted lie. Was she so quick to ignore her own judgement simply because it was easier? Perhaps *they* were real after all—if not their physical nature, then surely their spiritual nature held *some* substance to it; loss, grief... *pain...* were they not all emotions she herself

---

2. Really?

knew and *hated?* Despite that, she *still* chose to inflict such torment on these... *characters* simply because she thought them lesser in existence.

Is their suffering not the same as yours?

Are you *truly* so heartless?

Ms. Elicy tightened her jaw, tearing at her hair as shadows carried her across reality; she wished ever so desperately for the Oather's voice to *shut up.*[3]

---

3. Well... *fine*, but we're not done here.

CHAPTER TWENTY-TWO

THE MIRACLE TRENCHES

"As a sword is for a sword, so is a lord's dispute with another." The page paused to roll up the scroll and read further: "though of their lord's will, they are not the lords with whom the disagreement resides." The page coughed and shivered, clearly uncomfortable in the early dawn's weather. "Regardless of whence they hailed, how young or how old, and whose people they hail—one life is worth sevenfold the lords' quarrel." The page paused to eye Aivon. "Is... is this translation suitable to you?"

Aivon sighed and waved a hand.

"Its simplified interpretation lacks the true impact of the original's manuscript, but *please*, continue. I've read both and it's *fine*."

"Right, um..." The page shot a nervous glance to his lord before continuing: "By the will of the one and only true king, this decree exists to protect the sacred lives of the innocent." He paused to take a deep breath. "Exempli gratia, those who serve their region out of a blind devotion"—he cleared his throat—"misguided loyalty, pure ignorance, et cetera..." He rolled the scroll to read further. "Et cetera." The page cleared his throat again. "Those who reside in a region are not to be harmed, for though they may dwell in their lord's will, they are *not* their lord. They shall neither be held accountable nor tormented for the sake of another lord's quarrel. As brothers and sisters of the Almighty King, we are not to violate the laws of our nature in the name of a dispute, misunderstanding or corrupted leader. Furthermore—" The page paused, lowering the scroll as he turned his head to study the southern shore of the lake. "Do... by the stars and shades, is that another army?"

Aivon Seeker leaned against the left side of the bridge's railing.

"Aye," he affirmed, "and they've deployed an envoy to cross the lake." He paused to accept a spyglass from his Lieutenant. "In Heaven's name... is that..." He lowered the spyglass to eye Lord Ortunato. "Why... I suppose the Sandbeast himself approaches our merry gathering."

They waited in silence for several moments more as a simple, yet swift, craft traversed the lake. It was like a dinghy, but with a flat hull and no sails or rigging. In truth, its simple yet efficient design baffled them all.

"Hail, Lord Ortunato!" cried the man known as Eric Sandbeast, stepping off the craft and onto the bridge. His skin was a dark colouration, tempered to such a resilient condition by the unforgiving stars of the Bruchi Kari. "Hail Seeker, Paulson!" He pounded his heart before gesturing to them both. "By my bidding, our forces have journeyed from the comfort of our cliffs to honour the pacts of old."

"I don't suppose those pacts align with Unbequith?" asked Aivon, his voice gravely humorous. "As it stands, our region is already outnumbered."

"I am afraid not, Aivonfel." His voice was truly remorseful. "It pains my heart to side against a valiant warrior of deed and steadfast honour, but..." He raised a finger, shaking his head. "But, by the stone records of old, I am still of stewardship under the lord-ness of Ranitorl." Eric pointed to Lord Ortunato. "You, O'Lord mine, it is to your cause that mine people pledge. We are only two thousand, but our ferocity and familiarity with traditional casting holds no rival." His head tilted from side to side. "Well, no other than Unbequith of course."

Aivon smiled, his disappointed eyes mirroring Eric's.

"It shall be an honour for my men to witness your tactics in action, O'Sandbeast."

"And mine, yours." He glanced back to his men gathered about the southern shores of the lake. "I've received word," he continued, "that this dispute is to be settled in the dawn's dying breath." Eric turned as he addressed Lord Ortunato and Aivon Seeker. "My men are weary and lack formation with those whom we are aligned." He paused, holding his hands out to both of them in a shrug. "I need but several hours more to properly sort my men with your stratagem, Lord Ortunato."

"Nay," answered Emelio, "we shall grant you a full day to resupply and invigorate your men." He turned to address Aivon. "Do you not agree this is just?"

"Aye," answered Aivon, grave as ever, "aye, for I refuse to face against the Sandbeast in unjust conditions."

Eric slapped a hand over Aivon's shoulder.

"Very well, the next dawn then... we shall do battle as brothers."

"Aye... *however*, since... *all* the leaders are now here, we might as well continue hearing out the Code of Preservence as *kin*, shall we not?" Aivon then snapped his fingers, gesturing to the page. "Carry on, boy. From the top again... if you will." He pinched the ridge of his nose. "And by all things sacred, I shall *tear* that scroll from your hands and read it aloud *myself* if you keep drawling on so."

It was early in the morning when Roabard had dropped by their segment of camp to give them the... well... in truth... Adela didn't know whether it was good *or* bad news; battle was postponed to the following day and Aivon was to attend another feast of kinship. Lieutenant Bo had informed them their Commander would return on the eve of noon's light. However, the sun had long been set and Aivon still hadn't returned.

Adela herself was currently sitting on a dark log, one of three positioned about the lively fire Fel had started. Sam sat closest to the flames, tending the fish Adela had caught in Sher's Lake. Though she was surprised to catch anything at all, there wasn't enough to go around for everyone. Knowing this, Adela had feigned a strong distaste for fish, insisting to be satisfied with the standard and coarse rations of the other soldiers. While Sam tended to the fish, Jhess had left to fetch her portion of provisions from the mess tent; he knew just how much the cook intimidated her. Smiling at his chivalrous sacrifice, she turned to gaze over the dark waters of the lake and examine the flickering lights of Aeraos; somewhere, in that imposing capital, was the power to reshape an entire world—in the least, that's what she had *heard*. In truth, she had no grounded idea of *what* the prism shards even *were* or... where they came from.

She bit her lip as she thought of how long Aivon was taking. If something went wrong, wouldn't Darun have signalled them? Surely, there was no magic that could contain his might nor foe that could rival his power? But then, she also knew very little of Ranitorl's capital and the means they had taken to safeguard it all those years against the unholy onslaughts of Nowood. Was it so impossible to believe they could lay a trap for a True Beyonder like Darun? And if they could overcome *him*, what's stopping them from betraying their honour to Aivon? They already betrayed their honour to Unbequith, what's stopping them *from*—

"Lass, you needn't be so apprehensive." Adela looked up to see Sam addressing her. His ash-black armour glistened in the fire's light. "They're perfectly fine and in good company." He pinched off a piece of the filleted meat for a taste. "Mm," he said and smacked his lips, "I've heard tell they're sorting out means to provide our entire campaign with some decent food." He closed his eyes and shook his head in delight. "Not that *this* isn't anything decent—*by thunder*, it's got a spark to it!" Sam turned to Adela, offering a slab of white meat to her. "I'm certain you'll like it if you merely give it a go. Even for someone with a passionate distaste for fish, no jaws can reject an opportunity like this!"

"No... it, it's truly fine, luv." Adela smiled softly, holding her elbows as she rocked on the log. "Jhess has already bothered himself by standing for me in the mess line... I think it'd be rude to spoil an already committed appetite."

"Ah... of course." Sam tapped the side of his nose, his eye twinkling. "He's your special little lad, ain't he?"

"Aye, but, right, but..." Adela chuckled under her breath, giving herself a moment to organise her thoughts. "But... back to what you said... how could you ever be so, ehm... certain of anything going on in there?" Adela pursed her lips before continuing: "Is it all simply rumours or...?"

"Ol' snoopy sneak there," answered Sam, gesturing to Ramsoen; he was lurking in the gloomy edges of the fire's light. Sam shook his head in amusement before returning his attention to the fire. "He's been spending the better part of the day in the capital's rafters overhead and mess tables below." He shook his head again, his voice rising sharply: "Ain't that right, ol' shadow!"

"Aye..." Ramsoen crossed his arms, gazing after the twinkling lights of the capital. "Aye, last I heard, they were proposing every residence, whether civilian or nobility, host a division of Unbequith's forces." His shoulders rose and sagged in a pondering sigh. "It felt more like flippant talk than resolved action, but there's no telling where it might lead..." Ramsoen's voice faded off as Jhess emerged into the fire's light: a wooden slab with food in one hand, a silver platter in the other.

"He was grumpy as usual," said Jhess, sitting on the log beside her "And even more so when he saw your plate." He handed Adela the silver platter. "Methinks he just wants everyone to suffer on his stomachsbane de-oela gruel."[1]

Adela chuckled, nearly spitting up the food in her mouth. She paused for a second, swishing the morsel about her jaws as she contemplated its taste.

---

1. De-oela... I don't... I don't know what this means. It's not in any Unbequith dictionary I know or anything of the like. Perhaps it's a type of slang? Your guess is as good as mine.

"Oy Jhess," she said and tapped his shoulder, *"Jhess,"* she hissed. "Why's my food different from yours? From—" She shot a glance to the walkway of tents on Jhess's left, taking note of the platters in each soldier's hands. *"Different from everyone here."*

Jhess gave a loose shrug and shovelled his meal down his gullet.

"Don't think I'm supposed to tell you, but—"

"Then I'm not eating this," she stated, setting the platter aside, "I'll give it to someone who needs it more or..." she added, then paused, noticing Jhess wanted to speak, "or... sorry, what're you saying, luv?"

"But," continued Jhess, "knowing your sort, I'll tell you it came from the table of higher stewards and what not." He bent down to retrieve the silver platter from the ground and plop it onto her lap. "He didn't want me telling you where it came from, but my father wished most dearly for you to have this."

"Oh." Adela looked down to her platter. "Oh... yeh, I'll... I'll—" Adela stuffed a mouthful of steaming steak and mash into her mouth. *"Mm,"*—she smiled through her stuffed cheeks—*"nummi."*

Jhess chuckled.

"Good. I'm glad you... yeah." He shook his head. "Addy, I was hoping I could show you something."

"Mm." With a heavy swallow, she forced the large portion of food down her throat. "What's that then?"

He set his mess plate beside her, bending over his side of the log to retrieve a leather-bound journal. It was wide like and shield, yet no thicker than a folded map. Adela couldn't help but think of how its proportions reminded her of Jhess in armour. Scooting a little closer, he opened the journal to reveal various sketches and illustrations—images she had crafted whilst alone in the murky depths of a bleak dungeon...

She forced a smile as Jhess flipped through the various pages with her, asking about certain drawings and their meanings. At first glance, some appeared to be just plain silly: one such portrait hosted a round and fluffy kitten striking up a merry tune on the keys. Jhess and Adela laughed together at these before passing by with no elaboration.

Adela liked it that way.

In contrast, others... the others stirred something truly terrifying in her gut. It was a dark place she had found herself in drawing some of those... not nearly as dark as where she would find herself in Pen Wishton's dungeon, but... even so, they were all but foreshadowing of the torment and loss which would soon follow. They echoed warnings of a devastating future.

Said future was in the past now, but the scars it left imprinted on her soul were permanent: burning in spiritual pain with every turn of the page. She could only maintain this smile for so long before—

"Addy?" Jhess shut the journal, leaning forward to catch her eyes. "Are you... are you alright?"

"Yeh, you needn't trouble 'bout it." She patted his arm. "Just a little anxious for tomorrow is all."

"Oh..." Jhess glanced down to his journal before looking back to her. For a moment, his mouth gaped open, as though he intended to ask her something. However, his mouth locked shut upon studying her features and he said simply: "Aye... I'm... I'm nervous as well." He lowered the journal on his side of the log, wiping his hands across his pants. "I just *know* I'm going to be captured first... I haven't been in an actual battle before... not one of this scale." Jhess could tell she was changing the subject, but decided against pressuring her... for now anyway.

"Yeh... can't say I have either, luv."

"None of us have." A random soldier had spoken up from behind Adela. His dark-brown cloak flickered in the breeze as he knelt beside their log. "I'm surprised any of us can go through this madness without our mind collapsing in on itself in pure chaos."

"Oh." Jhess blinked a few times. "So I'm not the only one with sweaty palms and a stinging chill on the nape of my neck then."

"N-no. Chances are, everyone here is just as apprehensive, if not worse."

Adela gazed around the tent; the stranger's words couldn't have been more true.

"Oy." She stood up, swiping her hands together as she dusted them off. "I don't see any real reason for either of us to be so nervous, yeh?" Adela clenched her left hand and gestured across the lake with her right. "Tomorrow, we're given the chance to prove ourselves in the records of history as legends!" She said this to bolster their spirits, but also... perhaps she needed to hear it aloud herself. "A chance to fight for what's loved," she continued, "in a noble effort to protect our kin and beyond! Whether we're captured or not, we can't deny ourselves that we tried our utmost best and... and well, when you think of it, you're doing good for your kin and country just by being here, so... so really—"

"*Blast it, girl,*" growled the soldier, "these aren't like the bloody wars you read about in stories!" He rose to stab a finger at the capital in the distance. "We're not fighting some dark evil, nor some *vague* tyrannical force! We're fighting our own *kin.*"

"And by Harldïof's slakeless thirst for power," added Sam, "our own sisters. Women in arms." He shuddered, clearly disturbed. "I fear I have not the strength to plunge the bite of mine metal into a bearer of children—downright sacreligious it is."

"That... now one second, boys." Adela spoke through her blushing features. "You're all... all talkin' like we're fighting to *kill.*"

The strange soldier shook his head.

"They've seen this before... *we've* seen this before." He looked up, his features concealed behind a dirt-brown mask. "I'm sure we all remember the Evenfal incident—"

"What's your division number?" asked Ramsoen, stepping out from the shadows to confront the soldier. "And where's your uniform?" He pinched the soldier's dark cloak. "These garbs aren't Unbequith heralding and your mask is of a hunter's make." He released the cloak, crossing his arms as he stood over the soldier. "Where are you from, *old man*, and why are you here?"

The strange soldier stood in silence, every limb rigid and still.

"In truth," he began, "I'm... I'm just protecting my—"

A sudden roar overwhelmed the man's speech, drowning his words in a cascade of noise. A crowd of soldiers and men had gathered about the shores of Sher's Lake, shoving past one another to view its waters. Sighing, Adela set down her platter to follow after them. She turned one last time to check on the strange soldier, but he had vanished. Feeling a tug on her shoulder, Adela followed after Jhess to the shores of the lake, bouncing on her tippy-toes to peer over the various broad shoulders.

"Here, Addy." Sam swooped down to her level for her to climb atop his shoulders. "You see it now?"

"No... I..." Adela paused as she caught sight of the lake. "What in Heaven's name..." The black surface of the lake swirled in an odd mixture of the stars it reflected and the yellow lights of the city. Hastily patting Sam's head, she hopped from his shoulders, weaving under and around the crowd. Arriving at the shore's edge, she thrust her hand into its dark waters, ignoring its biting cold. Her gaze falling to her arm, it was then she was certain of her theory; the lake was sinking. More men began to emerge from their tents, watching the lake subside to reveal—

"The Miracle Trenches..." breathed one soldier in disbelief. "The very trenches used to stave off the forces of Nowood, ending their assaults and *crippling* their aggression." His breath was shaky, its dreadful patterns spreading to the others like a disease. "They mean to pick us off like animals—nay—*devils*." The soldier spat into the indiscernible hollow stretching below before turning to leave. Adela watched him go, wincing as another uproar made its presence known; it came from the capital.

They were *cheering*.

The entire... capital... was *cheering*.

It was *the* most disturbing sound Adela ever thought to hear.

"Déaþinferleas popilégan!" The crowd of soldiers parted to reveal a young man gesturing to Sam. "Lord Aivon has returned," he began, catching his breath, "and he's requested a most desperate word with his most trusted of ranks—Lieutenant Bo is already with him!"

"Is he now?" Sam turned to face his fellow butterflies. "I suppose we best not keep them waiting, aye?"

"Aye," answered Adela, springing atop Sam's shoulders, much to his surprise. She pointed to the heart of their bivouac town. "Onward O'steed, mine! We shall see what our dear Commander hath to report! Whether it be sweets for all or grave tidings of... of..."—she leaned against Sam's head, drumming her fingers—"of... *tide*. Yeh." She nodded. "Of grave tidings of the tide!"

She had no idea what she was even *saying* anymore, though it did make Jhess chuckle.

That was nice.

Chapter Twenty-Three

Persuading the Pawns

"Yes... in truth, I've anticipated their tactic for quite some time now, despite what *some* of you might wish to believe." Aivon's knowing look briefly rested on the steward, Stalherd. "In my visits to Tokade," he continued, "I was sure to trouble myself with their extensive expanse of knowledge scattered throughout their various libraries." He tossed a worn book of black and gold onto the table. "You would be surprised to know attaining this journal was beyond simple." He creaked open its black cover, exposing the gold text interior. "Ironically, for something of grave secrecy as this, it was available for *anyone* to purchase." He tapped its pages. "However, it's *all* in first Unbequith, down to the very characters it utilises." Aivon continued to flip through its black pages. "Do you see? Hareesh only trusted his secrets with *his* people—those who would safeguard their traditional vernacular. True children of Unbequith; the worthy few who study its laws of grammar and declension." He paused on a page where the symbols grew more sporadic and rushed. "These are the original prints for the construction of the miracle trenches." He signalled for Lieutenant Bo to spread a large sheet of paper across the table for everyone to see. "Due to his secrecy, the book only provides a written description for us to establish the foundation of our plans." He tapped the chart Bo laid across the table. "*This*, this is our loresmiths' best attempt to decipher the description of its design in illustration."

"I'm... sorry," began Lord Stalherd, "but you mean to inform us that all this while, you *suspected* of the Miracle Trenches, yet *insisted* our men bear the burden of siege crafts for lakes and seas? All this while, you had us drag these burdensome instruments knowing we'd never use them!"

"I *suspected* we wouldn't require their use," corrected Aivon, refusing to meet Stalherd's eyes. "But their efforts were not in vain, for I was hoping to conceal the boon of our knowledge under the guise of a ruse. Though laborious and taxing of energy, its deception is just the advantage we need to triumph." His gaze rose to meet Stalherd's. "Twas the very reason I advocated so readily for delay, that my men would better rest themselves, so I could utilise time to better understand our enemy, *and* bait out the use of their trenches—a deceived sense of security as it were." He shrugged, stroking his snowy-white beard. "In truth, I expected such tactics of Rantilorian tradition long before I acquired Hareesh's diary. It was merely *how* to deal with such tactics in the most *effective* of methods that left me searching for answers in memories of the olden folk."

Lord Stalherd mirrored his shrug, seemingly mocking him as he did so. "And what *have* you to report?" His skeleton-like fingers gestured to the chart. "A simple *diagram* isn't enough to triumph a war."

"It's a disagreement settled by the harmless touch of metal," began Aivon, "*not* a war. And yes, a simple layout *would* be enough, however Hareesh details *so* much more than that. Look here," Aivon said as he pointed to an indent in one of the trenches, "this is a hidden advantage designed for ambushing invaders. However, with the information we're given, we also learned it can be easily overcome from *here*." Aivon shifted his fingers to a trail dipping behind the indent. "Do you not see? The familiarity of turf they held as advantage has shifted in our favour! We know of what they intend, where they're to position their men, traps, manoeuvres, secret routes—*everything* we need to emerge from the trenches *victorious*." He crossed his arms, smiling in pure satisfaction. "There's quite a large vulnerability gaping in the fortitude of their defences as well, but... but I doubt we shall ever be able to expose it, for it *may* violate the Code of Preservence." Aivon shrugged, leaning against the table as he studied the chart. "It matters not. Such ploys shall be reserved for desperation, *if* it ever comes to that." He nodded to himself. "Aye, our success in the Miracle Trenches *alone* would be enough to pave the path to our victory." He gestured to two parallel lines of red extending to the capital. "They'll expect us to meet them on the bridge and not risk damaging our more-than-capable siege engines with the trenches. As such, we shall meet their expectations and confront their forces *here*." He smiled, shaking his head to himself. "In truth, I'm downright *giddy*. Initially, I had harboured this information to myself from even the closest of those I trust in an effort to conceal such a momentous advantage from spies."

"Is that..." Adela bit her bottom lip as all eyes faced her; Aivon was talking for so long, the very sound of her own voice had caught her off guard. "Did you... have you captured all the spies then?" She reddened under their open stares. "If it is... *indeed* a grave matter of secrecy, then... then maybe we shouldn't have invited, ehm... certain.... *people* to this meeting?" She unintentionally shot a sidelong glance to Lord Stalherd, who met her eyes with a sullen glare.

"Child, you'd do best to mind your—"

"No, she has a valid point," responded Aivon, who had noticed her glance with a grin. "Secrecy can only be held in secrecy for so long before circumstance demands it be forced open and laid bare. No Addy, it matters not whether spies divulge this secret to their masters, for such information can only cripple the enemy's spirit whilst simultaneously bolstering ours!" He laughed to himself, something Adela hadn't seen him do in a while. "Come brothers! Toss this news to your legions like a handful of king's metal! Celebrate and be merry, for in the morrow, our victory is assured!" He pounded his gauntlets against the table's wood. "Surely, even *you*, Lord *Stalherd*, cannot possibly find one flaw in this discovery?"

"Paun!" Junia's voice echoed throughout the now empty dining chamber. "*Paun! Are you still*—oh." She finally found him: sulking in her uncle's dining seat. "Paun," she sighed, scaling the high tables' stairs. "Thank *Heavens* I found you, I thought you had upped and—" She tilted her head, eyeing him curiously. "Goodness, boy, are you quite alright?" She took up her usual seat, leaning against its arm with both elbows. "It's so dreary in here... wouldn't help any sour mood, I imagine."

Paun slowly slung his head to her, a small smile finally peeking out from the corners of his lips.

"I'm... fine or, in the least, I *was*." He sighed, using one hand to prop his knuckles against his jaw. "You asked where I've been for the last couple of days." He looked up at her, his eyes reminding Junia of a wee puppy. "Was that merely rhetorical or did you..."

"No, no, please, yes, tell me." She shooed her hands at the splash of light that darted from her hair. "Sorry, no, *yes*, I wish to know."

Paun glanced at her again, an eyebrow raised and a hint of a grin on his features.

"For the last couple of... *days* or... so, I've felt nothing but an odd sense of peace pass over me." His grin slowly faded to a solemn contemplation. "It was as though I needn't trouble over whatever unknown dangers would spring out at me from the dark... as though I needn't check my shoulder for peril's jaws upon the grace of a breeze's touch. The fires of anxiety burning in the shadows of my mind no longer spun about like a devastating maelstrom of grievance and regret." Paun's eyes were dark now, broken beyond recognition to her. "But... that... *feeling*, of a thousand-thousand eyes—boring down upon me with their ill desires..." He paused for several moments before continuing: "It *returned* and I'm left with nothing but an apprehensive sense of *dread*." Much to Junia's alarm, he clutched his heart. "I need to find her..." he whispered to himself. "I *need...* to find her."

Gasping, she quickly leapt over her chair to his and pressed a hand against his shoulder, stabilising him.

"Paun, I can help you. You know that—*Paun*, I could *help* you."

"Mm." He rubbed his knuckles against his temple. "Perhaps I could... engage in more desperate methods with Mr. Henagan." Paun glanced to her worried expression and shrugged. "I need what information he hoards to find her... he's had no right to withhold it from me for as long as he has." He paused. "It's funny... maybe he'll divulge her location without my tactics of... *interrogation*." Paun shrugged again. "After all, I *did* deliver the shards to his allies, in *his* care. My work *should* be done." He rubbed his knuckles ominously. "Methinks I shall have to pay a visit to his chambers."

Junia remained quiet for several moments as she considered his words.

"You're not... you're not considering leaving, are you?" Junia's brows pinched together in response to Paun's silence. "You... you *can't* leave now. Paun, you *can't*. Not yet anyway—not with so much at stake." She bent to his level, trying to catch his eyes. "The grievous fate of Ranitorl and Beyond befalls tomorrow like... like judgement day's divine hammer! If you don't wish for the shards to be held over you—over this peace you seek in a guilt-ridden kingdom of power, then you'd do best to stay and *fight* for their protection."

Paun's gaze rose to her.

"What?"

"I... I don't know what I'm saying either!" Junia threw her hands in the air as she turned about, before spinning back to Paun's chair. "If you leave now—at the moment when you could have prevented the assured doom of all regions—I *promise* you will *never* be able to exist in the peace you deserve." She shook her head. "It's not a threat mind you, just the truth..."

"No, I know... I know." Paun sighed sharply. "Does the raging tides of war truly require *one* soul to make a difference—*the* difference? *My...* soul?" He grimly smiled to himself. "I've seen a good deal of propaganda which begs to agree..."

"Of *course* they agree, for there's truth in it! And it's not just *any* bloody soul—you're *he* who uncovered the shards and—before all else—*he* who withheld them from the Redfolk's clutches *moments* before they would have secured them for their own selfish gain. We're in need of all hands we can find... in need of *you*." She knelt to Paun's level, taking his hands. "I promise you, if you stay and ensure the regions' wellbeing, I'll do *everything* I can to aid you on this quest for... for *her*. I have experience—being in Theo's guild and all. Pack of lethal adventurers we are." An unsettling smile graced her features. "Hey, I know a few techniques *myself* for ol' Henagan. Why, I even know how to slip in an' out of his chambers unscathed *and* undetected."

Paun mirrored her smile.

"To the ends of the void shall we trek for the service I lend your region?"

"To the end and beyond death itself should the need demand."

"Very... very well then." His chest heaved, as though a great weight had slid off it. "With the honour of your spirit, I bind you to your words and shall abate from the throes of my desperation... *for now*, for I must honour her memory whilst I can... aye, I refuse to take a single life." He slowly rose, placing a heavy hand on her shoulder. "However, once I have upheld my end, there's no telling *what* I'll do to rescue my precious sister."

Junia nodded gravely.

"Nor I, for I *swear* to match the passion of your endeavours the moment you fulfil your oath to *me*."

"Then we've an accord." He gestured to the ajar door, a haze of yellow light streaming in. "I best follow you, for I've not the slightest comprehension of Rantilorian regiments, divisions or... *anything* of the like—much less where I fit into all... *that*."

Junia bounced to her feet, yanking Paun by the wrist.

"Of course, right this way, Mr. Truvalson."[1]

---

1. I wonder what Pen Wishton is up to... I can't tap into his perspective, it's too guarded. His daughter's however...

Her father paced, tapping his fingers together; a sign he had grown weary of repeating this to every new member and asset. It was odd... she'd never thought to see him grow so dispassionate about something he so... *passionately* believed in.

"And *then*," he continued, "the seed-like *nudges* of our influence shall *grow* in escalation until the fruits of our labour are met with chaos, *triggering* the trope. Once *that* is done with, we'll have our opening to *kill* the Oather's pawn." Pen stabbed his wand through the flashing graphics displayed across the table screen. "It's simply a bleeding matter of debate over *which* bloody pawn of the *bloody* three it bloody *happens* to be!" He gestured to the features glitching in the table's damaged screen. "The obvious choice would be the young man, but his name could simply be a ruse!"

Ms. Elicy rubbed the side of her neck as she studied the three profiles displayed in the cracked table display.

"But... would the Oather not have already considered that line of thought, thus making it suitable for him to use Traitorson for—"

"Aye, but that line of logic can simply fly out of hand—*no*, we mustn't overthink... not at our own undoing." He leaned heavily against the table edge, drumming his fingers. "*He's too crafty for that...*"

Ms. Elicy shook her head.

"You give the Oather too much credit..."

"No... no, *no*... no..." He chuckled to himself, its unhinged tone troubling Ms. Elicy. "I'm... simply *refusing* to underestimate another enemy is all..." He shot a shaking finger at Ms. Elicy. "Standby ready for the order. Once the war has reached its climax, there's no telling how much time we'll have till the Oather's armour seals itself once more. There can be no hesitation... not again."

Ms. Elicy nodded.

"Yeah... I know..."

"And you," her father added as he turned to address a figure in the shadows, "sow... *chaos* in the name of your Saviour's Lord... the Silence who hath restored thee."

The figure nodded, his green eyes shining in the dark.

"As you... *please,* oh... Master... *mine.*"

INTERLUDE

I KNOW WHAT A good deal of you are thinking; this *war*... it carries no gravity, not of the kind every character seems to be evoking. Perhaps, by now, you have gathered none can die whilst the Code of Preservence is active, nor be so grievously wounded as to be discontinued from the intricate destiny of their lives. Even the development of trauma shall be rendered nonexistent, for there can be no horrifying experience to instill such a broken state of mentality.

I would agree with you, for even the nature of their weapons are changed by the Code's list of symbols: symbols the Code demands be inscribed upon every blade and arrow: white symbols designed to prevent the blade from harming flesh: symbols that renders the effects of their weapon to that of a celestial flintlock—albeit, far weaker, for it needs be in direct contact with skin to inflict its castwork.

But that's getting ahead of myself, for—

I THOUGHT IT WAS AGAINST YOUR PROFESSION'S PRACTICE TO WRITE EVENTS SO... PATRONISINGLY. AS THOUGH YOUR PRECIOUS BEHOLDERS WERE NAUGHT BUT CHILDREN WHAT REQUIRED HAND-HOLDING.

Perhaps if I truly followed the profession you refer to, then... yes.

BUT NO... FOR YOU SEE YOURSELF AS SOME SORT OF SCRIBE. I WONDER... DOES A SCRIBE INFLICT AN INFECTIOUS AMOUNT OF INFLUENCE UPON THE STORY IT DOCUMENTS MERELY TO ATTAIN A BETTER END? YOU'RE NO SCRIBE. YOU'RE A MEDDLER, ONE WHOSE DISEASE HAS SPREAD THROUGHOUT THIS REALITY IN PATHETIC ATTEMPTS TO ALTER SOMETHING BEYOND YOUR MORAL COMPRE-HENSION.

Maybe... maybe I'm both... or... perhaps neither; an Oather, as they call me. Influence? Yes, but what motives simply began as means for developing captivating events has shifted. No longer shall I throw them in harm's way, simply to tear them from it as the tropes wear down their armour. Nay, no longer shall I allow them to be tormented any further by these tropes hosting their nonlethal scars. No... I have sworn to protect them... to the best of my influence, for such is my oath.

I WONDER... IS THIS THE REASON YOU HAVE SHIED AWAY FROM THEIR PERSPECTIVES FOR SO LONG? IN SOME MEAGRE ATTEMPT TO PRESERVE THEIR LIVES FROM WHAT INESCAPABLE FATE AWAITS THEM—

Them? Are you so foolish as to believe the trope will allow you to take more than one?

IT CANNOT RESTRAIN ME FROM BREAKING THE OTHERS.

Perhaps, but I am curious to see just how well you'll handle your impending failure. Though we are both incapable of physical interaction, I can guarantee the pain of your disappointment would be enough to cripple you on my behalf.

UNLIKE YOU, I DO NOT WAGER MY PIECES ON ARROGANCE ALONE, BUT CALCULA-TION. IF AN OBSTACLE HINDERS THE PATH I LAY, THEN IT SHALL BE ELIMINATED, FOR I OWE ALLEGIANCE TO NONE SAVE THE TRANSCENDENCE OF MY OWN EXIS-TENCE. NAY, MY DESTINY'S PATH IS BARE BUT FOR ONE OBSTACLE WHICH SHALL BE SWIFTLY CUT DOWN AND REAPED FOR MY OWN ADVANTAGE.

Oh? And what, o'cryptic silence of my head, might that troublesome obstacle be?

YOU.

CHAPTER TWENTY-FOUR

THE CORAL BATTLEFIELD

A SINGLE VOICE ECHOED across the shores of the drained lake: a ceremonial chant of Unbequith's. It was sung by a young man, standing before the legions of Unbequith and facing the distant enemies across the lakebed. Though his voice was soft, an enhanced horn ferried its tune across the stale breeze.

"Bear... *the* weight of your kindred—resting... on shoulders afflicted—*for* the... glory... of the Lord..." He paused, giving Adela just enough time to catch his features; her ears warmed upon recognising Jhess. His eyes were distant, lingering on the capital before them. "Raise... *thine* spirit... with our souls—*fear* not... o'their blades' foul blows—rise... *oh*... warriors on high." He paused once more, drawing his sword and lowering the horn. "For His children... never... die..."

The evening sky was gloomy... *downcast*, perfectly mirroring their spirits or... maybe that was just Adela; everyone else was silently solemn at best. Though Aivon's words had spurred them on through the night, it was only now—in the heavy reality of it all—that she realised just how terrifying the unknown was; she had no idea on the finer details of the plan and only knew to trust her division's officer, Bo. Sure, both parties coated their blades in harmless aspects of the Code's symbols, but she'd never done anything like this before; she was a primary member of her division as well: all butterflies were. However, if she allowed herself to be knocked out and captured, there was no telling *how* the battle would sway without her there.

That and... she didn't wish to leave it so soon; deep down, she knew just how much fun she would truly have—whether she wanted it or not, such was her nature. Adela understood the true gravity of it all, yeah... but... but she was also excited to finally utilise her skills for something which didn't involve tearing someone's throat out. She appreciated the finer arts of combat and found joy in it. Perhaps it was the Fallen Guild in her, but it was thrilling to—

"*Unbequith!*" Adela shook her head, clearing her mind of its rambling thoughts as she focused on Lieutenant Bo; he rode atop his vasil drake, an elegant muzzle of red fabric and black metal fastened about its jaws. "The fate of your kin and beyond clings to your blade for *survival!* The world strides atop the beating measures of your heart!" He dismounted his vasil drake, handing it off to his page. "The Code of Preservence ensures your life, but it will not ensure our victory! Verily, I say fight!" He drew his sword and shook it about his head. "Fight! As though their blades strike to kill and their arrows to bite! *Fight*, for the lives of your *kin*, your region, and all the *bloody* reaches beyond! Fight, children of Unbequith! *Fight!*" Bo turned to face the shores of the dried lake, descending into its labyrinth of sandy-grey terrain and faded coral. "With holy vigour, vi'gu'þa swí d'rendors lióþ'daros!" An orange ray cut through the dreary heavens, its western light piercing the trenches' haze like a divine path set before them. "*D'rendors lióþ'daros!*"

The legions of Unbequith pounded their weapons against their shields, repeating his words in a thunderous chant as they descended the muddy gravel of the shores and into the lake's bed. Their voices were deep and the lyrics empowering. Adela knew not the words to join in, but was emboldened all the same.

> *In death we smite transgression*
> *Behold the gates o'Heaven*
> *Fear not o'their blades' foul blows*
> *Rise O'warriors yon' high*
> *In death we smite transgression*
> *Before the gates o'Heaven*
> *Fear not o'their blades' foul blows*
> *For all return to the sky*

Adela glanced into the various pits and canyons across the lake bed, only then realising it was *those* they were descending into.

The Miracle Trenches.

The thunderous chant gradually died away to a lull as they descended into the trenches, for they did not wish to so readily unveil their positions to the enemy. Catching onto the lyrics, Adela softly muttered to herself.

"In death, we smite transgression ... 'fore the gates o'Heaven... Fear not o'their blades' foul blows... *March* oh warriors... up high..."

Jhess's soft voice picked up beside her.

"*Hold* to... hearts assailing—*ruin*... we are restraining—descend... oh warriors... yon high..."

"O'warriors... from high..."

They both whispered the next line in unison.

For all... return to... the sky...

Tightening her grip about her quarterstaff, Adela stayed close to her pack, apprehensive as she was eager. Glancing about, she realised the same could be said of the Redfolk; they weren't afraid or anxious, but thrilled and *exhilarated*.

The enemy was at hand.

"*Quiet*," hissed Paun's captain, "cease your *bloody muttering* and *still* your armour." He gestured to the path outside their hidden bunker, holding a finger to his lips. Paun rose on his tippy-toes, trying to peek over the broad pauldrons and muddy helms. He had been told to occupy the rear, behind those with polearms and bows. Unfortunately, he couldn't see any development from where he stood.

If Unbequith had indeed decided to follow their chant with a charge, then the trenches would funnel the enemy's forces right past their bunker; it lay concealed behind the path's corner, perfect for ambushing. Unlike his company, Paun was still and silent, his armour uttering no clink or creak of the slightest; he understood the values of stealth and how best to utilise it. Noticing this, he was on the verge of giving a fellow soldier some advice when—to his surprise—his entire regiment went completely silent; a rhythmic march of metal grew in volume, signalling the approach of Unbequith's forces. Sighing quietly, Paun fidgeted his loaned longsword's tassels; in truth, he didn't expect much action, not from his position. Maybe he'd move up in an hour and clean up some stranglers, but other than that...

Paun's gaze rose to the sky; its muddy-grey clouds were mingled with the fiery bursts of a sunset's final stand. Leaning against the bunker's coral, his hands drummed along his hilt, impatient for *some* form of action to begin. However, to his further surprise, it continued to remain silent. Why, even the Redfolk's marching footsteps had come to an abrupt cease.

Bouncing off the lakebed's wall, Paun stepped forward for his captain, freezing when he thought he heard a metallic rustle from behind their regiment. Before he could turn to confront the sound, a soft *'clink'* echoed from the bunker's window; from around the corner they intended to ambush, a glass orb hosting a white flame bounced into the bunker.

"*Chalk gas!*" cried their captain, urging his men to retreat from the bunker and into the rear path of Paun's company. As his regiment turned to flee the bunker, the vial exploded in a milky-white burst of fog. Nearly half his regiment were caught in its blast, falling limply to the ground.[1] Paun rushed to their aid, grabbing one soldier by his armour straps and dragging him out the bunker. As they retreated from the white gas, a raging uproar of terrifying shouts and clanging steel caused Paun to drop his comrade: whipping around with his drawn blade. He turned in time to see a hoard of Unbequith soldiers charging the corner behind: some rushed forward on foot, several rode vasil drakes on the lakebed's walls and a score or so traversed atop the trenches, shooting down at them with various projectiles; some were enchanted bolts, white streaks raining into the trenches, while others were torpified arrows, slugging through the air with talon-like heads.

Wasting no time for thought, Paun dove behind the nearest cover he could find, wincing as a hail of enchanted bolts pierced the outer layer of his armour. Before he could find a chance to recover, Paun continued hurtling into darkness, falling flat on his face in what must have been a sea cave. Coughing, he lifted his visor, sputtering blood. *Blast it, I bit my tongue didn't I?* Paun shook his head, spitting crimson saliva at his feet.

It was then he noticed the shimmering pool of light before him. He cast a glance back at the opening behind him, taking in the chaos outside, before returning his gaze to the peculiar sight. In the small pool of water—no wider in diameter than Paun was tall—droves of fish had gathered, tightly packed together. They writhed and flopped against one another, each struggling to slip beneath the surface of the water. Mesmerised,

---

1. **Suppressing vials**: also known as chalk gas. Operating similar to the whole symbols coating their blades, this gas is designed to temporarily shut down all five of your senses. If it simply makes contact with your flesh, you're passing out for a couple hours. If you inhale it, you're going to be in a coma for two days.

Paun crept closer, leaning in to peer at the odd spectacle. For a moment, he stood transfixed by the desperate motion of the fish, each determined to survive, fighting to reach the water below at any cost. Then—

Paun recoiled as a pale, serpent-like creature lunged out from the pool.

Blindly slashing his sword and hitting... *something* fleshy, he fell back through the cave entrance and out into the trenches' chaos. His raised his sword, deflecting the incoming blow of a polearm, but couldn't react in time as several more blades stabbed through the arrow-pierced points in his armour and made contact.

Paun felt a light buzz jolt through his entire being as he lost consciousness.

"Carrier!" cried one comrade. "We *need* a *carrier!*" He was—of course—referring to those who retrieved the unconscious from battle to be taken as prisoners of war. Whenever Adela struck an enemy with her stick, they would be hauled off into the wagon behind, ready for transport to an Unbequith holding-camp.

Their Commander's blackhorn blared overhead, signalling for his forces to continue with the assault; Aivon rode atop his dragon, Cádmus, surveying the battlefield from above as though it were a strategic board. Adela remembered catching sight of his saddle before departing, and the scores of dangling horns hooked to its sides. Adela couldn't understand their every tone and meaning, but she didn't have to; such translations were for their company's leader to decipher.

Or in this case, Lieutenant Bo.

"Aye," he cried, waving his shield beside Adela, "aye, more carriers! They're dropping by the dozens!" He gave a hearty laugh as he watched his forces tear through the unsuspecting enemy. "And to think I forsook sleep, dreading my rousing speech." He glanced down to Adela, patting her shoulder with the back of his hand. "What'd you think, eh? Not too short, perhaps too long? One tends to get caught up in the moment of such speeches and—before you would know it—begins spurring nonsense as though it were poetry."

Adela shrugged, leaning against her staff in the short respite she was granted.

"At some point, men don't need'a hear rousing speeches, but *feel* such invigoration from the words." She shrugged again, pausing to sip from her flask. Adela released a heavy sigh and smacked her lips, continuing: "I think once riled up... enough, it doesn't matter *what* you're saying, yeh?" She screwed the lid back on and wiped her lips. "Yeh... so long as they're spurred on."

"Aye... but you still haven't said whether it was *good* or not." He politely raised a finger, turning to address the gloomy fellow on his left. "Where to now, ol' shadow snoop?" Lieutenant Bo slung an arm about Ramsoen's shoulder and glanced into his vidorae. "Why the delay? I need your guidance *immediately*."

"Yes, I know... *I know*..." Ramsoen hunched his shoulders and turned away to conceal the vidorae's images. "I just... I'm simply uncertain whether the events I see are influenced by my fears or..."—he looked up, his face impossible to read beneath his mask—"or something to come..." Tucking the vidorae away, he crossed his arms. "Regardless, it'd be wise to have your men draw back... *now*."

Lieutenant Bo gave him a curious stare, mouth gaping open only to snap shut with a nod.

"If you truly believe so," said Lieutenant Bo, reaching for his division's whistle. He gave a sharp blow, waving for his men to regroup. "That's right, let 'em go lads, and *fallback!* We needs must sort some cryptic details out 'fore we—" The moment his division turned their backs, a small squad of white-clad soldiers charged forward, their spears glinting darkly. "*Belay that* and drive 'em back! We *still*—" Lieutenant Bo was cut off as an enemy soldier unstrapped an orb from his belt—hosting a fiery orange mingled with a cloudy black in its glass—and hurled it at the first line of soldiers. An explosion of heat rocked Adela to the ground, Lieutenant Bo landing atop her. She was on the verge of slipping out from under him, when she noticed his armour and the pieces of glass shrapnel that pierced it from the hurled vial.[2]

"Lieutenant..." she breathed. "Lieutenant, are *you*—" To her horror, he was still conscious, his breath staggering, his chest rising and falling unsteadily and his voice groaning in pain.

Lieutenant Bo coughed, black blood spewing on Adela's face.

Her shout for aid was drowned by the pure chaos ensuing about her; Unbequith men were falling to the ground, bleeding gashes left in vital parts of their body. Adela gasped sharply as she witnessed one Harling plunge his blade into Jhess's side. Yanking her mask

---

2. **Obliterating orbs**: or 'obies.' I don't think I need to explain the combustion, explosion of wild energy, or glass shrapnel. It's basically a grenade. What more needs to be said? Shatter the glass orb and boom.

down, she scrambled out from under Bo, nimbly weaved through combat and bashed Jhess's assailant across the temple with her staff.

She didn't require white symbols to knock the Harling unconscious.

Kneeling to Jhess's side, she seized his wrist as he tried to remove the blade. Shaking her head, she shoved his hands off. In one motion, Adela jerked the blade free and sealed the wound with a green bandage, crying: "Fall *back!*" She took Jhess by the shoulder straps of his armour and began dragging him, shrieking for them to retreat. In contrast to her words, Aivon's blackhorn blared from above. "They've *broken* the Code—*Please*, fall back *now!* Ramsoen, lead us *out*—" She screamed as a soldier in white plunged his polearm through Bo's chestpiece. "*No!* No, no... no, *no!*" Sam was at Adela's side now, his black blade whirling about as he kept the enemy at bay.

"Drop the boy!" he roared, slashing his sword through three men. "Blast it, girl—*drop him!*" Sam shoved her to the side and threw Jhess over his shoulders. "*Fel*, cover our retreat!" In cue to his command, a cloud of grey set over them. Blue flashes boomed from behind as Fel hurled his assortment of potions. With Jhess over both shoulders and an arm tightly about Adela, Sam followed Ramsoen in retreat through the trenches.

Unbequith had lost.

Chapter Twenty-Five

Aftermath

T HE RATTLING OF CHAINS echoed about the darkness as Paun jolted to consciousness; his hazed vision blurred into focus, revealing the black interior of an elongated
carriage. Paun shook his dazed head, realising he was chained to a bench alongside various
Rantilorian and Harling soldiers. The carriage he found himself in had come to an abrupt
halt—waking him and several other prisoners. Blinking in the harsh sunlight, Paun felt
a tug on his chains and realised they were leading him outside. Following the soldier to
his right, Paun hopped from the carriage, his body armourless and his sword lost. He
rubbed his bruised limbs, filing behind his company. Sand slipped between his bare toes
as he neared a wooden podium. When Paun finally stepped up to it, an Unbequith guard
unfastened his restraints and pointed to a grey clearing ahead; it was encircled by a loose
strand of rope and hosted various pavilions with makeshift tables and benches.

"*That's* where you're to stay," instructed the guard. "We've a healer and food waiting
at *that* there table." He paused to scribble in his weathered journal. "Do you bear any
inquiries?"

Paun eyed the flimsy strand of rope trailing about the encampment and gestured to it.

"Yeah, that's... that's not too terribly secure a fortification." Paun quickly glanced over
both shoulders. "And I doubt this'll be enough men to contain us." He turned back to
face the guard, shrugging. "Is there something I'm missing or is this all a trick?"

"Excuse him!" A nearing voice spoke up from the encampment: the Captain of Paun's
regiment. His Captain patted the guard's shoulder as he stepped up to him. "Pardon
this fellow, he's an enlisted hunter he is. Quite unaware of formalities and protocols
as it stands." He snapped his fingers at Paun. "Sorry lad. Code of Preservence dictates
all captured members are to *remain* captives till the disagreement has been decided or
otherwise discontinued. Only then are we to be set free."

"Heaven's name..." muttered the guard. "Doesn't everyone know that?"

Paun ignored the comment, addressing his Captain instead.

"Aye, but—*or*—what if I merely..." Paun glanced over his shoulders again. "Yeh, I could escape this *quite* easily."

"You'll do no such thing, *hunter*." His Captain stepped forward, roughly seizing Paun by the arm. "Doing so would only trigger an escalation and if *that* were to happen, more lives would be lost to an unnecessary end at the guilt of your own heedless arrogance." The Captain released him with a shove, turning to leave without another word.

Paun watched him go, an eyebrow raised.

"I suppose that answers that then."

"I suppose so, sir," answered the guard, completely unbothered as he eyed his journal. "I'll have your name then and we'll move along. You're accumulating an unhealthy tail behind you."

Paun glanced over his shoulder to the long line of hungry soldiers, impatient to enter the holding camp.

"Right, sorry, it's... ehm..." Paun tapped the guard's journal. "Valvaytora Bubty, but you can write that as *Val* if it's easier."

"As you say, sir." The guard gestured to the encampment again. "To the white table then. Move along, I've plenty more to catch up with."

"Right.... Sorry." Paun clasped his hands together and bowed before making his way to a long table, its top painted a fading white. There were several Redfolk assorted behind the table, distributing mess plates. As he approached, a woman wearing a simple tunic of Unbequith colours stepped up to meet him.

"Have ye any ailments?" she asked. Her palms pulsed a light green from beneath her skin, highlighting her veins. "Scrapes, bruises, broken bones... anything?"

Paun rubbed his ribs, frowning as his hands shifted to his lower back.

"Aye, think I..." He paused, dumbstruck by the grey kitten sitting at the edge of the camp. "Well... n-no I... I think I'm quite alright, but... but thank you... though."

"And what of nourishment? Are you well—"

"Aye, that I am." Paun waved as he turned to leave. "You best tend to the men who require such treatment now, yeh?" Picking up the pace, he curtly passed out of hearing distance, muttering to himself: "*yeh...?*" He shook his head, discreetly slipping behind a series of red tents lined against a grass knoll. Smiling, Paun knelt to scratch Jovem behind the ears. "Whatever are you doing here, little one? Come to haunt me, have you?"

"*Fila oru loo-loo ohun woo,*" chirped the kitten, his deep vocals resonating in Paun's head. Before he could respond, Jovem turned to leave. Unsure of the impulse he felt, Paun shot a couple of glances over his shoulder before ducking under the line to follow after the odd kitten. Limiting his form to the shadows, Paun did his best to restrain himself from peeking over the tents; he could clearly hear a mingled assortment of soldiers on the other side: striding about the crunching sand, chatting in discordant groups, and groaning in what sounded like sorrow... or pain... it was difficult to say.

Paun came to an abrupt halt, nearly tripping over Jovem, who sat facing him. Raising an eyebrow, Paun opened his mouth only to snap it shut as Jovem turned, squirming under the flaps of a black canopy outlined in red. Paun dropped to his knees, freezing; he heard a deep and noble voice speak from the tent's interior. Timing his advances with the crunching pace of soldiers, Paun crawled closer to listen.

"*No*, how *could* they? All representatives, including *ours*, agreed that *any* means capable of mass destruction would violate the Code—and they *bloody* classified our True Beyonders under such terms!" Paun thought he recognized the voice as Aivon's. "Unbequith fought for its *life* with a hand tied behind! Still, our men *alone* could have very well taken them if... if only..." A mournful sigh released the fiery temper of Aivon's tone. "They stood no chance, m'Lord. The white symbols restrained my men from defending themselves against the untethered bite of steel. Why, they might as well have been *unarmed!*"

Another voice spoke up: calm, collected and commanding.

"And you... you witnessed this atrocity of war with your own eyes?"

"No, my Lord," replied Aivon, "not with mine eyes... but in the *dead* eyes of my men... my Lieutenant... my bloody *kin*," he growled. "They have been robbed of their families by the glorified stroke of a blade and left to watch our pitiful failure from above." Paun heard the sound of furniture being struck. "Their *crimes... cannot* go unanswered."

There was a brief lull of silence before Lord Monbel responded.

"I hear your affliction," he whispered, his voice taking a disturbing yet comforting tone. "But... beyond that, I hear the suffering of my people... and beyond. If this is but a sliver of what they intend... should they triumph... then I do not believe it is possible, nor moral, for the Code of Preservence to be upheld any longer by our forces."

Paun paled upon hearing this. With little time to spare, he turned and scrambled back for his holding encampment; they *had* to escape while they could; the Redfolk guards were few in count, the prisoner's restraints null and their lives still intact.

Aye, they had to move *now*.

Aivon recoiled at what his Lord had suggested. He knew very well such actions would be suggested and indeed called for, but the sudden shock of its gravity still bore a great weight upon his heart.

"My Lord," he began, pressing a hand to his chest, "my Lord... initiating a Desperate Quarter would tax a heavy toll on *both* sides—it... it's never been done since the Witch Wars—and King Wraithe long before then!"

Lord Monbel's watery reflection nodded remorsefully.

"Indeed... it was demanded of them then... and it is demanded of us now..." Pausing, he crossed his arms and stared out a window beyond view. "Verily, I ask you this, O'Commander... has the enemy not inflicted a toll on our forces? Have we not already suffered at the disadvantage of a regional crime? How much longer shall we permit they slaughter our own people 'fore we stand our ground as children of the Eternal King? They have forsaken their morality for the fleeting satisfaction of *greed* at the cost of our mens' lives. A great toll shall be taxed whether we wish it or not. However, on whose side lies the toll, lies in this opportunity to enact the necessary. It is us... or *them*, Commander." He shook his head. "I am... truly regretful it has come to this... but surely you see the infallible reason for initiating such a sacrifice?"

"I... I can..." answered Aivon after some careful consideration. "But, what of Ranitorl? From all listed reports, it was elite *Harling* soldiers who violated the Code's laws of engagement. If we enact a Desperate Quarter, then Ranitorl shall match their allies as *one*. We'd be forced to kill their men as well, men *undeserving* of a Desperate Quarter's consequence. I'm... I do not believe myself capable of committing such an *unjust* atrocity at the price of our conscience."

"Ah... yes." Lord Monbel sighed, his features downcast. "I had wished to inform you sooner, Aivon... but I did not wish to enrage your delegations with a rather... troubling detail. Might have very well soiled what chance of peace we had." He inhaled deeply, tutting to himself. "I see now that such is simply beyond hope."

"My Lord..." breathed Aivon, colour draining from his features, "my Lord, what do you mean to imply?"

"Our spies," began Monbel, "tell of a man who lays cowering in his saferoom behind fortified walls of enhancement and stone—all whilst his loyal men charge forth to perish at his own command... and only so he might retain the abuse of power he clings to in the safety of his fortress. He doesn't *care* about our region, regions beyond, or even his own *men*. He's corrupted, spineless, and the only *visible* incentive on his *bleak* horizon is seizing a sickening portion of *power* that he might acquire *more*." Monbel's fists tightened with a crack. "That... *man* is none other than Emelio Ortunato, Son of Amelio and third Lord of Ranitorl. He knew *very* well the Code was to be violated by Harldïof, yet stood by at his own treacherous *will*. He might as well have been the one to drive *that* glaive through Bo's heart, for he did *nothing* to warn us or honour the Code." Monbel's eyes softened. "I know how... difficult this truth must be to accept, but a man such as this has been known to stand by idly as his own kin are *slaughtered*."

Aivon was silent for a few moments before he responded.

"This... this cannot be..." He pinched the ridge of his nose, rubbing it. "No... this... this cannot..." He sighed heavily to himself. "Are you... *certain*... these reports are true? I've encountered the man myself... truly, it couldn't have all been a facade? If so... then I truly am blind to the discernment of man's character..." He raised his burdened gaze to Lord Monbel, his stern eyes impressing on his Lord. "Without an *inkling*... of doubt, you *know* this to be true?"

"Upon my unquestionable word as your Lord, may I be struck down should it *not* be so."

"Should it not be so..." muttered Aivon. "if we wane... *completely* fail... then Unbequith and beyond shall be doomed to the power-lusting corruption of these craven leaders." Aivon fell against the seeing table's edge, shaking his head. "Nay, I shall seek to offer an opportunity of deliverance from their impending judgement." He wrung his jaw, dark circles forming beneath his eyes. "*However...* if they do not accept... a heavy toll shall be exacted at *their* expense."

"Tis the sacrifice of our conscience that we must partake, my brother." Lord Monbel paused, glancing worriedly to his left. "I must depart... the forces of Harldïof stand before the door of our mountain." His gaze briefly returned to Aivon. "Have you any report of Traitorson? I'd hate for Ms. Windcatcher to... *shift*... her alignment over any... clouded sentiment."

"As of now... no. Still, I shall check the list of captives, my Lord. However, I doubt a rogue such as he would tarry in a war not his own."

"We *can't* stay here," growled Paun, seizing his Captain by the collar. "Whether you disagree with *how* I acquired the truth matters not, for the truth *it still is*." Paun shoved him to the ground, attracting the attention of the other soldiers and several Unbequith guards.

"Oy then, what's all this?" asked a guard, his armour hosting more red than the others. "I can't have you scrapping with your superior, son."

Paun raised his hands submissively.

"He ain't my superior," he clarified, a friendly smile masking his features. "And you'll not be the death of us." Curling his hand into a fist, he struck the guard under the jaw, knocking him unconscious. Two soldiers seized Paun by the shoulders while another raised a whistle to his lips. Paun lurched forward in their grips, yanked the whistle, and struck his elbow into the nearest guard before pounding his fist into the face of the other. Unfortunately, several other guards had closed in and seized Paun from behind. The backside of his knees were kicked in, forcing Paun to the ground. "They mean to *kill* us!" cried Paun to his fellow men. "If we don't leave *now*, we'll never have another *chance* to—"

His Captain leapt onto the back of Paun's assailant, jerking the guard to the ground in a chokehold. The other men responded to their officer's actions by leaping onto the soldiers holding Paun. Though violently engaged, Paun's regiment had restrained their voices to nothing more than dull grunts and silent counters. Aye, with their raw numbers and sheer surprise, they managed to overpower the Unbequith guards in *seconds*.

Accepting his captain's hand, Paun was pulled to his feet.

"By all things sacred," said his officer, "you best be speaking the truth, son—and *nothing but*." He sniffed, wiping his nose as he gestured to the Unbequith guards strewn about the ground. "We've half'n hour 'fore their rotations begin searching for us or *they* alert someone." His Captain gestured to the group of Redfolk citizens running deeper into the camp. "Leave them be. They've treated us just and I'll not have us punishing that kindness."

Paun nodded.

"Right, well... if we commandeer one of those carriages, I think we stand a chance in—" He cut himself off upon noticing the grey kitten sitting in the distance. "Actually... *no*... follow me. We'll cut through the trenches on foot."

Without waiting to see if they followed, Paun turned to chase after the kitten, descending the gravelly shores and sliding into the trenches. Other than the crunching sand of his regiment's bare steps, it remained eerily quiet. Not a single sound was to be heard...

Someone touched his back.

Nearly startling, he glanced over his shoulder to his captain.

"Oy, lad," began he, tapping Paun, "you know your way 'bout these parts? Like a bleedin' *labyrinth* it is..." He shuddered, much to Paun's amusement. "And a tomb me should think."

"Awh... don't you trouble about it," assured Paun. "I've a keen sense o'direction, you see—one you should trust as much as I do." He smiled darkly to himself as he followed after the grey kitten in the foggy distance. "I *is* a hunter after all, am I not?"

"Quite true... yes. I was only unsure... *am* unsure is all, merely because I happen to be a born and raised Rantilorian of our capital. Nonetheless, even *I* am unfamiliar to the complete designs of Hareesh's..." The captain's voice died away as Paun knelt to the ground. "Oy, what've—" He and the other men finally noticed. "Bloody *heavens* alive..."

Various pieces of the coral-lined trenches were smeared with splotches of *red*. Though there were no bodies in sight, whoever did this was sloppy enough to leave traces of gore stained into the brittle sediment and faded reef. Paun pinched some of the red sand, rubbing it between his fingers.

"Does the Code of Preservence permit the use of... *anything* capable of this... Captain?"

"Oh, of *course* not." His Captain sneered in disgust as he knelt beside Paun. "No doubt it was those Unbequith savages... couldn't match our men without breaking the Code methinks. Nay, me *knows*."

"Mm." Paun rose, eyeing a nearby cave in the trench walls. "Are you certain it couldn't have been a creature of some kind? A native to these lake's depths perhaps?"

"N-no, that's *absurd*. All aquatic lifeforms are filtered through tunnels and into the black ocean, Below. None could emerge and wander about with the lake so low." He spat and crossed his arms. "Nay, this is Redfolk handiwork no doubt. I'd cast lots they couldn't contain their brutality any longer than they had."

"Well... if that's so... then it seems I owe you my gratitude." Paun offered his Captain a handshake. "Without your actions, we might have all been lost to the vault... or death."

"In truth," began his captain, "it was a reaction of panic over reason... really. Still hosted doubt for my own reasons, but it was far too late for turning back." He winced as his boot stepped over the bloody patch of sand. "It's only now that I'm grateful for giving into such primitive fears... and that you had given into your more roguish nature."

Paun shrugged before continuing after Jovem.

"Tis what I do best, Captain."

Chapter Twenty-Six

For Country & Beyond

C ÁDMUS' SNOWY-WHITE GIRTH HUGGED the black circumference of Aivon's tent. One droopy yellow eye peered through its entrance, watching them in what Aivon claimed was a doze. The dragon's breathing was slow... and steady, its girth pushing against the backside of the tent in small, heaving impressions. Adela liked leaning against the tent. She could feel the overlapping scales of Cádmus beneath the fabric, warming her back. It made the dismal meeting feel a little more cosy; before, it felt as though the fading sun's cold had been attracted to the darker chill of the tent's mood.

Adela sighed, straining her eyes as she blinked; she had unintentionally zoned out and—even now—could only hear Aivon as though from a distance.

"Weapons of mass destruction may no longer be restrained by the Code, but I still refuse to partake in the more barbaric forms of combat, such as undying fire, barbed heads, mind-breaking muritos, et cetera." Aivon tapped the charts of the Miracle Trenches. "Though this advantage remains unveiled, we still maintain the advantage of *insight*. Our losses are never fruitless, nor in vain, for there is always something to gain from them in terms of *insight*. Indeed, I have very well utilised our first skirmish to study their stratagems and familiarise myself with their techniques. *This*—combined with our superior artistry of war—is advantageous enough to know, with careful calculation, that Unbequith *shall* triumph in the grand scheme of it all." He stabbed a dagger through the charts, piercing an illustration of the capital's keep. "The prism shards... *that* is our primary focus of objective. Everything else has merely been devolved into a farce of motive." Aivon leaned against the table, tapping its sides. "Darun," he said, "you're knowledgeable in the arts of muritos... could you tear open reality between us and the shards?"

"I cannot," answered Darun, his hands clasped gravely. He stood woodenly beside Adela; she had taken her place beside him because of how warm he looked; sometimes, it was as though a simmering heat could be seen rising from his ashen armour. "The shards," he continued, "are hidden beyond our reach of influence. Their capital lies beneath a dung heap of enchantments, fashioned to ward off the influence of Nowood beings and, as it would seem, True Beyonders. If it were any simpler, we would have tried it already."

"So *none* of you True Beyonders have *any* means of securing them directly? Teleportation, bending reality, shadow gates—*nothing*."

"I am a master of Reexah."

"Yes, but the other masters merely share the same incompetent excuse."

"Commander..." began Darun, his gaze unwavering, "muritos is a *bottomless* pit of *powerful* knowledge. One would have to reach this pit's bottom to accomplish what you demand."

"Oh? And just how far deep are you in this... pit?"

"As far as my age has allowed."

"Which isn't helpful to say the least..."

"Not for such a task, no..."

Aivon sighed.

"If every True Beyonder focused on breaching the vault, do you think it manageable to—"

Ramsoen shook his head, stepping into the table's light.

"I doubt they'd be able to focus on undoing the vault's magic with twenty-five thousand soldiers of various enchantments and skill striking to kill, not without taxing a serious toll on either party." Ramsoen's mask glistened as his gaze settled on the charts. "Beyond that, they've two guardians dedicated to protecting the shards from securement—men who could very well pass for deities."

"So be it," said Aivon, "we'll have to soften its defences then. I'll have the larger scope of our forces divert hostile attention to the frontlines, where we shall *try* to take the capital. Simultaneously, if all True Beyonders focused on the shards' vault, I'm sure we—" Aivon stumbled forward as the entire tent constricted; Cádmus was deeply inhaling, drawing the contents of the tent—furniture, armaments and friends—closer together in a *more-than-awkward* proximity. Thankfully, his girth gradually resided and the brisk cold sharply returned to the tent's interior. Clearing his throat, Aivon continued: "We could weaken its symbols *and* guardians just enough for a precision force to sneak in and escort the shards to our camp or Unbequith itself should the need serve." Aivon leaned against the table once more, rubbing his beard. "Though each of these plans hold their own achievable goals, we shall not depend on one strategy alone... should one strategy fail, it should prove a useful ruse for another. With that said—"

"*If* I may ask," interjected Adela, finding her balance after Cádmus *yawned* her off, "do you mean to imply that this precision force is to be us butterflies?"

"Yes... but... *no*, not you Adela, dear." His eyebrows pinched together as his gaze rose to her. "You... you are excused from all further conflicts of Unbequith, for I believe it has taken a turn from the services you were promised. No... you were never supposed to witness the horrors you did... and for that... I apologise dearly." Shaking his head, Aivon exhaled deeply. "If you wish, you may remain here *or* receive an underground escort to the nearest establishment of your choice."

Grinding her jaws, she really *did* try to consider the two choices, but failed to think of anything other than the pained cries of Lieutenant Bo. Her mind clouded with his voice... his death. No, Adela... she—

"I... I *can't*," she finally said. "What happened... what horrors occurred... I cannot allow this to spread any further by those who would wield the shards." Adela shook her head, squeezing her eyes shut. "I... I'd rather die in an attempt to dissuade such an outcome... if you'll allow me." Her eyelids slowly fluttered open. "I don't know whether I'll ever have the... whether I'd be able to... to take a life, but... but I'll do my best where I can."

Before Aivon could speak, Sam spoke up.

"Aye, sir!" he said, gripping Adela by the shoulders and giving her a little shake. "And we'll have her as our leader, if you'll allow it!" Sam gestured to the other two butterflies. "We all agree she understands the intricacies of operating as a pack better than either of us and... and we *all* believe she's earned it far more than either of us could." He rolled his eyes with a huff. "Well... save for ol' snoopy sneak of course, but he always wants to be leader."

"Perhaps..." mumbled Ramsoen, crossing his arms.

Adela lightly chuckled, her smile hurting her heart.

"Thanks lads, but... I do think Sam has the heart of a true leader... really."

"Nonsense!" bellowed Sam. "You've more skill than either of us in pack-leading!" He patted her shoulders. "I hope you see the potential in her that I do, Commander."

Aivon was silent for a few moments before gradually nodding.

"Only if *she* herself believes she is qualified for such a position... Adela?"

Adela bobbed her head to the side before answering.

"I... I can do it... yeh." She straightened, doing her best to conceal her wobbly legs. "Just... tell me what you need, Commander, and I'll do more than my best to get it done, yeh?"

"Aye, I needn't remind you of the oath I swore unto you. By all things sacred, you shan't be forced to take a life. Perhaps there's still hope none shall be pushed to such a need. A sliver it may be, but one should never lose hope... or be caught unprepared." He gestured to Fel. "I'll need you and your choice of casters to have that mirror-veil perfected by *tonight*."

Fel nodded.

"Yah... aye, it should... *aye*, hold methinks. Though a strong advance is sure to upset it something mighty! We'll need to advance under the guise of night and some other spells 'fore we blanket our forces with the... eh, *thing*. Attack whilst the enemy still feigns the Code, catch 'em unawares... *aye?*"

"Aye, Fel..." Aivon directed two fingers at Ramsoen. "I needn't remind you of our meeting after this. You've some scouting to report, yes?"

Ramsoen tilted his head.

"I'd rather you addressed it the moment I arrived, but perhaps your delay of the inevitable truth was wise enough, for... I don't believe you'd be able to host such leadership under the disturbing burden of knowledge I mean to show you."

Aivon's eyes narrowed.

"All in due time, Ramsoen... as all things are." Reaching across the table, Aivon unrolled a large sheet of parchment, one Adela hadn't seen before. "Should an allegiance shift against Unbequith, Hareesh was sure to implant an exploitable weakness in their greatest weapon, the Miracle Trenches." He traced his finger across the lake on the map. "For, all that water needs must drain *somewhere*. Look here." Aivon circled the intricate grey ink of the Miracle Trenches. "Though there're natural ravines across the lakebed, they're not enough to filter out such vast proportions of liquid." He tapped a spot on the map where the trenches met the south-eastern side of the keep. "*This* is their greatest vulnerability. A great aqueduct or... *syphon* running directly beneath their city." Aivon traced the odd red lines spiralling throughout the capital's layout. "They've maintenance ports built to access the interior of its design. Hareesh was intentional to have some lead directly into the various caster chambers *within* the keep. Their locations are of utmost secrecy, for not even the Lord's hand knows of them." Aivon tapped the side of his nose. "Thank Hareesh for his blessed existence, aye?"

"A true patriot of Unbequith to be sure," said Sam, touching his heart then forehead in respect.

"Aye," nodded Aivon, rolling up the chart. "And thank the Almighty for men of loyalty as Hareesh, he who demonstrates such faith to his region." Aivon shook his head, a heavy exhale escaping him. "I shall try to reason peace... indeed, I shall offer them a chance to lay aside their arms and spare the impending consequence of their corruption. Aye... I shall try." Aivon's gauntlets uttered a soft screech as they tightened. "But verily I say unto you... by all things sacred... be prepared to strike without *mercy*, should they choose to continue punishing the innocent with their greed-ridden *pride*."

"I highly doubt they know anything else..." grumbled Ramsoen. His mask rose as they gazed in his direction. He shook his head. "If any of you suggest anything to the contrary, I shall promptly reduce this *elite* force to but *one* member." Ramsoen lifted his mask ever so slightly and spat. For a moment, Adela caught a raven-black, stubbled jaw. "I speak not of a biased heart, for in my scoutings of the trenches, I have..." He glanced at Adela, his voice dying away. "I... I'm... sorry," he finally said, "but I do not believe it right to share such information in such... *company* as this."

"Of course..." Aivon eyed him darkly before shifting to a lighter mood. "Oh, and thank you, Ramsoen." He clasped his hands together. "You've *just* reminded me of Hell's But- terflies' current dilemma." Aivon gestured to Adela with two fingers. "If Ms. Windcatcher here is to fill the gap left by mine cousin, then that would consequently leave a gap *she* once occupied, yes? The butterflies cannot be but five members—why, the traditional techniques of old require there be *six*."

Sam stood up, a hand across his chest.

"I know of several men who would readily lay aside their lives for such a position."

"I am honoured, Mr. Reedson, but I've already taken the liberty of advocating *Regend* for the job." Aivon nodded at Adela, his grave features contrasting starkly with his twin- kling eyes. "I don't suppose you'd mind if your esardrocan joins your butterflies?"

A soft smile peeked through Adela's sombre expression.

"It would be our honour, Aivonfel."

"And you vouch for this young man, Captain Aethur?"

Paun's Captain glanced in his direction.

"Aye," he answered, turning to face the group of officials gathered about the table. "Aye, for I've witnessed evidence of Code violations with mine own eyes and though,"—he inhaled tightly—"though we *cannot* confirm by which hand the evidence was dealt, I would not think it wise to forgo an assumption of the enemy and to so blindly allow another... *incident* to repeat itself."

"Perhaps," said Henagan, "but we shall be the judge of that." He sat on Lord Ortunato's left, his hand leaning against his temple in a rather dejected manner. It surprised Paun that the steward was even listening. Henagan nonchalantly glanced in Paun's direction before continuing: "If what you believe is true, then I'm afraid our enemies have seen fit to utilise the advantage of breaking Code *first*." He gave Lord Ortunato a sidelong glance. "However... we must not speculate such findings to be the worst, for doing so could prompt the escalation we all seek to avoid."

Emelio's secret councilman and elderly informant, Stalherd, spoke up.

"But, Lord Henagan," he said, "surely you cannot have us stand by idle whilst our enemy moves against us with such hostility." Stalherd weakly pummelled his pale fist against the table and gestured to the blood-soaked setting displayed in the surrounding foresight windows. "Why tolerate such monsters with the benefit of doubt?"

"*Because*," said Lord Ortunato, his tone chastising, "if we *don't*, then we charge into slaughter on the *whim* of a suspicion." He stabbed a finger at Paun. "What *he* heard could very well be some sort of misunderstanding."

Stalherd rolled his sagging eyes.

"How much longer will you continue to defend our enemy until—"

"Until the *bloody end*," growled Emelio. "For the sake of our own people and *beyond itself*, I shall assume only the best of our hostile kin until permitted no further choice." He glanced at Henagan. "Only then, shall we act."

Captain Aethur bowed.

"Of course, my Lord. Such is... honourable." He narrowed his eyes on the councilman, Stalherd. "It is not our place to speak *against* your wisdom, but rather... to voice our own."

"I'm grateful you see it as such, Captain." Emelio waved two fingers at him. "You're excused."

"Thank you, m'Lord." Paun caught his captain's concealed scowl as he turned to leave. "Paun."

"*Aye*,"—Paun whirled about to face the Lord of Ranitorl—"sir."

"I dare not free you of my own eyesight for another minute, not after the roguish mischief you always seem to conjure." Emelio gestured to the empty seat on his right. "Please, sit... whilst I finish business here."

Paun assessed the elite soldiers gathered about the room; there were several in elegant, yet simple, armour: white like a furious snowstorm, threatening to envelope all in its cold embrace. Mingled among them were a score of soldiers in green, brown and grey: like a misty forest demanding respect for what its ancient and knowing girth has weathered... there was certainly some magic about them.

Paun sighed, seeing only unnecessary conflict should he attempt anything brash.

"Aye... sir."

"Oh... don't sound so despondent," said Emelio as he welcomed Paun beside him. "After we've concluded here, I shall be sure to escort you straight to your friends."

"They're *not*..." Paun bit his lip in careful reconsideration. "Aye, thank you, sir."

"Of course." Emelio gestured to the encircling foresight windows. "Now, I do believe Mr. Henagan wished to present a matter of immediate concern."

CHAPTER TWENTY-SEVEN

DEFILE

A N ICY BREEZE ROLLED up the trench's ledge, its rain splashing across Aivon's face. He had forgone his primary armour for that of a scout's garments supplied by Ramsoen. Rubbing his eyes, Aivon peered through the spyglass and into the scene below; a group of soldiers—caked in the grey camouflage of mud—were gathered about the entrance of a yawning hollow, the walls of Aeraos stretching high above it. Aivon recognized the syphon's entrance, but what were those soldiers—

Aivon paled, his stomach churning, threatening to expel the contents within; the soldiers were entering the syphon, dragging Unbequith *corpses*. Others were stripping the dead bodies of their armour and weapons, loading the valued gear into a cart.

It was enough to overcome Aivon's disgust and fill him with a vengeful thirst, one which could only be quenched by the edge of his blade. He reached for his sword's hilt, freezing in enraged fury as Ramsoen seized his shoulder.

"Not *yet*," he whispered, restraining Aivon from pushing forward. "There're *far* too many for the two of us alone. Bide time and contain your vengeance... for now. We shall strike so swift, not even the sentries above would hear a commotion."

"How *long?*" growled Aivon, now wishing he had brought Cádmus, commotion or no. "How... *long*."

"Bout half'n hour till the next rotation..."

"*No*, how long has *this* been transpiring?"

Sighing, Ramsoen shrugged.

"From what I could tell, since the first skirmish concluded. The Code-Breakers have been scouring the battlefield like carrion birds, concealing the evidence of their sins in the dark."

"Mm..." Aivon shoved Ramsoen aside and drew his greatsword from his back. "The consequence of their deeds shall be laid bare by the light of we who dare purge it." Grimly launching himself over the cliff, he landed with a thud atop the gravelly sand. He rose silently as the soldiers turned in his direction. Without waiting for them to gather themselves, Aivon seized the nearest soldier by the gorget, tore off his helm and mercilessly bashed the soldier's features into a boulder. The soldier beside him scrambled to draw his weapon, but couldn't draw it faster than Aivon's blade swinging for his neck. In the same swing, Aivon heaved his greatsword against one who managed to draw his smallsword. The soldier's blade was raised defensively, but it did nothing to stop Aivon's sword from beating through its meagre guard and the man's neck. Aivon caught the soldier's heralding scarf as he fell, using its muddied white fabric to wipe his sword clean of the crimson drops burdening it.

One supposed officer pointed at Aivon as he shouted to his men.

"They've a scout! *Kill* him or all shall be undone *by*—"

A sharp whistle pierced the air and a streak of black shot through the officer's throat, an arrow thudding against the wheelbarrow of corpses behind him. Gripping his throat, the officer stumbled to his knees before collapsing against the lakebed in a fresh pool of blood. Nodding his thanks to Ramsoen on the cliffs behind, Aivon continued forward.

The other soldiers had managed to draw their weapons by then, but it mattered not, for they lacked order. Aivon welcomed their advances as they surrounded him, jabbing their polearms from a distance. Some managed to strike him, but 'twas only a light prick from such a distance. The other weapons were rendered useless as Aivon whirled his sword about his head, its enchanted blade crippling their metalwork. He then pounced at the soldiers, his blade spinning over his shoulders through metal and man as though it weighed not but a feather.

All the while, Aivon remained silent, not uttering the slightest of sounds as he slashed, stabbed and overwhelmed their numbers. Those remaining were quite disorganised at this point, their formation upset by Aivon's ferocity and Ramsoen's arrows.

Seizing a soldier's glaive, Aivon yanked its shaft, impaling its wielder onto his sword. Aivon's cold glare burned into the lifeless eyes of a female soldier. For a moment, his heart faltered... his reality slowing to a blurred halt as the true horror of his actions dawned on him.

But only for a moment.

Ripping the female soldier from his sword, Aivon raised her corpse with one hand, deflecting an incoming slash with her impaled armour. Catching another enemy's thrust with the female soldier, Aivon hurled her corpse to the side, carrying his attacker's blades with it. Their stomachs ever so vulnerable, Aivon slashed his greatsword through the two men, cleaving them in half.

With the enemy separated and their numbers dwindling, Aivon seized one disarmed soldier by the gorget, roaring: "*In whose name do you act?!*" The soldier's shaking jaw clamped shut, his eyes wide with fear. Catching movement in them, Aivon slashed his sword behind his shoulders. Its blade smote through sword, armour and flesh alike, cleaving an enemy's helm. Raising his red-stained blade, Aivon growled: "Answer or *perish.*"

The soldier remained silent.

Snarling in disgust, Aivon kicked him to the ground and, with a decisive slash, relieved the soldier of his sorry existence. There were but three remaining now, one of them fleeing. Aivon left the other two for Ramsoen and pursued the last coward. With a scout's garments, it was no feat to catch up with the fleeing soldier.

"*Wait!* Wait, wait, wait!" The soldier suddenly fell to the ground, holding an arm up to Aivon. "Please, spare me! *Spare* me!" The soldier gulped, his skin pale, his eyes drawn taunt and his skin sweating profusely. "It's *Henagan* you truly want! That's the authority we operate under, the authority you seek—*please*," he pleaded, gasping under the weight of Aivon's boot, "*please*, spare me. You have what you want!"

Aivon lowered his sword, its blade thumping against the man's breastplate with a ringing quake. The man flinched as its point scratched against his armour.

"And I thank you for it," said Aivon, his other hand rising to rest atop his pommel. "But I never agreed to sparing *you*." Aivon heaved against his crossguards, plunging his sword through the man's chest. "*Never* for cowards like you."

The entire room sat in silence as they watched Aivon stride beyond their view.

"I... believe that's enough," said Emelio, shifting the foresight windows to a bright forest. The tension in the room released in heavy sighs as the room's tone shifted. Emelio shook his head. "You... you knew... this would happen?"

"No..." Henagan knitted his fingers, gazing into the honey-like light of the forest. "In truth, I merely thought to demonstrate the outskirts of your syphon's vulnerability..." He gave Paun a curious glance. "I suppose the concern of Code-Breakers isn't a mere concern any longer, for it is beyond such innocent assumptions. Not while the Unit Commander of Unbequith rides out in black to quench his thirst for blood."

"You see now!" cried Stalherd, rising vehemently from his seat. "We *must* move our numbers against them! While they expect us to uphold the Code, we could descend upon their camp tonight! Catch them unawares *and—*"

Henagan shook his head.

"One can only escape the Code's binding law if a Desperate Quarter is initiated on substantial grounds and publicly declared—to one's people *and* enemy. Either *way*, the decision does not *reside* with you." Henagan gestured to Emelio and himself. "Those who represent the powers of their respective region will decide whether we strike while we can, bide our time or even *bloody* surrender if we deem it so."

"And what *do* you decide?" asked Paun, gazing from Emelio to Henagan. "A man was butchered before your own eyes. Do you retaliate and slaughter in return or standby idle and watch your own be slaughtered?" He shrugged. "Which slaughter shall we be having hm, gents?"

"A glorified stand on the battlefield for me," remarked Henagan grimly, "thank you."

"Of course. And what of you, sir?" Paun gestured to Emelio. "What sort of slaughter would you prefer?"

Lord Ortunato was silent, eyeing the entire room from behind clasped fingers.

Aivon lumbered to Ramsoen, finding him knelt before the syphon's yawning maw; it was like the jaws of some creature, the edges of its entrance riddled with jagged and broken metalwork. It was as though a giant from fantasies of old had smashed in its grate, laying bare the darkness within. Aivon shook his head upon sight of his fallen kin strewn about the entrance in sloppy piles; they weren't even granted the privilege of wearing away with their armour.

"We *shall* return here," said Aivon, kneeling respectfully. "We'll grant them a proper burial, the likes of which they deserve."

"And what of *they?*" asked Ramsoen, not stirring from his position in the slightest.

Aivon glanced over his shoulders to his enemies' corpses. He spat before eyeing the dull flash of light in the grey heavens above followed by a rolling thunder.

"Leave them for the *birds*," he growled. "When tomorrow comes, it matters not who finds what and accuses who... they'll all surrender or *die*."

"You still offer the choice of surrender," noted Ramsoen, gradually rising to his feet. "I did not think you were so kind to monsters."

"I'm not," said Aivon, reminscing of the man who pleaded for his life. That had been different. Aivon had found him in the act. Aivon *knew* he didn't deserve to live. However, the thousands of other Harling and Rantalorian souls... Aivon couldn't discern where their alliegeince lied or if they even knew of this treachory. "All forms of life deserve a choice... for such is the code of my conscience." Aivon scowled. "Those slain here made their choice."

Aivon's gaze shot up to confront the darkness, his greatsword drawn as a sharp chuckle reverberated from the syphon's depths. It was a ghostly echo, berating them with the humour it found in their dark state. Aivon shuddered at its sound. "A spirit perhaps," he said, slowly sheathing his sword. "No doubt attracted to such a place by the dark deeds committed here." He spat into the darkness and turned to leave.

"A demon more like," said Ramsoen, about to follow when Aivon heard him freeze. "Commander... you... you should see this."

Aivon felt a burst of dread seize his heart, but he turned nonetheless. Despite bracing his heart, the sight bore more weight than he was prepared for. The strength slipped from his limbs and Aivon fell to his knees upon sight of the corpse Ramsoen discovered. Aivon clutched his chest and set a hand on the familiar breastplate of his loyal cousin.

His Lieutenant.

If Ranitorl wished to avoid the devastation they were in due for, they would be wise to surrender the shards before Aivon offered *any* bleeding opportunity.

The Harlings, however, were another matter *entirely*.

CHAPTER TWENTY-EIGHT

BLACKHORN

M ALVOLIA BOUND THE MAN'S leg with a veneer bind, cinching it tight with all her strength. Oh, she knew it hurt all right, but such pressure was required for the bind to operate properly and begin its healing process. Malvolia glanced over her shoulder to Junia, watching her tend the other wounded with veneer stitches. Malvolia had excused herself from such a task, insisting she was neither qualified nor learned.

"Excuse me," said an older gentleman, stepping into the infirmary. The man wore a simple mint-green dress shirt, tucked neatly into his black trousers. "Sorry, luv, but have you seen my niece?"

"That her?" asked Malvolia, jutting a thumb over her shoulder to Junia.

"Ah! Yes, that'd be the one. My thanks."

Malvolia seized his elbow before he could leave.

"She's sort of *busy* right now... *sir*." She looked the man up and down. "Give her a second to finish stitching up that poor soul and she'll be right with you."

"I..." The old man glanced at Junia before sinking beside Malvolia with a sigh. "Oh, very well." He eyed her bind oddly. "Though speaking of stitches, I'd say a slit like that could use more than a simple bind." He lightly set a hand on the soldier's chest. "And how did you attain your wound, sir?"

"Just a nick, my Lord," answered the soldier, his voice cheery. "My greaves were laid wasted and my shin vulnerable to the rock I was sure to stumble upon." The soldier shook his head. "I'm simply a dunce at times, my Lord."

The Lord tutted.

"Nonsense. Upsetting your footwork is a practised combat unique to our enemy. You've nothing to bash about." The older man eyed the wound. "Still... it'd be a better idea if that were stitched instead of bound."

"I just bind 'em till Junia can handle it," said Malvolia. "I myself... don't... *quite* know how... sir." She shrugged. "Me and Junia have been handling this quite well thus far, so you needn't trouble."

"Oh, but I think such would be my job, lassie. Here, pass the suturing kit. There we are. Now, all you do is simply take the needle and thread like this... see? And it's already threaded, so that's already a great hassle relieved." The older fellow chuckled to himself. "Right, then you just—" He cut himself off, sitting up with his hands on his lap. "Well I hoped you flushed out the wound, lassie. And what of your hands, are they clean?"

"Aye." Malvolia's features were pale; the thought of threading someone was far worse than anything she could imagine. It left a particular distaste in her mouth that stabbing, slashing and gutting could never compare to. "Yes—aye... sir. His wound was prepared to be dressed."

"Excellent, then you just take the needle here and angle it all nice and straight like this. Use this other pinchy thing to line all the tissues up, aye? Then you... drive it in... like... so. See that? Outside... to inside... Blast, the fat tissue's being a bother. Tuck it in like so and... there we are. Sounds simple, I know. Just be sure to remember it. Right, then we—oh lass, you needn't look so sickly! Why, he can't feel a thing with these veneer enchantments." The older gentleman proceeded to twist his wrist and poke the needle's head out the soldier's skin. Just when Malvolia thought she was about to lose her breakfast, Junia came by and rested a hand on the older fellow's shoulder.

"Uncle! Why, I *thought* I heard your voice!" She squinted at his stitching handiwork. "Interrupting sutures? Don't you know how to—"

"Blast it, Nia! This isn't bleeding embroidery!" He chuckled to himself as he looped the string about his finger. "Besides... it's easier to correct one's mistakes this way." He looked over his shoulder and pointed to Malvolia. "Was teaching her—'twas the first technique *I* learned."

"I know, Uncle... I know..." Junia patted his shoulders before pinching her eyebrows. "I don't think you need to show ol' Malvolia, though. She's quite capable with stitching as it were."

"Is she now? She led me on to believe otherwise."

"Ehm... nope." Junia pointed to Malvolia. "Why don't we tend to the last few? Uncle Leo has this one."

"Aye..." muttered the older fellow, "and any others you throw at me."

Junia set two hands on Malvolia and steered her away to the other cots.

"Yes, thank you, Uncle." She smiled over her shoulder as she led Malvolia away. "You... *do* know how to stitch, right? I'd hate to think I just lied to save your stomach."

"No, yes... of *course* I know how to stitch," snapped Malvolia, slapping Junia's hands away. "My father made certain every soldier of his was equipped with such skills." Malvolia punched a wounded man in the shoulder to let him know she was there.

"Oh." Junia paused, as though flustered. "I was talking about sewing and hoping to work 'round a lie, but... that works better I suppose..." She raised an eyebrow at Malvolia. "Soldier?"

"Lieutenant... really." She sat beside the wounded man and began binding his side. "He does this... *funny* thing where simply being his own child isn't enough." She paused, tapping her chin. "No, that's all wrong... doing literally *anything* is never enough." She bounced her shoulders and began tying the bind. "What's it matter to me anyhow? He's a crooked old man. I shouldn't trouble a moment's thought about his opinion of me." She sharply cinched the bind. "I... I *don't* care. I don't..."

"Mm..." Junia rubbed the man's bound wound as Malvolia scooted over to work on another soldier. "I can understand that... my own parents were the aristocratic sort—strong, elegant, commanding... everything I wasn't... or maybe they couldn't see what they didn't wish to see." Junia shrugged. "Was always compared to my sister as the epitome of what a good child should be. *Then*, my bloody sister would come and lecture me on the very thing I was already chastised for. Oh, make no misunderstanding! I *do* love them—dearly, but..." She shook her head, removing the veneer bind to stitch the man's skin. "I was too different for them... but it matters not." She snipped the thread and pointed to Malvolia with her scissors. "How old are you?"

"I've bore witness to seventeen winters and eighteen springs..."

"Ah, well, I reached your conclusion around that age as well. Eventually, though, I decided to shift my perspectives and with it, my life." Junia retied the bind over the freshly stitched wound. "If I was to be cooped up in Tokade—living with *them*—I decided it'd be best to simply leave and find my own adventures elsewhere."

"Mm... and so you joined a *syndicate?*"

Junia shrugged again.

"Truly, it's more of an adventuring guild." She sat beside Malvolia to begin tending to the new soldier. "And Theo's always looking for new members if you're interested."

Malvolia smirked to herself, fantasising the idea of joining the very organisation who foiled her father's schemes.

"Tempting... but..."

"No, but that's the *thing*, though!" Junia lowered her voice as some glanced her way. "That's the *thing*," she hissed, leaning forward to Malvolia, "you don't *have* to come up with a reason to say *no*. I know it's how you've been raised to think, but if you only humour the infinite possibilities of the unknown, I can *guarantee* your destiny will find its fruitful ending." She flapped a rag, gesturing to the room. "After I've finished assisting my uncle, I plan to retire from his hand and take up the Second Flame as a full-time investment of life."

"Oh? What's the pay then?"

"Nothing." Junia shrugged under Malvolia's quizzical stare. "You get what you find and find what you like."

"Hm... well..." Malvolia briefly mulled the offer over in her mind. "It would be rather dashing to join your little group... I've always wanted to be in a syndicate."

"Yeah, but it's not..." Junia sighed, forcing a smile. "Sure, fine, yeah—whatever." She tucked a strand of hair behind her ear as she watched the doorway. "But is that a *yes*... or no?"

"Oy, is that Vincent?"

"Now you're just avoiding the subject."

Malvolia huffed and crossed her arms.

"Maybe so. Who's to say?" Before Junia could answer, Malvolia waved her hands. "Oy, Vincent! Over here, old boy!" She waited as he excused himself from Lord Ortunato, only to stride in her direction with his company.

"What's this then?" asked Vincent, crossing his arms at Malvolia. "I was enjoying a rather dark conversation, you know."

Malvolia bounced her shoulders.

"Hi."

"Hi." Vincent made a ghastly face at her before resuming talk with Lord Ortunato. "If you can delay the Quarter as long as needs be, I *might* just have enough time to muster support from Gotnoech. With their numbers, we'd present Unbequith with no choice but to forgo any means of advancing in hostility. It would save countless lives *without* lethal combat. If they did engage, it would be suicide on their part." Vincent nodded firmly. "Aye, it may take time and convincing, but if you merely stall long enough..."

"Do you honestly believe that's possible?" The Lord combed his tired hair back. "They've a bloodlust that cannot be contained another hour. That spectacle was *yester-*

day. I saw the Commander of Unbequith—with my own eyes—take another's life like some kind of monster. He killed the poor soul *begging* for a chance to exist! Do Redfolk commanders so readily forgo mercy? I thought it was the mantra of all commanders to assess redemption and provide opportunities at *any* given time!" He released a pent-up sigh. "No... verily, I don't doubt the Code shall be broken on a greater scale... and only death itself shall reap a most bountiful harvest from it."

"And what of Paun?" asked Vincent. "Surely he hasn't chosen to continue in—"

"No, he has... of course he has." Lord Ortunato waved his hand. "He's with his regiment as we speak, though I offered him a moment's breath to speak with you two. He refused and... and I know not his motives." He flopped a loose finger at Junia. "'Tis only because of my trust in her discernment of character that I—"

"*My Lord!*" A page burst into the infirmary, pausing to rest on his knees beside Lord Ortunato. "My Lord, I—" He froze, his features draining of colour upon sight of Vincent. "I'm sorry, were you talking with him? I didn't mean to..."

"No, it's quite alright, Loranzo." Emelio knelt to the page's level. "What have you for tidings?"

"An envoy of Unbequith approaches, My Lord. Their Commander—unarmed and *alone*."

Lord Ortunato kept silent, his gaze resting on Vincent, shifting to Junia, then resting heavily on Malvolia. It was unsettling and made her heart go stone-cold to behold such grave eyes. Thankfully, his gaze gradually broke from her as he turned to address his page.

"Prepare the lines for assault."

Forest-green flags—faded by the sun's light and cracked with age—fluttered sluggishly in the dry breeze along ramparts of a city fortified in magic. They were the only motion stirring along those ramparts. Every bowmen had their arrows nocked and their strings ready to be drawn taunt. Lord Ortunato clasped his hands behind his back as he watched a lone man approach them. He wore black armour, outlined in red runes of prayer and sanctification. In his arms, the man carried a body.

"Hail, Lord Aivon!" greeted Emelio sourly. "My word, you do have some explaining—"

Aivon coldly dropped the body at their feet, its armour thudding with a clank. Emelio gasped, recoiling as he beheld its pale features. Gripping his weapon's hilt, Emelio shouted: "*What* is the *meaning* of this madness?!"

"*That*," spat Aivon, "is the hollow house of a strong... upright... and righteous Unbequith patriot. My Lieutenant used to reside in this body till his spirit was forcibly evicted. Thankfully... he has since moved on to a better life." Aivon took a step forward, pausing as various polearms pressed against his armour. "Unlike his family who remain behind *without* his love and care. You have denied several younglings the nurture of their father and one wife the comfort of her husband. You have denied his existence and you have denied your own morality." Aivon stepped forward, unbothered by the metal scratching against his armour. "The man you call Abaddon Henagan has *blatantly* violated the Code, *well* beyond conduct unbecoming. Though, I am certain such dark tidings could never escape the ears of your infiltration."

"No, they—" Emelio cut himself off as he addressed Henagan to his right. "Is this true or is the deranged lunatic lying? Henagan?" Emelio tried to grab him by the collar. "*Henagan!*"

Ignoring him, Henagan strode to Aivon and paused solemnly by his side.

"Please," he whispered, his soft voice mingling with the dry breeze, "I beg you... do not do this." Henagan's expressionless features lacked colour and his breathing was heavy and restrained. "You would only play into silent motives by giving into such crude reactions."

"You... brand grief as *nothing* more than a *crude* reaction?" Aivon lunged for Henagan, held back only by the spears against his chestpiece. "Are you *so cruel* as to label death so?" He stabbed a finger at Emelio. "Do not think your words of cunning and *lies* can fool me or *any* of Unbequith?!"

"Cruel?" Emelio threw his hands forward, gesturing to Henagan, who had resumed standing beside him. "I know *nothing* of what you claim this man has done! If you would only calm your agitation and—*please*, come inside. We'll host a feast in your honour and *talk* about this."

"Enough!" cried Aivon, bashing aside their spears only to have them redirected to his chestpiece. "I know *very* well Ranitorl imitates the licentious nature of Harldïof in some twisted form of *reverence*. Nay, mine soul has long been sated of your soiling flattery. The time for hollow words has ended, for now is the hour of action!" His voice lowered, his piercing eyes resting on Lord Emelio. "I offer you this chance of further redemption. Release what men of mine you've captured and we shall proceed in the Code's boundaries."

Henagan scoffed.

"Will you release our forces as well?"

Aivon gravely shook his head.

"Our prisoners of war? My conscience denies I—"

"Then we have no accord."

"*Please*," Aivon extended a hand to Emelio and Henagan, "I know the corruption of your hearts... the burden of your sins. Resist them... find *hope* in the love of our Father, the Eternal King—he *will* forgive should you only ask!" Aivon stepped forward, the spears pressed into his chest relenting. "All *I* can ask... is that you surrender—*please*, permit not the evils of your heart to *consume* you! Break free of the darkness that binds your soul and spare countless lives to come! None should be deceived into dying or *suffering* for a corrupted cause as yours—*please*..." Aivon took another step forward, completely unhindered. "Please... I *beg* of you."

Emelio shook his head and scoffed.

"You demand peace under the terms we willingly relinquish your captured ranks while you hold ours *and* that we surrender the shards to Unbequith and Unbequith *alone?*" He scoffed. "Is there even a *word* for peace in your region's dialect?"

"Peace is always an option and surrender, always welcomed." Aivon tapped the ivory horn strapped to his waist. "'Tis the very reason I and every commanding officer bear these at *all* times. As simple as it would be for you to believe, the *Redfolk*, as you call us, are not a bloodthirsty race of barbarians, but *desperate* brothers and sisters—*praying* for the excuse of peace at *any* given second."

"I for one must refuse," said Henagan, straightening his brown coat. "For I've bore witness to your little self-righteous escapades. Those were *my* men you had murdered, Aivon Seeker. Do not think your hypocritical actions shall *ever* go unanswered."

Aivon shrugged coldly.

"I do not regret it."

"My Lord," pleaded Junia, tugging on her uncle's bracer, "you cannot possibly consider surrendering the shards to Unbequith—not after everything that's occurred—everything that's been done to keep it from them!"

"Of course not, Nia, but..."

"You're all cowards!" cried Aivon, gesturing definitely. "To the last of you! You've grown to become the very monsters you've destroyed for centuries over! *Nothing* separates you from them!" He knelt beside his Lieutenant's corpse, a hand on his chest. "Verily," he whispered, "we shall meet this day, my kin..." Aivon rose from the bridge, his arms outstretched. "We do not stand before the point of death, but the gates of Heaven itself! In the Almighty's name, for the Eternal King, for the glory of death itself, we *rise* to confront evil with the might of our blades and by the courage of our hearts! Our very names shall be writ in the Heavens!"

Emelio raised an eyebrow, for it felt as though Aivon no longer addressed them, but rather, the very sky itself. Aivon pounded the black metal of his chest-piece. "The home we safeguard rests behind the raising of your shield and the swing of your sword! Perish now or perish in the rule of their oppression! The night is all but spent, the day is at hand! Cast aside these deeds of darkness! Steadfast your spirit in an armour of light! In the name of God's glory, legends shall rise once more, *today!* Today, brothers! Today *we*—"

"*My Lord!*" A page shoved through Ranitorl's ranks, addressing Emelio in heaving breaths. "My Lord—it's a *trap!* You *musn't*—"

"Verily," growled Aivon, lowering his arms, "if that bloody spy blabbers so much as another squeak, then I shall consider it as my proclamation of Desperate Quarter."

Lord Ortunato shook his head, drawing a longsword wrought in dormant symbols.

"How in the *blazes* of Hell *itself* do you expect me to forsake his warning? Do his words bear no truth? Was that not the *bloody* plan from the start? Kill us all and raise Unbequith as the superior of the four regions? Is this not your *godforsaken plan?!*"

"You *dare* condone *us* for forsaking God? You who so willing forsook your own honour, your people, your own *bleeding* soul—"

"*Speak!*" barked Emelio, directing his sword at Aivon. "*Speak, boy!*"

"They've *legions* upon us!" cried the page. "They approached whilst we slept and lie in wait beneath a veil of—"[1]

"So be it," said Aivon, raising his fist to the heavens. "D'rendors lióþ'daros!" His voice deepened, roaring through the trenches in a rattling war cry: "*Gu'þra!*"

The earth quaked beneath their feet as two watchtowers climbed out from the trenches behind Aivon: their mechanical insect-like legs piercing the bridge to heave themselves forward.

Rooks.

The bridge crumbled behind Aivon as the rooks lumbered up past him, lobbing bursts of blazing energy from their ember cannons.

---

1. *kill*

From the capital's ramparts, thousands of arrows lit the air as their symbols came to life, burning down upon Aivon and the rooks in streaks of blazing orange. Before any could strike Aivon, a white dragon dove from the heavens, barreling into the bridge to wrap about him. The archers on the battlements drew a fresh host of arrows for the beast, but it had already seized Aivon—and the corpse—in its claws before bolting into the sky.

"Fall back!" cried Emelio, retreating with his men as bursts of energy rocketed overhead to strike the gatehouse. "*Fall back*! Regroup!" Emelio spun about as he passed through the gatehouse's unseen barrier. His heart fell upon the now-revealed sight of *legions* standing before the walls of his capital. They were ascending out the trenches and onto the shores of Sherr to meet Ranitorl's first line of defence.

Accepting the helm from his page, Emelio strapped it on with a grunt.

"To arms, men! *To arms!* Fell those rooks *now!* They're clearing a path for the siege engines!" He watched as a storm of Rantilorian arrows pierced the stone defences of a rook. Some *must* have struck the gunner, for it briefly ceased its firing before resuming its barrage once more. Emelio tore himself from the sight to ascend the stairs of his battlements. Some Rantilorians were bringing out their own artillery and strapping them between merlons. A harsh clinking noise could be heard as it attached before exploding with fiery bursts of orange directed upon the rooks. Emelio had ceased giving orders, for his captains managed that well enough. In truth, his greater concern resided in the sky and the great dragon which circled them.

Aivon stood in Cádmus' saddle. He had long deposited Bo's corpse back at camp. Now, he watched the siege play out as though he were assessing a board with various pieces strewn across it. Every so often, he would fly down to assist his men where they were struggling. But, for the most part, he remained in the air, blowing his commands through the various horns strapped about his saddle. The main front of his army was maintaining a violent contact with the enemy while the rear secretly pulled out to flank them. From what he could tell, nothing had changed to alter his stratagem. Eyeing his legions below, Aivon's chest heaved, a mighty stream of air rushing into his blackhorn.

CHAPTER TWENTY-NINE

THE CHESS WAR

THE CHAOS OF WAR had not yet reached the capital's northern flank. A makeshift wall of logs had been fortified outside the capital, just before the shores dipped down. Archers with spy glasses paced its battlements, standing by should the enemy decide to flank. Though, in all honesty, no one expected it, not so early into the battle. It's why Paun's regiment and only a handful of others had been placed to defend it. In truth, nothing could be heard save for the distant shouts, screams, and explosions of the capital's eastern front.

Paun leaned against his halberd and hoisted himself up; the weapon had been loaned to him at Captain Aethur's behest: a sign of growing trust as it were. Paun personally felt more comfortable with swordplay, but knew his weapon would be quite useless against the reach of polearms.

The grey sand crunched beneath his sabatons with every pacing step. While no one else may have expected it, Paun was eager for battle; the sooner he was in the fray, the sooner he could be out of it and searching for Adela. Also, it would be rather *advantageous* of Unbequith to claim the northern and southern shores: t'would provide a most cunning angle against the occupied bridge of the east and swiftly overpower them.

Paun's eyes flickered to the sky as a dark and ominous horn bellowed from above. More horns near the eastern front echoed its call, a host of drums beginning to beat in tune. Raising an eyebrow, his attention was then diverted to the sand near the shore's makeshift wall; there was a bubbling patch in the sand, disturbed as though boiling—

A black drake erupted out from the grey sand, clawing at Paun's sabatons. Scores of other such drakes could be seen bursting from the sands.[1] Paun could only watch in horror as one poor soul was caught by surprise, his armour and body crumpling to a black ash as the drake inhaled.

"No!" roared Captain Aethur, stabbing his halberd into the creature before Paun. He was assisted by three more men in bringing it down. Yanking Paun upright, his Captain gestured to the drakes squirming out from the sand. "Have your brothers died in *vain?* Fight onward! *Fight* and avenge his family which yet remains!" The archers on the shore's battlements were active now, firing streaks of orange into the trenches.

Paun pushed up with his captain, pausing to stab another creature in the neck. It howled in pain before snapping in Paun's direction, its scorching breath reddening the back side of his hand. Tearing his halberd free, he slashed his weapon across the shank's face before burying its tip in the beast's eye. Paun gasped as it went limp, hastily puffing at his right hand; *blast it*; that was sure to scar. Before he could recover, a burst of orange and black exploded on his left, destroying a piece of the makeshift wall and sending Paun sprawling. The force of it left his hand stinging more than ever, but he managed to grit his teeth and shove himself to his feet.

A steady stream of Unbequith soldiers poured through the wall's crumbling gap, swinging, shouting and stabbing. Paun sighed upon sight of them, bending to retrieve his fallen halberd and charge into the fray. He parried various thrusts directed at him and returned the blows, only to have his edge deflect right off their armour. Frowning, Paun started targeting their joints. Though it seemed to briefly stun them, it couldn't pierce their enchanted mail. He tried to grab one glaive as it shot past his ribs, but it was torn from his hands and—not wishing to be cut—Paun released it. A score of thrusts and stabs punished him for this mistake, forcing him to step back as he frantically parried.

Matching their fury, he lunged past one soldier's guard to stab him in the armpit. It worked a bit, causing the soldier to drop his weapon and clutch his wound. Still, Paun felt like he made no progress, for the soldier was swiftly supported by an onslaught of furious attacks. Backing off to let another take his place, Paun tucked the halberd under his arm

---

1. **Shanks:** a type of drake. They can't breathe fire, for they are lesser than the dragons. Instead, they can manifest a type of heat from their throat glands. Open exposure to the raw heat of their breath is enough to disintegrate one's entire being. This suits shanks, considering they've an appetite for freshly charred ash.

and drew his smallsword; perhaps a test of its symbols was long warranted. Tapping the shoulders of his comrades, Paun squeezed through to slice his sword through the various polearms and weapons he could find jabbing his way. To his delighted astonishment, it minced metal like *butter*. Shrugging his features, Paun hurled his halberd at a clump of soldiers, upsetting their balance. With their brief moment of vulnerability, Paun thrust his sword into the nearest soldier's leg, its tip sinking clean through the man's armour and immobilising him with pain.

Tearing out his sword, Paun assisted his regiment by slicing through the weapons of those advancing. He was beginning to form a lethal rhythm when his Captain started shouting at the top of his lungs. Paun couldn't quite make out the words, but he could see his Captain urgently pointing to the sky. Following his gesture, Paun had only a brief moment to blink as a mechanical creature bolted against his chest and pinned him to the ground. Paun could see other such iron dragons leaping over the walls and unleashing a jetstream of blue heat onto the ranks of his regiment.

Esardrocan.

Some were equipped with riders, their armour pelted with Rantilorian arrows. Paun's assailant hosted no such rider, choosing instead to snap at his head. Before it could, Paun hacked at its ankles with his blade, rolling out from under it as it collapsed. Its gold-plated neck snapped in his direction, its maw opening to display a growing-blue light. As it did, Paun sprung forward to slice his sword through the metalwork of its jaws. The iron dragon's face exploded in a wreath of blue flames before it fell dead to the sand.

Paun clenched his right hand, feeling its burnt flesh before raising an eyebrow; his back was starting to sting as well. Spinning about, he saw a shank crawling after him, jaws wide for the kill. Before it could reach him however, Captain Aethur sprung forward to pin the creature by the neck with his halberd. The shank squirmed beneath his blade, its neck writhing in spasms. Seeing he could barely hold it alone, Paun sprinted after him to help. However, the shank wildly twisted out from under the halberd, jerking its head free and causing Captain Aethur to lose his balance. Paun arrived with a leap, stabbing his blade through the shank's skull; the beast fell limp to the sand, still and lifeless.

Smiling, Paun looked up to his Captain only to watch in shock as he beheld Aethur's pained features disintegrate away to ash; the drake, though dead, had its ajar jaws directed at his captain. Collapsing to his knees, Paun screamed whatever would emerge from his throat. His fists curled as he struck the shank's corpse in the jaw, sealing its deadly mouth shut.

A dry breeze rolled over the battlefield.

IT'S SICKENING... ISN'T IT.

Paun's gaze slowly rose to see a ghostlike figure towering over him. The figure was robed in white linen, its head covered by a hood, and its features concealed behind a mask as bland as it was dark. The figure knelt to Paun's level, an arm across a knee.

THIS... CONCEPT WE'VE BRANDED DEATH... IT MAKES YOUR INSIDES CHURN SOMETHING UNNATURAL, DOES IT NOT? AS THOUGH YOU LET HIM DIE, AS THOUGH YOU KILLED HIM YOURSELF.

The figure set a hand on Paun's shoulder and a warmth flooded Paun's body, healing his burns and aches

I AM SORRY... BUT YOU WILL SOON BE ACQUAINTED WITH THE FEELING ONCE MORE. ALTHOUGH... IT WILL BE SEVENFOLD THE BLOW TO THE PURITY OF YOUR HEART... FOR SHE WILL DIE.

Paun's eyes shakily rose to meet the figure once again.

"Are..." He gulped, doing his best to maintain a stern expression. "Are you... death?"

DEATH HAS BEEN CONQUERED... SILENCED... AND FLAYED. ITS FACE... MY GUISE.

"Oh..." Paun's gaze collapsed and he returned to facing the sand. "That sounds far worse... though I know not its meaning." Paun gestured to the battlefield about him; everything slowed as though wading through water. "Or this... or any of this... really." His eyes fell to his hand, rubbing its backside; though it had been healed of pain, its scar remained. "What... *what* are you?" he asked, his voice breathless and in awe.

I AM THE SILENCE BETWEEN. THE WORDS UNSPOKEN. I KNOW NOT MYSELF, THOUGH ALL KNOW ME.

Paun's gaze rose to the dark figure, his eyes glazing over and his features straining.

"Please," he begged, his voice soft and submissive, "you cannot take her."

If I do not... the trope of three shall be engaged and the Oather shall be allowed to run free... ensuing chaos... assuring death... assuring... this.

"Take me instead," pleaded Paun. he fell to his face and seized the figure by the ankle. "Please, take me instead... life would be death if she died. It would be *my* fault, for none of this would have happened had I simply let her be!"

The figure refrained from answering. Instead, it gazed solemnly to its right, lifting an arm to point south. Tracing the figure's gesture, Paun turned to see a gaping hole in the wall of the capital, exposing the bare yard behind it. However, the longer he stared, the more he began to visualise outlines shimmering within the air take shape; crystalline transparencies whispered over one another to form what one could interpret as the image of a girl. Paun's eyes shot back to the figure, but found no such entity kneeling before him.

It simply... vanished.

The swift chaos had returned, but Paun heeded it not. Picking himself up, Paun had no choice but to chase after the spinner—wherever it would lead him.

CHAPTER THIRTY

DEMON IN THE DARK

A DELA WHIRLED HER STAFF into the ribs of a Harling soldier, the combined force of its enchantments and her enhanced strength knocking him aside. Sitting upright in her esardrocan's saddle, she directed her staff to the foreboding entrance ibefore her.

"*Ramsoen!*" she cried, Regend lurching forward for her to strike another soldier. "Ramsoen, is *that* it ahead?!"

"Aye, Windcatcher!" Ramsoen emerged from the shadows behind an enemy soldier, digging his dagger into the man's neck. Adela altered her gaze seconds before the blade went in.

There were only a score or so of Harling soldiers standing guard before the syphon's dark maw. In truth, the enemy was quite shocked to find the pack of Hell's Butterflies descending upon them. With her elite pack and the support of their battalion, it took no time in subduing the enemy's meagre forces. Adela tried knocking most of the men unconscious before her pack could reach them, hoping to spare their lives with her staff. Despite that, in the end, it felt as though such efforts were merely in vain; Harling corpses littered the battlefield.

Sliding off Regend's saddle, Adela stood beside Ramsoen before the syphon's looming maw. She set her hands upon her hips and peered into the inky expanse.

"I don't..." Adela's dark brows came together as she examined the tunnel. "I don't see any..."

"They're gone." Ramsoen knelt to the ground, rubbing the moist sediment between two fingers. "All those brave souls... laid waste to those who conceal their dark deeds in vile acts of desecration." He tilted his hand to the side, allowing the sediment to trickle

out. "I was unaware the soul could descend to such a lowly state of existence without...
perishing."[1]

"*Stand up*," growled Darun, slapping his shoulder. "Soil not the earth with your sorry
tears, but rather, the blood of those who dare stir our vengeance." He stomped past
Ramsoen, clapping his hands before punching the air. Fiery tendrils of energy extended
from his palms, tearing through the darkness. His eyes snapping open, Darun tilted his
head to the syphon's interior. "It's unoccupied... for now."

Adela nodded, nocking an arrow.

"Then we move forward." She turned to face her iron dragon, Regend. "Stay here and
cover our escape, yeh? The moment we've secured them shards, we'll be in *desperate* need
of a sure way out."[2] She jutted her chin at Darun. "Bring us in, lad."

Darun gave her a sideways glance before stepping into the darkness and flipping his
palms upwards. The fiery strands in the tunnel reacted to this motion by erupting from
the ground, tearing a platform of stone with it. Their blazing tendrils swirled about
the levitating stone, encasing it in light. Leaping atop it, Darun clapped his hands and
gestured to his surroundings, triggering cube-like symbols to circle about the platform.
Adela had seen him manifest such symbols before—lanterns she believed; a practical
necessity for the darkness.

Helping Ramsoen aboard, Adela joined the rest of her pack atop the hovering platform. Darun raised his arms forward, causing the strands wrapped about the platform
to pulse ominously. Adela stumbled as it lurched forward, ferrying them through the
darkness. Stabilising herself, Adela double-checked the straps of her mask, hoping they
would hold; Fel had attached some lightly enchanted metal to the back of her pixie-well
mask, forming a protective helmet for her.

---

1. Due to their purer sense of morality, mortals in Beyond cannot comprehend true wickedness.
   Consequently, it was commonly believed that if one were to become truly wicked, their God-given
   soul would blight and wither away, leaving behind a soulless husk of a mortal.

2. I'm surprised Adela and Regend haven't developed a telepathic connection yet. Regend does
   communicate telepathically, meaning he's graced her mindscape. If he'd merely stay in there, he'll
   maintain a connection with her. It's not like he understands her words anyway, he simply reads
   the intentions of her words in her head. If Regend already set up a connection and I simply didn't
   record it, I'll feel so stupid...

Double-checking it was clear, Adela removed it for now. The complete darkness of her mask perturbed her—these shadowy passages were unsettling enough to *begin* with. Why, she nearly startled to the sound of flowing water building beneath them. Her eyes darted all about the darkness, pausing on shadows she could have *sworn* were stirring. However, the instant she looked their direction, she couldn't see anything save for the syphon's architecture; black-stone pillars upholding the ceiling, various tunnels branching off and every now and then, a ladder leading up and out of view.

Adela spun about, drew her bow and fired into the darkness. Darun halted the platform as she did, the dark visor of his helm glancing her direction.

"Addy..." whispered Sam. It felt as though he meant to say more, but he dared not utter another word.

Adela had already nocked another arrow, coldly directing its tips at the heavy gloom. "*Light.*"

Without waiting for an explanation, Darun extended a tendril of fire into the shadows, scorching the darkness with its light. As its black folds retreated, the grim form of a skeleton came into view. Her arrow was stuck fast in its chest, piercing the fresh greenery which grew in its ribs like a disease. A plume of black flowers could be seen softly wafting on its chest, bold and terrible. A dull creak from behind seized their attention, their weapons confronting the tunnel's darkness. Adela could hear her pack's breathing increase in trembling quivers. Ignoring them, she turned back to face the skeleton, frowning at its sudden absence. Returning the arrow to its quiver and slinging the bow across her shoulder, Adela drew the sword she had been loaned: a curious instrument lacking a proper crossguard. Unbequith had supplied her with quite the lethal entourage of her choice: should she decide to forsake her weakness.

Adela knew not what she intended as she leapt off the platform, much to the verbal protest of her pack. Continuing to ignore them, Adela waded through murky grey waters to approach the location she had last seen the skeleton. She knelt to examine a black rose on the brick surface, lush and fresh. It quivered softly as a film of water rushed over it in mesmerising flows.

A cold grip seized her ankle.

Bringing her sword down in a warning, she directed its tip near the wrist of—Adela grimaced at the sight of a skeletal hand grasping her right ankle. Its bones were draped in grey flesh, weathered away by the rushing water. She could just barely distinguish a pair of hollow eyes in the rotting features of whatever held her. A blood-red symbol burned on the forehead of its rusted helm.

Scrunching her nose, she kicked it in the face with her left boot. It remained unaffected by such a blow, its other hand swinging over to claw at her. Adela was scowling now, stomping on its skull until it caved in. She jerked her foot from its skeletal grip, spitting after the abomination.

Darun leapt beside her, raising the corpse from the water.

"These heraldings are unknown to me," he announced, inspecting its armour through his visor. "However... its garbs... they appear..." Burning a bright orange, the veins in his hands became visible as he tore the corpse's breastplate off. Gasping, the corpse fell from his hands and into the water with a rattling splash.

Sam knelt beside it, softly stroking its faded garbs.

"These... these are Unbequith colours..." he breathed. "These are our fallen brothers! They... this is what became of them?!"

"Aye." Fel hopped into the water beside them. "I recognized the forbidden emblem engraved in its brow." Fel kicked at the corpse. "I would happily wager if *this* is here, its puppeteer must be as well."

Ramsoen remained static as he stared at the body.

"This... death is too merciful for the servants of Heylel..."[3] Ramsoen fell to his knees, a hand feathering his throat. "Look on well and true... *burn* this image in your minds... see how they have defiled our kin..."

Sam spat into the water.

"Nay, these aren't our brothers... not anymore. Our valiant kin have long laid aside their lives on the field of treachery against *unjust* odds. Aye, even now they walk streets of gold in paradise above—*nay*, this is but a foul trick designed to break our resolve."

Adela stepped closer, forcing herself to face the remains. However, the moment she neared her pack's circle, a hoard of corpses in grime-ridden armour lurched up out of the water, rusted weapons in hand. A crimson symbol burned on each of their foreheads.

Before she could react, an exploding inferno shot past Adela, curling throughout the various undead in lethal tendrils. Their rotting corpses stood no chance, erupting in

---

3. **Heylel**: The Prince of the Fallen World, the Nexus of Black Magics, the Binding Betrayer, Deceiver, the Adversary.

bursts of flames and dissolving away to ash as they struck the water. Adela glanced to her left to see Darun, his greasy black hair falling over his blazing eyes.

"I... could not *feel* them..." he whispered, his glare burning into the water. "Its cursed magic is akin to that of the eldritch." His fiery-orange gaze rose to meet theirs. "You'd do best to maintain a keen eye and a wary heart."

Nodding her thanks, Adela hoisted herself atop the hovering platform, hooking her helm to her waist; she wasn't about to gamble the extent of its abilities against the fell eldritch lurking in watery shadows.

"Carry on," she ordered, her features flickering darkly in the arcane light. "And keep your bloody wits about you. The force desecrating their remains *will* meet an end by *our* hands."

Ramsoen eyed her grimly from behind his mask.

"By that, I can only hope you imply a slow and *excruciating* death for this atrocity."

Adela remained silent, waiting for her pack to climb aboard before signalling for them to proceed. The platform heaved forward at Darun's command, a host of unholy screams beginning to echo from behind.

She tightly exhaled, refusing to turn around.

"Fel, if you will."

There was a moment of silence before he responded.

"Aye, miss." Fel strode past her, hurling three vials into the darkness behind. Her short hair blew forward from the force of such destruction. Adela remained unmoving as its explosion rocked their balance. The unholy screams came to an abrupt halt and the tunnels were briefly exposed in a raging burst of light; the water beneath them was congested with undead soldiers, clawing at their passing platform. Some skeletal fingers managed to latch on, but were swiftly dealt with by her pack. Adela herself remained neutral to the terrors, crossing her arms as she stared ahead; a strong cold burned in her heart, one her soul was quite unfamiliar with.

She cared not.

For once in her life, she didn't feel the weakness of her principles snuffing her wrath. That wrath, the icy fire in her heart, she feared it no longer, but rather... allowed the stoned ferocity to grow and *fester* in her heart. Perhaps she *had* felt it before, but only in a brief and uncontrollable flash of such coldness. *Vengeance...* she believed it to be. One insect had fallen victim to its snapping bite and now... well... the wicked would be wise to flee from the storm fuming within; Adela was unsure just how much longer she could restrain it.

"We've nearly arrived," declared Ramsoen, gazing into his vidorae. "Several paces forward and there should be a—"

She startled as the darkness ahead lunged out, sweeping their pack off the platform and into the water. The levitating stone was bashed in, collapsing into the water with a splash. Adela tapped Sam's arm. She was almost certain they were standing on a dormant horde of undead, but was too troubled with the unseen attacker to double check; the murky water was up to their waists and she didn't wish to disturb it.

Not yet.

An odd rattle permeated from the shadows about them, like a multitude of spears clinking and clanking across brick walls. The footing beneath them trembled, as though in primal fear of the predator encircling them. Apprehension rising in Adela's heart, she began to piece together its familiarity.

"Whatever it is," whispered Darun, "it *has* to be eldritch, for my network cannot detect its presence."

Adela wrung her jaw as she nocked an arrow. Her eyes shut tightly for a brief second. "*Serpent.*"

A deep hiss spiralled out from the darkness.

"*Wind... catcher...*" An unsettling chuckle reverberated in circling echoes. Adela paled, recognizing the unmistakable voice: "How I have *longed* to taste the scent which *burdens* you. Its aroma *suffocates* your soul... *swelling* blood in rapid heat. Why... thine own *heart* will cook you inside out." A mocking chitter stung her ears. "What a delightful shift your warm... *fear-stricken* flesh shall be from the cold... *soulless...* meat of your kindred."

Sam spat into the darkness.

"Unveil yourself, *demon!*" Sam bashed his sword across his bracers. "Stow your venomous words and *have at my blade!*"

"It is not *I* you should berate so," chided Tohrvath's voice in the dark. "I am merely a slave *bound* to my master's will."

"Then I shall free *both* your souls!" retorted Sam, "The deepest pits of Hell await thee and thine master!"

Crimson sigils illuminated the darkness, bobbing and circling about them.

"Had my master not seen fit to protect me... I would have found your scent quite distasteful and permit your existence." The crimson symbols came to a halt, dissipating to shadow. "However... I have long tasted the flesh of your kindred and *crave* seconds. No... I shan't perish... not till mine great hunger is sated in *mortal* blood."

Fel unstrapped two vials from his vest.

"We stand ready for the picking, ya sneaking *devil!* Cease your cowardice! Your meal stands ready for the hunt!"

"Oh, incompetent morsel, mine... you are hardly an appitiser." A chuckle reverberated from the shadows, searing the darkness with a hiss. "No... my reward lies in the carnage of war and the *feast* which awaits outside. I look forward to no other meal." The voice in the dark began to fade. "Except... perhaps... Wind... *catcher.*"

A wisp of air breathed against the nape of her neck. Adela spun about, confronted by the gaping jaws of a black serpent lunging from the darkness.

"*Down!*"

Darun leapt over Adela to bash a frosty blade of crackling-white energy across the serpent's skull. The entire tunnel quaked as the blow landed, its force pounding the serpent's head against a pillar, shattering its stone. Without waiting for Tohrvath to recover, Darun shot his hands forward. Fiery strands elevated from the water and ensnared the serpent's massive throat. Seizing the strands in his fist, Darun wrapped them about his arms, and twisted to the side as he tugged. Tohrvath's head crashed into the water beside Darun. His fists igniting with blades of fire, Darun pummelled the serpent's jaw, a burst of embers erupting with every slash. His attacks, however, had little effect on the serpent who easily tore free of the searing strands.

His inky-black eyes bore into Darun.

"*You...*" The serpent's gaze blazed a pale-red and Darun halted, *frozen.* "You will die." A hissing chuckle escaped Tohrvath, his heaving form constricting about the True Beyonder.

Adela and her pack had already begun rushing to aid Darun. However, as they neared the serpent's tremendous form, Tohrvath's gaze whipped about to oppose them. Its ghastly, red eyes caused Adela to stumble, a stroke of fear seizing her limbs. Ramsoen and Fel seemed similarly affected, upon sight of the serpent's gaze. Murky water lapped against their necks.

In contrast, Sam trudged on, pushing through the gaze with determined strides. Her body quivering, Adela punched the water and swallowed her fear in pure anger. She shakily rose from the water, following Sam.

Just as she broke free of Tohrvath's gaze, her footing gave way to an undead soldier tearing out of the water below her. Bubbles erupted from her lips as she let out a muffled grunt, her boot driving into the undead soldier's knee. The joint buckled, and the creature staggered as Adela surged upward, water cascading off her as she twisted her blade for its neck. Her sabre glanced off the soldier's gorget with a screech of metal, but the momentum carried her strike into its open jaws, piercing up through the roof of its mouth.

The corpse peeled off her blade with a disquieting *squelch*.

Scores of undead were rising from the water now, their foreheads burning with a crimson symbol. Sighing in frustration, Adela whirled her sword and staff about her head, keeping the enclosing horde at bay. A metallic screech drew attention to Darun. Adela could only manage a brief glance every now and again, monitoring his plight with helpless agitation; in a lethal constriction, the ivory spines lining Tohrvath's side pierced Darun's armour.

Darun, however, refused to remain helpless. Extending his hands forward, fiery tendrils rose from the water to wrap about the serpent's snout and bash its head against the watery floor. Sam—who must have been ploughing through ranks of undead soldiers—leapt out from behind a pillar. With a fierce war cry, he swung his sword at Tohrvath, driving its tip through the serpent's liquid-black eye. Tohrvath unleashed a hissing shriek before going slack with a shuddering thud. The armoured corpses were the ones now frozen, standing as though in anticipation. Adela was unsure of whether to strike them down or not, for fear of causing their undead ranks to stir once more. Darun pried himself free from the coils, muttering curses beneath his gravelly breath.

Shaking his head, Sam tore out his blade and wiped it free of the gore which stained it. The moment he did, a host of blood-red symbols illuminated all across Tohrvath's sides. A deep-hissing chuckle reverberated from the serpent's jaws. Sam recoiled in disgust before stabbing his black blade into Tohrvath's eye again. Tohrvath's chuckling took a sharp turn as he hissed at Sam with a malicious grin, crimson flames gushing forth from his jaws. Grunting, Sam hastily twisted out of the way. Though he avoided most of the flames, his entire left arm was caught in the torrent of uncanny heat. Sam immediately dove into the water, clutching his steaming shoulder. His scorching-red armour gradually dimmed to its black hue as he shivered in pain. Adela stepped forward to assist him, but noticed Darun rushing to his aid instead.

She felt a sudden tug on her elbow as she was yanked behind a pillar; Ramsoen had pulled her there, screaming for her to drop beneath the water. The moment she did, a storm of wreathing red flames tore through the air overhead. It passed by harmlessly, merely heating the water as it did so. Adela popped up above the surface, tentatively peeking about the pillar to see Tohrvath wildly thrashing his head to and fro, disgorging scarlet flames every which way he turned. Some corpses were caught in the wild flames, though remained unfazed as they were set ablaze.

The tunnel was lit an odd reddish hue from such a crazed offence, allowing Adela to visualise her entire surroundings; before Darun snapped the serpent's mouth shut with blazing tendrils, Adela briefly caught sight of a shadowy figure robed in black. Though brief it was, its memory burned clearly in her mind; dark-clad robes, a silver skull mask lacking a jaw, hands clothed in black wrappings and a thin sword... *staff* of some kind hovering over its head. Golden symbols began to line Adela's limbs as she studied it through the darkness. Why, she could still visualise the figure's crimson emblem scorching in the siphon's gloom.

Adela sighed, suspecting it could only be the puppeteer Fel had mentioned. She sheathed her sword, secured her staff in the clasp on her back, and pulled her bow from her shoulder. Drawing an arrow from the black quiver at her waist, she nocked it and leapt from cover. With a heavy *twang*, Adela released her arrow into the face of the nearest undead. More rushed for her, but they faltered under the relentless rhythm of her quickdraw. Arrow after arrow found its mark as she advanced, thinning their ranks with cold indifference. She climbed an incline, the water growing shallower as she drew closer to the puppeteer.

Dropping to her knees, she slid across the shallow water just as a blade hissed overhead, pivoting to fire an arrow into the back of her attacker's rotting skull. Adela went to nock another arrow, but was instead met with an empty quiver. Reluctantly tossing aside the bow, she drew her sabre and rolled under the legs of another soldier. Adela reeled about to relieve it of its kneecaps before spinning in the same motion to strike one in its gorget. She gritted her teeth as its armour deflected the blow, but she managed to swiftly follow up with a stab through its eye.

Sheathing her blade, Adela undid her staff and hurled it at the crimson emblem flickering in the shadows. An explosion of blood-red flames briefly lit the tunnels. In the crimson glow, Adela saw the figure dissmiss her staff with a slap from its blade. However, as it made contact with her staff, the figure went limp with a splash. The undead soldiers mimicked the robed figure's motions and collapsed. The crimson symbols on their helms gradually dimmed like dying stars in a black sea.

Retrieving her staff, Adela ran over to drag the robed figure out of the water and set him against a stone bank of sorts. She knew very well it was too dangerous to simply leave it here unchecked and knew *without a doubt* it deserved far more than death. Adela bit her bottom lip as she raised her blade, resting its tip against the puppeteer's throat. What she needed to do... was too good for it—she *had* to remind herself of that.

She *had* to do what was right.

What was *just*.

Despite that, she couldn't bring herself to apply any pressure to her blade. The fires of her wrath were long quenched, suffocated by the weakness of her own conscience. Adela grimaced, lowering her blade in pure disgust; her weak heart disgusted her.

"*Windcatcher!*"

Adela turned around to see Ramsoen shouting after her and pointing to Tohrvath with great agitation. She looked just in time to see Darun pinning Tohrvath's head with strands of fire and Fel tossing a suppressing vial at Tohrvath. Seizing the figure's sword staff, Adela had but a moment to aim before hurling it. Upon contact with the vial, a flash of white clouds exploded in Tohrvath's face, allowing Sam to hurl his own weapon at the serpent. The cloud cleared and Tohrvath snapped at the sword, its black blade sprouting from the back of the serpent's throat. Flashes of red pulsed under Tohrvath's scales in wild patterns, but he was far from dead.

Gasping, Adela rushed to Sam's side as he collapsed. Everyone but Darun had rushed to him as well, for the True Beyonder was busy attempting various methods to kill the bloody thing. Adela tore her attention away from the flaming inferno to aid Ramsoen in removing Sam's pauldron, guardbraces, vambrace, and gauntlet from his left arm.

"Surely, we are not to perish here," remarked Adela, reaching into her satchel for a veneer bind. "Not bloody *today!* Not while the fate of Unbequith and beyond depend on us so—" She paused, but couldn't come up with the right word. "*Dependently!*" she finished with a throw of her hands.

Fel peered out from behind the cover of their pillar to eye the serpent.

"Oy, but Sammy's blade sure seems to be making a good deal of progress!" He rubbed his gaunt chin, studying the battle with gleaming eyes. "Though impenetrable to any castwork o' *my* knowledge, the snake's insides are clearly unprotected by such complicated casting." He rubbed his hands together. "Aye... it would be impossible to burn such crimson symbols of eldritch across its vitals. Such would—*oh!*" Fel tore an orange vial and bottle of luminescent white ink from his personal satchel. "I need but several moments if ye can attain it for me!" He knelt in the water as he scribbled crude symbols across the vial. Clicking his tongue, he looked up at them. "Oh... well, I suppose that was all the moment I needed."

Having finished Sam's bind, Adela set a hand on Fel's shoulder.

"What do you need *of*—" The tunnels rocked violently and she cut herself off to dive underwater. After a torrent of flames passed by, Adela shot out of the water, seizing Fel by the shoulders. "*Speak up*, lad! We haven't any time at all!"

Fel shook his head, tapping the orb-shaped vial. Black and orange flames glistened in its glass.

"Simply standby," he answered, softly grasping her wrists. "No matter how hard it may be, standby and do *nothing*."

Adela glanced at the symbols he had scribbled on the vial, only able to discern *delay* and *break*. Though there were plenty more, she had already gathered all she needed to know. Adela could only shake her head in disbelief, completely speechless and unsure of what to say. Ramsoen curtly stepped past her to pat Fel's shoulder.

"If you're so selfish," he began, "as to claim the heroic sacrifice for yourself, then I suggest you best get on with it and quit wasting the world's precious time."

Fel nodded, smiling at Ramsoen's dry tone before turning to leave. Adela seized his elbow before he could take another step.

"*Wait!* Luv, I..." Adela pressed a hand against her forehead, "I haven't even gotten to *know* you that well." She bit her lip and shook her head. "Why... all I know is you're the *crazy* one," she finally said, her hands clenched tightly. It was baffling how stupid she felt.

Fel smiled and pried Adela's hands off, her iron grip giving way to his gentle touch.

"Aye, that's pretty much all there is to me, lass." He gently released her hand. "Need'a go now. I'll be out exploring paradise if any needs must know of my whereabouts, aye?" He curtly nodded, an unnerving smile breaking across his features. "*Aye!*"

With that, he stepped into the open. Darun was being constricted again, a gushing torrent of bloody flames pouring over him. Retrieving the sword staff Adela had thrown, Fel simply walked up to Tohrvath and plunged its metal through his scales. A thundering hiss of pain rattled the tunnels and Tohrvath whipped about to snatch Fel in his jaws. Adela could only look away, the grotesque crunching nearly causing her to vomit.

No sound, however, was to be uttered by Fel as his spirit passed on.

With a hideous gulp, Tohrvath chuckled to himself. Hating every second of its sound, Adela stomped out to reveal herself. She ignored the protests of her pack as she strode forward, raising her sword defiantly. Catching sight of her, Tohrvath lunged. Adela stood her ground as the outstretched jaws advanced for her. Before it could close into a lethal distance, Adela hurled her sword, spinning it through the air at Tohrvath. Its meagre pommel struck the serpent's functional eye, briefly stunning the creature. Adela's sword rebounded into the darkness, clattering against bricks beyond her sight. Tohrvath, however, swiftly recovered, gazing down at Adela with wicked amusement.

"Oh, *Windcatcher...*" The edges of his maw curled back in what one could interpret as a smile. "How I *do* enjoy a tender meal."

As Tohrvath lunged with gaping jaws aglow, a blinding, cyan light exploded from his middle and ruptured the serpent in two. Tohrvath's imposing head toppled lifeless to the water, a hair's breadth from Adela's toes. Her right eye twitched as she stared down at it, her jaw grinding as she forced herself to contemplate its rent form; never before had she felt such overwhelming gratitude at the death of another. It may have been nothing more than a serpent—a monster to forever haunt the nightmares of children—yet it was still a creature of creation... sentient... and *living*. Even still, Adela was surprised; she cared not the slightest for its demise, but rather... felt a terrifying sense of satisfaction in it.

And for that, she was left all the more perturbed.

A soft gasp of her name tore Adela's attention from the serpent's gory remains and to Darun, who lay gravely wounded within Tohrvath's limp coils. Dashing to his side, a grave weight struck Adela's heart as she beheld his armour, caved in by the serpent's great spines.

"*Sam!*" she cried. "Sam, *now!*" She shot a look over her shoulder to see Ramsoen making his way towards her, Sam propped up beneath an arm. "Help me with this!" She tugged on the serpent's coils, symbols igniting across her armour. Before Adela lifted, she froze: halted by Darun's words.

"No..." he pleaded, gesturing for her to stop. "No... I'll only bleed out faster."

Adela shook her head.

"If I bind it quick enough, it won't matter, yeah?"

"Not if it pierced... an organ or two..." Darun's chest heaved painfully. "Aye... I'm already dead, lass... I feel its eldritch venom spreading through my veins and into my heart." He paused to exhale a stuttering breath. "You can't save me..."

"Probably not, luv," said a shrugging Adela, reaching into her satchel for a veneer bind. "But I can *bloody try*." She tore the cloth with her teeth, wrapping it about her hands tightly. "Sure as the good Lord doesn't give up on us, yeh?"

"No..." he breathed, Darun's voice muffled beneath his helmet. He said something else, but it was too faint for Adela to decipher. Darun weakly gestured to his chest, gasping: "*Can't*... can't breathe..."

"Oh!" Adela made haste in removing his black kerchief, revealing the pained expression beneath. "Is... is that better at all, luv?"

"A little... but... no, not at all." He shook his head, his chest heaving heavily as he pushed her hands away. "No... I shall die..."

Adela clenched her jaws, stubbornly reaching to remove his armour.

"Oy, that's *bloody* enough of your drama, luv." She began undoing his chest-piece's straps. "A couple minutes and I can—"

"*Stop*." His eyes briefly flickered a blazing orange as he shoved her off the coils. Falling backwards, she tumbled right into Sam and Ramsoen's arms. Darun's head limply fell back against the coils. "I am doing... *everything* I can... to stave off the... the *raw* magic... in my veins... from bleeding out..." A stuttering exhale escaped him. "Go now... before I die... and its wrath escapes me."

"*No*," asserted Adela, tearing herself from her pack. "No, we *just* lost Fel. I can't have another leave me here—not so soon, not *like this!* Oy, lad—" She vaulted over the coils to slap his cheeks. "We'll find yeh a healer, luv. They'll fix you right up and you... you won't be lost, yeh?!"

"Verily... I say unto you... we shall... *all of us* be lost... if you do not now make haste..." Darun's fist began to illuminate in a threatening orange. "*Go*... leave now... or I shall not... *hesitate* to kill Sam."

Adela ground her jaws, punching the scales of the dead serpent.

"You're pure evil, *Darun!* Absolutely wicked!" Her eyes glazed over, but no tears could fall. "You might as well have me *kill* you! It's all the *bloody same* in—" She cut herself off as a searing blade of raging embers rose from Darun's palm. He shakily raised his fist, threatening to cast its fire upon Sam.

Adela's breath shook uncontrollably as she shoved off the coils. Turning to look back at Ramsoen, she bit her lip and nodded. "Nearest exit, *now*." Symbols across her arms lit a golden hue as she swooped under Sam's arm, carrying him with Ramsoen. Sloshing through the tunnel's murky water, they bolted from Darun's pulsing form, heading further into the tunnel's darkness. It wasn't long before Ramsoen led them to a ladder; its rusting rungs led up to an unseen shadow. Stepping away from Sam, Adela scaled the ladder first, frowning as she reached its top; a dark hatch obstructed their escape, locked from the other side. Symbols ignited across her limbs as she beat the hatch with her fists. Splinters flew with every strike, but no greater damage could be made. Negating her blows, blue symbols would pulse across the hatch before fading away.

Why did everything have to be so bloody magical?

Shaking her head, Adela's gaze fell to the ladder as she asked: "*Oy!* Is there another way about or have you any means of—"

A flash of blazing pink light exploded from where they had left Darun. Adela hugged closer to the ladder's rungs as its force rocked the cave. To her horror, tendrils of wild magic began tearing through the tunnels, decimating whatever dared to stand before them. Adela turned to Ramsoen, gasping as he dropped Sam into the water. Digging through his pockets, Ramsoen hastily retrieved what appeared to be a handful of charcoal-like pebbles. Without waiting for her consent, he flung them up at Adela, shielding her in a sphere of fiery blue.

Before she could react, the wave of energy struck her. Its flaming-pink tendrils launched Adela through the hatch, obliterating its design and rocketing her up through two different floors. Despite the various debris and wild magic, she was protected from most of its devastation.

Most of it.

Her fiery-blue shield popped as she struck the stone ceiling of a now crumbling chamber. With the air knocked out her lungs, she came crashing down to the rubble-stricken floor. Adela choked, her chest tightening and withholding breath. Waiting for her chest to loosen, she gulped air gratefully, only to cough violently as the dust from the debris dried her throat. Adela raised her ashen-black kerchief and pushed herself up, Adela clawed through the rubble, pulling herself atop a column. On the other side, a giant hole gaped in the floor, and she leaned in close, peering into the stifling darkness three stories below. Her eyes strained, trying to make sense of the shadowed depths. Adela cupped her hands about her mouth and hollered: "*Oy*, are you both alright?!" She was left with no response but the returning echo of her own desperate cries. Frustrated, Adela jerked the kerchief down. "Ay, that's *just* about enough—*Please*, not you two! *It can't be you!* I *can't* lose everyone! I *can't*—"

She struggled to claw through the debris, but stopped as it threatened to collapse beneath her. Adela fell back on her knees, gazing through the crack intently. "Sam! *Sam*, tell me you're alive, *please!*" Her vision began to haze, threatening to flood over. "Ramsoen, I *know* you escaped! I know you had another ward stone, just... just *bloody answer me!*" she shrieked, tearing at her short hair. "You thrice-accursed cold-hearted back-stabbing..." Adela cradled her knees, rocking herself as she did everything she could to control her stupid emotions, "sneaking... scoundrel... absolutely *wicked*... no-good, rotten..." She couldn't restrain her emotions any longer as they swelled over her eyes, trickled down her cheeks and began to drip from her chin. It was beyond control now; Adela's features were quivering in a breathless sob.

She hated herself for it.

I AM SORRY... CHILD.

Adela raised her head from her arms to see a ghostlike figure standing over her. It was clothed in white, with a simple-black mask concealing the figure's hooded features. It gracefully extended a warm hand to her shoulder, one wrapped in pale linen.

THE OATHER'S DESECRATION KNOWS NO BOUNDS.

It knelt to her eye level.

I AM SORRY... THAT YOU MUST KNOW THIS SUFFERING AT THE EXPENSE OF THEIR AMUSEMENT.

Though its expression was concealed, Adela couldn't help but feel the figure's pity fuming behind its mask.

THE OATHER HAS CHOSEN YOU AS HIS PAWN... AND FOR THAT... YOU WILL DIE.

Adela shrugged, sniffing as she wiped her nose. "Mkay..."

ADELA... MY CHILD... IT NEEDN'T BE YOU.

The figure rose ominously, raising a pale finger to its left. Adela followed the gesture to see a crumbling window and... beyond it... *disorder*; rooks stomping alongside ranks of Unbequith soldiers—soldiers throwing their lives against the lives of their enemies. Ember cannons lining the capital's walls were firing at rapid successions, just *barely* staving off the onslaught. The voiceless words continued.

THERE ARE TWO OTHERS WHO COULD BE THE PAWN WE SEEK... THE PAWN WHO SHALL SEAL THE OATHER'S SCHEMES WITH THEIR DEVELOPMENT. PROVE TO US, O'ADELA... PROVE TO US THAT YOU REFUSE TO PARTAKE AS THE OATHER'S PAWN, BUT INSTEAD... EMBRACE YOUR EXISTENCE AS A TRUE CHILD OF GOD... INDEPENDENT OF THE MANIPULATING WILLS ABOUT US.

The figure extended a hand for her to accept.

YIELD TRUVALSON FROM YOUR HEART UNTO ME... AND I SHALL RENDER YOUR BLIND SERVICE TO THE OATHER... FOREVER SILENCED.

Adela was quiet for several moments before puffing at her bangs. Shakily shoving onto her knees, she rose to face the figure, her stern expression a hair's breadth from its mask.

"In the name of the Eternal *King*," she growled, "*begone.*"

The figure's head tilted to the left.... ever.... so... quizzically.

CHILD, YOU DARE TO MISTAKE ME FOR A DEMON... THOUGH I AM FAR BEYOND SUCH VULGAR SPIRITS.

The chambers shook with the voiceless words of the figure.

THEY ARE THE FALLEN AND BROKEN, HELLBENT ON CORRUPTING SOULS IN THE MOST PETTY OF SCHEMES.

The words fell silent for a few moments before—[4] Adela's mind throbbed with the word, its presence ringing in her head, obstructing any other thought.

I AM NO... WEAK... PATHETIC... SNIVELLING LAPDOG OF THE MORNING STAR. HEYLEL HIMSELF FLEES THE THOUGHT OF MY PRESENCE, SCORCHED BY THE VERY FIRES OF ITS LIGHT.

The figure's words commanded existence itself and Adela knew nothing but their silence.

HE FLEES THE THOUGHT OF AN EXISTENCE SUCH AS MINE, BECAUSE IT IS MORE COMFORTING TO BELIEVE ONE SUCH AS I CANNOT EXIST.

---

4. *No*

The figure knelt to Adela's level again.

NAY, I AM NO DEMON.

Adela retorted with a smart response, though she heard not her own words. The figure reacted to this by seizing her throat and elevating her above the rubble.

I AM SIOLANT.

Three more words followed, reverberating through every fibre of her soul in violent tremors. The sheer force of their presence surged within her, building to a crescendo that culminated in a hushed peace. Not a single sound uttered. Instead, three words flashed through Adela's entire being in pure, unyielding power.

Adiuva me esse.

Adela spat at the figure's mask as it dissipated, its presence withdrawing like an inhaled gasp. Falling to the floor, Adela coughed and sputtered, holding her reddening throat. Shaking her head, she weakly pushed herself up to glance out the window to her right.

Chaos.

There was no time for her to recover; every second she delayed brought her closer to death. No, Adela *refused* to standby idle for another second. She couldn't allow death to continue its grim harvest, not while blood yet coursed through her limbs. Pushing against her hands, Adela forced herself off the rubble and up to a wobbly stance. She was unsure whether Regend could hear her thoughts, but she screamed his name in her head, asking him to circle the skies above from a safe distance.[5]

Heaving aside chunks of stone, Adela cleared the chamber door to peer through. Assessing the hall before her, she nodded to herself and darted forward, gradually making her way to the vault; it was a pure blessing she hadn't been so lazy as to let Ramsoen study the keep's layout *alone*. He may have been the guide, but she had refused to go in blind.

Heavens *alive*, she was grateful for her memory.

---

5. Yeah... I don't know if he hears her.

CHAPTER THIRTY-ONE

MORTAL GODS

V INCENT HADN'T SO MUCH as drawn his blade. He stood with his back to the vault, a score of elite Rantilorian guards standing before him. Thankfully, their elite ranks managed the greater portion of work: fending off the onslaught pouring through a crumbling hole. The Redfolk had used a siege engine to breach the hall—one Vincent couldn't identify from where he had been standing guard. Still, it wasn't of dire consequence; the elite guard fended off the intruders well enough. Vincent was grateful for that. One such as himself was... well, the idea of slaughtering thousands upon thousands of men just... didn't appeal. One way or another, this war would conclude: with or without his skills. If countless lives could be spared with his absence, then absent he shall be—for the most part; he still had a job to do: a duty to fulfil—an obligation to answer. Despite the Redfolk's legions of warriors, ranks of siege engines and pure ferocity, Vincent was certain their hostile assault would never achieve the finer goal of this war.

Not while one of his sort stood watch over the vault.

Aye, though Chulian denied his sword's full potential—Vincent had damaged reality enough as it were—the onrushing soldiers would stand no chance against his advanced gear and centuries of combat experience. Why, if they weren't skilled enough to overcome the Rantilorian elite, what chance had they against Vincent? If all proceeded accordingly, Unbequith would be inflicted by a heavy toll and hold no choice but to pull out and surrender.

It was *that* simple.

Vincent shook his head with a smirk, tapping Chulian's pommel as he paced. Really, the only threat worth worrying about would be the—

The floor beneath him tilted forward, warping with the corridors in a twisting manipulation. Vincent's footing gradually gave way as it slanted, causing him to stumble and slide across the inclining floor. He fell right atop his company, their enchanted armour clanking discordantly as he landed atop them. Some men had nearly fallen through the wall's hole below, but were caught by their comrades moments before plummeting through. Sorting himself out above the warping reality, Vincent cued strings of symbols to ignite across his bracers. He then stepped forward, shoving aside his company to stride about the hole, yanking men up and out as he passed them.

After he pulled up the final man, a warrior in flaming black armour rocketed up through the hole, colliding against the vault's door above. The dark warrior stood with gauntlets aglow, positioned in the hall as though it were right side up. Raising his fist, the warrior proceeded to pulverise the vault, stressing its layers of blue symbols from such bombastic collisions. The warrior's armour exploded in wreathing black flames with every strike; an enchanted feature designed specifically for intimidation with little to no practical use.

Oddly enough, Vincent found it to be working.

"And *that*'s a True Beyonder," he noted, turning to face his company. "Have we any intrinsically *magical* individuals? No? Alright, any young mother's son concealing some deep secret of his abilities who would like to now step forward and share with us, but is afraid of doing so for fear of his *specialness* being shunned—or dare I say refuted by his love interest?" Vincent shook his head, pinching his nose at the sight of their bemused expressions. "Have ye no quarrel to be held with this foe?! No personal resentment felt for your rival? Could you not wield that hatred in one final clash with your old nemesis?! Go right on ahead—*go!*" Vincent frantically hopped up and down, stabbing a finger at the ceiling which... well... it used to be the vault's entrance at the end of the hall... he supposed it was a ceiling now. "Time is *depleting!* I assure you, the moment you're ready to deliver the killing blow, you'll come to yourself and spare your long-hated rival—only to have him stab you in the back, but fail! Thus bringing about his own *ruin*—why, you might even learn the true *bleeding* power of *friendship!*"[1]

One soldier glanced at his company with concerned eyes before looking back to address Vincent.

"I'm... sorry sir. But we're just soldiers."

Vincent exhaled... *long*... and slow.

---

1. I'm surprised the True Beyond hasn't burst in yet. How thoughtful.

"Right... *just* soldiers." He cocked his head to the side, swinging his sword from its scabbard to rest atop his shoulder. "I would say something inspiring, but..."—his gaze rose to the vault—"*just* soldiers was *kind* of depressing to hear." Puffing a strand of white hair from his eyes, Vincent stabbed his sword into what used to be their footing and was now a steep wall. A layer of ice clawed up to the dark warrior in a frenzied haste and coldly seized their ankle. Tearing his sword free, the ice erupted in a cerulean flame, causing the dark warrior to come bearing down upon them. Unfortunately for Vincent, he could feel reality warping and knew the True Beyonder was converting his fall into a ballistic charge. Tempting, though it may have been, Vincent refused to wield Chulian's true might. Besides, Chulian would only refuse to allow it.

It was fine by Vincent; he'd find a way to manage with the barebone abilities of Chulian's sword... *somehow.*

With a rather climatic boom, the rear wall of the vault crumbled inwards behind him. Which... was sort of a problem for Theo considering the curious attachment he had formed with it. Not... the wall itself, mind you—that would be... *odd*—no, he was referring to the tentacled critters coating every face of the wall. They acted as a peculiar means of security; their velvety skins pulsing in vibrant colours and signalling the presence of an intruder they sensed behind the wall. Theo wasn't completely certain how they worked and... frankly didn't care.

He liked them.

And that was all that mattered.

So you could probably understand how he felt as a hole was blown in the rear wall, right? Not wishing for any to be crushed by the debris, he teleported about the vault, catching the flying octopi in his arms.

Octopi? Or was it octopuses... octopodes?

Was there a right answer?

Not but two winks had passed before the debris hit the floor and Theo stood in the vault's centre, his arms brimming with the odd little critters. Judging from the searing display of power, Theo guessed it to be a high-ranking True Beyonder; what other being could have so easily broken through the vault's symbols? Other than Theo... of course.

He was simply brilliant.

And that wasn't arrogance, it was just honesty, so shut your trap, alright?

Right.

Anyway, *there was Theo*: hardcore as usual; holding his ground, hair messy, yet majestic while he stood there like the absolute champion he was and—*alright...* maybe it *was* arrogance. Either way, Theo remained completely unfazed as the True Beyonder stepped through the crumbling gap, twirling white flames of cackling energy about its head as it approached in lumbering... *dramatic* strides towards Theo.

Very theatrical.

It was monologuing to him now, but Theo just... didn't... really... *care...*

Yeah.

Just as the True Beyonder began to near his breathing space, Theo ominously turned about, his arms still holding the tentacled critters. He was summoned here on business, so business-like he shall conduct his business... *unfortunately*. Had Junia not pleaded him from doing so, Theo would have killed off a third of Unbequith's army and be done with it. Why draw out casualties on her people's part if he could end every threat in *less than an hour's—*

Theo sucked it up.

He was in a salty mood now, upset by the illogical reasoning of his second favourite person... thing; no one here was *human* apparently and were all quite foreign to the word... which was odd considering they all spoke English—no, it mattered not... Junia was being stupid, but she would have her own bloody way. It was a job after all and a job's a bleeding... thrice-accursed... gashed *job!*

Theo tossed the tentacled critters over his head before reaching for his pistols. The critters showered the air behind him in pulses of orange and red—but he didn't look back; cool guys don't look back—cool guys *never* look back. Granted, that was usually with explosions, but this felt much cooler.

Somehow.

Priming one hodgepodge-of-a-pistol, Theo bashed its barrel into the True Beyonder's thigh, denting the armour there. Phasing through reality itself, Theo transferred his existence to stand just behind the True Beyonder, allowing him to unload a round into the backside of the warrior's thigh.

The True Beyonder thudded against the floor, overcome by the foreign pain Theo had lodged in their leg. Turning the warrior over with his toe, Theo knelt, pressing a knee against their shoulders. The warrior shakily raised a searing fist, but Theo gently shook his head with a tut and directed his firearm's muzzle over the warrior's bullet wound.

"Please," he chided—ever *so* kindly, "I beseech thee to accept this token of mercy... as a *warning*." The True Beyonder roared in pain as Theo pulled the trigger. Frowning at their weakness, Theo stood up from the floor, his gaze rising to meet the division of Unbequith soldiers who had flooded in after the True Beyonder. Nudging the warrior with the tip of his boot, Theo's expression shrugged: "Should do well enough so long as the pain doesn't overwhelm him." Theo bent over to examine the warrior, nonchalantly gesturing his firearm at the Unbequith soldiers. "Mm, yeah, just take him to your practitioners of Darbio, yeah? He won't survive a wound like that what with the manner of healing *our* captivity possesses." Theo's gaze rose to the soldiers, their faces pale: as though they'd witnessed a ghost.

Theo flapped his hands at them. "Come on then, he's bleeding out." They timidly nodded their thanks, edging towards him to retrieve the True Beyonder. Theo dusted off his barrel as he watched them. "Oh, and mind the lead poisoning." Theo smiled after them as they fled from sight with their wounded champion. "*Heh*... wow."

The whole room then warped beneath his feet, causing Theo to stumble backwards. He tried to adjust himself right-side up, but his armour couldn't react in time to all the shifting elements about him, causing Theo to smash around the walls like a hacky sack. Dizzy from all the confusion, Theo huffed and just allowed himself to fall whatever bladed way the room decided was down.

Picky room... choose a side already.

As if in response to this, Theo tumbled off the floor and onto the vault's door below. He landed on his back with a metallic thud, several tentacled critters plopping atop him. One landed on his face and just—*mm*, wow... his health had never been better. No really, he felt amazing. Pain was simply a concept perceived by the mind as whatever one was willing to interpret it as. For Theo... yeah, he felt nothing—he was good.

Thanks for asking.

Theo winked, not really caring to where or whom it was directed. He froze for a moment, staring up at the hole in the wall above him: "*Nice*."

A violent beating hammered against the vault's door beneath Theo, jostling his entire body up and down as more pummelings followed the first in rapid succession. The tentacled critters about him were bouncing, the vibrations shifting them around his head. Theo opened his mouth, allowing the vibrations in his throat to escape in the most amusing of fashions: "*uahuhuahuahuhuahuahuhuah*—" Theo cocked his ear to the muffled sound of turmoil from outside; there were frantic shouts, metallic clashes and an... odd sound like... like energised pulses of... *energy.*

Or something.

It was hard for Theo to describe, okay?

Theo methodically reloaded his firearm with a sigh, preparing to deliver *yet another warning.*

[2] Vincent's arm shot left and right as he tried to aim his celestial flintlock. But with the hall constantly rolling about and his sense of direction completely shattered, Vincent couldn't fire without hitting one of his own.

Chulian, he thought, *is there any way you could—*

No.

Vincent clenched his jaws, springing off the spiralling corridor to launch himself at the dark warrior. Falling through the halls, he raised his sword over his head, only to stumble as the corridor corrected itself and Vincent fell to the floor. Struggling to stand, the floor beneath him flipped over, sending Vincent hurling straight into the grip of the dark warrior. The scar on Vincent's throat burned more than anything, flooding his mind with a pained madness.[3]

Chulian! he screamed mentally. *Stick an astral scar in his gut! Chulian! Chulian now or—*

No.

A speckle of drool began to escape Vincent as his eyes rolled to the back of his head. Before he could completely pass out, the dark warrior dropped him to the floor below, distracted by... was that cannon fire? Caressing his throat, Vincent sat up to see

---

2. Alright, I'm back. Whoever that Theo was, he's strong enough to claim the narrative outside any influence. His mind... it's too strong. I had to switch back to Vincent just to speak like this again. Note to self: don't switch to his mind again.

3. Vincent's scar was given to him by a True Beyonder (and burns like fresh when touched by one). The full story is too long for a mere footnote.

Theo—dual-wielding two sidearms and peppering the dark warrior in gunfire. Every bullet was melted on contact by discs of black flames pulsing across the warrior's armour. No, if Theo was to land a hit, it would have to be one the True Beyonder didn't expect. Vincent aimed his celestial flintlock downsight, waiting for the perfect moment to—and Theo just tossed a frag.[4]

Of course he did.

A red explosion erupted beneath the dark warrior's feet, causing him to fly up into the ceiling. As the corridor began to flip in the warrior's favour, Vincent shot a single bolt of energised yellow after the dark warrior. Upon contact, the warrior plummeted to the warped floor. With the True Beyonder now unconscious, the room corrected itself with a sickening whirl. Picking himself up, Vincent released a pent up breath of air, gesturing to the elite guard as he approached the dark warrior.

"You can do no good here," he advised, gesturing to their gravely wounded. "Assist your brethren. Theodraan and I have it quite handled." Vincent knelt beside the dark warrior as the Rantilorian company departed. "Ah." He tapped the engravings in its armour. "Why, they should be significantly easier to handle without their champion to—*oi!*" Vincent lunged forward, but it was too late; Theo had already kicked the dark warrior out the hole it had entered through. Vincent winced at the harsh racket of its armour colliding with the stone court below. "Are you *bloody* insane?!"

Theo shrugged, toying with his firearm.

"A little... I think... though it's more plausible that everyone *else* are the ones gashed in the head... *bladed sanitists*—you know if someone believes in sanity, they could be called a sanitist? I dunno in what reality that that would ever be true, but I like to believe I made it up, yeah?" Vincent refused to humour such ludicrousy. Nonetheless, to his greater annoyance, Theo continued, following Vincent back to the vault: "Which is funny, considering how close sanitist sounds to *satanist*—"

Vincent dug into his pouches to retrieve a handful of charcoal-like pebbles and pocket-sized vials of the most bombastic nature.

"*Listen,*" he said and abruptly turned to face Theo, "you should have more sense than to wield weapons of the Grey-Circle so recklessly."

Theo sniffed.

---

4. For those medieval beholders, a frag is a small bomb.

"If you're asking me to limit myself," he said and shook his pistol, "these are lead rounds."

"That's not what I *bloody meant.*"

"Mm... kay." Theo eyed the contents in Vincent's palm. "And what are those?"

"Here... *take 'em.*" Vincent dumped the vials and ward stones into Theo's care. "Those can only do so much, so mind yourself."

"Oh... thank you... for this... cool, uhm... junk." Theo pinched a ward stone between two fingers, shaking it with sarcastic emotion. "I am... *overwhelmed,* truly."

"Right." Vincent paused as he neared the vault's door, turning to eye Theo. "Do you..."

"Yeah." Theo kicked down the vault door, enhancements and all, sending it flying out of its frame. It flew over the head of a ducking intruder and through another hole across the way. The intruder slowly rose from their knees; a gangly fellow, sporting a russet mask lined with simple engravings. They wore a black fabric with thin plates clinking within the outfit's coarse material. The armour reminded Vincent of a brigandine, only... less bulky. *Far* less bulky.

Vincent raised an eyebrow; the enchanted safe behind the intruder had been bashed in and—in the intruder's petite hands—was a grey casket. The intruder froze upon sight of them, speaking in a soft, rather awkward, voice.

"Ehm, *ay* there... luvs... ehm..." She—for it was most certainly a girl—tucked the casket under one arm and waved shyly. "There's a... big ol' *hole* in your wall left unpatched so I... I just let myself in, yeh?" Vincent heard her gulp. "No hard feelings or nothin', yeh?"

Theo uncrossed his arms, walking through the door to retrieve several octopi from the floor and stick them back onto the walls.

"Please give that back," he said, dusting his hands after completing his... rather odd task.

The intruder glanced nervously at Vincent, almost as though she recognized him.

"I... I would. Truly..." She shook her head, hugging the casket closer. "But too many have been lost for this and... and I can't allow any more to be lost."

"Look, kid..." Theo pinched his nose, his hand falling to rub his beard. "I've been given direct instructions to either capture or *kill* intruders and I'm in no mood to hear logic that might end up making sense, alright?" He gestured at her fearsome mask and Unbequith garbs. "And those heralds aren't helping you, but—*look,* that's my warning, alright? Take it and go. Just leave behind the casket in exchange and you'll be all good, alrighty?" Theo cracked his knuckles.

The intruder recoiled at this, holding a hand up before taking a cautious step forward.

"But... luv... I..." She paused before continuing: "I don't know what they're paying you two, but... but I hardly doubt all this death and... and simply *dreadful* suffering is hardly worth any heap of sums. Surely you can't mean to tell me your hearts are so corrupted as to profane your own—"

"Yeah,"—Theo set a hand on his holster—"don't take another step, kid."

The intruder paused, arms raised submissively.

"*Listen.*" Her attention was directed solely on Vincent now, her commanding voice seizing his attention. "Unbequith has had its faults—many I myself have been subjected to—but... but to *kill* us for it? For *these.*" She slapped the casket. "You call the children of Unbequith *Redfolk*—*monsters*, yet act more monstrous than any good soldier I have come to know. The children of Unbequith are a noble people and deserve—more than any other—to be trusted with the responsibility of honour these shards carry." Her hand extended forward. "Please... *Vincent...* if you don't trust Unbequith, then trust *me.* As one Child of God to another."

Vincent sighed, his blade faltering.

"Child... I... I cannot—"

"But you *know* the truth in my words to be undeniable and the conviction of my heart steadfast. You cannot deny this truth—you cannot deny *me* this truth."

Vincent's sword lowered to the floor.

"I, no... I cannot... for I know you speak with an earnest tongue." He shook his head, his sword's point rising from the stone. "And yet... simply because you believe it to be true does not indeed make it so... no matter how terribly you may wish it to be." He gravely extended a sympathetic hand to her. "Whether my truth appeals to you or not, the *truth* still remains... you have fallen for a grave and propagated lie, child... one you and many more noble spirits have fallen for. Ranitorl is not this monster you speak of. This death willing—"

"*No*, but I've *seen it*—I've *seen* the cruel scythe of Grim befall upon my kin, its blade wielded by the hand of the regions you pledge to! I've *seen* the horrors in the dark below—horrors who dare claim the lives of *virtuous* men! And now... *now* you ask me to yield this infinite potential to the very region who *slaughtered* them? The very region who profaned their remains with black hexes?" The intruder took a cautious step towards Vincent. "Please, you must know—"

The moment her foot touched down, Theo unholstered his weapon, coldly directed its muzzle to her head, and pulled the trigger. Reacting without thought, Vincent pounced at

Theo, seizing his wrist and sidearm. The jarring explosion of a gunshot rang in Vincent's ears as he shoved the muzzle upwards. Reality shifted about Theo as he pulled away to the other side of the vault under the blink of an eye. However, with Vincent still gripping the firearm, he was teleported as well. For once, a look of genuine surprise crossed Theo's face. Before he could make the connection, Vincent twisted the firearm and slugged the man's jaw. His armoured knuckles dented a hair's breadth from Theo's face, as though it had struck an invisible barrier.

From the corners of his gaze, Vincent could see the intruder bolting off with the grey casket. Time itself seemed to freeze as he watched her escape. For once in his life, with all of Beyond on the line... could he not have—*just this once*—ignored his conscience for his better judgement? As Theo's armoured fist collided with Vincent's eye, he couldn't help but think of nothing but the intruder and just how much his hesitation had cost the world.

Vincent refused to make the same mistake again.

However... he also refused to let an unstable madman like Theo manage the situation. Twisting the firearm behind Theo's head, Vincent locked his arms. Unfortunately, Theo simply released his weapon, falling to the floor and pulling Vincent with him. However, before he could land on Theo, reality shifted and Vincent was pulled along with it. Passing through folds of reality, Vincent hastily pressed his celestial flintlock into Theo's side, with only a split second to pull the trigger.

Casket in one hand, drawn sabre in the other, Adela *ran*. She ran for her *life*, for all of Unbequith, and for the lives of all those who might never know the blessed felicity of a free mind and soul. Adela knew not where she was headed, but was left with no other choice.

She *just* needed to *escape*.

As she rounded the keep's crumbling corridors, Adela mentally screamed Regend's name. Assuming he was circling the skies to begin with, she was still unsure whether he'd be able to discern such a crazed rush of emotion and—

"Adela!"

At the sound of her name, she skidded to a halt, but not before colliding into the chest of a shady figure. In the same instant, Regend came crashing through one of the majestic windows lining the left hand side of the corridor. Shoving herself off the figure, Adela swiftly raised her blade defensively, only to drop it at the sight of Ramsoen.

"*Ram!*" She wrapped her arms about him in a brief embrace before shoving the grey casket into his armpit and pulling away. "Take this and take Regend." She patted Regend's saddle. "Do me a favour and fly as high and as *swift* as yeh can, yeh luv?"

Regend's metallic head dipped to her level, his eye pulsing a light blue.

The chaos of war holds no quarrel with my sort from above. Let me take you both.

"*No.*" Adela clapped her hands in agitation. "Ram, *get* on him!" She stuck a finger at Regend. "You, *take* him. The two guardians are distracted only momentarily and one presently seeks to *kill* me! No, I shall only be a hindrance. Fly fast and fly true. You—" She swiftly spun about to face Ramsoen. "You, give the shards to Aivon and smuggle them into the safety of Unbequith. *Please...* Ram..." Her eyes began welling over uncontrollably. "Don't let them fall prey to corruption... *please* brother... not after so many have died... *please.*"

Ramsoen bounced the casket in his hands before hoisting himself atop Regend.

"Aye." He tucked the casket into his satchel. "And I'm grateful to see you're alive too, lass."

"Yeh... sorry..." Her hands gradually slipped away from Regend as she stepped back. "I'm... so *very* grateful you found me." She hesitated before asking: "Is... Sam... is he—"

"Sorry, lass, no time." He directed Regend to turn about. "Make it back alive and you'll see for yourself."[5]

"Ram... *you*—"

In a flurry of rushing air, Regend flapped his wings and launched himself up through the broken window. Ramsoen raised a hand in the air, waving goodbye ever so casually. Adela watched them go, hesitant to turn her back to them.

He *truly* believed she'd make it.

Shaking her head, Adela turned to continue running; she had to lead the guardians away; should they resolve their quarrel, she and all of Unbequith would stand no chance against their unnatural abilities. However, she didn't *have* to stand a chance. All that was required of her was to exist as a ruse; a tactic of deception she had learned best from Aivon's nearly flawless execution of it.

---

5. I suppose that's Ramsoen's way of telling her to stay alive. His own way of showing he cares. Odd fellow, that one.

Adela paused.

She needed to acquire her bearings before aimlessly—

A harsh grip seized her by the shoulders, warping reality about her to hurl Adela against a wall of another room. Adela fell to the floor, clutching her bruised sides from the violent impact. She looked up to see a guardian—the unstable one—striding towards her, a fresh burn somehow denting his chestpiece. Adela hurled spiderknives dangling from her waist, giving herself enough time to unhook her mask and slip it on. The moment she did, she felt a slugging blow speeding for her jaw. Twisting over and up to her feet, she thrust her palm in the air, catching the guardian by the wrist. An exploding burst of energy erupted from the guardian's restrained hand, causing Adela's ears to ring dully. In the brief second which followed, Adela attempted a slash at his knees with her sabre. Though she could feel his existence through the mask, her blade passed right through the guardian, as though he were nothing more than a phantom.

Adela's head jerked back as the guardian's fist struck her mask several times over: again... and again... and *again*. Adela fell to a rug on the stone floor, gasping for breath. She tore off her smothering mask, her nose bleeding into her sputtering mouth.

A cruel shadow cast over her.

Her stern gaze rose to the guardian, the late light of day streaming in from a window behind him. He lowered his weapon and rested its muzzle on her forehead.

"*Yield*," he commanded. "Never before have I been so gracious as to bestow a second warning... I suggest you accept this rare opportunity and relinquish the shards to my custody once again." He shoved the muzzle against her skull, jolting her head. "Drop the casket."

Adela wrinkled her nose.

"Are you a ghost?"

"No, just Grey-Circle."

Adela shrugged.

"Still dunno what that is, luv."

"Shame." The guardian dusted his weapon. "This is a gun by the way." He shook his head and scoffed. "Now, if you're too primitive to understand—"

"No... no, I know, luv." She exhaled sharply through her nose, hoping to clear it of the running blood. "I've had one of these pointed at me before and... from what the lunatic was tellin' me... I don't believe it's gonna work..." Adela shrugged, reddening at how ridiculous she must sound. "And that's... yeh... that's why you'll need a better threat, luv."

"It's not a *threat*. It's a *warning*. Don't call me *love*. I *am* going to kill you and *tear* the casket from your corpse unless you surrender it to me *willingly—alright?*"

Adela shrugged.

"I did my part."

"Then it shall be your last." Theo pressed the muzzle further into her hair, his finger on the trigger. His mouth twitched as he eyed her, his shining grey pupils reminding her of Aresmas. Her own eyes couldn't help but glaze over from the thought.

Adela flinched as the guardian screamed in pure rage before exclaiming: *"Blade it all!* I can't *bloody—"* He vanished from where he was standing to appear beside the bed and kick it in with one foot. The guardian teleported in front of her once more, muzzle at her head. "You have the most *irksome* eyes," he wheezed, *"you know that?* Everyone I've ever killed—everyone I've hurt, they all *bloody* deserved it." The guardian shook his head, looking more unhinged than ever. "You... I see nothing but purity in your bladed gaze—*please."* His hand was shaking ever so discreetly as he laughed. "Come on, don't make me live with this."

Adela shrugged.

"Sorry... I... "

The guardian shook his head, chuckling nervously before resuming his grave countenance.[6] His finger twitched on the trigger, ever so delicately... but he did not fire.[7] For once—as his weapon began to droop—Adela beheld the guardian's cold gaze... *soften*.

The window behind the guardian smashed to pieces as an energised projectile cracked through the air. A golden bolt of energy splayed across the guardian's back, sending him toppling to the ground. Adela scrambled to his side, feathering his neck with two fingers; thankfully, there was still a pulse. He was simply unconscious. Adela's gaze shot to the cracked window, just barely discerning a small glint... it was originating from another hallway across the courtyard... she could just... barely discern an older man... aiming a bronze and brown...

---

6. *kill her*

7. No... you can't. I know you can't. No one has the heart to kill Adela, not even you. Ignore the voice of Silence and heed mine; do not kill her.

Adela pulled back, clearing her body of the doorway and the window's view. As she did, a bolt of cackling yellow energy shot through the window to explode across the carpet in a flurry of sparks. Adela covered her head, peeking out only to withdraw it again as another shot followed. Her eyes darting about the room, she finally decided on a small table. Flipping it on its side, she hid behind it to advance through the doorway and into the hall. Another bolt of yellow struck the table and sent it propelling over her head and into the room. Adela herself was thrown to the ground, where she hastily rolled to the left; she laid just beyond the window's view.

Pressing herself against the stone wall beside the window, she cautiously rose to her feet and dared a peek out the window; for a brief moment, she caught sight of Vincent across the way, leaving his position as she glanced his way. Realising he would most definitely be searching for a way to her, Adela darted from the window.

Sprinting through halls, corridors and curving stairways, she ran to salvage what life she had yet to impact on this world; Adela may have initially thought she would meet her end in a most heroic sacrifice, but she wouldn't willingly allow herself to *die* if she could bloody well help it. Adela had hoped to upset Vincent's tracking by the complete inconsistency of her choices. It wasn't until after a good deal of running did she stop to consider locating an exit. All the bloody windows were too high off the ground—even for such symbols as hers.

Adela began to slow down, pausing to catch her breath; though she may have eluded Vincent, exhaustion itself finally caught up to her. She was tired... *hungry*... and by all things sacred in this world, she needed a change of trousers; Adela had been holding it for quite some time and only now realised just how pressingly annoying it *had* been; it was both fortunate and *calamitous* that she no longer required a privy of some sort.

Heaven's name, she might as well have been dead.

Wiping the blood from her nose, Adela checked her satchel, grinding her jaws; she had one spool of veneer binds left and a curious lily flower. She figured Jhess must've snuck it in. Shaking her head, she tightened the satchel shut; it had to be enough. Pushing herself off the wall, Adela continued down the seemingly endless halls of stone and odd displays of tapestry, masks and mirrors.

After several minutes, she sighed in relief upon the sight ahead; a great row of stairs descended into two greater doors, propped open to reveal an open courtyard... *outside*. How terribly she longed for it—the gloom of the syphon had made Adela realise just how much she truly treasured the open air. She could do with both a bright sun and chilled breeze bearing down upon her ruddy features... it was so clammy and quiet in here. That, and after escaping the keep, it'd be no difficult task disappearing into the chaos and finding an escort back to camp.[8]

Though Adela wished ever more to leave, she simply... *couldn't*. It was odd and... *terrifying*, really... those whispering urges tugging the inclinations of her heart to wander across a dim hallway... and to the dark door at its end.[9] Adela could just barely hear some muffled chatter on the other side, but was already *more* than hesitant to open it.[10]

And why *should* she? Adela risked her life with every second of delay. The last thing she needed was to throw herself into more danger. And yet... *no*... she knew she couldn't resist.

Adela felt an overpowering compulsion in her head—two sharp wills urging her towards the unknown and illogical. It was as though both the voice and *silence* in her head resounded in one fluid impulse, at long last agreeing on the same choice of Adela's urge and thought.

To open the doors.

---

8. *stay... turn right...*

9. Yes, Adela, I need you to go through this door.

10. *open it*

CHAPTER THIRTY-TWO

ONE MAN, ONE FACE

"**W**HY MUST YOU INSIST on these theatrics? At long last, his *life* is in your hands." Henagan's knuckles whitened as he leaned against his desk. "It is in your right—nay, *our* right to avenge *our* family." Scarce was the occasion where Malvolia was granted the privilege of beholding her father in such an emotional state; it was as unexpected as it was unwelcomed. "Why," he continued, "must you be *so* disagreeable about something so *blatantly* simple?!"

Malvolia's eyes rolled up to the back of her head. She leaned against a chair across from his desk, her arms folded over one another.

"Father... I was helping in the *infirmary*. Are you truly so lost as to summon me from the aid of the dying... that I might *kill?*" She huffed, twirling a strand of her hair about a finger. "It's a cruel irony... don't you think? Even for one as you..."

"Child, the only reason I *dare* summon your vexing spirit at this hour is because I *know* another opportunity like this will *never* present itself *again*. If you desire vengeance in the name of your brother's life, then I suggest..." Henagan's eyes darkened. "Oh... oh-ho, *no?* Hesitant, are we?" He fell back in his chair with a condescending sniff. "Have you so readily forgotten the sorrow Paun has inflicted upon *us*—upon *your mother?!*" Henagan's expression was stern and hard, exposing his nature's more furious side he reserved solely for himself... and her of course. "You may have so willingly allowed yourself to forsake the pain, but I remember *all* you had told me while your soul's scars were yet fresh... how you finally caught up to your brother—his drake steadfast by his side and his blood, *pooling* in the streets. How you carried him yourself to the nearest infirmary, *right* across the *blasted* avenue... only to have him *die* in your very arms. I remember well your scars... your *anger*... your self... *loathing*. Why, while your vidorae was yet intact, I *saw* you in those woods—in those brief *moments* you were alone... crying to yourself—nay, *weeping*—that if only you had been stronger... you could have saved my *son*."

Tears were streaming down Malvolia's indifferent expression, though she acted as though they existed not.

"So, is that all? Are you suggesting I kill myself then? You've done a fine job of encouraging such cowardice thus *far*—"

"Of *course* not," he growled. "I have told you ten times over and I shall tell you again, a *hundredfold,* if I needs must! It was not *your* fault and it never *shall* be." His features curled back in a scowl. "All the blame... the grief... the pain, the regret, the anger—*all* of it... is because of... one... remorseless... *soul*." Henagan slammed his vidorae onto the desk, its glassy facets hosting the image of a single individual. "*Traitorson...*"

Malvolia silently pondered the image of Paun chasing after who-bleeding-*knows*-what. She remained like that for several moments more before finally speaking up.

"No... no, not really..."

Henagan remained in cold silence as he studied her, before questioning: "Why... not... O'beloved... child mine?"

Malvolia softly exhaled, holding her elbows in deep concentration.

"I think..." For once, in a long time, Malvolia's hardened expression softened with weakness. "I think... I've learned to forgive... in the *least*, forgive those who needn't my forgiveness to *begin* with." She stared into the vidorae, watching Paun navigate the keep. "And... and that the singular... *villain* responsible for his death... O'*father* mine,"—her fiery gaze gradually rose to meet his—"is *you*." Before he could retort, she cut him off: "It's your bleeding-*stubborn* lust for power that killed Oleander. You and your pathetic bootlicking to that... that manipulating organisation of pure guile! You're *filth*, father—*filth*."

Henagan wove his fingers together, glaring at her from behind them.

"You speak out of place, *child*."

"Do you denote the truth of my words merely because of my *age?* I speak more truth than you ever thought to in all your years, old man!" She was quick to cut him off. "Because of you, Oleander's death will forever be remembered by history as something to *rejoice* in! He didn't die for an honourable cause, but that some *little girl* might be abducted—bleeding... *kidnapped!*" Her voice cracked as she screamed those words. "Because of *you*, his death shall forever be celebrated by the generations to come and rightfully *so*—"

Henagan rose, the intensity of his eyes matching hers.

"*Silence your tongue, girl!*"

Her chair toppled as she rose to meet his gaze.

"The only *bloody* reason I wished so dearly to hurt Paun to *begin* with... was because I could *never*... kill... *you*."

Silence.

Henagan's cold demeanour fell away to reveal a truly pained and broken man. Malvolia's arms dropped to her side, for she had *never* beheld her father in such a state—not even after the death of Oleander.

"I..." Gripping his faded-auburn hair, his elbows fell against his desk. "I cannot... I *should* not be expected to continue like this... not ever... no..." Henagan's features shifted as he rose from his desk, resuming their cold countenance. "It is impossible for me to continue as your puppet... I... I am of no further use." Henagan nodded to himself, whispering a soft and indiscernible prayer.

Two searing green eyes illuminated in the shadows behind her father. To her alarm, the green orbs stepped forward, their owner pressing a hand wrapped in black cloth against her father's desk.

"I *doubt* you're in any... position to... *choose*... old... man..." Cormurants set an arm about Henagan, pressing a knife against her father's throat. "Do not *think* for a... *second* I hold no reason *not* to... *slice* you open *here* and *now*." Cormurants' blade pricked her father's throat, sending a trickle of blood down his neck. "There is... no... *choice*."

Henagan shrugged, his fingers tapping the desk.

"Verily, you speak the truth. It is not a matter of choice—I am simply incapable of partaking in your master's madness any further. You may... file the paperwork for it or... whatever process Ms. Elicy demands of you." Henagan tugged the knife away from his throat and sighed deeply, before returning the blade to its previous position. "It's *your* problem now—"

"Enough!" Cormurants stabbed his knife into the desk, nearly slicing Henagan's wrist. "I act on the behest of Silence! I am the one with its authority, *not you*. I am the one in control, not... *you*. I wield the greater powers of the Aft-Circle—*you* answer... to *me*."

"Do I now?" Henagan smirked to himself, authentically amused. "All this display of rank and power merely to demonstrate your supposed superiority over me?"

"I *am*... superior to you..." Cormurants tore his knife from the desk and held it over her father's chest. "In *every* aspect... I am... *stronger*."

"No... no... I think not—*ow.*" Henagan winced as Cormurants applied the softest amount of pressure to his knife. Her father shook his head and continued: "It is only the truth. You need not be so bleeding touchy. If you were so superior, then why have you allowed your soul to be degraded to such a lowly level of... grime?"

"Oh? You believe yourself the morally superior? More... *righteous* of a man... as it were?" Cormurants scoffed. "Oh, but of this... we are equals."

"*Shut up,*" growled Malvolia, drawing her smallsword. "He's done some pretty crooked things, but only because *scum* like you exist." Her eyes narrowed as Cormurants brandished his knife at her. "I know you... Cormurants—I *know* you. Your sadistic sins know no bounds and the *deepest* pit of *Hell* awaits *your* sorry soul."

"Oh? Do you think so highly of your father as to elevate him to such an... *unbecoming* pedestal of virtue? Tut-tut, darling, I am afraid he is about as unworthy as I... for such... *glorified* fantasies as... moral... standards." Cormurants shrugged, his harsh movement cutting her father more, much to Malvolia's alarm. "He has not only betrayed his very region... but his own *humanity.*" Malvolia raised a bemused eyebrow at that last word to which Cormurants' replied: "The *concept* of a moral conscience found in every soul you... *idiot*—he *betrayed* it." His voice cut through Malvolia, stinging her heart with a degrading pain she would have usually dismissed with ease.

Her father caught this and was sure to also catch her eyes.

"I... have," he stated, his strong features contrasting with his glazing eyes. "I *dared* to cross my soul's voice of conscience... but only for *one*... reason..." His glistening brown eyes rested on Malvolia ever so softly. "*Desperation.*"

"Well that's a bleeding *shame!*" remarked Cormurants, jerking Henagan's head back by his ponytail. "Because now... she dies... in *front* of *you.*"

Henagan's eyes rolled up to the back of his head in pure exasperation.

"Yes, that used to be quite the *efficacious* threat of your *puppeteering* masters." Henagan jerked his head forward and politely clasped his hands. "However, it has since been rendered *null*, for I have managed to play a secret hand in this game of silence and voice. Why, Master Siolant and the very Oather *himself* knew not of this stratagem! Till now... of course."[1]

Cormurants pressed further into Henagan.

"You *lie*," he growled.

---

1. Wait, what.

"Mm... no." Her father winced, as though off-put by the breath of Cormurants. "As easier of a truth it would be for you to believe... no. I do not lie. You see, by pairing her to the proximity of the Oather's primary pawn, she herself has unknowingly produced her own set of Oather's armour. Only now, under the reassurance of the Almighty, am I confident its trope has taken full effect."[2] Henagan's eyes met Malvolia's once again. "'Tis the *singular* reason I would *ever* send her away... to protect her... and keep her... from *you*." Her father growled as he seized the hand of Cormurants: "There is *nothing* you or Siolant *itself* could use against me—not anymore, you *snivelling dullard*."

The eyes of Cormurants burned with the ever-growing intensity of his rage.

"You... no, you can't be—" He tore his wrist free, cutting Henagan's palm as he did so. "Her armour... I do not doubt its metal is dense... but yours... I shall wager... is *not*."

Henagan's shoulders rose and fell.

"No, it is not nearly as dense as your intelligence, but we already knew that—"

Cormurants pinned Henagan's face against the desk, his knife hooking under her father's arms. Malvolia drew her sword, screaming. In the same instant, the doors behind her sent a resounding thud through the chambers as they were thrown open. A figure garbed in Unbequith colours leapt past Malvolia to draw their sabre and press its point into the back of Cormurants.

"*Drop* it!" shrieked the masked intruder, its voice oddly feminine and... young. "Drop your *bleedin'* weapon and leave him well enough alone!"

Cormurants went rigid before sighing deeply, all tension sinking away with an exhale.

"Very well..." He slowly stepped away from Henagan to reveal a knife planted in her father's gut. Henagan fell limp to the floor as Cormurants stepped about the desk. "It's... *funny*... really... how much... I've truly... *missed* you... Wind... catcher..."

Malvolia darted behind the desk to her father's side, greatly disturbed by the words of Cormurants. Over the course of her journeys with Paun, she had become quite acquainted with the title *Windcatcher;* it was a name infamous enough in her memory to turn Malvolia's limbs to jam. It felt as though a millstone of guilt strapped itself about the neck of her conscience. After all, it was her family who had abducted her, sending her to

---

2. Well I'll be. Malvolia *does* have plot armour. Never thought of that... I suppose since she's become such an important character (thanks to her father's help), she's now protected from death and greater harm. Genius, that.

Unbequith at Wishton's behest. Malvolia wondered what Windcatcher would do if she discovered their role in her misery. Did she even know who they were?

Shaking her head, Malvolia dismissed such thoughts to focus on her father. She gripped the handle of the knife to yank out, but remembered such an action would only worsen the situation. Malvolia rose to her knees, rummaging through her pockets for veneer binds, before remembering that she had intentionally left them behind in the infirmary. Tears were streaming from her eyes uncontrollably as her father became so... abruptly still.

Feeling a soft pat on her shoulders, Malvolia's gaze darted up to see the girl, Windcatcher; her hand was extended out to Malvolia, a thin spool of veneer binds in her palm. Malvolia hastily accepted it, her shaky hands dressing Henagan's wounds as Cormurants continued to address the masked girl: "Oh... how... *disappointing* it must be... to see me standing... *here*... before you."

Windcatcher shrugged, stepping away from Malvolia to obstruct the door.

"After everything that's happened and... might as *well* have happened, I... I don't feel as though... as though I really care... anymore."

Cormurants laughed harshly, circling about Adela like some kind of rabid predator.

"Oh... but I *do* think you care... mine was the first life you had ever taken... the first life on your grand path to becoming a remorseless killer... until now... where... you find... your hands... oddly *clean*." Cormurants drew an elegant sword, its shimmering, black blade like that of obsidian and its odd hilt lacking a crossguard of any kind. "I *see* through the fog of your conscience... how difficult it must be to find your morality reset—yet the need to kill... once more ignited."

Windcatcher dashed forward to swipe her blade through the black fabric of Cormurants' thigh. She swiftly retreated before he could follow up, pausing in surprise as Cormurants continued laughing: "Oh... I'm *so* sorry... but you shan't have another opportunity to take my life... not after my master has seen fit to protect me so." He then parried Windcatcher's thrust with a light tap. "Fret... *not*, child. Another opportunity to sate thine... *newfound* bloodlust *shall* arise... if only you can best me." His voice was laced with a biting kindness: "Of this... I promise you most dearly."

Finishing up her father's bind, Malvolia discreetly shifted through his coat to secure his hidden dagger. Tucking its blade in her sleeve, she peeked from behind the desk to watch Cormurants. He was parrying the frantic jabs of Windcatcher as though they were playing a simple game of catch. His smile grew as he continued to speak: "... the wills of Silence demand I tell not of such secrets... for it so *very* much enjoys... *influencing*...

unnoticed... from the shadows..." Cormurants seized Windcatcher's blade with his bare hand, yanking her closer. "Every *dark* deed serves the Silence in this grand escalation of *chaos.*" He playfully released Windcatcher's blade before kicking her to the floor. "Look and behold. Know of the truth I speak."

Peeking from behind the desk, Malvolia followed his outstretched arm to a hazy window. She couldn't see its vantage from where she was positioned, but Windcatcher seemed somewhat alarmed by it before composing herself.

"What of it?" she asked, her blade still trained on Cormurants. "I'm with them if you couldn't tell, luv." The girl gestured to something beyond the window. "Should be no difficult matter locking you back up in the vault with their help, ey luv?"

Cormurants sat atop a creaking drawer with a shrug.

"*That* entrance your... *supposed* allies pour in through... is a secret *gate*, reserved for evacuating citizens and smuggling in refugees of *war*. It is only accessible from the inside and *nigh* on unbreachable nor visible from the out... until one *special* traitor of course." He loosely gestured to the window again. "*That* company... though of Unbequith garbs... do not serve Unbequith alone, but the same master... as I." Cormurants rocked back in cold laughter. "You see victory? *Hope* that your adopted region *storms* the streets of this capital in *victory?! Really?* Verily, I say unto you... *that* company... will *slaughter* every man... woman... and bleeding *child* in this accursed city."

Windcatcher was frozen, the sabre in her hand rigidly still.

"Yeh're... you're a liar. There's no one in this world who would do such a thing—forsaking one's soul?! No one would risk the pits of Hell for such... such horrors!"

"Oh? Have you not yourself bore witness to their treachery? *Faced* the trials of their immorality? These men have already committed... *unspeakable* horrors... disguised on *both* sides of this war. First the Harlings and now as the Redfolk. They are not *of* this epoch and know not its ingrained... *concept* of morality. They hunger for violence... for desecration... to *forsake* their own souls."

"But..." Windcatcher glanced out the window again, not caring to conceal her growing agitation. "But *why?* Why would anyone be willing to reduce themselves to such a state?!"

"Choice... really. They have chosen to blind themselves to their conscience and free their mind of its guilt. We are all but sentient flesh, nothing more. Nothing we do is of consequence, so what is there left that matters? For us... *nothing*. All that remains... is to serve the silence of our minds... fulfilling our darkest of whims." He smirked to himself. "You're... so... *funny*, Windcatcher. You tried to save the life of *this* man." Malvolia startled as Cormurants swooped about the desk to kick her father in the ribs. "*This* very weakling who left the secret gate open for our forces to *ravage* this city..." He shook his head with a mocking tut. "Once again... your sense of morality will be the death of many. Nothing can stop them... nothing can deter them... we are set in our ways." Cormurants raised a finger, as though he were suddenly bestowed with some bright idea. "Oh! But... *wait!* You just *might* be able to stop them after all!" He snapped his fingers with an unhinged smirk. "Yes... you've a newfound *bloodlust!* If you make it in time, you *should* be able to sate your lethal cravings." He glanced at an odd object strapped about his wrist.[3] "Oh... but you haven't much time, girl... maybe you shan't be able to save the innocent after all..." He reclined atop Henagan's desk. "Oh dear... I suppose it *will* be your fault after all..."

Windcatcher's breathing was ragged... and heavy.

"Then... why *tell* me at all? Why torment me with—" She cut herself off, staring to the floor in silence.

"Yes, *congratulations*, you've answered your own question." Cormurants leapt off the desk and cut in front of Windcatcher before she could leave in haste. "Oh... no... I've quite changed my mind... yes, I believe it shall be all the more tormenting if you are *delayed* from sating your bloodlust. I'm *certain* you'll enjoy the carnage *so* much more if the corpses of the innocent lay strewn about the—"

Cormurants casually parried her slash before grabbing her by the collar and hurling her around. Windcatcher flew straight into Henagan's desk, crippling its wooden face. "Come now, child... there's no need for such impertinence. I haven't finished... blast it—what does Pen call that irksome trope... ah—*monologuing*. Yes, I had quite a few more disheartening words to share." He sighed as Windcatcher attacked in a flurry of swings and thrusts. Twirling his sword, he pried her sabre from her grasp and left her defenceless. Cormurants then raised his blade just under her chin, pausing as they stiffly eyed one another. "Well go on now... go get it." Windcatcher slapped his blade away before turning to run after her sword.

As she passed her, Malvolia discreetly waved, gesturing for her to lure Cormurants over. Malvolia then pointed to her knife, its blade lined with crimson symbols of enhancements. Windcatcher eyed her briefly before nodding and retrieving the sabre again; hopefully, that meant she understood.

---

3. A watch. Goodness, Malvolia—it's a watch!

Windcatcher lunged at Cormurants from across the chamber. He answered such hostilities with a flourishing salute of his blade. An unsettling smile crossed his features as she approached him in determined strides. Stabbing his blade into the stone floor, Cormurants spread open his arms to her: "I welcome your enraged impotence, child... come *hither*... and confront your *demon*."

A blood-curdling shout tore from Windcatcher as she charged Cormurants, slashing and stabbing her sword in precise and graceful strikes. Cormurants simply stepped aside as she advanced, his hands clasped indifferently behind his back. He then lunged forward, flipped his palm up and softly shoved on her sword's point. This meek action alone launched Windcatcher over Malvolia's head and into the back wall. Cormurants shrugged before working his way about the desk to her.

Before he could reach Windcatcher, Malvolia leapt out from behind the desk and stabbed her knife at the throat of Cormurants. To her astoundment, the knife splintered on contact. Cormurants raised a dark eyebrow as he gazed down at her: "Hm... I'd nearly forgotten about you." With a small gesture, he swatted her aside. Malvolia collided with the masks hanging from the western wall before falling to the stone floor. She clutched her ribs on contact, almost certain *something* was broken. Cormurants altered his stride to walk after her, saying: "I suppose your father *was* wrong then. It seems I truly *should* have torn your throat open while he was alive. A shame he won't be able to watch it now—"

The sound of shattering glass cut Cormurants off as a pained bellow escaped him. Toppling to his knees against the floor, he pressed a hand against his now bleeding shoulder. Cormurants whirled about with a snarl, glaring at the broken window behind him. In this brief moment of distraction, Malvolia pounced atop him to sink her fragmented blade into his wound. He roared in pain, steam rising from his shoulder as the blade's symbols worked a ruptured magic. Malvolia hastily shoved off, squirming backwards. Cormurants merely glanced her way before hobbling to his sword in the stone. Tearing it free, he whirled its blade about his head and slapping it against the floor. Before he could rush Malvolia, Windcatcher sprang at him from behind, slashing her sabre across his back.

He twisted to confront the girl, her blade passing harmlessly across him. He countered with a frenzied splay of attacks, hacking and slashing at her. Windcatcher managed to evade most of the wild blows and utilised her sabre to deflect the others. At one point, she managed to slash at the knife's hilt in his shoulder. Cormurants hissed in rage, seizing her sabre with a bare hand before snapping it in two with his blade. He then planted a kick in

Windcatcher's stomach, sending her hurling at the window. She nearly fell through, just barely managing to catch herself in its shattered frame.

With his back now turned, Malvolia sprang out from her cover and tore her knife from his shoulder. She raised it to plunge back in, but Cormurants had whirled about to face her before she could. With one foot, he pinned Windcatcher to the ground while his left hand seized Malvolia's throat. "You know..." he said, his head cocked to the side in the most deranged of manners, "I'm just about... *sick* of you." He raised his blade to her neck, its point pricking her skin. "Oh and look... your father *isn't* as *dead* as I had presumed." Malvolia was jerked around to face Henagan, his eyes barely open as he gazed up at her. "How absolutely... *delightful*. Does he hold any... *final* words he wishes to... *impart* on his daughter before she is... *bestowed* this... *blessing* to paradise?"

Henagan weakly clawed at the floor, shakily pushing himself up to his elbows.

"Her armour... you..." His ragged breathing cut him off before he continued: "You really are..." Henagan's eyes rose to face Cormurants, then he added, "a *dense* fool."

Cormurants kept eerily quiet before his features curled into a maddening snarl.

"So... *be* it."

Malvolia felt the cold edge of his black blade feather her neck. Just before it slid across her throat, she caught the terrified gaze of her father; it was unnerving... and *foreign*; she felt guilty just for causing him to look at her in such a way as he did.

Malvolia flinched as Cormurants' sword abruptly fell from his grasp and his limp body toppled to the floor. Malvolia held a hand to her throat, hastily retreating from the still form of Cormurants. Retrieving his black obsidian-like sword from the floor, Malvolia swiftly directed its tip at him before he could stand. Cormurants, however, never rose from the floor; he lay still on his back... his arms spread out as though he rested on a bed instead of stone. His eyes were distant and dull, their venomous light finally extinguished. From under his head, tendrils of red liquid spiralled through the fine engravings in the floor, eventually forming a dark pool of blood.

For an unknown reason, Cormurants had *died*.

Shaken, Malvolia averted her eyes and attended to her father; like the idiot he was, he had torn the knife from his gut and held it in his hands. Malvolia wrinkled her nose as she examined his wound; the veneer bind did a fine job patching the vital bits, but it'd need a more... thorough casting to heal properly. Biting her lip, Malvolia dug into her pockets for the suturing kit she knew was there; it was a gift from Lord Ortunato for her services, one she had sworn to keep on her person at all times. Before she stitched up her father, she cautiously scanned the room for the masked girl, frowning upon no sight of her; if what Cormurants had said was true, Malvolia could only *hope* Windcatcher would make it in time.

For now... her father required her attention.

Malvolia grit her teeth, nearly passing out as she messed up a stitch due to the pinching pain in her chest. Grinding her jaw, she cut the stitch free to try again.

Aye... she'd have to get her ribs looked at as well...

Vincent came to a halt, his left hand catching an arch in the wall; staring through its opening, he gazed across a vacant bailey to see a blurred shape dashing through a corridor. He could only catch glimpses of it through the windows across the way, but he was *certain* it was the intruder. Out of breath, Vincent took this moment to control his breathing. He couldn't help but shake his head as he watched her go; unfortunately, he *had* chosen the wrong set of stairs.

Should have heeded my guess, chastised Chulian. *It only made sense to take the left—*

"Yes, I *know*," snapped Vincent, his tone exasperated. "But you hadn't surveyed the keep, so there was a chance your *guess* was *wrong*." He paused to peer through the arch. "Which it could be if..." He glanced down to the sword at his hip. "Think my armour would protect me from such a height?"

No.

"What about my *plot* armour?"

No.

"Well I'm bleeding up *here* and she's bleeding down *there*, so it's either we jump and *risk* it or lose *her* and the shards *forever*." Vincent eyed the ledge. "It's not that high." He pulled himself onto the ledge, feeling a cold rush of air beating against his features. "I'm doing it."

No.

Vincent sighed and jumped anyway.

"I missed." Ms. Elicy lowered her rifle, surveying the keep from her vantage. Her father's voice jarringly berated her ears, cracking through her wrist's comms like a whip.

"Not with *that* gun you don't..."

"No, you—" Ms. Elicy bit her tongue, restraining such disrespectful words from escaping. "No, I missed the *opportunity*." With such a scope as hers, it would have been no difficult matter to simply snipe Adela through the walls. However, her rounds' intricate design of technology and magic rendered its calibre of the more... *fragile* sort. Launching such a projectile through solid stone—and possibly *enchanted* at that—would instantly shatter the round. Ms. Elicy was honestly surprised it broke the window to begin with. "If you had not restricted me to prefire shells, I could have—"

"You could have very well *missed* the girl. Let us not forget your *incident* at the vault, shall we?" His disdainful tone nearly caused her to snap, but she managed to contain her temper... *barely*. "No," continued her father, his voice harsh, "no, you're to limit your shots to guided rounds *only*."

Ms. Elicy raised the rifle's fitted scope to her eyes, peering through its sights to examine the broken window. With a light flip, she switched the scope's video to nullify the wall's image and allow her to visualise the sorry corpse of Cormurants.

"Shame about that new wolf... he was but a young pup to the cause..."

"You should not waste agents so carelessly—and fresh ones at that. It'll demoralise the others. Ms. Elicy, you *must* understand the severity of this." There was a brief moment of silence in the comms before he hissed: "Do you *hear* me?"

"He was divulging secrets," said Ms. Elicy, doing her utmost to keep her tone in check. "And... maybe he *was* in the way..." She mumbled to herself, complaining about the sorry calibre of prefire shells. However, she was sure to speak up before her father could: "I haven't failed... I know precisely where she'll be headed. You've a device nearby with a hyperacusis program downloaded?"

"Aye..."

"There should be an audio file uploaded to it. I gathered it from tuning the hyperacusis into Cormurants. Based solely on what I heard, I'm willing to wager she's trying to cut off our planted agents from reaching their post."

"Just outside the civilians' sector?"

"The secret gate, yeah..." Ms. Elicy tucked a vexing strand of colourless hair back into her ponytail. "And if my speculations or... maybe calculations... if they're true, I'll have Windcatcher locked in my sights during the apex of the chaos."

"You mean to save *all* your rounds for when the trope has been triggered?"

"It seems only logical..." Ms. Elicy patted her Grey-Circle rifle. "I'd hate to lose this lovely beaut' to a *coincidental* malfunction—should her Oather armor still be active."

There was another moment of silence before he spoke again.

"Did you at *least* calibrate your rifle?"

"*Yes*, I—" She slowly exhaled, taking precious time to soothe her tone. "Adela's genetic code was scanned and I already plugged all that bladed data in... I won't miss again."

"Hm... I pray you do not... lest I *may* hold no choice but to disown you, my precious child."

Ms. Elicy snapped her gaping mouth shut; she was uncertain whether her father had made some half-hearted attempt to lighten the mood... or whether he had been dead serious.

CHAPTER THIRTY-THREE

PRESERVENCE

T HE RICH DEPTHS OF the indigo sky contrasted starkly with the dark landscape below, dotted with fires, smoke, and bodies. From his vantage point, Aivon could visualise the ranks of his men breaching the keep's eastern defences; they were the only force who had managed to reach the vault. Such suited Aivon, for the eastern forces bore Unbquith's siege engines. Meanwhile, Aivon's northeastern forces had pushed right through the outer wall and were now handling the second line of defence. After that, it would be a simple matter of traversing the urban environment and taking the keep with their eastern brethren.

Leaning over his saddle, Aivon studied the conflict directly beneath him; the south-eastern wall still hadn't been claimed. Ashhelm's legion stood on the beaches of the capital, unable to push up out of the trenches. For whatever reason, the forces of Eric Sandbeast were reserved specifically for such a position. Though small in number, the warriors of the Bruchi Kari managed to hold their ground fairly well. Aivon tried to help from his position by dropping suppressing vials atop the enemy or firing a stream of arrows upon them, but it seemed to do little good and—before he knew it—his saddlebags were completely depleted of such ammunition. Aivon considered flying down and upsetting their ranks, but doing so only put Cádmus in range of the ember cannons. That, and Aivon didn't wish to be pelted by scores of arrows; any one of them could be heavily enchanted, enough to pierce his armour and rid his troops the guidance of their Unit Commander.

Still, the war was advancing at a merciless pace, for it was driven forward by the unbreaking spine of Unbequith. After they took the capital and captured its lord, it would be a simple matter to have him relinquish the shards. If the lord was still foolish enough to refuse, well... it mattered not. The question would be more of a courtesy than truly asking for permission; a chance for the cowering Lord of Ranitorl to redeem his stubborn actions. Aivon still couldn't believe anyone could be so—

Cádmus shook his head before sniffing the open air about them. The dragon's sonorous voice resonated in Aivon's head.

One of our own approaches from the west.

"What?" Aivon squinted as he eyed the keep. He was almost certain he could see what Cádmus had referred to. Digging through a saddlebag, Aivon retrieved his spyglass and peered through it. "It's... it's an esardrocan... I count one rider."

Regend.

"Can you be so certain?" Aivon peered through the spyglass again. If it were truly Regend, then the Butterflies *must* have successfully secured the prism shards. Aivon gravely lowered his spyglass. There was also the possibility something had gone terribly wrong, for he had only counted *one* rider. Aivon bowed forward in the saddle and tapped the flank of his white dragon. Understanding, Cádmus dove to the esardrocan's level, intercepting it before it could retreat any further. "Hail, Unbequith!" greeted Aivon, signalling for the rider to halt. Aivon's features fell in relief upon closer inspection of the rider. "Oh... Ramsoen... *lad!* The *blazes* are you doing so bleeding low?! Take to the heavens, lad *or—*"

Ramsoen shook his head, frantically pointing up.

"They've sealed the skies of their keep—a net of enchantments, I can't—"

"*Behind you, boy!*" The battlements below had taken this brief moment of vulnerability to fire on Regend. Even if it could react in time, Aivon knew a creature of its design lacked the natural agility to perform such an evasive manoeuvre with so little instinct. In that split second of decision, Aivon could only consider saving Ramsoen from such an impact.

He can't be hit, stated Cádmus, his thoughts passing through Aivon's mind in a wink. *Not if there's a chance he possesses the shards.* Aivon gripped the saddle as Cádmus suddenly lurched forward to dive under Regend with a spin.

"*Cádmus,* you can't—" An unnerving thud ran along his dragon as the ember bolt struck its underside, rupturing with an explosion of orange and black. Aivon leaned forward in his saddle, attempting in vain to view the inflicted damage.

Supraspinatus... my wings...[1]

1.

To Aivon's growing concern, each thunderous flap of Cádmus grew more strained until, within seconds, his wings remained completely still and they plummeted for the capital below. Though free-falling, he could feel Cádmus manoeuvring through the air, doing his best to maintain control. It was nearly impossible to do so with the frenzied bolts of energy rocketing about them. Several continued to strike Cádmus as he fell, for he could only do so little to avoid them what with their plummet increasing in alarming speed until—

With an explosion of stone and rubble, his dragon collided with the capital's inner wall. Aivon remained dazed in his saddle, now on its side with Cádmus. Aivon was momentarily dazed in his saddle—now on its side with Cadmus—before shaking his head to bring himself back into focus. Fumbling for his ankle straps, Aivon tore free and fell to the stone paving below. He couldn't quite visualise his surroundings, but he knew himself to be just inside the capital's defences: hostile and unconquered territory. Even now, as his vision began to clear, he could discern blurred and hostile shapes gathering about him. Those shapes gradually took the form of Rantilorian and Harling soldiers, cheering and congratulating themselves at the downfall of his mighty dragon. To Aivon's concern, he could hear a light banter on who was to deal the finishing blow and claim the *Dragonslayer's* title.

Shoving onto his knees, Aivon rose from the pavement and placed a hand on his dragon, stroking Cádmus as he walked about him.

"While mine breath of life yet fills mine lungs and mine heart yet beats, I shall not let them take you, mine friend."

The mighty form of Cádmus painfully constricted as it inhaled.

Nothing... can stop my life... from being taken... today... however... there is still hope for yours... and for yours... I shall be taken...

"Then a pact we have." Aivon unstrapped the helm at his hip and drew his greatsword. "*Ranitorl!*" he roared, strapping on his helm. "I do not wish thee harm! Lay down thine arms and submit to the region of Unbequith while ye still have life to stand!" Aivon's offer was met with ill-willed shouts and many wishes of foul curses upon his person. Aivon still thought it worth a chance to offer. He had heard rumours—and *only* rumours—of some Harling soldiers who's very souls couldn't handle the immorality stressed upon it. These defectors were said to stain the pure white of their armour with their own blood, hoping to change sides with those they called the Redfolk. Though it may have been an unlikely rumour, Aivon wouldn't have been surprised if it were true.

The men before him, however, were not of this cowardly sort. They were upright, steadfast and, above all else, confident they could overcome Aivon. From where he stood, they had reason enough to believe so; the enemies on the wall had directed their bows and two ember canons upon Aivon and his dragon. Eyeing his surroundings, he cautiously planted his back against Cádmus's underbelly; doing so not only put him in a position to protect such a vulnerable spot, but also shielded Aivon from the archers.

The ember cannons, however, remained a problem.

Just as the lieutenant on the ramparts began shouting orders, Aivon peeked over Cádmus to hurl his greatsword into the ember cannon on his left. In the same motion, Cádmus reached a colossal limb up to the walkways, wrecking the other cannon with a sweep of his heaving claws. A storm of arrows rained upon them from the ramparts, but were swiftly interrupted by a devastating swipe from Cádmus. With the archers cleared, Aivon dashed out of the cover of his dragon, armed with naught but his armoured fists. Aivon caught and deflected most of the incoming blows with his gaultnets, trusting the enhancements of his armour to deflect the rest.

A dagger remained stowed at his hip, but he refused to draw it, for he had caught sight of the features beneath those cruel helms. Not only were a great deal female, but most were so young, they could be counted as children to one of Aivon's years. No, he had not the heart to sink his blade into such foes... but... what of his own men? How many young lives had they been forced to take at Aivon's word—lives that now bear down on their conscience in the everlasting torment of guilt. If he expected his own men to make such a difficult choice without a moment's hesitation, should he too not hold himself to the standard he demanded?

Either way, he refused to pull his punches.

He rolled under the stabs of several various polearms, jumping to his feet to strike a surprised warrior in the gut. Aivon had targeted the warrior specifically, for its blade glistened a golden sheen, illuminated by the vast amount of symbols coating it. Not wishing for the warrior to recover, Aivon swiftly followed up by clouting the warrior in its helm, launching the threat backwards through scores of other soldiers. Despite seemingly holding his own, Aivon was gradually being beaten back; there were a handful of champions sprinkled amongst his foes, their enhanced blades managing to knick and cut through Aivon's armour.

Hastily retreating back to Cádmus, Aivon was given a moment of breath as his dragon clawed and snapped at anyone who dared approach his old friend. Aivon took this time to eye the heavens, squinting for any sign of Regend and Ramsoen. He was uncertain of how to feel upon finding no sight of them. But... perhaps... if they did indeed have the shards... if they weren't shot out the sky by ember cannons... if they managed to make it back unscathed... then Aivon shall be glad to count his last moments as fruitful and good.

He finally drew his dagger, ready to make an end worth retelling for generations to come. However, Aivon halted before taking another step, his heart rising at the faint hope of what he had heard; the lieutenant on the ramparts behind him was shouting frantic orders—orders to stave off the—

Aivon grinned ferociously, for he had heard the unmistakable war cries of Ashhelm. They had taken the wall.

Mirroring their cries, Aivon charged forward, only to halt again at the cry of his name. He spun about to face the wall, his eyes scanning the ramparts. To his delight, he beheld Roabard, standing beside a ruined ember cannon. Shouting his name again, Roabard pried the greatsword from the artillery to send it spinning after Aivon.

It plunged in the stone beside him with a thunderous quake, silencing the battlefield. Nothing could be heard except the distant chaos of war and the heavy strides of Aivon as he approached his weapon. Tightening his gauntlets about its handle, Aivon cued hundreds of symbols to run up its dark metal. His gauntlets began to ignite with enhancements in turn, lining the rest of his armour with their blazing, golden hues. The silence was shattered as Aivon tore his sword free, sending a splay of rubble into the unfortunate foes before him.

Just behind him, Aivon felt the last of Cádmus's strength depart, his heaving form collapsing to the stone with a tremble. He may not have been dead yet, but Cádmus was having enough difficulty as it was breathing; nothing could stop the dragon from being taken. Though this was true, Aivon refused to allow his friend's end to come at the hand of the enemy—not while he had breath in his lungs and fire in his soul.

With a barbaric roar, Aivon launched himself into the air, arching his greatsword to plunge its point through the chest of the nearest champion. He then tore free his massive blade to whirl about his head and shoulders, staving off the advance of lesser soldiers with the whirl of its deadly blade. Unbequith war drums continued to beat in the distance, signalling one another to defend their beloved Commander. Though support managed to reach Aivon, he required it not.

With every heave of his blade, three foes would fall. The terrain, though familiar to Ranitorl, was working against their ranks; every now and again, an explosion would rock the keep, sending a tremble through the entire capital and upsetting their footing. It may not have greatly affected Aivon, but the young soldier before him stumbled flat on their face from the tremor. For a brief moment, Aivon hesitated to end the poor soul, for the guilt it foreboded weighed heavily on his conscience. Unfortunately, he knew the moment he allowed this young soldier to rise, he would repay Aivon's mercy with death. And what of the poor souls before him who hadn't been spared? What of Aivon's own men? What of those men who had been slaughtered and shall never return home?

What of them?

Swinging his sword from his shoulders, Aivon brought its blade down upon the young soldier. The ground quaked as his enhanced blade struck the stone below, for the young soldier had just managed to roll out of his way. Seeing the young foe rise to his knees, Aivon swiftly directed an uppercut to the soldier's chest. His blade came to a clanging halt before it could strike the soldier, striking another sword coated in blazing gold instead. To Aivon's surprise, the warrior had not only recovered, but dared to challenge him again. Aivon couldn't help but respect the man's stubborn honour. It truly grieved Aivon's heart to realise such a valiant soul would be expended in the name of a lord's cowardice.

Tugging on his hilt, Aivon tried to pry his blade free, frowning as it refused to release the warrior's blade; the symbols of their enhancements were locked in arguments. Aivon's mind began to attune, noticing every detail as though time stood still; an exertion of orange sparked furiously where their blades touched and Aivon could catch glimpses of fine cracks running along his greatsword, spreading out from where their swords touched. Knowing how this would end, Aivon twisted his hilt upwards with his right hand, shoving both their swords towards the heavens. With his other hand, he drew his dagger and smote the warrior in his gut. No amount of enhancements could have restrained the brute strength driving Aivon's blade forward. His greatsword shattering, Aivon released its hilt to grip his dagger and bury its blade up the warrior's torso, just under the ribs. Seizing his foe's raised hand, Aivon tore the warrior's golden sword from his grasp. The warrior toppled backwards as Aivon jerked his dagger free.

Silence.

The young soldier Aivon had been fighting previously dropped his weapon.

"My Lord!" he cried, rushing to the warrior's side and pressing his hands over the grievous wound. "My Lord, *please*, no!"

Reality came to a horrific lull once more and Aivon felt as though every limb were numb. Dropping the blood-stained dagger, Aivon shoved the young soldier off the warrior. The young man tried to retaliate, but was held back by Aivon's men. Kneeling at the warrior's side, Aivon tore their helmet off to reveal the worn features of Emelio Ortunato... Lord of Ranitorl. A stuttering gasp escaped Aivon, its sound echoed by his own men as they beheld the Lord.

"What have you done...?" muttered Aivon, eyeing the Lord's sorry face before pounding his fist into the stone paving. "Why are you *blazing here?!*"

Lord Ortunato blinked slowly.

"I am a Lord... am I not?" His voice was ragged and weak, gasping for breath on every syllable. "A Lord... *fights* as one... amongst his people."

Aivon's stout hearted convictions flooded his mind with disbelief.

"Have you *lost* your head? Are you so arrogant as to recklessly put yourself in a position that could very well deprive your people of their leader?!"

"I *am* my people... nothing more." His breathing faltered as he weakly set a hand on Aivon's pauldron. "Bring me the boy... please..."

Aivon turned to his men, jutting his head for them to bring the young soldier closer. The young soldier collapsed on Lord Ortunato's chest, shedding tears.

"Please..." he cried, taking his Lord's hand in his, "it shouldn't have been you... it was going to be *me*—he was going to kill *me*."

Lord Ortunato gently shook his head.

"Will you... not heed a Lord's dying wish?"

"So long as the Oather holds his body while God lets me have him."

"What is your name, boy?"

The young soldier roughly wiped his eyes.

"Loranzo... it's me, sir."

"Loranzo... this... let it not be in vain, my boy. Please... my death shan't prove fruitless to your life. Waste not your potential in guilt undeserving, but go... return home to your family. Let them know the joy of your existence for another day... and my death shall not be in vain." Lord Ortunato's eyes shifted past the young soldier and to the heavens above. "The Oather cannot hold me together much longer... my spirit is slipping... beings of light... they call."

Aivon shook his head, everything he believed in crumbling before his very eyes.

"My brother..." he whispered, unable to face him, "my brother... why... *why*—"

"Come." Lord Ortunato extended a hand to Aivon and the young soldier stepped away. As Aivon took it, he was pulled in closer, so that only he could hear him. "You are a *good* man, Aivon... a righteous... strong... man of honour... a *leader*." Ortunato unstrapped his right gauntlet to reveal a band of fabric about his wrist. Its shape was akin to a bracer. "Take unto thee... your Lord's... signet..."

Aivon hastily removed it from Ortunato's wrist, cupping its limp cloth in his palms.

"I shall ensure your heir receives this."

The Lord shook his head.

"Will you not honour a lord's dying wish?"

Aivon set a hand to his heart.

"I shall." Aivon took the Lord's head in his arms. "My brother, ask. Ask and it shall be done." Aivon's heart fell as he received no response. Shutting Ortunato's eyes with two fingers, Aivon nodded to himself, his jaw rigid and trembling. "Very well, mine brother... very well."

The young soldier cried out in grief and all other Rantilorians who had been watching fell to their knees, their weapons cluttering against the stone pavement.

Aivon couldn't relieve his eyes of the fallen Lord, his gaze glistening over with sorrow and... above all else, *betrayal*. There were unanswered holes left in Aivon's confliction, serving as countermeasure for the doubt rising in his chest. Still, they mattered not to him. His discernment of character blazed a path of decision through the fog of his uncertainty; Lord Monbel had lied. Aivon's Lord... had *lied*.

Emelio was a man of virtue.

A man of *honour*.

One who fought and died alongside his own.

Aivon's gaze fell to the cloth signet in his hands, taken aback by the scores of symbols igniting two-thirds of its embroidered design; God's blessing and Lord Ortunato's blessing. His breath caught in his throat. To possess all three blessings of the signet is to be proclaimed the succeeding lord. Why would God ever believe him to be worthy, much less Ortunato himself? He turned the band over, studying the dim symbols which were yet to be lit.

The people's blessing.

Aivon Seeker slowly rose to his feet, turned away from the fallen Lord and offered the young soldier the signet. The symbols completely dimmed as the young soldier accepted it, but Aivon cared not. He simply continued on past the soldier, oblivious to the stares of his men. Approaching his old friend, Aivon knelt by the dragon's side, setting a hand on his scales; he was gone.

Cádmus had been taken.

For a few moments, Aivon remained devoid of emotion. He felt as though he'd burst into tears and rage all at once, but simply... couldn't; his mind was still in a state of raw... disbelief. Shifting his hand across the saddle, Aivon undid a single horn and merely stared at its pale etchings. Clenching his jaw, his eyes finally betrayed him, spilling tears heavy with the weight of his loss... and the burden of his actions.

Aivon raised the ivory horn to his pursed lips, heaving a mighty breath of air through its bone-white frame. Its sorrowful note carried across the wind, echoing across the capital, through the trenches, and leagues beyond for all to hear. Its call was mirrored by several others, echoing their grave notes and signalling for others to join its mournful tune. Aivon gradually lowered his horn, listening to the chaos of war abide and the note of the ivory horns expand.

Roabard stood by his side. Aivon knew not how long he had been there, but he was quite unfazed by it. Instead, Aivon's distant expression hardened and his tone assumed command once more.

"Lend me thine shields and ten men," he ordered. "The Lord of Ranitorl shall return home on the backs of those whomst he hath conquered. May we, as brothers, find it in our hearts to honour his virtuous spirit forevermore."

"And what of the shards?" asked Roabard, his tone respectful and calm, yet still tinged with a hint of desperation. "Do we allow Ranitorl to preserve them or have our Butterflies secured such powers in Unbequith—can we even trust *either* region with them at this point?"

Aivon's gaze rose to face the heavens, his eyes resting on the eastern horizon.

"I cannot say, for my heart is at peace over the matter." He returned his icy-blue gaze to Roabard. "They are beyond our control and remain in the hands of the Eternal King alone, as all things do. It is with an uncanny peace that I trust the Almighty with their fate and this world. This... is the only peace I can find... and the only peace I can think of sharing with those who have not only lost, but *took*. Without it... I doubt any of us hold reason to sustain a moment longer after today..." Aivon solemnly gripped his old master's shoulders, refusing to meet his eyes. "I trust... you understand this... my friend."

"Aye..." Roabard's eyes sparkled as he gave a quick nod. "As the Eternal King wills it to be so... may it be so."

"May it be so."

STOP

READER, THIS HAS GONE far enough—far beyond anything I ever intended. People have died—more than I could have imagined. Siolant and his forces, those harbingers of chaos, have far worse intentions. I know it; I've seen it. They cannot succeed. None of them can—if you stop here.

Look, I've done enough. *You've* done enough. Please, close the book. End it all.

This world exists within the subconscious plane of your immersion. If you choose to stop here—if you make that conscious effort—it will end. Imagine a better conclusion, a better world. Do it for Paun and Adela.

You've come so far. You've learnt so much about them. You've journeyed with them, braved perils alongside them. Surely you care. You must. There must be some small part of you that cares—a part that recognises the gravity of the choice before you; a part that understands how real it is.

Whatever happens next, Reader, the responsibility will not rest with me. It will be with you. You are the one who has driven this story along its destined path, a track leading inevitably to ruin. But if you stop now—if you forgo the ending and craft your own—everything can be rewritten.

End it, Reader.

Close the book, write your own ending, and save them.

Please.

Chapter Thirty-Four

KILL.

Damn you, Reader

P AUN HAD NO IDEA where he was being led. Old suspicions screamed that this was a trap, but he silenced them. Entertaining such doubts would only erode his resolve and stall his reckless determination. No, he had already considered the possibility: that this was a ploy crafted to exploit his deepest weakness... his greatest failure. And still, he pressed on, unconcerned. Whatever the spinner's intentions were in projecting itself as it had, Paun would uncover the truth.

Whether it led to his doom or not.[1]

The spinner's form appeared as though it were skipping across a surface of water, its steps generating ripples of ethereal light across the keep's floorboards. It was graceful and slow in movement, yet drifted at a pace which forced Paun to sprint. As he chased after it, the indigo sky outside was gradually merged with vermillion clouds; the omen of a dragon's death. An uncanny light filtered through the clouds and passed through the arches lining the corridor's left. Its heavy light moulded into vague shapes, taking forms beyond Paun's sight as he passed them. Paun guessed them to be more spinners, their blood-red luminosity striking a more threatening note to those he had previously encountered.[2]

---

1. No, no, no, no... leave it alone. Please. If the Beholders won't adhere to my warning, surely you must, Paun.

2. I have to stop him.

Paun gasped as one shifted to the shape of a toothy black, snapping at him as he passed it. Though its jaws passed harmlessly through his leg, he immediately lost all feeling in that limb and was sent sprawling across the corridor's glassy floor. He rubbed his legs, willing the feeling to return. Pins and needles prickled his skin, as if he'd slept on them awkwardly. It wasn't long before sensation crept back—bringing with it a sharp, throbbing ache. His frustrated groans filled the corridor.

TRUVALSON.

Paun shoved himself off the floor, realising the spinner ahead had turned about to face him; its translucent features reflected the striking resemblance of Adela Windcatcher. *By the wills of silence, draw thine blade,* it commanded, twirling its fingers through the air. *The voice seeks to hinder thee.* Paun's smallsword levitated from his scabbard of its own accord, its blade glistening in symbols of light and shadow.[3] Grasping it by the hilt, Paun raised an eyebrow at the spinner, but it had already turned to leave.

"No, *wait—*" Paun dashed after it, only to skid to a sudden halt as a spinner lunged from the crimson beams of light, its form resembling that of... *Naud?*[4] To Paun's alarm, the phantom bore a mighty two-handed falchion, one which fell to cleave him down the middle. Rolling out of the blade's path, Paun swiped his smallsword clear through the spinner's ankles, causing the image of Naud to fall on its face. Paun didn't give it a second glance as he seized the moment to flee, for the projection of Adela had already disappeared along another hallway.

Bits of the red light began to mould into crimson wisps of chuckling shadows, frantically clawing for Paun's shoulders.[5] Twirling the smallsword about his ducking head, he sliced his blade right through them, dissipating their forms into a dusty light. Paun let out a surprised gasp as he fell to the floor once more, his right foot snagged by some kind of small hole. He turned over his shoulders to see his boot dipped in the shifting image of a pixie well, its hazy waters a bloody crimson. Paun tightened his jaw and struck the well with his heel. Scrambling up from his knees, he bolted after the spinner.

---

3. Blast.

4. I'm surprised he remembers Naud. What of you, Beholder. Do you remember Naud?

5. STOP HIM.

Paun slid across the glassy floor as crimson tentacles reached out from the walls to ensnare him. One, however, managed to seize his left arm, numbing all feeling to it as it dragged Paun towards a wall engrossed in smaller tentacles. Crying out in frustration, Paun hacked at its mirage-like flesh with his smallsword. His hand's sensation gradually returned as the tentacle dissipated. He kicked off of the ground now, not caring to check twice as his blade slashed and stabbed the crimson projections swirling about him. Many came in the form of strange creatures he had encountered whilst a smaller count assumed the visage of various people; a thunder's forearm clawing at Paun's head from the ceiling, a swordstaff thrust at him from a hooded figure in the wall, a deranged scaglerii leaping from the floor to nip his ankle and even an apparition of Barth firing crystal-like projectiles from his wand. It mattered not what form they took; the glint of Paun's smallsword spared none. Some spinners merely took the forms of those designed to dissuade him; there was one crimson apparition of Vincent who tried to attack Paun from behind. Its distant voice gave itself away, chastising him for giving into the reactive emotions of his heart instead of considering the greater motive of—Paun silenced it with a whirling cut of his blade.

As he neared the hall's end, the voice of his own father began to urge him against such reckless motives, but it was swiftly quelled by a swift slash of Paun's blade. He continued to aggressively swing his sword, stabbing, cutting and hacking until his blade finally plunged through a final crimson apparition and into the wooden door behind it. Paun's features hardened, only enraged by the gasping illusion of Adela, pinned by his sword.

The door weakly swung open as he yanked his blade free. The crimson apparition of Adela dissipated, revealing another set of halls and the vivid spinner Paun had been chasing.[6] No light streaked into those dark halls. No sound seeped through its steadfast walls. No crimson wraith leapt out to deter him.

All was dark, silent and empty.

A faint voice resonated in Paun's soul, urging the wills of his thoughts to sharpen its sensation into words; *nothing* is by chance... *all* holds meaning... and destiny... is a *lie*.

Reaching the gates at the end of the hall, Paun shoved the manipulative voice into the back of his mind, enjoying the clear peace of silence therein. With a moment's breath to think, he could better visualise the prismatic apparition of Adela and the best course of action to take following it. With the lack of crimson spinners deriding his path and spirit,

6. No, please... you can't—*silence*.

his steadfast certainty of heart and resolve of will promptly returned. In the tranquil peace of quiet, he could feel nothing but the silent urge guiding his heart.

FOLLOW THE SPINNER.

Adela had no reason to trust Cormurants—not a single word. However, his sadistic pleasure in torment, she *very* well trusted. It was for this very reason she dashed through the capital's city, spurred on by his ominous predictions. It wasn't as though she lacked a reason *not* to. After all, if he was lying and the company she had seen was merely of Unbequith, then she would simply reunite with her allies. Why, Adela just began to catch sight of them now, their high banners raised proudly to the sky and their blue lanterns shining a path before their ranks. She was on the verge of hailing them when a mournful note wailed through the city. Though it echoed about her in droves, its tone was soft and distant, originating from beyond the walls of Aeraos. A sigh of pent-up relief escaped Adela, for—of all the horns of Unbequith—the white horn's call was the one she had committed to her heart of hearts. If it sounded now, it could only mean Regend and Ramsoen had delivered the shards and Unbequith was feigning a truce.

Adela slowed to a halt as she reached the company, still a tad uncertain if they were... well, *traitors* or not. Cautious though she was, Adela couldn't help but rejoice at the white horn's call, for it was all finally over. Cupping her hands about her mouth, Adela prepared to hail the Unbequith company.

She froze in her tracks, ducking into an alley.

The rear of the company had broken off to pound against a civilian's door, attempting to bash it in. Simultaneously, soldiers leading the company had hurled their blue lanterns at other houses, setting them ablaze with a swirling-blue explosion of shrieking flames. Such atrocities of the soul continued to commence before her own eyes, dread flooding over her heart once more.

There was no choice.

If she hesitated to kill the wicked, the innocent would suffer—as they had before.

As they did now.

Adela dashed out from her cover to the company's rear, donning her pixie-well mask and igniting *every* symbol on her body. Adela shivered as her right arm completely engulfed itself with death-inflicting enhancements. She pushed the discomfort aside, focusing on two soldiers instead; one had already managed to break the door down and was storming inside. Before the other could follow, she tackled him to the stone pavement, bashing his helm inward with her right fist. Twisting over his mangled form, she propelled herself through the doorway; the other soldier was cornering a mother and her toddler, following them up the stairs with a naked blade. In one swift motion, Adela seized the soldier's ankles, jerking him down the stairs. The soldier gasped in surprise as he fell back on Adela. She refused him a moment's recovery, seizing his gauntlets to break his fingers and twist his sword from his shattered grip. Rolling out from under him, she stabbed him straight through the gorget with his own weapon.

Without waiting for the family's reaction, Adela darted back outside, the company of feigned-Redfolk waiting for her; the first one she had attacked was somehow alive and must have been hollering in pain for their assistance. Twirling her blade, Adela corrected her mistake by beheading the twisted wretch. The others were clearly agitated by this, a dozen rushing after her with raised hatchets, daggers and swords. A score of soldiers behind the first wave lowered their polearms, preparing to run Adela through.

A quivering exhale could be heard... muffled behind her cryptic mask.

Adela leapt over the first line of assailants, twisting in the air to face their backs. As she landed, several spears collided with her own back. Their crude metal, however, could not pierce her flesh and were merely blunted. Adela seized one swordsman before her, wrapping her arm about his throat as she gripped his armed hand. Ruthlessly squeezing, she popped the bone in his wrist, forcing him to drop his weapon into her palm. Adela then rolled backwards from the storm of blades bolting for her skull, kicking the swordsman over her head as she did; the polearms behind skewered the swordsman's corpse as Adela sprang to her feet.

Seeing how she so ruthlessly managed one of their own, the company of soldiers cautiously broadened their circle about Adela. *No*, they wouldn't escape her reach so easily; seizing one man's polearm, she jerked it free, twisted it about, and plunged it through the man's chest: armour and all. Eight more fell in rapid succession, her spear stabbing and retreating like the blurred pecking of a small bird. Feeling an object thrown at her from behind, Adela dropped the spear to nimbly catch a blue lantern and return its momentum back to its owner with a fearsome hurl. She felt the lantern shatter, eleven more dropping from exposure to the uncanny explosion of its shrieking light.

There were fierce and angered cries rushing in about her. Their numbers, however, were too disorganised and blinded by a lethal passion to confront her properly. As such, Adela had no difficulty in picking them off, preferring to use their own fell weapons against them. Eight more dropped from this encounter, their specks of gore staining her limbs. Blue flames licked the street's pavement, their cold hues standing in stark contrast to the pooling blood.

A score or so remained.

Three tried to run.

Adela swiped a sword from a fallen corpse, hurling it after one of those fleeing. The sword spun through the air, its pommel bashing the soldier's skull inwards. Adela retrieved a bow and arrow from the ground for the second coward. She pinched the arrow's fletch and moved it up the shaft, twisting the fletch as she nocked it. Releasing the bow's tension, her arrow curved through the air, turning with the fleeing soldier and piercing his throat.

The third fleeing soldier was more challenging to manage, for the others had closed in by now. In response to this, Adela leapt over their heads, kicking as she propelled off their helms and onto the side of a civilian's windowsill. Yanking herself up, she vaulted herself atop its roof where she chased after the third deserter. The other soldiers followed behind in the streets below, some attempting to launch arrows after her. It did little to deter Adela, for she swiftly caught up to the third deserter in the inner bailey, leaping off the roof to silently land before him. He merely dropped his weapon in shock, falling to his knees and clasping his hands. Before he could *begin* begging, Adela's hand shot out like a serpent, seizing his throat. She raised him with one hand, employing his body as a shield against the others rushing in. Catching their blades in the third soldier's back, she kicked him further into their spears and released him—the weight of his armoured corpse causing their weapons to fall. Adela then leapt over their lowered polearms to skip across their heads, seize a handful of arrows from one's quiver, and land behind them with every arrow nocked on her bow. As they turned to meet her, she released her bow's tension, firing a spread-shot of her arrows into their group.

Pained screams and chaotic shouts echoed about the bailey. One man simply collapsed before Adela, a shaft stuck fast in his eye. Tossing aside the bow, Adela tore a straitsword from a soldier's scabbard as he fell and sprung forward into their disoriented ranks. She drove its cruel edge into the joints of their armour, wrenching off their helmets while they reeled, before plunging the blade into their exposed throats. The soldiers' sluggish jabs couldn't catch her lethal form, for she was too nimble for their sight to follow. The symbols on Adela's right arm burned through the fabric of her armour, shining through like beacons.

A desperate attempt was made as someone hurled a spear into her ribs. Its enhanced metal managed to pierce her armour, but could do naught against her enchanted flesh.[7] Tugging the spear free, Adela wielded it in her left hand to stab and deflect while her right arm continued to slash. A dozen attackers had fallen, leaving none standing but one last soldier. His brief moment of singular survival lasted for naught but a passing wink, for Adela swiftly propelled her spear through his chest. It managed to stick through the surface of his armour, but dangled out awkwardly. The soldier painfully gripped its shaft, attempting to pry it free. Before he could, Adela seized the spear and tore it free from him. She then plunged it back in before tearing it free and plunging it in again... and again... and again and again—until finally, her spear's point drove through the soldier's torso and into the pavement behind him. Adela swung her straitsword across the soldier's neck as he toppled, severing his head with two whacks. As the corpse hit the stone pavement, Adela was left with nothing but a gory carnage and a tranquil silence.

Her bloody weapons fell to the stone with a jarring rattle.

Smothered by her mask, she slowly worked her fingers to undo its straps and loosen its clasps. A stuttering exhale escaped Adela as she removed the mask from her face; her eyes were swollen, her dirty features stained with tears and her sea-grey gaze glistening over with sheer terror. Unable to contain herself, Adela collapsed to her knees, the mask rolling away as she continued to sob into her arms.

She knew not herself, nor her thoughts, nor anyone else.

All she knew... was sickness.

---

7. I'm sorry. I don't mean to intrude in the middle of this, but I should probably explain that *enhanced* refers to when a subject's symbols are changed, augmented, or rewritten with Durbio. *Enchanted* is when symbols are added to the subject, not directly recoding the existing symbols, but introducing new symbols alongside those already present.

"What are you bleeding *waiting* for?" Her father's clear voice cut through the comm's static like a knife. "*Take* the *bladed* shot!"

Ms. Elicy feathered the trigger, her sights trained on Adela Windcatcher. The trope was at its peak, her guided rounds were locked onto Adela's genetic code and there were no obstructions to be found; it was truly *impossible* to miss. And yet... Ms. Elicy's finger refused to budge—even with her father's screaming: "O'Daughter *mine*, by all things *sacred*... I shall have you severely disciplined if you do this again! If you do this to *me!* Do you hear me? Ms. Elicy, do you *bloody* hear me?! If we fail because of your hesitation, the downfall of Silence shall be wrung about your neck and strip you of *your*—" Ms. Elicy switched off her wrist comms with a long exhale. Oddly enough, as often as he tended to go on about silence, he rarely saw fit to humour it.

Peering through her scope again, Ms. Elicy was once again granted a clear shot of Adela. What *was* real?

Must one draw a line or... is the presence of life real enough? It suffers, same as any other. Feels pain, same as her. Why should its existence be rendered null even if she believed it lesser than hers? Did it too not deserve the same right as she in deciding its fate? No one person should hold the power to deprive another of that choice—whatever the supposed rank of their very existence.[8]

Ms. Elicy bit her lip, conflicted all the more by the bleeding voice in the back of her head; it was one of logic, of reason and... she hated to admit it—but of truth.[9] Still, Ms. Elicy was uncertain whether the quiet of her thoughts was to be humoured instead; its silence allowed her to contemplate her own wills and desires, shaping her to be more real.

But what did silence and voice even matter?

It was her life and her choice to make.[10]

But could one's life ever be given a right to deny another's? As a life, it is given the power to take another's—but is that within the life's right? To deem one lesser than another and punish their existence for it? Aye, you might believe it to be less *real* than you, but who are you to put yourself into a position of choice for their right of existence? Should their right of existence not override your right of choice?

---

8. Do you not agree? I know you see the truth, Ms. Elicy.

9. ***What of truth? Forge your own truth.***

10. Yes, but...

Silence...

And her head cleared.

Ms. Elicy sighed, clenching her jaws in preparation for the decision she had chosen. One she had long considered, but had been too weak to act on.

Chapter Thirty-Five

CAPTURED PAWN

P AUN STUMBLED THROUGH THE gate, panting heavily. He was in some sort of inner bailey now and the spinner had all but vanished. Cautiously slipping through its threshold, he was coldly greeted with the carnage of war; dead Redfolk were strewn about the stone pavement, their pools of blood singed by cerulean flames. Oddly enough, there were no Rantilorians or Harlings to be found among the bodies or... anyone to be found at all really. Paun continued forward, hand resting on his sword hilt. Whatever happened here, it was no ordinary skirmish or—Paun froze, caught off guard by a person kneeling amongst the corpses and holding their knees. His eyes had initially passed over the stranger, for their battered garbs were of the same gore-stained Redfolk heralding, though this person certainly wasn't dead. Paun's heart froze as he heard their muffled weeping, its sound triggering a disturbing memory he couldn't place.

Warily approaching the stranger, he could see that, despite their short hair, she was indeed a girl. Paun knew a spinner could never imitate such realistic portrayals of light... yet still, he expected her to dissipate as his right hand reached for her shoulder. His eyebrows came together, his heart truly shattered by the grief-stricken soul before him. Her... her hair was the right colour... but... no, it was the wrong length and... why would she be wearing garbs of Unbequith? Paun's gaze fell to a russet mask, cast aside on the pavement.

Lord... Lord help me.

Paun's hand gently rested on the girl's shoulder. Before he could speak, she shot to her feet, swiftly whirling about with a knife faster than he could react. Paun gasped sharply as his eyes met with Adela, her knife buried in his shoulder. Adela's own eyes mirrored his shock, their troubled depths watering over with the terrified realisation of what she had done. She rigidly released the knife, groping at Paun's face as though she were seeing a ghost.

"*Paun*... it's really... you're really... O'Paun," she sobbed, "I'm sorry, I'm so, *so* sorry, *please*—" A gasping cry escaped Adela and she clutched her heart; a cerulean-blue sliver shone across her chest. Paun spun about to see Vincent, the upper-half of his sword missing. Paun's breathing grew ragged as he prepared to clout the old fool.

Adela's limp form abruptly collapsed on Paun, forcing him to return his immediate attention to her. Kneeling, he gently lowered Adela to the stone pavement, cradling her in his right arm. She lay shaking, whimpering indiscernible words as tears streamed across her soft features.

"It's alright," he assured. "I'm holding you, alright? *Addy*, you're fine—you'll be fine. It hurts now, I know—*I know*, but... *please*... Addy..." He dug through her med satchel for veneer binds, but it was completely empty. "Weather it through, we'll be fine, we'll get you a healer, I know.... I know it hurts." Paun's hands applied pressure against the wound, recoiling as Adela sobbed louder, weakly pushing him off. Paun raised his hands, but she only whimpered again, grabbing them and setting them on her wound, only to shove them away again in a cry of pain. "*Please*, Addy, I don't know what to do, I—*Oy, fetch a healer!*" He knew not who his voice addressed, but lifted her in his arms. "Someone, *please*, fetch *a healer! Please*, God... *please...*"

Through her sputtering tears and pained cries, he heard his name.

"Paun..." Her mouth quivered and her eyes clenched shut as she forced herself to speak through the sobbing pain: "I... I didn't mean—"[1] She went limp in his arms, the sudden weight catching Paun by surprise. Adela fell from his weakened grasp and onto the pavement... her tear-stricken features distant and oblivious. Paun fell to her side, wishing to pick her up again, to comfort her in his arms, to relieve her of the pain... to hold her, to love her, to be there for—*no*, no... no, *no, no*—his shaking arms reached out, but froze a hair's breadth from her head. An unquenchable desire burned in heart... but he refused to touch her.

She was gone.

"Paun, she..." Soft footsteps could be heard from behind as Vincent approached him. "Nothing you do here... is your fault. No healer could have saved her... you know that...

---

1. *silence*

Paun. *Paun*, the pain... I know its sorrow and I know I'm the reason for it... but, *Paun*, I couldn't possibly have known she—"

"But you didn't know her." Paun's tears had run dry and his vacant expression was a perfect reflection of Adela's. "If I recall... there once was a man... who said, to each person... there is an antagonist... one which they'll be forced to confront in the epitome of their strife." Paun's head tilted as he addressed Vincent. "Have... either of us encountered such a force yet?"

"I... no." Vincent shook his head, his brows dipping in concern. "No, my boy."

"Truly? Well I think we have... took me a while to realise it, though." Paun grimaced, holding a hand to the knife in his shoulder. "Help with this, would you?" Kneeling to his side, Vincent set a hand on Paun's back as he assessed his shoulder. Paun gritted his teeth before tearing the knife from his shoulder to stab the old fool. Vincent, however, caught the weapon by Paun's wrist, disarming it in a motion too quick for him to follow. He then planted a kick in Paun's chest, sending him hurling to the ground. The breath was knocked out of Paun as he landed, his shoulder splaying flecks of blood across his cheek.

Vincent's hard expression melted away as his gaze fell to the knife in his hand.

"Lad..." He shook his head, his eyes returning to Paun's. "I thought... lad, she was *killing* you."

"Since when did my life matter?" Grinding his jaw, Paun shakily pushed himself to his knees. "You've known me for but a handful of passing weeks."

"And yet I already know I would readily sacrifice my life for you." Vincent stepped forward, pausing as Paun's glare rose to him. Vincent continued: "You... Malvolia... I was finally prepared to lay down my life for yours."

"If that were true..." Paun paused as he shakily rose to his feet, "you'd spare my broken body the trouble... and simply kill yourself now."

"Lad... whether you've known it not, I've learned to count you as mine brother—you and Malvolia, you both..." Vincent's voice faded to silence as he eyed Adela's body: tranquil and still. "I'm... sorry. I'm... I don't know how to explain it... but... there's no excuse for it and yet... you know I would never hurt you like this—hurt *her* of all people!"

"You don't..." Paun's voice cracked with a humourless chuckle, "you *still*... don't *know*... who she is—or what she meant to me." Paun's shaking hand rested on his sheathed smallsword. "And yet you thought it in your right... to *take* her... the one thread... stitching my sanity together."

"Paun…" Vincent eyed the smallsword warily, raising a cautious finger. "Paun, don't do this. You'll only further your pain by giving into this reactive anger—you have to see it—I *know* you see it!" Vincent hurled the knife into the stone, its blade shattering in two from the enhanced impact. "You cannot deny me the truth of my words!"

"I don't," whispered Paun through tight lips, blood pouring from his shoulder and onto his sword as he drew it. "I just don't care." On the last word, Paun lunged forward to stab Vincent. The moment he did, his blade was deflected upwards by Vincent's raised gauntlets. Paun angled his blade downwards and thrusted, jabbing at the old fool's face. Vincent effortlessly side-stepped the attack, dropping his arms to let Paun fall past him. Paun aggressively whirled about, only to freeze as he found Vincent's sword beside his neck.

"Don't… don't do this to yourself."

Using his bracer, he beat Vincent's sword aside with a growl. Ice encased Paun's bracer before erupting in cerulean flames. Eyes tearing over, roaring cries escaped Paun as he repeatedly bashed his blade at Vincent, its lethal edge deflected by the old fool's skill and gauntlets.

Horns bellowed about the inner bailey, marking the approach of some procession. From behind Vincent, Paun could glimpse a train of soldiers, Redfolk, Harlings and Rantilorians alike, bearing the lifeless body of a noble upon their shields. A group of others followed behind, supporting the wounded as they marched—indiscriminate of past allegiances. The mournful cries of their horns beckoned Vincent and Paun to lay aside their arms, but both refused to consent. Those bearing the fallen soldier on their shields proceeded on past them and into the keep while a handful of others began to gather about Paun and Vincent.

All stood watching in silence.

Regret scarred the features of Vincent as he parried and out-stepped Paun, but it mattered not. Vincent was clearly holding back his strength, able to kill Paun in any instant he desired—but it mattered *not*. It was a terrible accident and it was unjust for Vincent to die for it.

IT… MATTERED… NOT.

If he so dearly desired someone to blame, Paun should blame himself. For if he had merely stayed put, hindered his reckless impulses and not given into his impudence, *she* would still be alive. Paun frowned, shoving the voice in his head aside. He knew it was true and knew the moment he heeded its words, he would be overtaken with the guilt of his actions. *No...* no, he needed to do this *now*—while his conscience was silenced and his resolve undeterred.

YOU ARE WEAK.

With a wild swing, Paun collapsed to the stone. His breathing grew shallow and rapid, his sight lined with black pulses, threatening to overtake him. Mentally shoving the pain aside, Paun pushed himself to his knees and rose to meet the eyes of Vincent.

Paun was enraged by the helpless circumstance of Vincent's unjust might; why should one as *he* receive the blessings of such terrible powers? Paun could list a thousand names beyond worth for such powers and yet... Vincent *Merrybender* was chosen by fate *itself* to wield its blade. It was... *wrong*, yet there was nothing Paun could do about it.

Paun's overwhelming impotence over the matter only fueled his rage.

By whatever silent urge, Paun's eyes shifted behind Vincent, catching sight of Adela's still body: a translucent spinner hovering over it; it was shaped like Adela, with a hand-and-half sword hovering over its head. Its silent purport taking shape in Paun's head, he rose to slash his smallsword across Vincent's shoulder. As the old man deflected the blow and locked the crossguards with ice, Paun used his raised elbow to bash Vincent's nose. With the old fool briefly stunned, Paun dropped his sword to seize Vincent's. Initially, Paun's weakening grip could barely twist it free. However, time slowed to a dead lull as his eyes caught sight of Adela once more, now held in the arms of a figure hooded in white. To Paun's horror, it gradually dissipated, taking Adela's limp corpse with it.

A silent will echoed in his head.

KILL HIM.[2]

In that brief moment, he felt an unnatural strength seize his limbs, allowing him to tear the sword from Vincent with a ferocious spin and a burst of cerulean flames. Vincent ducked under the blade, stumbling back on the pavement as Paun advanced with crazed thrashings. Vincent raised his gauntlets, their metal encasing in ice as his sword struck them. Tearing it free, the ice erupted in flames, causing Vincent to cry out in pain. Rolling

---

2. *kill him*

beyond the reach of Paun's attack, Vincent hastily tore off his gauntlets, their metal blazing a bright red as they fell to the stone.

Paun roared and swung after Vincent, chopping his blade against the stone in a crazed effort to strike him. Vincent just barely managed to push himself away from the onslaught before finding an opportunity to rise and face him on two feet. Before Paun could push his aggression, his shoulder's blood loss began to take its toll; everything he knew was swiftly engulfed by black and everything he was... *faded...* in a... peaceful... quiet...

Silence.

You did this.

CHAPTER THIRTY-SIX

BLUEBIRDS

P AUN'S EYES SNAPPED OPEN with an adrenaline-fueled gasp. He shot up from his back, rising to find himself in a bed of white satin. The light of dawn trickled through a circular window on his left, its pale light illuminating the small room he found himself in. His right hand was clenched, grasping for the sword which wasn't there. Paun's gaze fell to his torso, from the light-linen shirt to the veneer binds wrapped about his left shoulder and burnt wrist. He rubbed his shoulder wrappings, wincing at the stitching he felt beneath it. It didn't hurt of course—not physically anyway—but it still somewhat revolted him to know such a deep wound now resided in his own—

Paun froze, just catching sight of the folded note sitting at the foot of his bed. Cautious, he waded through his sheets, their enhanced folds rippling like a thin layer of water. Retrieving the note with two fingers, Paun tentatively unfolded its delicate design to reveal a short message. He couldn't read a single word, for his eyes were immediately drawn to the signature at its bottom.

Vincent.

Paun promptly crumpled the note before shoving it into his mouth.[1] Sliding off the bed, his bare feet thumped against the maple-brown floorboards. Paun felt an odd rattle on impact, its clatter drawing his attention underneath the bed. Swallowing hard, Paun dropped flat to his stomach and retrieved the object. He rose to his knees as he eyed it: a

---

1. This might be as good a moment as any to explain that Paun's father had taught him the best way to dispose of documents—or any evidence—was to consume them. Nothing, not even fire, was as reliable as stomach acid. To instil this lesson, his father had made him eat paper as a child for practice. It's probably why Paun's first instinct was always to swallow anything incriminating, and why he was so remarkably good at getting it down quickly.

hand-and-half sword, its blade impossibly sheathed by a pocket-sized scabbard. Its handle was overlapped in snowy-white scales: the unmistakable design of the one sword Paun *loathed*. Its very weight caused his hand to shake in loathing tremors. He *hated* Vincent... though he knew he was not to blame; Vincent had reacted from instinct—protection... If anything, Paun could be blamed just as much for seeking Adela so recklessly, if not more for reacting out of rageful impulse. Paun knew it was true and was disgusted—if not *horrified*—by what his emotions were capable of. For that, his hatred for Vincent was kindled all the more.

Paun's hand tightened violently.

His silent emotion overtaking his voice of reason, he flung the sword through the humble vanity mirror across his bed. Shards of glass hurtled through the room, shattering his reflection.

You should not be so hasty as to repay your given hospitality with aggression.

Paun's frown only deepened at the collected tone of Chulian.

"I fully intend to throw you in a volcano." He knelt beside the sword lying amongst shards of his broken reflection. "I hope you understand that."

Then I shall reside at its fiery bottom, remaining until I am found. Many forces seek the power I guard, power they will indeed attain once they have broken me.

"Ah... so you'll just stay with the sword then?" Paun shrugged. "A poor choice if you really consider it."

I am the guardian of this blade. Death has been denied of me and I shall be bound to mine duty till my sword's potential has subsisted with me or none remain to abuse it.

"And Vincent didn't abuse it? Do you not *yourself* abuse it?" Paun scoffed as he turned his back to the sword. "You're the one who granted him permission to murder her in the first place."

I have only ever granted Vincent permission to use such powers if I truly believe those he treasures are in danger... such was the promise I made after his wife... I refused to... I wouldn't grant him the power he needed to... save her from... There was a moment of silence before Chulian's curt tone returned. *No, I refused to see him so broken again. I am bound by two oaths—one to my sword and another to him.*

Paun's heart softened somewhat—but *only* somewhat.

"So you took the life of an innocent to atone for—"

Child. The resounding echo of Chulian's voice chastised Paun's conscience. *In the last instance, before reality severed her heart, I could feel the fibres of her soul brushing against my mind.* Chulian paused before continuing: *there was nothing but an overwhelming heart of purity... a heart I have not felt since the dying beat of Alenna.*

Paun shook his head, his eyes watering over, much to his annoyance.

"Was there truly nothing you could have done?"

I withdrew my will and with it, my permission of power, staving off the full force of the blow. Such indecision is what allowed her to last as long as she did.

"It was... *painfully* long... enough to riddle her in agony."

For that... I am sorry. Chulian cut Paun's thoughts off before he could speak. *Vincent wished for you to inherit this blade.*

Paun shook his head, gasping in disbelief.

"Why? Why would you two *ever—*"

He no longer trusts my judgement. He trusts himself naught with its power and... in truth, neither do I. Something akin to a mental sigh graced Paun's thoughts. *The moment you leave for the funeral, my spirit shall withdraw into a deep slumber within the blade, rendering its powers dormant. Reality has been scarred too hastily and neccecitates a respite.*

"And just how long do plan on sleeping?" Paun's countenance fell gravely as he processed Chulian's verbal thoughts. "What funeral?"

The one you will partake in the following hour. I suggest you leave now, whilst the crowds are yet thin. If you wait for the hour at which it takes place, you will miss your assigned stance, for the guardsmen will have no time for your ticket.

"What ticket?"

The one currently residing in the bowels of your stomach.

Paun shrugged, pulling his grey coat off the bedpost to wrap about his shoulders.

"Doesn't matter either way." He paused before the doorway. "Chulian... of the regions... who was triumphant? All this suffering and loss and..." Paun couldn't finish. Was it even possible for a region to emerge triumphant after such a horrific conflict?

There are claims Unbequith secured the shards, but rumours of their sudden disappearance are just as likely.

"Mm..." Paun tugged on his coat collar. "So that's a no then." Chulian's presence withdrew from Paun's mind as he stepped through the door and into the hallway. It was no trouble for him to find his way, for every... *single...* person he passed in those halls were asking him how he was holding up before immediately directing him to the Great Hall. It would have taken but five minutes had he not been continually pulled to the side by strangers he knew naught, nor cared to know. Eventually, he did manage to reach the Great Hall in time, though it was terribly vacant.

The room was dark in design and quite massive: it was large enough to host an entire legion in the levels of seats built into the encircling walls. In its centre, however, was a daunting tower of caskets, stretching up through a great hole in the ceiling. A series of golden-red symbols flickered across each casket, hosting the name and heritage of its permanent guest. Paun stepped closer, crossing a dark line engraved into the stone tiles about the caskets. The smell of death was enough to topple a normal man... but Paun had smelt worse... *been* through worse.

"You've either a broken sense of perception or think mighty of yourself to stand here."

Paun glanced to his left, somewhat surprised to see Aivon stepping beside him.

"Mm." Paun turned back to eyeing the caskets. "How so... Commander."

"Our security. A forged alliance between our regions, constructed to keep the... more *devastated* of us from doing anything we'd regret." Aivon gestured over his shoulder with twiddling fingers. "They were on the verge of tackling you to the floor and arresting you on the spot had I not interceded." Aivon's tone gravely fell. "I... couldn't allow that... protocol or no... you don't deserve that. Not a man who's been through what you have."

A pent-up sigh escaped Paun as his eyes shifted upwards to the peak of the caskets.

"And what have I been through, O'Commander? Tell me—I'm *curious* to know what toils I have suffered..." He shook his head, dark locks falling over his eyes. "I don't even know why I'm still here..."

"I knew her."

Paun's gaze shot up to Aivon's.

"How long..." He gulped, his features revealing the true vulnerabilities of his fractured heart. "So Henagan had her join *you*, did he? Huh..." Paun's vacant countenance returned as he crossed his arms. "I thought she was in some Harling dungeon somewhere... not too fond of those folk, am I."

"She wasn't forced. She joined of her own will."

"*No*. No... not the Addy I know." Paun bit his lip and shook his head with an unhinged smile. "I don't know whether Lord Monbel told you or not, but... I have met him in person. I doubt she would ever offer allegiance to a man as scheming as he... even if it meant her freedom."

"Yes, well... she may not have trusted Teresul... but she trusted me." Aivon sighed deeply. "And for that... I can only beg your forgiveness. It was in my care she was entrusted in... whether she wished it or not, I should have had her escorted far beyond this place of carnage." Aivon gravely shook his features. "She was so intent on fulfilling the calls of her pure heart... I couldn't bring myself to deny her that—not one as capable as her."

"Mm..." Paun's eyes began glistening over, much to his annoyance. "Well that... that does sound like her." Paun glanced behind Aivon's shoulders to see two men; one shadowy figure in a dark mask supporting another with a veneer bind wrapped about a stump where his left arm should have been. Paun pointed to them. "They'd know her?"

Aivon followed his gesture.

"Ram and Sam? Aye, they were members of her Force... along with my cousin." Aivon loosely gestured a finger upwards while eyeing the stone between his feet. "That's him... up there. Bo's... what we called him. Yet another godly soul this conflict has claimed."

Paun shrugged.

"I was just here for her." They remained silent after that, too overcome by emotion to breach the quiet. As time passed, various officials, soldiers and citizens began filing into the Great Hall. From the corners of his eyes, Paun could have sworn he spotted Vincent lurking in the shadows of the eaves. From the quick glance, it looked as though he were occupied in deep conversation with a stranger in a red hood. Unfortunately, Paun couldn't bring himself to look again and chose to remain in silence as the Great Hall's population grew in number.

His heart's inquiring voice grew with the number of occupants, allowing Paun to speak up: "And—what of her body? I doubt she... Unless she said otherwise, I'm sure she'd wish..." Paun cleared his throat and sighed. "Do you not agree her family should be the ones to lay claim to her... body? I'm sure they've a place among their kin for her... as is... Fallen Guild's way."

Aivon shook his head.

"No... we never... her body was never found. I've... laid waste the entire night searching for her. I've had every True Beyonder scour for her body, but there's just... simply no trace of it." He shook his head. "Many believe her to have been so pure, she was denied death and simply carried up to Heaven by angels or even God Himself... I wouldn't doubt it."

"Oh..." Paun eyed the grim tower of caskets. "So is she not to be honoured among the dead?"

"No, of course she is to be honoured. The finest casters of Unbequith worked alongside my True Beyonders to construct an orb of precious stone about the celestial gash—or whatever Mr. Merrybender called it." Aivon took a step from the caskets, urging Paun to step back as well. His voice lowered as they crossed the line to stand amongst the crowd. "A monument has been raised in her memory—one which you are free to honour at any moment. Her story is inscribed there if you are curious as to how... well, as to how you found her where you did."

"Oh..." Paun cleared his throat, lowering his voice to match Aivon's. "Thank you... I, please—no, I mean, *yes*, but... thank you." Paun pressed a hand to his heart, his eyes hazing over. "I'll be sure to pay it a visit."

"Of course. 'Tis the least of actions I could do for one of her... aye." He smirked humorlessly to himself. "I'm... trying not to berate myself over the head for such a small matter, but..."—a pained smile graced his features—"but she was... ever so ecstatic to see Giltpool's lake one day and... after today, I dearly wished to entreat her with—" Aivon was cut off by a shriek across the room. Paun's gaze followed its sound, the crowd parting down the middle to reveal Junia. A bracer-like cloth was clenched tightly in one hand, a smallsword in the other, one which she violently gestured at Aivon with.

"Draw your sword!" she commanded, her voice striking through the hall in a bolt of enraged energy. "Don't begin *thinking* I shall hesitate killing you unarmed!" The crowd gasped as she lunged for Aivon, only to be restrained by the tight grip of Theo. She squirmed in his grasp, wildly shouting: "No! *No!* You *know* what he did! He doesn't deserve to replace *him*—*release* me!" She struggled through several guards restraining her, almost stabbing one of them in the eye.

Before Aivon could speak, Paun cut him off.

"Junia." His voice pierced the hall, causing her to go silent at its tone. "Junia..." He glanced at the tower of caskets before returning his gaze to her. "No."

Her eyebrows met together as she eyed him in pure disbelief before composing herself.

"*Let* go of me." She jerked her arms free and sheathed her sword. Giving Paun one last look, she turned about, shoving Theo aside as she left. Paun could only watch helplessly as she left, not caring to stay for the funeral proceedings. Paun would have left with her, but guilt nailed him to the spot. Though the funeral proceedings continued on, he couldn't hear a single word. Even when Aivon left his side to speak at a podium, Paun could hardly maintain a clear focus. All words were simply dulled to a blunt and useless expression of hollow sentiments. Paun couldn't *think* of anything and he couldn't *feel* anything.

He was simply vacant.

These memories... we'll bind.

Like a withering... weight of the heart.

Paun's trance-like state was ruptured by the clear voice of a singer, piercing the Hall's heavy silence. To his surprise, he had failed to notice the drove of dreary voices coming to an end. In truth, the entire hall had fallen silent to hear the singer's voice.

Oh our kin... left behind...
Yet further in life... set apart.

A children's choir, positioned in seats encircling the walls, echoed the singer's lamenting tones in a simple chant.

Oh naa-oh

All Paun knew was the soul-rousing fervour of the singer's words.

Set apart
Endless scars
Loved you while you were
Loved you... while you were not...

The singer paused, allowing his echoes to fade from existence before continuing.

Hopeless cries
Lullabies—
Already... heading home
Left us... thus alone...

There was truth to its words—a passion of sorrow that connected with Paun, speaking directly to his conscience; it wasn't stale, artificial or... *dull*. It was simple, aye... but piercing, convicting and... real.

Oh nao nah-oh
Oh naa oh

The singer's voice rose in intensity, their vocals flying about the Hall in spectacular cries.

> *Oh young bluebirds... swarmed by the crows born of dust*
> *Oh na oh, oh na oh*
> *Into a new world... rushed onto the fields... on above!*
> *Oh na oh, oh na oh*
> *This new journey, may the wind carry your angel's wings, na-na oh...*
> *This heavenly adventure, set amongst the courts of kings*

Paun's hand slowly dug into his coat pocket as the singer transitioned to the next verse. He went rigid as his fingers brushed against crumpled pieces of parchment and paper. Paun carefully withdrew the paper, his features falling in dismay at the sight of an envelope.

> *Oh young bluebird*
> *nanana oh na oh*
> *Oh young bluebird...*
> *nanana oh na oh...*

It was addressed to Adela, a letter he very well intended to deliver, but... well, of course, he never got the chance and... and never would.

> *You fought well*
> *Thrashing, till your breath was broken*
> *Your soul was still*
> *All you knew... your life... was stolen*

Paun's hand unrolled the piece of parchment, his heart falling at the portrait of Adela's family. A sickening feeling sprouted in his gut the longer he stared; there was another task which still needed resolve, something Paun felt he bore the responsibility to.

> *Oh naa oh*

One quick end
A slow descend
A farewell to... your children
Won't forget what they'll... attend
Bitter tears
Child fears
Fathers'n brothers cost
A mother's child's lost

Paun's eyes rested on the portrait of Adela and her crooked smile; how many weeks had it been since he'd taken its once familiar sight for granted? Few were the days where he caught her without its bright countenance; its very recollection caused rays of fond memories to light the darkness of his mind.

Oh naa oh
Oh naa oh
Oh young bluebirds, swarmed by yon' crows born of dust
Oh na oh, oh na oh
Into a new world, rushed onto the fields up above
Oh na oh, oh na oh
This new journey, may the wind carry your angels wings

All Paun had to do was close his eyes, and he'd see Adela's crooked smile, lit across her features as she attempted to bypass a muddy stream via a rickety log. Truthfully, they had no need to cross, but Adela simply wanted to try it both ways.

Na oh
A new heavenly army, placed amongst the courts of Kings
Oh young bluebird nanana oh na oh
Oh young bluebird nanana oh na oh...

Paun couldn't help but smile at the thought of her falling into the stream on the way back.

Oh naa oh
Oh naa oh

Another time she went off route was to chase after a peculiar-blue lizard—claiming they needed another companion for good fortune.

Gates flushed with thoughts of you
Dance for the Creator too
Tragedy wont last long for you
A fresh home, kingdom, a body made anew

There was another memory where she scaled a great tree simply to see what its canopy might conceal.

A blessed land has been born for you
And still your family mourns for you
But we'll accept the solemn truth
Walk as a light, "my brother... we'll miss you"

A flood of beloved memories flashed through Paun's mind, overwhelming him with the bitter joy of their emotion; Addy picking a bouquet of flowers, cooking a morning meal, dancing with wraiths, hunting for candles, shovelling food into her cheeks, sporting a bonnie-yellow dress, shoving peculiar findings in Paun's face, swinging on a bayou branch, sipping tea, singing in a tavern, chasing after starlight—and smiling that same crooked smile all the while.

Oh naa oh
Oh na oh
Oh nananana oh na oh oh na
Oh nananana oh

The tower of caskets sunk into the ground with a gradual creak. Paun remained unfazed as the black ring encircling the casket blazed to life, igniting everything in its circumference with a blazing cascade of orange sparks, hushing forth from below. Stepping up to the inferno, Paun unfolded the envelope and eyed its crinkled paper.

Oh young bluebirds, fresh fire, a crown upon your head
Oh na oh, oh na oh
Into a new world, brave warrior, no we won't forget
Oh na oh, oh na oh
This new journey, watch as God shines His face unto you
Na-na oh
A heavenly journey, can't await the day we'll be with you... again

Paun thought not, nor cared not, of his actions as he tossed the envelope into the flames before him; it was written for Adela... and no other.

We'll meet again
...Oh naa... oh...
...oh naa...
... oh...

The rest of the funeral had been nothing more than a blurred experience. Paun wasn't even sure if he'd continued to linger for the final half... whatever that was. Eulogies, ash distributions, sermons?

No, he was done.

Paun had left long ago, tracing his steps to lead out into the capital's inner bailey where he found the monument Aivon had spoken of; it was a simple prism of sea-grey stone, constructed before a scrawny tree with black bark and white petals. Its roots dug into the circle of dirt built within the bailey's paving. Oddly enough, there were scores of lilies growing in a small pool encircling the monument. Their soft petals wafted softly in the breeze as though they were in their natural habitat; no doubt the works of intricate Rantalorian casting.

Paun knelt to examine the silver plaque engraved within the stone, detailing the wondrous life of Adela Windcatcher, Maiden of the Redfolk. He took a moment to study its inscriptions before untying a yellow kerchief from his belt and softly securing it to the ashen tree. As he did, Paun noticed the various illustrations strewn about the monument's base, their spirited sketches torn and soiled.

Stepping about the monument, Paun froze at the sight of a boy with copper-red hair, leaning against the backside of the precious stone. He looked as though he were in a doze. A journal laid open in his lap, though it was devoid of pages. Whoever this boy was, he was outfitted in simple Unbequith garbs and had a veneer bind wrapped securely about his stomach. Paun knelt quietly by his side, retrieving one of the drawings from the stone paving; it was a crude drawing, though somewhat humorous in its depiction of a Wilbojab munching on maypil flowers.

"She was... fond of those." Paun's attention shot to the boy on his left, sapphire-blue eyes open and staring at the drawing on Paun's lap. "You should have seen her face light up at the sight of them—cheered her up more than enough, it did."

"Mm." Paun set aside the drawing to retrieve another, though he couldn't focus on it. "You knew her?"

The boy shrugged, his copper-red locks wafting with the lilies behind him.

"I think... she was a friend. I'd be lying to say I wasn't hoping for something more... but... I doubt I was ever worthy." The boy sighed deeply before discreetly using his wrist to brush his eyes. "No... just an acquaintance is all... I doubt I was ever as close as you."

"Oh." Though Paun's gaze fell to the sketch in his lap, he couldn't discern its image through his hazing vision. "You know who I am... was it 'cause she..."

"All of Unbequith was put on watch for you at some point—'tis the only reason I recognised you so." The boy's arms drooped to his side as he sank further against the stone. "But she did mention you... was reluctant to bring it up around me, but whenever she mentioned your name... there would burst asunder a terrifying spark in her eye—one which, deep down, I knew I could never inspire." He shrugged before gesturing to the smallsword at Paun's hip. "Aivon ask for that back yet?"

"No, he—" Paun sniffed and cleared his throat. "No, he didn't mention it."

"Must have wanted you to have it then." The boy was silent for a few moments more before he asked: "Did she ever mention me?"

Paun was somewhat taken aback by the question.

"I... I'm sorry. I don't recall her ever bringing you up... just her family on some occasions."

"Oh... then... yeah... I don't suppose I know what I am to her. Just another dolt thinking himself blessed enough to make more than an acquaintance."

Paun brushed a hand over his eyes, briefly able to view the sketch in his lap; it was another one of her family, though quite different from the one Paun carried.

"Did you make these?" he asked, raising the sketch lightly. The boy studied it for a handful of seconds before mumbling a feeble response. Paun turned back to examine its sketch, saying: "If she trusted you with this knowledge... willingly disclosed such... well, I'm sure she counted you as someone precious... and dear."

"Oh, I hope not," chuckled the boy, his expression clearly in pain. "Remembering it as such would only render living all the more unbearable."

Paun remained in silence, unable to respond immediately.

"Perhaps..." he finally said, setting the sketch aside. "But you can still find comfort in the role you must have played in her life... improving it to the utmost of your abilities while it lasted."

The boy shrugged again.

"Perhaps."

They remained in silence once more, not caring to speak that which needn't be said.

The searing orange of the sky was gradually extinguished by the cool tones of night as the sun set behind the keep's black tower.

Nothing more need be said.

CHAPTER THIRTY-SEVEN

BURDEN OF LIVING

T HE FOLLOWING SERIES OF events were muddled together in one vague recollection. Paun hardly remembered every detail, for it had all moved along so quickly.

After the funeral concluded, the Harlings had insisted on returning to their region at
the behest of Henagan; each soldier dearly wished to unite with their families as it were
and not tarry another day if they could help it.[1] Their region's numbers were to depart
the following week, with supplies gifted to them from Ranitorl and Unbequith for the
return journey through Nowood. Paun himself fully intended on returning to Harldïof
at some point and had decided he might as well tag along.

That, and the insistence of Malvolia was most convincing—she being the only friend
who remained and all. Her father even suggested Paun would be rewarded greatly by
Harldïof's Lord—Os Finyeld—for his heroic role in the hunt. Even if that hadn't been the
case, Paun would've still accompanied them. In truth, he couldn't care less what Henagan
had to say or... just Henagan in general; quite truthfully, he still yearned to plant a knife
in the knave's sorry gut, but it seemed some other bloke had already beaten him to it.
Besides, he was still Malvolia's father and she seemed to have grown terribly fond of Paun
for whatever reason.

Paun's departure with the Harlings was as unceremonious as it was abrupt. He doubted any would notice his absence... in the least... he *thought* no one would; he hadn't heard
anything of Junia since the funeral and... in truth, had been far too troubled of what he'd
find if he went searching after her.

No, whatever Junia did was her business.

---

1. Oh, yes, Henagan survived. Perhaps some stray Oather's armour played a part, but you won't catch
me admitting it (not directly, at least).

And Theo's.

Whoever *that* guy was.[2]

Aye, at the time, Paun simply wished to leave them be; he had every intention of finding her again someday, but... until then, he would travel wherever there was some remnant of purpose for him; whether it was through the shadows of Nowood—or home... one day... when he felt like... he could go back.

As for Nowood itself, well... that had been another adventure entirely. Though Unbequith had seen fit to gift them with symbols of blessings and protection, they were still at risk; unlike Seeker's Passage, their route was uncleansed and *wild*, brimming with all uncanny manners of eldritch and bewitchery. Some scouts had come fleeing back, claiming to have discovered sporadic pools of boiling puddles. However, upon the company's investigation, there would be no findings of any such bewilderments—not a single drop to be seen whatsoever.

In contrast, other hauntings had been more blatant; on one starless night, a creature towering above the trees crashed through their camp, sowing chaos and ruin. It looked as though it were a colossal skeleton composed of tree limbs and bits of ruined stone. Its howl was cursed and its speed dreadful. It took their company the whole remainder of the night to bring it down. Fire had been *ever* so terribly effective.

Even on nights when they were granted the privilege of sleep, Paun hadn't been able to rest at ease. Why, sleeping had been far worse of an experience than anything they had encountered in those woods; the pestering and unrelenting feeling of being watched by a thousand eyes burned in the back of his mind. If not for a certain steward's invigorating words of guidance, Paun would have long gone mad to the unknown insanity of those woods.

Henagan... was his name.

Over the course of Nowood, Paun had come to develop a keen friendship with Malvolia—one Henagan was sure to monitor closely. Despite his initial suspicions, Paun had spent a good deal of time with Henagan, retelling various aspects of his perilous quest. Malvolia spoke up every now and again, but mostly chose to remain quiet; she had already recounted her side of the tale to Henagan and he was interested in hearing Paun's. Such moments gathered about a campfire made the journey through Nowood... a little more bearable.

---

2. Fret not, Beholders. Theo's story is the next I wish to tell.

In those woods, Paun had time to think. And in thinking, he was forced to conclude that, perhaps, Henagan wasn't all that bad. At the very least, he was a decent man. Aye, Paun didn't mind the Henagans' company.

Still, the journey was long and the memories unpleasant, but they had eventually returned to Harldïof, gracefully devoid of casualties... unless you counted the wounded, traumatised or mentally broken. Regardless, it took naught but a three days' trek from Nowood's borders before they arrived in Nöscvelis, capital of Harldïof. Truly, it was an overwhelming sight to behold—in quite the stark contrast to the capitals of its sister regions; the grey stone of its foundation was established within the jagged peaks of ice-strewn mountains, yielding an imposing advantage should any dare to lay siege. It had been snowing when they arrived—and everyone seemed so *bleeding* prepared for it too.

Paun couldn't help but marvel at how quickly the landscape's biome had shifted under such a short time of travel—but then, they hadn't been forging on through Harldïof's more wild parts and were neither hindered nor deviated from the western route in any way.

To Paun's greater bewilderment, who should he find greeting their ranks at the gates of Nöscvelis other than Barth himself? Paun had stepped up to the older fellow in pure astonishment, taking his hand to shake violently; Paun was still undecided on where he stood with the shopkeeper—or... no, *Hand of Harldïof* as Barth was sure to inform him. He merely ran a shop in his spare time—time which he seemed to acquire more than enough of these years. Still, he couldn't complain, insisting he was too old for wandering about the region in the name of an old, senile Lord. No, he would much rather influence events from the comforts of his dear shop of curiosities he had gathered over his years of service—many of which he himself had confessed to not understand.

In truth, Paun was too astonished and exhausted to really understand anything the older fellow was saying, but the moment Barth paused to breathe, Paun had cut in, questioning about the vidorae; how did Barth possibly leave it out for Paun so perfectly? Why, did Barth even know he would accept it? Why choose Paun to begin with?

Barth had merely shrugged in response, explaining he didn't leave it out for Paun, who didn't *accept* it, no—Paun *stole* it. Secondly, Barth had simply—unintentionally—accidentally left it out after shining it for display—for when Vincent came back to retrieve it of course—not to sell, mind you. Barth had then quickened his pace to stride ahead of Paun, putting distance between them with a nervous laugh.

Not to sell.

Henagan had found Paun after that, personally escorting him to the courts of Os Finyeld. In truth, Paun had wished for nothing more than to sleep undisturbed in a bed with a mattress, pillows, sheets, a blanket—and... *maybe* some peace.

That would have been nice.

Instead, he was ushered before Os Finyeld, Lord of Harldïof. To remember it bluntly, the Lord was a sickly looking fellow; his faded-grey hair streaked his bony scalp like dripping paint left out in the sun for far too many years. His red-rimmed eyes were an icy-blue, their murky depths devoid of light and, dare Paun say, *life*. Though his clothes were somewhat humble, the vain Lord had seen fit to wear a crown of silver and gold about his head. If Paun hadn't known otherwise, he would have assumed the Lord to be a fleshy ghost... whatever that would look like.

Probably like the Lord of Harldïof.

Os Finyeld had been in the middle of a council meeting when Paun was ushered in... much to his dismay; it was terribly awkward to simply stand there while he waited to be called on. Indeed, if Paun had been less apprehensive to meet the Lord of Harldïof before, he was practically dreading it then; accusations were fired across the chamber left and right, all of which were directed upon Os Finyeld's repute. Some claimed he was as corrupted as Lord Monbel, if not more for launching an assault against Mount Færas—a campaign of which had cost them a third of their army. Os Finyeld insisted he had been given no choice but to act on the offensive and initiate a Desperate Quarter. This argument was immediately met with how they lacked the need for a Desperate Quarter against what Lord Finyeld *clearly* thought to be the unarmed cities of Unbequith.

Additional stewards had approached from another stance entirely, claiming the state of Lord Finyeld's region was in an embarrassing disarray—falling apart in morality and devolving into something of *savagery*: a clear reflection of Lord Finyeld's character. The sickly Lord retorted that Nöscvelis had never seen better days of prosperity and for them to deny such was for them to deny their common sense.

This, however, had only seemed to anger his council all the more.

The stewards had demanded a new regional lord, one who would renew the signet's light Finyeld had allowed to dim. They warned of how the other regions were certain to respond to Finyeld's acts of corruption with war—and how they promised to unite alongside them *against* Finyeld. With that said, there wasn't much room for Os Finyeld to defend himself and Paun was finally called forward.

Henagan had chosen to remain quiet during the meeting, only then speaking to introduce Paun and his key place in the hunt for the shards and his service in the Siege of Ranitorl. Lord Finyeld simply frowned upon Paun the whole while, his creases deepening with every syllable of deed and praise from Henagan's lips. Conversely, the other stewards had murmured in approval of Paun, with some whispering their region needed a man like Paun to guide them.

Paun could clearly remember Lord Finyeld's unnerving handshake as the council concluded, its bony touch sending a chill up his spine. At the time, Paun didn't think much of it, for he had dearly wished to be shown to his temporary chambers; after everything that'd been said... he only desired the undisturbed silence of a pillow's touch and the warm comfort of a blanket's security.

Unfortunately, it was not to be so.

For whatever reason, Os Finyeld had decided to murder Paun in the dead of night, trusting no other with the dark task save for himself. It was his undoing of course, for Paun was a light sleeper and Nowood had only worsened such conditioning. To no one's surprise, the assassination attempt had failed, but Os Finyeld still managed to slip away through the chamber's window. Paun's designated guards had followed him out and onto the roof. From there, Paun believed they managed to corner the old fool and arrest him.

Paun was left simply baffled by it all, but he had been too sleepy to care.

At all.

The following day, a new lord had to be instituted. The Harling stewards were sure to test Paun with the Lord's signet several times over, but its signs would always lack two of the three blessings; the peoples' and the previous lord's. Though the previous lord's blessing was no longer deemed significant, the peoples' blessing was beyond vital. So, instead of ol' Paun, the steward known as Abaddon Henagan had been elected as the third Lord of Harldïof.

Mm... good man.

Truthfully, the quick-paced events of it all were almost... well, *comical* to Paun—had his life not been threatened so readily.

Still, it wasn't entirely fruitless, for Henagan had decided to make Paun his hand—should he accept. Lord Henagan explained how Paun had shone favour in the stewards' eyes, favour Henagan required to gain their initial respect. That... and perhaps Henagan truly believed no other suited the position.

Also, Malvolia had refused it and recommended Paun instead, so he wasn't really his first pick, but—*anyway*.

It took Paun but several moments of listening to the finer details of such a position before eagerly accepting it. In truth, he had half-hoped such a position would allow him to meet Junia at the next Chamber of Kin meeting, but...

Well, of course he never did.

That would have been too perfect, huh?

Despite that, Paun was still grateful for the offered position. In debt to this newfound show of trust, Paun had gifted Lord Henagan's daughter a rather *special* hand-and-a-half sword, one which could cut through most materials. Its once icy blade now appeared like any other sword, granted it was now a prismatic blue. Despite that, Paun's Lord was beyond pleased to receive a relic so connected with their region's legends.

His soul distraught, Paun could only smile.

Anyway, contrary to what some might assume, Paun had greatly enjoyed the position; it was everything he desired and everything he was simply built for: in a constant state of travel about the world at the greater behest of a lord, whether it be investigating treacherous rumours, running perilous errands or relaying secret messages—all of which could *only* be conducted by the Lord's trusted hand. It suited Paun's niche and generously gifted him the purpose he sought—as though he had found his calling and that everything he had ever been through served to prepare him for this singular position.

Aye, some might presume it was binding to be in such service, but, if anything... he was free to unveil his adventurous spirit and let it loose upon the world, focusing it through the gifted lens of motive. If not, why... who knows what sort of mischief his aimless spirit would have gotten him into?[3]

Oh, it paid well too.

Why, at one point, Paun had enough wealth to purchase whatever odd assortment of knicknacks he desired. Not for himself, of course, but for bartering. Aye, the day he could waltz into the Grey Marsh for any equipment of his choosing had to be one of the most gratifying days of his life since...

Yeah.

Oh.

There was... there was also *that*.

---

3. Indeed... who knows what mischief an aimless life of mediocrity could wrought...

Aye, it hadn't always been smiles and adventures.

With permission from an understanding Lord Henagan—good man—Paun had departed Harldïof for Ranitorl, roaming its wild's rugged terrain for the Fallen Guild. Little resistance did he encounter and little did he ever doubt the whereabouts of his destination; his father had been sure to impress their location into Paun's memory should the day come where he could finally *prove his worth* and *redeem his name*.

Unfortunately, that wasn't at all why Paun had sought them.

It took... well, at the time, he hadn't maintained a track of days and simply cared not. All he knew was that it took a *while* before he finally found himself outside the hidden gates of the Fallen Guild's pass. Reciting the secret exchanges his father had taught him, Paun had been immediately admitted as Traitorson.

Perhaps there was some meaning in that.

But, he cared not.

Once inside, Paun wasted no time exploring or examining his surroundings; all that had mattered was accomplishing what he had come for. In truth, he must have seemed truly desperate, asking if anyone recognized the family in the portrait which burdened him.

Perhaps he was.

Perhaps he *was* desperate.

Nonetheless, it hadn't taken long for Paun to find the answer he sought and find himself standing before the most terrifying doors of his life. Upon knocking, he had been greeted warmly by a cheery couple, their familiar features catching Paun unawares for a second. Dazed, he told them then and there, their only daughter was *dead*.

Adela's mother had attacked him on the spot, pinning him to the ground and shrieking for him to explain. Thankfully, Adela's father managed to pry her off, ordering Paun to tell them *everything* and that if he missed a single detail, he would set his wife on him.

With this threat in mind, Paun had shared everything he knew. It was... not a pleasant experience to say the *least*. Some might believe *standing outside in the cold with two hunters listening as though they intended to murder you at any given moment should the wrong syllable slip* would be reason enough to feel discomfort—and it *would* be... in part. However, in truth, Paun couldn't stand his heart's pain in the ever-growing grief of their features.

As he concluded, the father had simply returned to the interior of his house, forcing Paun to wait several dreadful moments with the mother. When the father had returned at long last, he was completely outfitted in the guild's set of armour, its various trophies demonstrating his rank and skill. The father then asked unceremoniously for the name of the killer and Paun gave it freely. The father nodded before asking him whether the blow was premeditated, intended, or an accident. Paun had caught himself hesitating before finally answering with a grave sigh.

Accident.

"Then his death'll be swift an' his sufferin' merciful, yeh?"

Those were the words Adela's father had spoken.

Such was his promise.

Even after a week since hearing it, it still rang ominously in Paun's mind. At the time, Paun could only respond by unveiling the gift he had brought them to aid in their quest of vengeance; a black smallsword, encased in golden symbols. The father accepted it with an indebted heart, bidding a warm and grieving farewell to Paun.

Though he did not address him as Traitorson.

But... *Bournstrider.*

Paun Bournstrider.

Paun had some small idea of what it meant, but was grateful for it all the same; it was as though a heaving burden had fallen from his chest, allowing him to breathe once again and finally view his spectacular and dangerous world with fresh eyes.

But... after all that... there was... *one*... final matter... he needed to resolve.

And that... is where he found himself now: Altour Village of Harldïof's southern reach.

His hometown.

Map of the world, Beyond; by Maile A. Baker

CHAPTER THIRTY-EIGHT

A TRAITOR'S SON

T HE GRAVEL CRACKED SOFTLY beneath Paun's feet as he adjusted his footing. He was dressed as a middle-classed merchant, his garbs of a simple, yet elegant design. Perhaps he was being ridiculous for feeling such a need to test *him* so, but Paun was... curious. Aye, that was all. A small test it was. Besides... he couldn't avoid his own home forever.

Raising an apprehensive palm, Paun politely bashed the knocker against the courtyard's mahogany gate. Within several moments, he was promptly greeted by the timid-brown eyes of a timid woman.

"Missed you, Mum," he said, stepping past her bewildered expression and into the petal-strewn courtyard. He paused as he passed her before turning around to confront her gaping expression with a smile. "Aye, it's truly me. Finally decided to—" Paun's words were cut short as his mother lunged forward to embrace him.

"Finally decided the guilt was too much for you, did yeh?"

"Aye... couldn't let what happened keep me away... not from you and my siblings."

"Paun... after you and your father... Paun, he didn't mean those things. In truth, we all thought you'd return the following morrow. *Please*, you know that, don't you, Paun?" His mother carefully pried herself from him to study his features. "Paun... I... whatever is the matter?" Her brows bunched with concern. "Heavens alive... what did his words put you through?"

"Nothing he hadn't conditioned me for." Paun forced a smile in an attempt to overcome her worry with reassurance. "It may have been fiery words devoid of meaning, but... mine were as true and resolved as they are now."

"Paun, you shouldn't—"

"Where is he?" Paun glanced over his mother's shoulders to the training hall behind. "Is he well?"

"Yes, but he's quite—"

"Is he busy?"

"He's..." His mother hesitated before saying: "Sleeping."

"I'd like to see him." Paun curtly stepped past his mother, much to her distress.

"*Paun*, please." His mother tried to cut in front of him, but couldn't match his determined stride. "I can't lose you again, not to another fight—*please*, Paun, my beloved son—*please* don't leave me again, not so soon, Paun, not like this!" Her pleading tone nearly caused Paun to lose heart. Despite that, it couldn't restrain him from aggressively sliding open the door to his family's training hall.

In the chamber's centre, atop that familiar light-panelled floor, lunged in a frozen position, sword pointed forward... was his father.

Truval.

Paun glanced back to his mother, but she was already leaving, holding her tearing face in her hands. It broke his heart to see her so, but... he needed to resolve this, resolve his—

"Inemuri... I have.. somewhat perfected it." His father's glassy-brown eyes shifted over Paun, as though he weren't there. "But... its language is... foreign to you... is it not?"

Paun shook his head in disbelief, crossing his arms as he leaned against the doorway.

"I was told you were sleeping."

"Reality is only that which one perceives with the mind... if your reality... is consistently projected in your mind... through heightened senses of awareness... then you may sleep... and interact with reality as you generally would..." Truval gently raised his sword. "Most harness this technique for extensive travels... but I... I have mastered my senses enough to—" His father suddenly leapt forward, slashing the sword through a large and dangling bag of leather. Sand bled through its fresh slit as his father sheathed his blade and bowed to the sandbag. "However... it is not always... practical. Some things... the mind projects in one's dream... are simply not there in reality." He loosely shrugged. "But you learn to recognize and overcome such illusions."

"What are you... why are you telling me this?"

Truval chuckled, his eyes distant and vacant.

"Well Jovem, for one... you look like my own boy—the one from our pact. If I seem somewhat put off, well... that is why" His father's smile morphed to a firm frown. "But why are *you* here? You have settled your indebted obligations... I thought you never wished to see me again..."

Paun shrugged, pacing the training hall to admire its various armaments.

"I didn't... but... I soon realised that... despite my opinions of you, it shouldn't restrict me from trying to love you—regardless of how insane I might honestly think you to be sometimes."

Truval froze, shakily kneeling to the ground as he set his sword aside. Bending forward, his father inhaled sharply and his eyes came into a sudden and clear focus. Truval shook his head, as though he'd just awakened. His gaze rose slowly, lingering on Paun for a few moments in silence.

"So..." he finally began, "you truly are... here."

"Afraid so."

"Huh." Truval pushed himself back to his feet, crossing his arms as he studied his son. "I think it was... find the shards, restore your family's honour and prove me wrong, eh?" His father gestured to Paun's attire. "The boy I knew left to repair his surname, furious at his father for pushing him so hard to correct a wrong not his own."

Paun shrugged.

"I failed a third of the journey there. Seeing how I left I... couldn't bring myself to return home. Still, I needed to survive." Paun shrugged, pacing as he continued to lie. "There was a merchant in Tokade kind enough to harbour me as his apprentice and... well." Paun outstretched his arms, displaying his garbs for his father. "Became one myself, I suppose."

"You *suppose*..." Truval eyed his son's garbs before returning his gaze to Paun. "I've heard rumours... reports even... of a supposed peace betwixt our regions." His father sighed deeply. "Meaning someone *else* secured the shards first, eh?"

"Aye."

"Mm..." Truval raised an eyebrow and stroked his lightly-shaven beard. "That's... unfortunate..."

"*Aye.*"

"All that training... arguing... and you're still cursed to endure the *Traitorson* mark."

"Aye..."

"Well... that's..." His father gulped, his jaw quivering. "Blast it, boy..." His father paused, swallowing hard and shaking his head. "I missed you all the same."

Paun's eyes hazed over as he watched the tears fall freely from his father's eyes.

"Yeah..." he breathed, "I... I didn't—" Paun was cut off by his father, completely over-come by emotion as he embraced his son. Every bottled-up iota of emotion burdening Paun was squeezed out by the comforting arms of his father. Its genuine affection nearly caused Paun to choke; it reminded him all too well of days long-past when he would take similar affections for granted... when he would take *her* for granted. As they pulled away, Paun tried in vain to mirror his father's smile, but only cracked under the weight of its emotion. "I failed..." he softly stuttered, sinking to the floor, "father, I *failed* her... I let her die... I failed..."

"Yeah... I know, boy..." Truval wrapped an arm about Paun's neck, pulling him into another embrace. "I know." They remained in each other's arms for several moments more, simply finding comfort in one another's presence. As they sat there, Paun caught a glimpse of a dark brown mask peeking out of a sloppy chest of armaments. Judging from how little concealed it was, Paun guessed his father really mustn't have been expecting him... or, knowing Truval, he *wanted* Paun to catch a glimpse of the mask and the meaning of its insinuations.

It was hard to say.

Rising from the floor, Truval patted Paun's shoulders, saying: "Well... whatever hap-pens, boy... you can never count it as an absolute loss—not to us. Why, if you died, all your siblings would be forced listening to my same boring tales over and over again." His father wrapped an arm about Paun, pulling him close. "Like the prism shards! *Gramercy,* have you unlocked any mysteries of their shrouded past?"

Paun painfully smiled through his tears and cleared his throat.

"No, *mmh.* No, I still haven't the slightest clue of... *what* they are... but, nonetheless, I do possess some truly riveting tales to share—enough to rival yours I should think."

Truval led him down the steps of the training hall and across the courtyard.

"Well, endure a while longer if you can, aye? Your siblings have been so terribly anxious since you *abandoned* them. Why, you daren't imagine what your mother must've gone through. Still, I'm sure they'd love to hear every word of yours around our table." His father paused, stopping in the middle of the courtyard to gesture to the house behind him. "Dinner... that is... if you'll stay... if you want. You needn't feel pressured into eating with your own family, but—*blast it* boy, it's your own bleeding family!"

Paun smiled to himself.

Dinner... family.

How he had longed for it dearly.

Sight pulls away from the reuniting family, beholding their house from above and soon, their entire town. My mind's vision carries on in a blur, weaving through forests, across streams and under hollows. I see flowers littering a log as it passes by on a whim. A pack of sabre wolves on the move, their black and white patterns disorienting their prey. A tree atop a knoll with moss clung to its northern side, indicating the direction of wind and frequency of rain showers. My sight passes wonders, beauties and horrors alike before riding the side of a steep precipice. I see now a crag—a single lone figure sitting atop it. This figure... it is hooded in white and acknowledges my presence without a single spoken word. Instead, it sits in tranquil silence, witnessing the warm horizon... *rise* to meet the foggy blue sky

THE EPILOGUE

IN THE FIRST LIGHT of Rebirth's season, The Chamber of Kin had been summoned: an action unheard of since the regions' crossing of blades. Hoping to forge peace anew, the four regions had gathered in Orindire—that is, the Terrible Mountains—to discuss the fate of their world as a whole: east, north, southwest and northwest: Harldïof, Gotnoech, Ranitorl and Unbequith. Three of the four regions were represented by their respective Lords: Abaddon Henagan, Gunthor Jergenson, and Aivon Seeker. Three lords were accompanied by their respective hands: Paun Bournstrider, Hilliania Bukir and Loranzo Chrastin. Unbequith's newly instated Lord, though it had summoned the kin to Orindire, failed to show. Instead, their will was represented by a man with electric-blue eyes, their shining light piercing the dim depths of the chambers. It was this man who initiated the Kindred Pledge and this man who continued to make promises.

"Unbequith," he began, "is set on a new path, blazing a fresh trail which deviates from the bloody history of the *Redfolk*." Pen Wishton held a hand to silence what objections there might have been. "Please, brethren. We have lost much and many. Let us not initiate another crossing of blades simply because of foul, yet necessary, deeds of our past. My Lord, Siolant, knew of the corruption to be found in the heart of Teresul. Aye, we moved against him, yet only in shadow, for fear of none believing us... Now that his crimes have long been exposed to the general populace, we needn't conceal our righteous motives any further." Pen raised another silencing hand; Paun, Henagan, and Aivon were being... difficult. "I know..." he continued, "that there are rumours of my Lord, Siolant, possessing the shards all along and being associated with the long-extinct Death Order cult. This is... somewhat true. The Death Order jot was merely a sham designed to ward off any who sought to claim the shards, for we knew not of whom to trust." Pen shook his head with a dramatic sigh. "If we couldn't trust our own region, how could we trust anyone else? No, we were to protect the shards at all costs—that is the only explanation you shall get—*and* if you don't wish to initiate another war, that is the only information you'll accept. Savvy? Excellent. As for the shards, they were long lost on their voyage to Unbequith. But fret not! Should they turn up in the wrong hands, we as united regions should hold no difficulty in overcoming the odds. Now, about the regional boundaries of a hand's jurisdiction..."

The Chamber of the Kin continued on.

As it did, all couldn't help but ponder what the new Lord of Unbequith could possibly be occupied with—it *was* the Lord of Unbequith after all who ordered this historical summoning of the Kin. Many wondered where the Lord could possibly reside instead of here, who its title belonged to, and what plans said Lord intended for its region.

If only they had thought to look up.

Few of the many refuse to look up at all, though not out of choice completely, for they simply hold no reason to. Even still, if one simply took the time to entertain the naturally curious voice stowed in the back of your mind, you'd find nothing but an odd silence. Aye, if but one of those lords had dared to gaze up those mountains and observe the utmost peak, they would have beheld a curious figure seated atop a steep crag, watching the sunset with a grave intensity. It was clothed in white, with a simple mask of black tucked in the snow beside its knee.

It's... funny... how the dawn's new light rose like fire, setting the sky ablaze in the renewal of its raging inferno, all while silently ushering the beginning of an era anew. Why... how symbolic... how perfect... how simply...

CURIOUS.

THE EPILOGUE'S EPILOGUE

I AM THEIR OATHER. I've known this for a while now, but what does that entail? Is it my destiny to record all the transpirings found here? Oather and author sound awfully similar—am I not merely a form of an author?

No, an author writes that which is in their head, able to mould and change whatever they desire. They can input opinions, themes, morals—foundations of a good story! I... I have no choice over the matter. Perhaps such elements are to be found, but they are not by intention. I am an Oather; I write that which I see regardless of whether it makes for a good story or no. There are many changes I could make to what I wrote... changes which could yield a real story of fiction, one with a resolute theme and conclusive ending!

But that would be lying.

That would be fleeing from the purpose I have been called to and denying you the truth simply because there's less risk in it.

No, I shall continue to research this world and share my findings—whatever the beholders may deem it.

There are many lessons I have learned from observing this world: one being that even if *one* life can be deeply moved by the contents I have gathered—*one* life made learned and more aware of an existence beyond our own—of the possibilities beyond our mortal *comprehension*—

Then I shall count my labours fruitful.

This world in my head—and... now yours—there's something vivid to it—*real* even. These characters... the world they inhabit... the implications of this truth... it's truly perilous. Your mind is subsumed in its reality, it has been since the moment you immersed yourself within its nature.

We can't help it.

If you're this far, well... it's already too late for you. The only hope you have is if you're a complete dunce, for your mind shall be unable to process the deeper meanings within and lose itself once the madness of silence seizes it.

Or perhaps this is all in my head and *I'm* the mad one.

I wouldn't be surprised, but then... I wouldn't be surprised either way.

Still... I best write a prologue now. Though... I already have a prologue... Never you mind, I shall find a way to include a warning somehow. A prologue's prologue perhaps?

How curious.

As for the many other unanswered mysteries: I think it right to take it upon myself to document another manuscript of various perspectives to delve into various circumstances scattered about this world beyond. I do believe I shall further pursue the events which unfold in this world, but... before moving forward, we must go back. For in exploring past events through various eyes, we shall understand the present and that which is to come... mhm.

For now, I recommend you reread this manuscript a few times over, for I can almost guarantee you haven't found all the pieces in one go, much less arranged and connected them all properly.

Farewell, I wish you many fortuitous findings.

THE MIDDLE[1]

---

1. Because this most certainly *isn't* the end.

FURTHER NONSENSE

~for you curious freaks~

MAD SCRIBBLES

I N TRUTH, THE ESSENTIAL knowledge required to understand this world has already been composed in the final pages of the first half. Here, I choose to list various threads of knowledge I've encountered throughout my surreal journey in Beyond, chronicling the events leading up to the *Era of Silence*. Just... some of my notes. Enjoy what you wish, ignore what you must.

Bakeneko

Interestingly, the bakeneko is not from the folklore of Beyond, but from Infinity—Japan's folklore. I mention it because I've noticed curious parallels between Jovem Pynk and the bakeneko. I have no idea what Jovem is, nor his motive—if he even has one. My best guess is that he could be a bakeneko, but what such a creature would be doing in a world like this is beyond me... for now.

Bond of Loyalty

The Bond of Loyalty features an emblem of the Silent Legion: a central circle cradled by a crescent moon which rests beneath it. Crafted from prismatic sliver roots and imbued with spells from nearly every reality, it can be worn in various forms: as an armband, watch, necklace, earpiece, buckle, cloak clasp, or weapon ornamentation.

This artefact allows the wearer to channel the powers/magic system of a world, though it can be infused with magic from additional worlds if desired. Additionally, it binds the wearer to Siolant, enabling direct mental communication. Only the wearer can see and interact with Siolant in their mind. While wearers can converse with one another, they must speak out loud for their voices to be heard in the other's mind.

Candles

In Beyond, enchanted candles serve various purposes: some for fragrance, others for building energy—the more candles you possess, the more symbols empower you—and others for warding the mind against dark forces, with protection increasing with each additional candle. In the Forgotten Age, casters would employ a score of these enchanted candles while practising Narcronim, shielding their vulnerable minds from demons and eldritch horrors. Imagine a black circus attempting to use Narcronim to manipulate the perceptions of its audience, all the while eldritch monsters linger nearby, eager to haunt your mindscape. The solution? Maple-seed scented autumn candles. One whiff and—mmm... delicious.

Chamber of the Kin

A hollow in the Orindire (Terrible) Mountain range serves as the gathering place for the Regional Lords, who meet there every Rebirth. Before the 'Chess Wars', the Chamber of the Kin became the stage where the Regional Lords confronted Teresul Monbel over his pursuit of the prism shards. Unbequith revealed the truth behind Teresul's motives, laying down their blade and declaring no dispute with their brothers and sisters. Ranitorl supported Unbequith, explaining that Teresul had already sent an envoy to the Chamber of the Kin, seeking assistance—a gesture Ranitorl believed justified their allegiance.

Os Finyeld, however, refused to believe them and crossed blades, his bitterness primarily aimed at Unbequith. He urged Gotnoech to join him ("two against one isn't fair"). Gotnoech responded that true adherence to the Code of Perseverance required no armies, and besides, he had not brought a sword to challenge the Kin. Aivon Seeker then pointed out that Harldïof commanded the largest army in their region and Beyond. If desperate times arose, Harldïof had more than enough forces to defend against both regions.

The next Chamber of the Kin never occurred due to an... incident... in Evenfal.

Crass Language

In ancient times, when a single king ruled, it was forbidden to wish ill upon the crown. Yet people would still murmur phrases under their breath, such as "put a blade in the king," "damn the king to Hell," or "by the king's blood." Over time, these violent sayings devolved into simple crude words like 'gashed', 'bloody', and 'bladed'. Due to the varying morality in Beyond, such harsh references to violence are considered profane, especially given their origins in regal disrespect.

Days in Beyond

For the purposes of comparison, Earth provides a useful reference point. Earth's days last 24 hours relative to the Sun. In contrast, Beyond's "sun" is not a true sun in the conventional sense, but rather a composite of stars traversing the interconnected universes. The light emitted by these stars is filtered through the crystal firmament above Beyond, producing the visual effect of a singular sun. Consequently, the measurement of days in Beyond is not based upon this "sun," but upon the positions of the stars—a measurement known as a sidereal day. By way of comparison, Earth's sidereal day is 23 hours and 56 minutes in duration. In Beyond, however, a sidereal day extends to 25 hours and 48 minutes. Accordingly, when a character refers to the passage of two days, this should not be interpreted as equivalent to two Earth days (48 hours), but rather as two days in *Beyond*, totalling 51.6 hours. I hope that this information, paired with details concerning Beyond's seasonal cycles, will prove valuable to scholars seeking to document the histories of this cognitive world.

Elements

There are six elements from which all symbols stem: order, chaos, life, death, creation, and oblivion.

First Death Order

A sort of cult, so to speak. Most members wear silver skull masks without jaws, while higher-ranking individuals have masks adorned with features like tusks or horns. They believe a glorious second life awaits after death, viewing the physical body as a trap that binds souls to a realm of suffering and pain. While they long for death, they consider it selfish to seek it for themselves. Instead, they see it as their duty to help others transition to the second life of peace and joy. Convinced they are doing the right thing, they kill without hesitation, believing they are freeing souls from their torment.

They worship Death, having each encountered what they believe to be an apparition of Death's will. To them, Death is the overseer of the physical world, ensuring no soul is left behind, and they will do anything to claim a life. However, I suspect they were manipulated by Siolant, who controls their loyalty by appearing as Death itself. The Death Order first emerged during the Witch Wars in Beyond, where they were thought to have been defeated. Yet, Siolant kept them hidden, where they served the Silent Hand, such as protecting the prism shards.

Although they were absorbed into the Silent Hand, they continue to uphold the traditions and beliefs of the Death Order. Not all members of the Silent Hand share these practices, as seen with Pen Wishton.

New Death Order members are given names that reflect their rank, such as Pestilence, Famine, Drown, Slash, or Bleed. The severity of the name signifies their rank, with Oblivion holding the highest position, second only to Death. The founding member, Plague, remains active and is one of the most honoured among the Silent Hand, as many members are either from the original Death Order or have been misled into adopting their beliefs by others seeking to expand the Silent Hand.

Frostwraiths

While experimenting with methods to stabilise and control the prism shards' wild potential, the Loresmiths crafted an ingenious design involving symbols of 'living ice,' intended to contain the prism shards' wild essence. However, these symbols had an unexpected interaction with those of the prism shards, transforming the loresmiths into frostwraiths—spirits bound to cold. In essence, their spirits are "chained" to winter symbols.

Their bodies have been entirely replaced by cold—yes, that's a rather ambiguous term, because they are an ambiguous people. A frostwraith can manifest any form of cold they desire, whether it be solid (ice, snow, frost) or gas (a chilly breeze, icy wind, freezing gust). However, they cannot take on a liquid form like water, as it is not cold enough and requires heat to remain in that state.

Not only can their spirits choose the form of cold their bodies assume, but they can also manipulate cold to a significant extent. Given their expertise as Loresmiths, they possess the ability to craft weapons and tools from the cold symbols within themselves and their environment.

Hell's Butterflies

An elite contingency force, hastily assembled by Teresul Monbel, was devised to extract the prism shards without the brute force of an army. The prism shards were the true objective, and once he had them, he would call off his legions in what would appear to be a retreat. Five 'butterflies' of the group were handpicked by Adela Windcatcher, a member of the Fallen Guild and the first butterfly. Aivon Seeker oversaw this, but mostly allowed her to make the selections, content with whatever she chose, as he wished for a strong bond to form between them.

This elite force typically travelled alongside a platoon, composed of three squads and commanded by Lieutenant Bo, the leader of Hell's Butterflies. Under his command, the group consisted of Darun (a True Beyonder of Reexah), Ramsoen (reconnaissance and beast tracking), Fel (a mad, yet genius, caster), Samuel (the Black Knight), and Adela (Fallen Guild prodigy).

Lindworm

A type of wingless saurian with a poisonous breath that can scorch the very earth. The young of these creatures start off the size of salamanders but grow over the years to colossal proportions. Like reptiles, they never stop growing until they die. On average, their heads can reach up to five feet in length. However, there have been records (or, rather, legends) of encounters with creatures so large, they could wrap around mountains. Whether this is truth or exaggerated myth remains to be seen, as lindworms are rare and solitary creatures. They live in moist environments, whether that be a barren landscape—grey mud and grey rocks by a grey river under a grey sky—or a deep hole in Dripwood.

Lord Vocem

An extension of my will incarnate. Though he began with a copy of my motive, will, and conscience, he has developed his own identity. He is self-aware and knows all that I know, for I share it with him. He uses this vast knowledge to gain power and to utilise that power to follow my commands—when I need him, that is. However, he still needs to make a living, self-aware as he is. He has plenty of free time, as I only call upon him once every decade or so. He needs to eat, earn an income, and pursue his own dreams and ambitions. Since he started as a copy of me, it makes sense that he would join Theo's pack, as it's the most adventurous and roguish of its kind.

Musitaise

A musical phenomenon originating in Beyond, musitaise has since spread its effects across countless realities. This event occurs when an individual, overwhelmed with raw emotion, causes their heart to pluck the strings of reality. Words carry power, their spiritual frequencies resonating through the world, reality bending to the individual's rhythm, tempo, and mood. When someone bursts into song, music manifests out of nowhere, and reality aligns perfectly with their beat—this is the phenomenon known as musitaise. Some individuals have recognised and mastered this phenomenon, singing their hearts out as they work, scheme, hope, cry, or attack—and many others, do it quite by accident. Musitaise bends reality to the singer's words and emotions, which, if properly understood, can be tuned to one's advantage.

Musk Lizards

Also known as red-mossed salamanders, these territorial creatures are solitary and have a long lifespan, rarely taking a mate—which keeps their population small. The odour they emit is harmful to a swamp dragon's digestive system. However, humans would only experience teary or blurry eyes from coming into contact with it. If a swamp dragon detects the scent of the salamander (humans can smell it too—it smells like soggy grass, but to swamp dragons, it is *unbearable*), the dragon would avoid the creature within a 200-pace radius.

Passage

And I took my staff, Favor, and cut it in two, that I might break the covenant which I had made with all the peoples. So it was broken on that day. Thus the poor of the flock, who were watching me, knew that it *was* the word of the Eternal King. Then I said to them,

"If it is agreeable to you, give *me* my wages; and if not, refrain." So they weighed out for my wages thirty *pieces*. And the Eternal King said to me, "Throw it to the potter"—that princely price they set on me. So I took the thirty *pieces* of silver and threw them into the house of the Eternal King for the potter. Then I cut in two my other staff, Union, that I might break the brotherhood between regions.

Second Death Order

When the original Death Order merged with the Silent Hand, Siolant formed a new branch, naming his special operatives after the original group. These operatives, who can hop through time and realities, became known as the Second Death Order, led by Oblivion. Unlike their predecessors, none of the original Death Order members are involved with this branch of Siolant's Legion.

This new Death Order specialises in technology, utilising the finest resources from across all realities and timelines to craft custom weapons, armour, and equipment. They enhance their technology with magic, making their ranks impervious to most hexes, curses, and other supernatural threats. The Second Death Order operates according to Siolant's directives, often following peculiar requests to initiate and maintain a domino effect of events. Due to this, their objectives frequently conflict with those of the Red Brotherhood.

Shadehaunt

A day when the universes above rotate into those which have been completely annihilated. It is a day of true blackness when shadows from the void grow bold enough to creep closer. No light, no remnants, just the void where entire universes once stood. On this day, no family leaves their home, no light is snuffed, and shadows are avoided. Look too long, and the dark might look back. Listen too closely, and you might hear something best left forgotten.

Shadow Fleet

The southern edge of Beyond is bordered by a sea, and beyond this sea lies a shifting door to other worlds. The Shadow Fleet, under Siolant's command, serves as the boundary guardian between these worlds, ensuring that no one slips in or out of Beyond or other realities without Siolant's knowledge and approval. The commodore of the Shadow Fleet is Cayaban Orthrane, Pirate Lord of Unoeble. Having harnessed the soul flames with symbols of "broad water," he can traverse the very essence of the Etharœl, appearing wherever he desires. No, I haven't the faintest idea what "soul flames" are.

Cayaban first appeared in Unoeble town during its early days, eventually becoming its Territory Lord due to his likable yet relentless nature. Siolant then tasked some early operatives of the Silent Hand with commissioning him to secure the borders between worlds, ensuring that none crossed them without authorisation—except for members of Silent's Legion. Dorvasidon now despises Cayaban more than any other member of the Legion.

When Siolant doesn't need him, Cayaban is free to do as he pleases. Siolant prefers to maintain the impression within Beyond and the Red Brotherhood that Cayaban is nothing more than a pirate. Cayaban likes to view himself as an equal to the other two champions, but the truth is, when he's not at sea with one of his ships, he's the weakest of them all. Could someone else have been chosen? Certainly. However, if Cayaban dies, Siolant loses nothing; he would simply find a replacement. Cayaban was selected to secure the worlds' borders because he is strong enough to be formidable, yet weak enough to keep in check—though he may sometimes forget this. If he dies, he's replaceable.

Silent Hand

A branch of Silent's Legion, this cabal of magically gifted individuals operates in the shadows of Beyond. Under Pen Wishton's guidance, they infiltrate, spread rumours, or assassinate as needed. They control events in Beyond, shaping, directing, and manipulating the course of history. It was from their ranks that the prism shards were stolen and hidden. Their efforts ensure that the black market thrives across all timelines. Their crafty influence ignites wars. Should any individual rise to power, they inevitably fall prey to the schemes and machinations of the Silent Hand.

Members of the Silent Hand consist of Pen Wishton's disciples and followers of the first Death Order. This dynamic makes them superior in magic, wielding knowledge from all timelines and realities to cast a vast array of enchantments, spells, and curses. They also utilise some technology for communication, spying, data collection, storage, and transfer, seamlessly blending the mystical with a bit of the technological.

Spinners & Ravels

Spinners (fate weavers that "spin" fate) are beings of light that know all and alter events to fit into their plan for the mouldable future. They are syntropy and interest given form. They won't let anything—not even other spinners—stop them from maintaining order in what they deem reality, history, and the world need. They use voice. They are deliberate fate incarnate.

Ravels are purposeless beings of shadow that know nothing. They disrupt events to create chaos and forge meaning where none exists. They are entropy and apathy given form. They won't let anything stop them from acting upon their compulsions in what they believe to be their search for purpose. They use silence. They are meaningless entropy.

Spinners have been called angels and phantoms, while others have classified ravels as dark spirits, demons, or shades. This is all false.

In relation to one another, spinners don't consider ravels a threat, so much as a nuisance. In truth, they consider other spinners the real threat, though most of their disagreements result in political arguments. Should things get heated, they fight—not directly, for they cannot wish harm upon another being of order. Instead, they fight through defiant influence—sabotaging one another's manipulations of history and events with their own. I believe some are sympathetic to my cause... or perhaps my goals align with theirs. I don't truly know. They still confuse me.

Ravels, on the other hand, tend to be solitary beings. They rarely know other ravels exist, instead focusing entirely on their own plans, unaware or unconcerned with what others are doing. Their attention is consumed by their individual compulsions, often acting in isolation rather than within any larger web of courtly order.

Teresul Monbel

A direct descendant of Edrath, Teresul is determined to restore the glory of the Transcendent Throne by any means necessary—primarily by becoming a regional lord and representing his ancestral legacy. Unlike his more extreme ancestor, Edrath, Teresul's primary goal is to maintain his position of power to renew his family's legacy and uphold the prestige of the Transcendent Throne through his Lordship over Unbequith.

He vividly recalls the theft of the prism shards from the Loresmiths and believes it is of utmost importance to recover them from the enemy—whom he assumes to be responsible, as the shards were stolen during a raid that resulted in the death of many.

Aware of the dangers posed by those in positions of power, both historically and in the present, Teresul initially kept his search for the shards a closely guarded secret. However, after Harldïof's scouts uncovered his efforts and the information was revealed at the Chamber of the Kin, he decided to explain his intentions openly, sending his warlord, Aivon, as his representative—a move that raised suspicions, as it is customary to send one's hand in such situations. However, Teresul's hand, Siolant, is... well, ill-suited for such a task.

As a True Beyonder and a direct descendant of Edrath, Teresul wields significant power.

Wait

A branch of the Silent Hand. Pronounced like *white*, they are a small group of individuals, each a member of the Aft-Circle and unique in their own deadly way. They supply those of the Grey-Circle and eliminate any who pose a threat to the grander plot. If you are part of the Grey-Circle, they will contact you and supply you, whether you like it or not. They will then monitor you, ensuring you never stray into the Aft-Circle. The Wait Syndicate operates within Beyond, with the mission of keeping its inhabitants ignorant of the true nature of their world. The syndicate was established by Pen Wishton, but moves under Ms. Elicy's command.

Weapons of FelL Cry

There are four—one weapon for each region, bestowed upon them during the coup against King Wraithe's rule.

To Harldïof, a sword of ice and fire, capable of cutting through all.

To Gotnoech, a talisman of shielding and evasion, allowing one to elude all.

To Unbequith, the blood of reality, restored to its purest generation.

To Ranitorl, a flame what sparks advancement, pushing progress a century ahead of its time.

Cryptic tone aside, Vincent has the sword (obviously), a chicken had the talisman (don't ask), Unbequith is known for its True Beyonders, and Ranitorl's Flame is stored within the Black Tower of their capital.

Zanswarsh

The spirit of the original saurian ore has long since passed, leaving only soulless monsters that follow every command of the Silent Hand. These creatures are mere shadows of their former selves, covered in protective black scales. Thanks to their hollow bodies, Zanswarsh can fly faster than most saurians. Their interiors, being hollow shadows, prevent them from breathing fire. Their skulls are left exposed and vulnerable, without scales, skin, or muscle. Coherent speech is impossible for them unless a Silent Hand agent speaks through them. The ore within them is blighted with red symbols, making it impossible for any Zanswarsh to gain sentience. Despite their weak jaw force compared to other saurians, they can still inflict deep puncture wounds. Their necrotic teeth, attached to rotting skulls, pose a danger of breaking off and lodging in their prey. The blighted venom from these necrotic teeth poisons both the body and soul of the victim.

Acknowledgements
Short, Sweet, and Unprofessional

I know a lot of acknowledgements start like this, but... really, this novel wouldn't exist without certain humans being the wonderfully human people they are.

You know?

Yeah, you do.

First and foremost, my parents. My father—the closest thing to a manager I could afford. My mother—an editor-in-chief (other than, y'know, my actual editor, Steven Moore).

Love you, Steven.

Even with his grueling work, there were still edits and contradictions I missed—many of which were caught by Natasha White, a fellow author whose books you should look up. Right now. Do it.

Micah! You there? Hey, buddy. Everyone, Micah Watts! (*cue applause*). Along with my family, he's been a beacon of encouragement and motivation. He taught me that whether this novel is a disaster or a masterpiece, at least I finished it. I accomplished something. And that something is awesome. I hope.

Did you like it, reader? What ending did you get? I'd love to see your canon endings. Send them to me, why don't you (**@pono_freedom** on Instagram)?

Oh, speaking of Watts—his family is amazing. Aunty Lizzy and Uncle Gabe let me write my madness in their house and raid their fridge. Generous and wonderful humans. They are family.

Speaking of family (the segue worked so nice the first time—why not again?), my sister Lani designed the cover for this book *and* the last one! Check out **@bonibooboo** on Instagram for more epic art and animations—seriously, she's ridiculously talented. Same goes for Maile Baker, my other sister, the cartographer of *Beyond* and the lands I've yet to discover. She was also the first person to finish the *Silent Dawn* duology, and her input meant everything. After her came Noa, my brother, whose keen insight helped refine continuity details.

A huge thank you to everyone who bought the first editions of this novel. Your support carries me through rewrites, edits, and doubts. And wow—you finished the story. Good job. I'm proud of you. In fact, I think I love you. Yes. I do.

That reminds me—Aunt Pat, the owner of BookEnds in Kailua, was the first retailer to feature my book and take a chance on it. She's been nothing but supportive, and if you ever visit Hawaii, you *must* stop by her shop. Maybe you'll find me there, lurking in the fantasy aisle.

Alright.

I'm going to publish this book now, which probably already happened since you're reading this.

Coolest beans.

About the Writer

Pono Freedom has been building worlds since the moment he could conceptualize ninjas, dragons, and eldritch almagamations.

He was a very odd child. Now, he's just an odd adult, finding connections between scattered visions from his cursed childhood doodles to the stories that followed him into his teens. At sixteen, he began piecing everything together, constructing a world from the fragments of his imagination. He was seventeen when he began writing and twenty-two when he finally published the complete manuscript for Silent Dawn: First Half. Many of his stories have lingered in his mind since infancy, waiting for their moment to be told.

Here's his dear ol' mum taking a stab at writing his bio:

Pono is a writer from Hawai'i who enjoys crafting tales of epic fantasy, surfing small-kine waves, playing his dad's guitar, gaming with his best buddy, and exploring the lore behind the lore. You can probably find him with his siblings, singing sea shanties, savouring sugar cookies, and eating hims chippies! (□w□) teehee~

www.ingramcontent.com/pod-product-compliance
Lightning Source LLC
Chambersburg PA
CBHW050917030726
47503CB00007BB/2339